ON THE EDGE

Revised Edition

Life Changing Adventures in the Wild

RICHARD D. JACKSON

authorHOUSE®

Other Books by Richard D. Jackson

Yesterdays Are Forever
A Rite of Passage Through the Marine
Corps and Vietnam War

The Last Fast White Boy
A Memoir of Athletics at Marshall University

Too Stupid to Quit
Banking and Business Lessons Learned
The Hard Way

Dedication: To my grandchildren and future explorers Richard Taylor and Christopeher Kyle Jackson, and for all those people who want to become explorers.

Appreciation: My gratitude to Mack Butler, Jim Box, and Chris Jackson for their support in the creation and recall of these stories.

Cover Photo: Taken by Jim Box from Elk Mountain of the peaks in the Sangre de Cristo Range in the Santa Fe National Forest.

Author Contact: dickjackson@mindspring.com

AuthorHouse™
1663 Liberty Drive
Bloomington, IN 47403
www.authorhouse.com
Phone: 1 (800) 839-8640

Published by AuthorHouse   07/09/2015

ISBN: 978-1-5049-1811-4 (sc)
ISBN: 978-1-5049-1812-1 (e)

The Original Old Explorers
Mack Butler, Jim Box, and Dick Jackson

The New Breed Explorers
Richard Taylor Jackson and Christopher Kyle Jackson

What is life but a series of inspired follies?
—George Bernard Shaw

The possible we will do today. The impossible,
well, it takes a little longer.
—US Marine Corps

I learned early that the richness of life is adventure.
Adventure calls on all faculties of mind and spirit.
It develops self-reliance and independence.
Life then teems with excitement.
—William O. Douglas

Two roads diverged in a wood, and I—I took the one less
traveled by, and that has made all the difference.
—Robert Frost

This is the word I bring you from jungle and from town,
From city street where weary feet are seeking vague
renown. From cotton fields to northern snows,
or where the west winds cry. This is the word
I bring you: Keep strong or else you die.
—Grantland Rice

Contents

ORIENTATION

"If you don't know where you are going, any road will get you there." This is a famous quote by the English novelist Lewis Carroll, from his story *Alice's Adventures in Wonderland.*

Unfortunately, from time to time many of us may suffer from the dilemma of not knowing where we are going, so during the course of our travels, we must make adjustments or even change direction altogether. Finding our way when we've gone off course requires some effort in *orientation*—the process of determining where you are, where you want to go, and the most expedient route to get you there. This is not rocket-science stuff, but it does require some diligent effort to reach the desired destination.

When I started writing this real-life wilderness adventure book, I had to orient myself a couple of times. It was originally titled *Eagles with Clipped Wings.* The story was about a group of men, e*agles* if you will, who had soared high, living adventurous and exploratory lives for years; then slowly but surely, they began to decline physically from the wear and tear on their bodies and normal aging. At this point in their lives, with their wings clipped by these maladies, the wilderness adventures they undertook became more moderate than their earlier hard-core expeditions.

Yes, most assuredly these explorers were still visiting the backcountry regularly and still doing much more than the normal person would even consider, but *they had lost a step or two,* as is often said about old athletes who are no longer in their prime.

However, as I wrote and probed deep into the recesses of my memory, researched my notes, looked at maps, talked with my fellow explorers, and then counted the number of expeditions that had been taken over twenty years, I hastily came to another conclusion.

We did live on the edge in everything we did. We were risk takers, adrenalin junkies, sports enthusiasts, athletes, and dedicated professionals in our chosen fields of work. We loved the outdoors—the hikes, camping, climbing, and going where few people would dare to venture; we enjoyed being together, involving our children, and sharing in experiences that would give us a lifetime of stories to relive and relate to our friends and families. It was a thrilling and soothing balm for our souls; it made us who we were, and it gave meaning and direction to our lives.

Outward Bound was the initial motivation for the expeditions, but after nearly depleting ourselves physically from these strenuous activities, we chose to do our own adventure programs—seventy-five over a period of twenty-five years. Certainly enough for most lifetimes.

Here within these stories, you can travel with these explorers on their Outward Bound experiences and many other adventure journeys to vast parts of this country, including climbing mountains; canoeing rivers, swamps, and rapids; rock climbing; and trekking through dense foliage and along unspeakably beautiful mountain trails.

These trips are a travelogue of sightseeing and excitement. They will entertain and enlighten you as you hear about the explorers' humorous escapades in the backcountry, learn about the topography of this country, and discover how it was formed by yesteryear's cataclysmic forces.

Of particular interest to some will be the reflections on jungle survival and combat experiences in the marine corps and Vietnam War. These compelling stories contrast the relationships between the harsh reality of those challenging experiences and the difficulties usually undertaken by explorers during their wilderness adventures.

Learn about Lewis and Clark and their expedition across this country from 1802 to 1805. Vicariously travel with these explorers to the same locations and campsites that the Corps of Discovery visited two hundred years ago, and learn how this experience helped us to discover more about this country and, most importantly, about ourselves.

Read about fieldcraft techniques, navigation, cooking, and trip planning. You'll find many points that will be useful, even amusing in some cases, especially for those interested or experienced in the backcountry.

Most importantly, I hope the reader can understand how we kept going, pushing on with the challenges we loved, even when we could no longer perform at our peak. Yes, we had slowed down considerably—who doesn't?—but we did not quit; a few of us are still at it today, albeit at a much-reduced level. This is our legacy and the lessons we learned, perhaps the hard way. And now, the message of this book, the take-home value, if you will: Never quit doing the things you love, be an explorer, and seek out the unknown. There is always a trail to follow; you just have to search and find it. So keep looking, and don't forget, "When you're through, you're through."

ONE

STARTING OUT

It was the monsoon season in Vietnam in 1967 when those devilish rains began and seemed as if they would never stop. It was a drenching, never-ceasing kind of downpour that appeared to have a life of its own, and it would not end until it eventually pierced the very marrow of our bones. *How could it be so damned cold in a semitropical climate?* we continually asked ourselves, trying hard to stay warm and somewhat dry as each wintry, sopping day passed without any imminent respite on the horizon.

We had heard about monsoons, but this type of continuous bombardment of water was never mentioned in the training manuals or in the classes we were required to attend before deployment to fight in this crazy, almost maniacal, Asian war. Not only did we have booby traps to traverse daily while on foot patrols, but we also had enemy artillery and mortar fire to keep our attention during the day and the long, forlorn nights. And now, of course, we had the monsoon rains!

During the weeks of heavy rain, it was not unusual trying to sleep on a secluded hilltop in a defensive position in "Indian country"—enemy territory—with our writhing, cold, wet bodies wrapped in a rubberized poncho for protection after a lengthy day of patrolling. It was normal.

Water gushed around, over, and underneath our quivering fetal bodily forms as we lay on the chilly, soggy ground, diligently trying to capture a few intermittent hours of sleep that were continuously interrupted by rifle, mortar, and artillery fire.

It was during times like this when I vowed secretly to myself that I would never sleep outdoors on the ground again—if, and it was a *big* if, I was fortunate enough to survive this insane war.

Several years later a close friend, Mack Butler, an attorney and outdoor enthusiast who was legal counsel for my bank, asked me on numerous occasions to go camping. My standard response to him was, "I have no interest in the woods, hiking, or camping. I do not want to *ever* sleep on the ground again. I had all of that crap I could take in my eight years in the marine corps, and especially in the Vietnam War."

In fact, my feelings were so strong and my body so over-conditioned to these hardships that I wouldn't take my own son, Christopher, camping during his youth. Later my attitude changed. It took twelve years for me to break my vow to myself, and this was caused by a business necessity, not a resurgent desire to go back into the woods and live like an animal.

In 1968, after spending my time as an officer in Uncle Sam's fighting elite, the United States Marine Corps, and after leaving Vietnam disgruntled and distraught with that fruitless war, I was prepared to try a less demanding, more comfortable existence without the everyday rigors associated with that occupation. I also wanted to spend more time with my family and see my children grow up.

The banking industry appealed to my thought process, and I ultimately chose this field for my new career. As a consequence I would devote more than thirty years of my existence to this profession. Actually it was a good choice; however, I soon learned that people could become casualties in civilian life as well as in the military, unless they were routinely cautious, though ambitious and hardworking, and did their homework constantly.

Ostensibly there were no real bullets, mortars, artillery, or booby traps to circumvent; however, the business world could inflict great pain and discomfort at the slightest provocation. For example, when organizational changes or the injection of new senior management occurred, when acquisitions were made, or when fluctuations and changes impacted the economic environment. These misadventures in business are more common than not, due to the nature of the beast. That nature is normally driven by the demand for sustained profitability in the company, shareholder return, and often individual egos. Incidentally, those egos normally belong to the owners, the board of directors, or not uncommonly, someone more senior than *you.* Consequently corporate gamesmanship is always prevalent, and it is essential that you know how to play; otherwise, you may become one of the "walking wounded" or even a complete casualty in short order.

A wonderful slogan I have always admired seems to be most fitting for anyone in a major leadership position. It says, "The higher the monkey climbs, the more his or her ass is exposed." I was fortunate enough to climb to a small summit in business, not from high intelligence, but mostly from just working hard, being diligent, and having a great staff around to protect me from my own errors of sound business judgment. Still, with my limited amount of success and my senior position in those business endeavors, I had to cover my ass and deflect criticism more than I care to admit. I climbed this corporate ladder enthusiastically, believing with all my being that if you make a commitment to something or someone, you should give it all you've got all the time or not attempt it. I like to think I gave it all I had for thirty years, and that was enough, at least for me.

After reaching a high plateau in my profession, I finally decided to call it quits, wanting to do something else with my life—something more gratifying and fulfilling, at least for someone of my age and energy level, particularly after fighting all the corporate and combat battles that had been cast upon me during my lifetime.

Having enough to live on in a comfortable manner was good enough. Being wealthy beyond all imagination and destroying myself to do it, which seems to be the mind-set of many business folks today, never appealed to my mentality.

I had many friends with similar attitudes as mine, and in many ways, we were all considered to be *rare birds*. Like me, they enjoyed playing the game, but they also had varied interests. They enjoyed traveling vigorous and daring trails, living a hardy life, being consummate risk takers and adrenalin junkies. But always, over the horizon, they could see a bluish and radiant sky, and they marched toward it with unabated passion.

Years ago I read a quote by an anonymous one-legged female mountain climber that has remained in my subconscious mind over the years. She said, "Life without risk has no excitement."

Understandably, some people are not destined to be risk takers, nor are they motivated or excited by a constant release of adrenalin in their systems. They may be adventurous, even explorers, but if the risk or hardship they encounter becomes considerable, they will frequently and quietly alter their course and move in other directions that are more suitable to their liking. Many risk takers cannot explain why they act as they do. Is it the challenge, the adrenalin high, or the drug-like feeling that comes from surviving some breathtaking experience? That tendency can occur in many areas, not just in the outdoors. It can be in an occupation, athletics, war, business negotiations, investment decisions, relationships, or any other situation that requires a person to face peril or the unknown in whatever endeavor they are engaged.

Armchair adventurers or those less inclined toward taking risks of any kind might look at these people and wonder if the actions and mentality of risk takers center on a death wish. Possibly they may believe these folks are not normal human beings. Physiologists seem to think that risk taking is subjective and that one person's risk is another person's hobby or skill. Some say that these thrill seekers are people for whom life is nothing unless they continuously test themselves physically—in some cases, even testing their own mortality.

I have heard the term adrenaline junkies mentioned throughout my life on numerous ocassions and have been called one by some of my close friends. It is used to describe people who thrive on stress, risk taking, overcoming physical challenge, and the thrill of living life on the edge in many of their strenuous activities.

I would offer the proposition that these unusual people build fires just to put them out. This will keep the adrenalin going.

The French refer to this attitude as *sang froid* (cold blood). Ernest Hemingway termed it *grace under pressure*. For many adrenaline junkies and risk takers, *it's their raison d'etre.*

Putting all of this into perspective, particularly for me and I would think probably for most risk takers and real adventurers, I cannot help but recall the anxiety and even the fear that I felt in my gut while playing athletics in my school years. At times before taking the field, I would actually throw up from the apprehension. Once the games started, I could settle down and go about my job, but it was always challenging, and the contest would test my mettle to its fullest every time I competed.

The same kind of pervasive feelings would often occur in Vietnam before going on a combat operation. I would be fearful, both for myself and my men. It was then that I had to reach down, do a gut check, and do what I had to do, find some strength of character, overcome my personal fear, and mentally deal with the potential loss of life that might result when the action began.

I've always preached that it is okay to be afraid, but you must work though it; being afraid keeps you on your toes. It makes you do your homework. These feelings help you stay alert and avoid attempting stupid and unsound acts.

So, maybe fear is good, if used as an asset and not as a liability. It can jump-start the system, pour adrenalin on the fires of action, and help people accomplish things that otherwise they might not have attempted or even considered possible. Perhaps there may be something that needs to be done, and then suddenly, someone with or without courage, even fearful, steps forward and just does it.

The interesting aspect about all of these adrenalin-pumping occurrences is that when they are over, there is always a feeling of great relief and personal exhilaration. At times there may even exist in the mind a great anticipation of doing it again. It is the high that always follows a successful but stressful venture.

I cannot tell you how many times I have experienced these sensations in my life nor explain how good I felt afterward. There was an overwhelming consciousness of gratification and satisfaction. I would be intoxicated beyond words, and it would feel great. The next question would be, "When do we do it again?"

Some of the best sensations that many people have ever felt inside themselves, although they might not understand or even admit it, were when they pushed themselves to the limit. Remember, the best and most exciting times are frequently the most demanding.

Henry David Thoreau wrote in his book *Walden*: "The mass of men lead lives of quiet desperation," and many obviously do. But, he also wrote, "Men spend the first half of their lives learning how to live the second half." That is what we should all be about.

All that we do early in our life contributes to our future and influences our ultimate destiny. Many people do not realize how much they impact their own destiny by the decisions they make, or don't make for that matter, along life's turbulent highway. Hopefully we have all learned to appreciate these efforts and have found those things that will work for us as we go about living a productive and interesting life. Launching a direction and gaining a foothold in our lives is critically important to our success, and it can be done in many dissimilar ways.

From reading this narrative, I hope you will understand how one group of men did it. It was difficult, but it was certainly fun; it was also crazy at times and highly controversial. But it worked for them.

Once again I quote Thoreau, who wrote, "If a man does not keep pace with his companions, perhaps it is because he hears a different drummer." The music they heard inspired their souls, and they responded in the only way they knew. What else would you expect from people who also apparently lived by the maxim "If stupidity got us into this mess, why can't stupidity get us out?"

What else is there in life for those individuals who enjoy new adventures, challenge, the unknown, a constant adrenaline fix, and importantly, living their lives with a smattering of risk and some modicum of madness? Living as if there is no tomorrow and always reaching out for the *golden ring of daring experience,* and then, upon grasping it, holding on to it with all the fervor of youth until the next opportunity appears. Never asking why, or questioning their own personal motives, but constantly doing those wonderful and fulfilling things that gave meaning to their lives while living *on the edge.* Always exploring and searching for a life filled with excitement, anticipation, and the unrelenting thrill of new journeys and explorations. Constantly seeking new highs and pursuing challenges that might turn others back. Not caring what the world thought about them, but knowing deep in their souls that they were right with the world; never tiring from their efforts, never relenting from their quest, always and always asking the question, "Now what?"

TWO

OUTWARD BOUND

In 1968 I resigned my commission as a major in the marine corps after eight years of service, and joined The First National Bank in Atlanta. A few years later, I accepted a position with another Atlanta bank, First Georgia, and was made president in 1975. It was a daunting experience, because that bank was about to fail as a result of the bad decisions of former management and the accumulation of a loan portfolio that was a disaster waiting to happen, and it did, unfortunately on my watch.

Upon accepting the position I was not business-savvy enough to understand the seriousness of the situation. This was one of those bullets not fired from a gun that could kill you. But alas, because of my lack of business experience, I was unable to read the situation properly. Consequently, I took the position to enhance my career, to increase my salary, and naturally to inflate my ego. I was now chasing the golden chalice of success and monetary reward with all my personal vigor. I was also now trapped like so many others.

By the grace of the Almighty, a wonderful staff, and many other industrious and loyal supporters, we pulled the bank out of its downward tailspin, and after a couple of years of hard, dedicated work, we finally obtained solid profitability.

Life and profits were good for a few years; then in 1982 our executive management team, reading the handwriting on the wall, realized new initiatives were needed if we were going to maintain a successful march toward sustained success.

The business areas receiving most of our attention were the team building, morale, and training of our staff. We knew we had to ask more from them and we had to get it someway. How to do this was the big question, and we didn't have the answer.

One of the bank executives, Jim Box, the chief financial officer, finally arrived at a solution. It was a dilly, to say the least. He had researched and suggested that we send our key staff members to a nine-day Outward Bound course conducted in the mountains of North Carolina. Jim believed that this training would be a good vehicle to build and install camaraderie among our staff, and unquestionably, he assumed it would eventually dribble down to their subordinates, subsequently resulting in improved performance throughout most of the departments of the bank. After some deliberation on the matter and following my experience and instincts from the marine corps on their outstanding team-building tactics and training, I agreed. However, there was a *catch-22* in his proposal.

From my previous life, I recalled an old adage on leadership that would remain with me throughout my business career. It ran, "Never ask your people to do something you won't do." If I followed this creed, I would have to personally undertake the course and endure all the discomforts that went with it before asking our employees to commit to the training. Obviously this meant more suffering and the likely encounter of all kinds of precipitation, critters, and all the other elements associated with the outdoors and the wilderness. In other words, more pain and certainly more rain. "Maybe it wasn't such a good idea after all." I began to reconsider after thinking through his recommendation with more objectivity and reflection on the discomfort factors.

None of the other managers, including me, had developed any positive ideas about our quandary, and so it seemed that I was probably stuck with Jim's suggestion. As Thomas Paine wrote at the beginning of the American Revolution, "There is no power like the power of an idea whose time has come."

It appeared the power of Jim's idea had now arisen, and the timing was unfortunately appropriate. We had to stay the course and give it a try if we were going to achieve our objective.

▼

In my earlier years of athletics, our ancient coaches had always told us that when we were hurt, we should run though the pain or just shake it off. I am no stranger to this malady and have probably run 10,000 miles based on that philosophy.

In the marine corps, we were also taught to tolerate the pain and that it was good to do so—a hardy lesson, to say the least, and to most civilians, not acceptable under normal conditions. The atypical people who chose the corps savored it. It was definitely macho to be a marine, and we were supposed to be macho hunks. Anyway, that's what the marine corps recruiting posters alleged.

Set the example, never complain, take what is given, and never, never, give up under any circumstances. I had done this for eight years; wasn't that long enough? Why, now, should I have to continue suffering and tolerating pain and discomfort after all of these comfy years as a soft civilian in the world of business? These were the questions cascading through my brain before I finally relented and accepted Jim's harebrained idea. The thought of sleeping in a tent or in the open on the ground nearly prompted return of the delayed stress disorder that had affected me for several years after returning from that jungle war. But this was not war in the traditional sense, and I made my decision. Just get on with it before I chickened out.

▼

Late in the year, Jim enrolled us in the Outward Bound mountaineering course at the North Carolina school; the class was to start in March 1983. We would try it out as a possible teaching technique for our managers; if we had a successful experience, we would then begin sending our managers to future courses. At least that was our initial thought and our plan.

It is frequently said that good things happen to good people; however, early spring is not necessarily a good time for good people to be outside camping, hiking, or canoeing in the Carolina Mountains. Although we did question the time frame, we would quickly learn the truth about this query.

After becoming fully engaged in the experience, we would eventually discover that we actually enjoyed this rigorous activity. Of course, this occurred after we became fully acclimatized to the program and mentally accepted the physical challenge and the consistent daily hardships thrust upon us during the course. More importantly, it would have a significant impact on our management styles and actually be a turning point for the way we lived and how we would elect to spend much of our future leisure and recreational time. This was all positive and healthy.

During the length of the course, we honed our outdoor skills to a fine point, although we constantly did stupid things in the field, regardless of the fact that we were backwoods-savvy. I suppose one could assume it was the result of wanting to live somewhat dangerously *on the edge* or possibly going over the edge by constantly challenging ourselves and trying new things.

Working and living without some degree of risk did not seem to hold much excitement for us. We wanted change and stimulation in all the things we did, not just in our profession, but we had to learn this the hard way. Outward Bound was the impetus and the answer.

▼

I have no idea how many people have attended an Outward Bound program, but I am certain all participants have learned things about themselves if they went into it with a positive mind-set, as Jim and I did when we attended the school in North Carolina. The impact of this experience was so significant that we later enrolled in several other courses around the country. We definitely were into pain, but it was a good pain, or so it seemed.

Outward Bound, a wonderful organization, provides wilderness adventure-education programs offering a broad array of courses that typically run from four to twenty-plus days. Training and adventures in mountaineering, general exploration, sailing, canoeing, and backpacking are included in their broad educational syllabus. This organization focuses on teaching values related to leadership, individual confidence, teamwork, and personal growth, which imbue in their students, of all ages and interests, a great sense of personal pride and accomplishment in themselves. The outdoor courses were originally designed during World War II to provide young sailors with the knowledge and skills to survive if their transport ships were attacked in the North Sea by German submarines or battle cruisers. After several successful years, these programs were subsequently customized to fit the corporate world. Many large and highly successful companies have used this training to affect their corporate culture and to build stronger, more vibrant organizations to meet the challenges within their particular industries.

Outward Bound courses can be modified to meet specific corporate goals based on the needs and objectives of an individual company. Highly trained, enthusiastic, qualified, and knowledgeable instructors are available to guide the students toward the desired learning objectives.

Later, after attending several of these courses, we incorporated a variation of wilderness-adventure programs into our bank's training syllabus. The impact of this training on our managers and staff assisted greatly in the development of a thriving business culture.

Today, hindsight always being 20/20, when we look back on that time and the programs we attended, we are most thankful that we ventured forward with this program, albeit I went into it kicking and screaming. Jim, on the other hand, was highly enthusiastic and welcomed the challenge with open arms. Personally, it was my strong conviction that I had experienced all the physical challenges I needed in my past life in the marine corps. But I was wrong.

▼

My career in the marines started in March 1960 and concluded in January 1968. After completing college I attended the Officer Candidate School in Quantico, Virginia. My duty tours during those years included stints at Quantico; Camp Lejeune, North Carolina; Cuba during the missile crisis in October 1962; a Mediterranean cruise in 1964; Camp Smith in Oahu, Hawaii; and jungle-warfare training in Malaysia. It ended with a paid-for "vacation" trip to Vietnam for thirteen long, tough months. Being an infantry officer meant lots of foot travel wherever I was sent.

Jim had not served in the military because of an early marriage and young children; however, just as I had in the corps, he would soon learn to respect and acquire the necessary skill set required to operate in an unforgiving environment. Mack Butler, our other prominent, full-time explorer, did not attend the course in North Carolina, but he had spent a great deal of time in the woods growing up in South Georgia, and later on numerous hiking and camping trips with his friends. He had already developed an affinity for the wilderness before we started our recent wilderness travels.

▼

In early March, after making umpteen trips to the local High Country outfitters store in Atlanta to purchase the necessary, and some unnecessary, gear for the trip, we piled our costly equipment into our car and began the trip to the headquarters of the North Carolina Outward Bound School, some 150 miles north of Atlanta.

The school was located near Morgantown, North Carolina, within the Great Smoky Mountains range adjacent to Table Rock Mountain. The physical site of the school provided our small group of students a beautiful nightly lit view of this small, quaint city. That is all we ever saw of the town or the view, because the instructors, changing venues, and constant movement during the length of the course kept us occupied day and night while we were in those mountains.

The first day they issued additional camping items they said we needed, although we doubted we needed anything else for the course, as we had nearly depleted our savings by purchasing every conceivable camping item that the outfitter had on their shelves. Besides, we reasoned, we couldn't possibly carry any more stuff in our already overweight backpacks. But we took the gear anyway.

Who knows, we may have forgotten something, although we couldn't imagine what it could possibly be. In retrospect, our packs, with the extra added weight including the food we carried, probably weighed close to ninety pounds—not a smart way to commence a hiking trip that would eventually require all the physical energy and strength that we possessed within our unconditioned and softening bodies. However, in time, and not necessarily by our choice, they would soon become very lean and very hard.

In the marine corps, if and when we had carried a backpack, it was recommended that our pack be no heavier than forty-five pounds and certainly no more than sixty pounds. Normally, on patrol or sweeps in Vietnam, we carried a poncho tied around our waists to sleep in, two canteens filled with water, rations, our weapon, two hand grenades tied to our suspender straps, compass, maps, knife, and ammo—actually, lots of ammo. You could not survive without ammo, and most of it was very, very heavy.

▼

Overburdened as we were, the next stop, as the hours grew late, was to pick up our food. They led us to their food storage, which was nothing more than a small wooden shed within the camp. Opening the door we were introduced to a canvas bag containing all of our meal supplies. After opening the small bag, we remarked to the instructors that this would make a great meal for the first evening, but reality was soon to became our constant companion when we were informed by our leaders that the meager supplies, as we called them, were to last the group of eleven students and two instructors for the next nine days! Shaken, we thought, *"They must be insane; that couldn't possibly be enough food to feed us for that lengthy period!"*

The idea, we were told unabashedly by our instructors, was to do exceptionally good meal planning, to conserve the food, to use everything prudently and not be wasteful, because if were, we would *go hungry.* It was as basic as that.

Some of our primary staples were cabbage and cheese. You will not believe how long a large head of cabbage will last in the woods and all the variations of meal preparation that it can be used for. I still can't believe it after all these years.

The reason for the abundance of the white cheese, we learned later, was because vast amounts of cheese had been donated to Outward Bound as a charitable gift by a major food supplier. Consequently, we were the ultimate beneficiaries of this bequest. It was amazing what you can do with cheese in the woods when that's all you have and you are hungry. But that's another story.

▼

We carried C rations with us on operations in Vietnam. Normally the cardboard box contained a small plastic package of miscellaneous articles and three small cans of basic foodstuffs. Items frequently packed in these rations included a small cigarette package, coffee, sugar, powered cream, toilet paper (an item always in demand), plastic eating utensils, fruit, peanut butter and crackers or white bread, a can of fruit, or some other major food delicacy like beanie weenies, ham and lima beans, scrambled eggs, fried ham, beefsteak stew, or turkey loaf. A small heating fuel bar was included with the rations so that we could warm the canned food without building a fire. Heating the stuff did assist greatly in the taste category.

I have forced myself to forget most of the other stuff in the ration box, but the food was filled with solid protein and carbohydrates, and we could gain weight eating this chow if we could sequester additional items from our fellow troopers.

Carrying the rations was not a problem. Usually we would dump the contents of the box into a long boot sock and then tie the sock at chest height on our shoulder suspenders, which also supported a cartridge belt worn around the waist to carry ammo, small arms, compass, K-bar (a large knife), and a first aid kit.

A plastic spoon or fork was generally carried in a breast pocket, and a midget can opener was commonly affixed to the dog tag (identification) chain worn around our necks. These two items had to be readily available, because most of the time during the daylight hours we were required to eat on the move.

At the end of the day, the sock would be empty. The next day when we were resupplied, usually by air, we would fill it again; this same ritual would be performed every day when we were on patrol.

If you could confiscate a large metal spoon, which I ultimately did from a mess hall, it was the preferred eating utensil and could be carried ad infinitum in your breast pocket and used expeditiously whenever food was available. It was wise to always be prepared to eat when the opportunity arose, especially if it was *real* food.

▼

We prepared a small repast for the evening and gobbled it down like a pack of hungry wolves. By then it was late, and we were told it was time to hit the sack. They took us to a screened wooden hooch—it had a roof and screened half walls—to spend our first night in preparation for our forced march the next day. By the way, our worst fears about the mountains at this time of year were realized sooner than we thought. As we had earlier assumed about the weather prior to our departure, it was cold, raining like mad, with intermittent sleet thrown in for good measure when we crawled into our sleeping bags.

"The more things change, the more they stay the same." I always seemed to recall this old adage whenever familiar but unsavory conditions surfaced. The next day brought sunshine; albeit, the wind-aided temperature produced a penetrating chill. To warm us up and to work out the kinks in our hungry bodies, the instructors took us on a hilly two-mile run in short-sleeve sweaters and shorts. At the conclusion of the run, which had produced a fair amount of body heat and perspiration, we were required to jump off a small hilly rise into a mountain stream. The water felt like it was ice-cold; remember, it was early March in these mountains, and our bodies were submerged below the near-freezing surface. After jumping from the rocky precipice, we wondered if we would ever recover our breath when and if we floated back up to the surface.

It was terrible. The sudden surge of cold water shocked our entire system into almost total numbness; it had captured all the strength from our struggling bodies. After bobbing back to the top, we could only hope that we would have enough strength left in our debilitated bodies to pull ourselves from the water.

After regaining our composure and some degree of vigor, we prepared breakfast from our already shrinking food stores, and then organized our gear to move out on a forced foot march into the mountains. At the time we did not know that this hike would last until zero-dark hours, meaning very late that night.

The group climbed from our base camp up the mountain until we reached the top of Table Rock, aptly named because it was totally flat; from a distance it looked like the top of a table. It was only 5,000 feet in elevation, which is high for this part of the country, and the views were stunning. Then we descended into a deep valley by sliding down a steep mountain gully on our butts, dragging our gear behind our fannies. It was much too steep to traverse upright on foot.

We had been given maps and compasses at the start of the course, and this initial cross-country venue was our introduction to *orienteering*. Our instructor-assigned mission was to find our way, as quickly as we could, to a distant objective. According to the map, it appeared to be an extremely long and difficult hike; we would discover just how long and tedious it was twelve hours later. I was the only person in the group who had had previous experience in map reading and compass work, so I was summarily appointed, maybe I should say anointed, by the instructors to start with the first leg of the wearisome course.

It was an interesting and challenging cross-country hike. The route took us to the tops of mountains and hills and then back down into the valleys, then back to the top again, back to the bottom, and on and on throughout the long day. This is not the easiest or most expedient way to travel by foot in the mountains. Following the contours of the land is the preferred method of hiking in steep country. These are distinguishable on most maps. We clambered along in single file in the thick vegetation following the readings on our compass, as dictated by our map and our instructors—upward, downward, and inexorably onward toward our assigned objective.

Unfortunately, I had led our wavering group of explorers much too long as we fought our way through the thickets, so that at about seven o'clock that evening, I became inoperative and unable to lead the team. I was so tired physically and mentally from leading the column that I was not lucid and could no longer function or reason intelligently on our course direction.

At that time we had reached our midway point, as indicated on the map. We were elated and hoped the instructors might allow us to stay there for the evening, since darkness was now approaching and we had done so well on the first leg of our journey. Foolish people can often have foolish thoughts. "No way, José," our diligent instructors cruelly informed us. "You have a mission, and you will complete it today," and they emphasized *complete it today*.

Another member of our team took over the lead replacing me, and I retreated toward the rear of the column out of harm's way, badly in need of rest and recuperation. I had reached my physical breaking point, and it was not pretty.

My replacement did an admirable job the rest of the day and into the nighttime hours as we plowed our course onward toward our final first-day objective. It was well after midnight when our hungry, tired, and frazzled group finally arrived at our destination. Actually, I was so tired that I was unable to eat anything and immediately crawled into my warm sleeping bag. The remainder of the group did the same thing.

▼

As we went about our trials on this march, memories from the past crept into my mind. I couldn't help but reflect on our combat patrols in Vietnam. The pain and discomfort from this hike were the same as we had experienced in the jungles. However, our group did not have to contend with booby traps, punji pits, and other surprises that had been left for us by the ruthless enemy when we circumvented our way through the heavy underbrush.

On most occasions when searching for enemy bases and hidden caches of supplies, we were required to do cross-grain patrolling, in single file, from ridgetops to stream bottoms. This type of search-and-destroy mission was necessary because of the way the VC and NVA (Viet Cong, the insurgents in South Vietnam; National Vietnam Army of North Vietnam) would locate and attempt to conceal their various combat base camps.

Their sites could be found on the top of a mountain, on the steep sides of hills, or located deep in a valley adjacent to a small brook. In all cases their base areas would be heavily fortified, dug in, and booby-trapped. There was no set-piece (fixed) method routinely employed by them. It all depended on the nature of the terrain. Sometimes the obvious was not the obvious at all. This was the nature of guerrilla-warfare tactics—to keep you guessing and off guard. The enemy—most especially the NVA—did a damned good job and in most cases was fearless when encountered in battle.

The extreme difficulty of our compass march on Outward Bound was similar to that experience on our combat patrols, and the mountain landforms had some paralleling characteristics. One item that was definitely comparable between the two situations was the exhaustion we felt throughout our bodies at the end of the relentless day. The major differences we had to deal with in Vietnam, of course, were the heat, monsoon weather, the stressful anticipation of combat, and the possibility of men being killed.

▼

Using the compass and map to navigate in thick brush is quite a challenge, especially if you have no prominent terrain features to guide by or if visibility is limited by thick vegetation.

On the Outward Bound course, we did have hills and mountains displayed on the map, which provided solid and obvious reference points for our travels. In the heavy vegetation of the jungle, about all we could see much of the time as we moved about was the brush.

Compass and map-reading training was a major subject matter taught in the marines, with classroom instruction heavily reinforced by practical application in the field. Your life and mission could easily be impacted by the proficiency or lack of proficiency you had acquired on this subject. Fortunately for my needs, in 1964 I obtained additional practical application on the use of the compass and map by attending the British Army Jungle Warfare School in Malaysia. This instruction, under trying conditions—heavy rains and dense terrain—would be of immense help to me in the thickets of Vietnam.

▼

Compass and map reading are difficult subjects for many people. But there are a couple of good rules to remember. First, it is imperative that the compass and map be oriented with the terrain features. Second, it is important to remember that the magnetic declination from true north (compasses always point to magnetic north) is different the world over by a few degrees, meaning the compass and map must both be aligned (oriented) and the compass set to point toward true north and not magnetic north.

Magnetic north is the direction the compass actually points toward. The magnetic declination or difference between true north and magnetic north is typically depicted at the bottom of the map page. An error in calculating this declination by only a few degrees and setting your compass to account for the difference can create an inaccuracy in direction that will take a group or individual off course by hundreds or possibly thousands of meters depending on the distance traveled. Fortunately our orienteering team did a good job of interpreting the map and compass settings so that, after covering several arduous miles in the bold mountainous terrain, we only missed our initial midpoint on the course by less than one hundred yards.

▼

Upon completion of this *death march,* as we later called this highly challenging hike, we were transported to the Chattooga River, near Clayton in North Georgia, for our canoeing expedition.

The Chattooga is a wild and scenic river sequestered by tall timber and natural vegetation. No structures or development of any nature obliterate the wonderful scenery and serenity it provides for people canoeing or rafting this rampant stream. This whitewater river winds through the canopy of trees from its origination point near Cashiers, North Carolina, forming the boundary between the two Carolinas, and continues through Georgia. It is filled with world-class rapids and cascades. Many sections are too dangerous to navigate by either raft or canoe, thus requiring all ambitious boating travelers to portage on and across the rocks around them. This feat can sometimes take several hours, depending on the severity and difficulty encountered while toting the craft over the impediments.

All of these features add to the luster of both the river and the excitement level of the adventure seeker. Navigating this river will definitely force one toward the edge of his or her endurance and courage. Many of you may remember the Chattooga River from the seventies' movie *Deliverance,* which starred Burt Reynolds. We canoed through some of the same areas as those shown in that award-winning film. Fortunately we did not meet any of the ornery mountain folks who were depicted in the movie, but sometime later, in Mountain City, Georgia, I did see the young man who was in the banjo scene of that film playing *Dueling Banjos*—just a little nostalgia for the movie buffs of the world. He had become a hometown hero to the locals.

When we arrived at the river, the weather was once again our enemy. It was raining and sleeting mildly when we took to our durable aluminum canoes. The temperature was also dropping rapidly, so naturally we questioned our sanity once again. The instructors had forgotten the wet-weather gear, and we had to improvise with the few clothing articles we had available. Most of us wore a long-sleeved wool shirt underneath a rain jacket; however, this combination of clothing attire provided no protection if your canoe capsized and you were dumped into the water, as several of us were early in the trip. When the shirts became wet, they were almost useless. Some of them became wet very quickly. Several members of our errant group had never canoed before; as a consequence, as soon as they climbed clumsily into their canoes, these neophytes managed to turn them over, spilling bodies and gear into the cold river water before they even pulled away from the shore.

Raining and sleeting, with some of the bodies and gear now totally drenched, was not an auspicious way to start a three-day canoe training course or an extended waterborne expedition. Nonetheless, we headed out into the unforgiving river toward our first night's camp objective.

We spent the day on our knees in the two-person canoe paddling hard, trying to warm our bodies, while navigating a few small rapids. Finally, just before dark we reached the take-out point for the first leg of the trip. After leaving the river for the night, a new and critical challenge emerged. Two of the students, a man and a woman, began to have chills, the shakes, and a dangerously low body temperature. They were sliding precipitously into an early hypothermic condition.

Hypothermia is caused by prolonged exposure to cold and dampness, which we had sustained for several hours. The afflicted must receive immediate first aid treatment, or they will pass out and can possibly die from the effects of this condition. Just plain body heat, if no other remedy or medical help is readily available, is a quick and safe way to tackle the problem. Thankfully our instructors provided the solution for this crisis. Our group formed a tight circle around them compressing our bodies against theirs, while a few people removed their shirts and pressed their warm skin firmly against theirs. This huddle retards the cold air. The condensed body heat from a person(s) will warm the affected individual(s) after a few minutes. This effort will normally restore equilibrium to their failing systems if the condition has not deteriorated to a highly critical point requiring expedited major medical attention.

It worked. They began to regain normalcy as we continued to press our bodies against theirs. It probably took almost an hour before they fully recovered. We broke our healing circle and began preparations for the night. After some hot coffee and chow, they seemed to be functioning properly.

Incidentally, food is also a great heating source for the body and can greatly help in combating this condition before it erupts into a serious situation. The message: Eat frequently if it's cold, even if you are not hungry. Also, drink lots of water to keep your body hydrated, especially in hot weather. If you should notice your urine is bright yellow, you are becoming dehydrated and need fluids.

The next day was more of the same as far as the canoeing went, but importantly, the weather broke and the rain and sleeting stopped, although the river water was still extremely cold.

Speaking of the cold water, one of the most humorous events of the trip occurred that day when Jim Box's boat companion tipped over their canoe on perfectly flat, slow water and dumped them and all of their gear and supplies into the river. To say that he was really pissed at his canoe mate would be a large, blatant understatement.

My canoe was close by when the incident occurred, and my partner and I attempted to help them recover their canoe and their wits, which had almost faded into oblivion.

Jim had already hastily crawled from the icy water and scrambled up onto a large, flat rock in the middle of the river, close to their accident. He stood erect on his lone, granite platform and began to berate his companion, still struggling in the water, with the most foul and angry expletives that he could spew forth from his furious, cold mouth. His tirade went on for several minutes. I must admit he was quite funny-looking, standing on a rock in the middle of the river, drenched to the bone, shaking from the cold air and totally wet clothes, cursing violently and finally threatening the instructors and everyone else within earshot to leave the course and walk back to Atlanta, some sixty miles distant. In the meantime, all their scattered gear and canoe, which was now upside down, were floating peacefully downstream. After his tirade finally concluded, I yelled to him, inquiring how he was planning to get out of the river without swimming in the cold water to the distant shore.

Finally, cooler heads prevailed. He and his partner retrieved their canoe and gear with the help of the rest of the group, and then both of them unceremoniously crawled back into their bathtub of water, the canoe, and continued with their wet trip while bailing out the accumulation of water with their coffee mugs.

His breaking point, or trial under fire, had now passed, and Jim was back in control of his emotions, ready to proceed with the next challenge. But it took some serious mental readjustment on his part.

▼

Generally it is believed and practiced that during times of stress, strong, committed people will ultimately move up to a higher quality in their thought process and accept the hardship and challenge that befall them. Once this understanding is reached mentally, they do something about it. This is commonly referred to as moral fiber; however, we all have a breaking point, sometimes several, that must be dealt with from time to time in our lives. Especially if we live a life filled with change and stress.

This is normal in the life of risk takers. I experienced my breaking point on the so-called death march. You may recall that I nearly *lost it* after leading the pack of hikers for several hours. I was stressed out, physically spent, disoriented, and unable to continue with my mission. In addition, I had to retreat to the rear of our column to regain both my composure and strength. Jim experienced his breaking point during the canoe expedition. He was cold, wet to the bone, and pissed-off at that time with the course, his companion, the instructors, and the situation. If he could have been flown off his rock and back to Atlanta at that moment, he might have accepted that solution. Who knows? But Jim overcame his breaking point. He went on to successfully complete the program and gain full enjoyment and satisfaction from his trial and the experience in general. As stated earlier, this is called moral fiber or character; it is also tenacity. Some refer to it as *stick-to-itiveness*.

▼

We finished the canoe venue the next day none the worse for wear after shooting a number of compelling rapids. We then headed by van back to the base camp in North Carolina. This had been an eye-opening experience, and we were happy to leave it behind, at least for the time being. Later on, we would successfully undertake additional canoe trips in several locations around the country. We gained the necessary skill to operate in most any kind of riverine environment, except for world-class rapids, and thoroughly enjoyed each and every awesome new experience.

Our next challenges in the course on the following days were rock climbing, rappelling, and the dreaded ropes course. Dreaded, because it was a series of rope obstacles constructed in the treetops, all suspended about seventy-five feet off the ground.

It was the ultimate in obstacle courses and a fantastic confidence builder once you conquered your initial fears. All participants had to ensure that safety ropes were adequately affixed to the harness they wore before they attempted to negotiate the various and sundry barriers. Any failure, especially if there had been no safety lines, could definitely result in serious injury. The rope safety lines were tied tightly around our waists and to the harness, almost squeezing the breath from our shaking bodies. The height of the course in the treetops was as frightening as the physical challenge was demanding. We spent an entire day in this setting learning how to swing like monkeys in the trees, while trying to dispel our fears about heights. We learned the techniques of using the safety harness, meaning that it needed to be hooked up properly to the supporting ropes as we moved through the course from one obstacle to another.

Thank goodness everyone ultimately made it though without any mishap. Obviously, the course was designed to help conquer one's personal trepidations and enhance his or her confidence level. Safety was not an issue unless the suspending ropes broke, which was highly unlikely. At least that is what we were told later after successfully completing the course.

Rock climbing and rappelling were also great fun, although injury was possible if you miscued and crashed into a rock while clambering over, around, and up and down the granite rock faces. We were also required to wear safety harnesses for these events, which helped alleviate some of the anxiety when we climbed up a high distance or rappelled from a particularly lofty, daunting cliff. Both of these events were exhilarating.

Although the course was now winding down, Jim and I were personally gaining momentum every invigorating day. We began to feed like hungry animals off the thrill and spills created from each new experience. It was as if we were approaching nirvana or some level of Zen in our minds. Sounds weird, I know, but it was a fact.

Maybe it was a combination of the elevated altitude and better physical conditioning. It might have been an influx of confidence in our abilities to meet whatever was thrown in our direction. Or it could have been an amalgamation of all three of these possibilities. Whatever it was, it was working on us in a super-hyper mode. We made the most of it and began to extend ourselves more with each undertaking. We were on an adrenalin high, and it felt great. But what goes up must come down. We would eventually crash—not from the course, but from exhaustion.

It was easy for me to identify with these feelings because I had experienced them many times while playing on various athletic teams in college, during my early military training, and later in combat in Vietnam. This incontrovertible mental condition can be somewhat scary and dangerous, because a person may begin to believe he or she is both invisible and invincible. This is not good, and as a matter of fact, it can be downright scary. People can certainly get badly hurt by taking chances or assuming risk without sound forethought and proper inventory of their motives. Fortunately and thankfully, in my case, I did regain a modicum of reality about the situation before doing something too stupid or out-of-the-box crazy. This was not always the case, but it was particularly important during the war when lives were at stake.

Confidence is a great attribute, but never allow yourself to take anything for granted. Think and then think again. Understand your capabilities and learn to work around your liabilities. Furthermore, everyone should remember the old adage, "If you think you are indispensable, place your finger into a bowl of water, and then remove it, and notice the hole it leaves."

▼

We had another couple of hikes and nights to spend in Mother Nature's North Carolina playground, and naturally it had to rain at least once before the trip ended; otherwise, we might have felt that we were not treated with the proper respect from Mother.

But before it was over, we got that and much more, and it was all white and cold. The snow started during the day before we found our campsite for the night. We looked like little white bunnies running though her winter wonderland. I know it sounds like fun, but it was anything but fun. The classes did not usually carry tents on these trips; we used ground cloths and tarps to sleep on and shield us from hostile weather. The quandary that night was to determine how to house thirteen people from the wind and snow, and not to experience a repeat hypothermia performance similar to the one we had had on the Chattooga River.

Our instructors decided that we should tie our tarps together under some dense trees on a hillside, to aid in protection from the bad weather and blowing snow. After joining them together, we tied one end of the tarps much lower to the ground to form a protective, sloping roof to facilitate the runoff of precipitation and to retard the blowing, cold wind. The sides and uphill front were left open. Then the entire group crawled under the tarps and aligned their sleeping bags side by side, as close as possible, in a long lateral column.

Togetherness and some amount of close familiarity seemed like a plausible course of action to take if it would help keep us warm. We huddled together, pressing our sleeping bags as close as we could to one another, seeking any body heat that would emerge from the crowded arrangement. We stayed warm, at least those in the center of our human body pile did. Those folks on the open ends of the shelter did not fare quite so well.

The next day, after successfully weathering the storm, someone in our group remarked that they thought they had heard a few sleeping bag zippers being worked during the night. Perhaps some members of our crowd had cuddled together more closely than others. It may have been nothing more than creative imagination that fostered the comment. Even though a few of the mixed group had possibly found a better, more palatable way to stay warm that dreary, cold night, it made little difference to most of us. We had survived, and that was the issue. As was said earlier, *"In times of stress, people always try to move up to a higher quality."* This is human nature and normal, in case you are wondering. After completing this ill-fated overnight segment, we headed back to the base camp for our final challenge.

The following day, we cleaned our gear and then spent most of that day on our solo. This was time by our lonesome in the woods making notes on the course, detailing what we had learned, and generally putting our thoughts together about how we could use the experience to create a better life. This experience was followed by a competitive and tortuous five-mile mountain run, mostly uphill, that terminated at the camp headquarters. It was a fitting end for the course. After a wrap-up of all the loose ends, we were treated to an all-vegetable pasta respite without any alcohol, naturally, to celebrate our graduation. And it was great. After the sparse food we had eaten during the tenure of the course, we ate our chow like wildly crazed, hungry animals.

We were debriefed the following morning, said our good-byes, and headed out to our respective homes. It was finally over. For Jim and me, our first stop as soon as we reached civilization was to buy hamburgers and a couple of beers. Some pundits say old habits die hard, but I think in this case we were just plain hungry!

▼

Upon returning to the bank, Jim and I spent considerable time evaluating the potential of using this course in our management-training syllabus, and after considerable reflection and discussion we elected *not* to go forward with it.

The nine-day program was outstanding in all respects; however, we believed it was too long for our purposes, and probably too physically demanding for the mostly female and older members of our staff. Also, we thought it might send the wrong message to our troops if they were tested beyond their capabilities. We were greatly concerned about this aspect of any future program and did not want our managers to think they had been put through a survival course, since it definitely was not for the fainthearted and we were concerned that some of our officers might relate negative feelings to future attendees. Of greater importance, we believed a three-day course would be more appropriate, and we preferred to send a group of at least ten to fifteen managers to each class. We thought that a larger group over a shorter time span would promote better camaraderie and teamwork in the company. Consequently, we decided to look into some other executive outdoor-training programs, knowing that if we kept searching, we would eventually find the perfect fit for our specific company needs. In many respects, we were saddened that we were unable to use Outward Bound; it was and is an outstanding training program.

In the eighties, executive wilderness programs were just beginning to come into vogue in corporate America. Ultimately, First Georgia Bank would be one of the early pioneers to use this method of training for key members of their management team.

Some months later, we located the program that fit our precise needs. Actually, it was an Executive Wilderness Program hosted by Boston University and conducted in conjunction with a local Atlanta company, Executive Adventure.

After successfully enrolling a large component of managers and receiving much attention, primarily because we were the only bank and probably one of the first companies in Atlanta to employ this unique and new training technique, the Atlanta newspapers and business magazines refered to our staff at First Georgia in various articles as *"the bankers who swing from trees,"* more or less a reference to the ropes course employed in the training. Our staff loved this unique recognition, and so did our customers.

Our competitors, on the other hand, thought we were crazy; after all, no staid, boring banker would do things like this. It just didn't seem to fit the mold. But it fit *our mold*—and it worked for us. This training became a hallmark in the development and implementation of our dynamic business and sales culture, and eventually promoted the accomplishment of all of the future goals that we had initially identified for the bank.

As for Jim and me, well, our new interest and adventure had just begun. It would last for many years, almost a quarter of a century, and carry us to many exciting places involving quite a few people.

These adventures would also leave us with enough thrills and stories to last a lifetime. Matter of fact, we still tell them today, that is, whenever we can find someone or anyone who will listen. If we can't find an interested party, we repeat them to each other, over and over and over. Amusingly, they do seem to get better with time. Read on, and you'll understand the reason why they do.

THREE

APPALACHIAN TRAIL

When the summer months arrived in Georgia, Jim and I took to the woods once again. Still enamored and thrilled from our Outward Bound experience and finally at ease with the outdoors and satisfied with our improved fieldcraft, we were now eager to apply our improved skills in the bush and to continue with our invigorating open-air adventure program.

We had all the gear we needed, and after a few blisters, we had broken in our relatively new Danner boots from our previous trip to a comfortable fitting level. We were ready to get on the trail and give it the old college try once again.

When I thought about or used this new equipment and compared it to that issued to Marine fighting units in South Vietnam in 1966, it was almost impossible and definitely impracticable to try to compare the quality or functionality. The latest equipment technology was so far superior that it made the old military stuff look almost primitive.

▼

Marines were issued a pair of jungle boots when they first arrived in-country. These boots were lightweight and not totally waterproof. The upper part of the shoe was made from a fabric-type binding that seemed to soak up the water after it had been worn and exposed to the elements for any period of time; however, the soles were durable. A metal-type innersole insert was also provided to help mitigate the effects or penetration of certain kinds of booby traps; however, the regular rubber sole of the boot was not stout enough to prevent the barbed point of a bamboo stick with a metal tip attached, hidden away belowground, from penetrating it. The metal innersole insert was supposed to help protect the foot from injury when these booby traps were encountered.

The enemy would assemble these injury-prone devices in concealed or camouflage holes dug a few feet below the ground's surface. They would often defecate on the sharp, pointed tips to help inflict rapid infection when an unsuspecting soldier stepped on one and it pierced the sole of his boot and jabbed into his foot. These nasty booby traps were commonly called *punji pits.*

Booby traps in general were probably responsible for as many of the debilitating injures to American servicemen in Vietnam as any other weapon employed, including artillery bombardment, mortar fire, rocket attacks, and small-arms' fire.

It was amazing how effective these crude instruments were. The momentum and weight of a man's falling body becoming impaled on a fixed, sharp barb cut into the tip of a bamboo stick, buried below the ground, could create a formidable situation for serious injury to the foot soldier.

▼

Hiking boots should be sturdy, especially when carrying a backpack, and large enough to accommodate the swelling of the foot after several miles of hiking. The fit should include extra space in the toe box so the toes do not jam-up against the front of the boot when descending steep slopes. This applies to any kind of walking shoe worn when hiking in the mountains or even for leisure walking.

Also, it is necessary to wear a good pair of reinforced socks. Most times a thin liner sock worn under your outer wool sock will provide protection. Frequent waterproofing of your boots is also a good idea; this can be done with a product sold at your local sporting goods or outfitter store.

Boots or hiking shoes made with Gore-Tex will mitigate water seepage and are generally your best bet for hiking. Just in case blisters do occur on your pinkies while hiking, be sure to carry a package of Band-Aids or moleskin with you to place over the sore to lessen any discomfort and infection.

These things were learned the hard way, and there is no better teacher than experience. But I would encourage everyone to always try to learn from others' misfortune whenever possible. No one should have to practice to be miserable. It comes naturally in the backcountry with the rugged terrain and bad weather.

There were times on combat missions in South Vietnam when we were required to scout out flowing streams while searching for the enemy. Due to the wet nature of the terrain and contours of the land, much of that time was spent walking in the streams. After a couple of days, immersion foot would spread to almost everyone in the unit. At one time over half of my rifle company, seventy-five men, was incapacitated with trench foot.

It was necessary to halt our operations for several days to allow my men to recover from this problem and to regain their operational effectiveness.

Whenever your feet are wet, it is essential to find the time to dry them out—the same for your boots; otherwise, this constant wet condition can deteriorate quickly into a major medical issue. Also, it is always a good idea to carry several pairs of socks and to change them whenever the feet become damp or soaked with water. When our socks were wet and we were on patrol during the day, we would put them inside our shirt next to our body. The heat from our upper torso would dry them out within a few hours. At night, after a hard, wet day in the boonies, we would place them next to or under our body, or use them as a kind of pillow to help with the drying process. It was important to take proper precautions to ensure that we had dry socks on our feet the next day when we continued with our combat operation.

As noted earlier about our experience on the Chattooga River with two of our companions, body heat can help restore functioning equilibrium for the outdoor enthusiast in many unique ways.

▼

Our explorer group tried to be prepared for these contingencies during our adventures; this kind of preparation is very important, especially if a person is hiking ten to fifteen miles per day. Let me assure you, if you don't already know from past experience, it is miserable to hike for a long distance with festering sores and bleeding feet.

These early hiking and camping experiences took place in the North Georgia Mountains on the Appalachian Trail, which begins about sixty miles from Atlanta. About seventy-five miles of the Appalachian Trail is in Georgia and is locally accessible to the hiking aficionado. The southern Appalachian trailhead is located on Springer Mountain. It traverses from there through fourteen states to Katahdin, Maine, some 2,160 miles.

However, we had no plans or time to undertake this challenge. Conversely, our trips were to be weekend forays at the most, with only one or two nights camping. We did not want to overdo our program and bring this new undertaking to a rapid end by overextending ourselves in the early stages. Later on in our explorations, we would nearly foolishly accomplish this deed while attending more strenuous Outward Bound courses around the country over the next few years.

Our plan was to hike various sections of the trail in Georgia, primarily to save travel time and allow for more time in the woods. We probably had more eagerness, motivation, and diverse hiking opportunities for this new venture than we had good sense. Nonetheless, we launched our efforts enthusiastically, with the vision of becoming bold and hardy mountain men, just like you see in the movies. We began living their lives vicariously as we continued to expand our efforts and time in the backcountry. Frankly, we did well, many times hiking in excess of twelve miles per day while enjoying the beautiful mountain scenery. Then as night fell, we would establish well-positioned campsites in the mountains, with wonderful views of the surrounding valleys and numerous water elements.

We always tried to leave our camping sites cleaner than we found them. Many times we spent extra time cleaning up the mess that previous campers had deposited. I cannot understand why people leave their camps in such disarray, almost as if they could not care less about the environment or the next group that would want to camp in a nice, clean camping area. Oh well, it is human nature for some, I assume, particularly those people who have little regard for anything but their own personal gratification. Our meals were usually prepackaged freeze-dried food, purchased from various outfitter stores, and cooked on a small, compact gasoline-fed Coleman Peak camping stove.

We had been taught to travel with minimum gear to keep the load under sixty pounds, but we did not always follow this very appropriate and comfortable guideline. Our inbred comfy instincts had not yet been jettisoned from our city minds; consequently, our tired bodies would speak to us wisely at the end of the day and tell us, in no uncertain terms, that our loads were much too heavy. We tried to listen; finally we made the adjustment after much pain. For example, both Jim and I carried a tent and some special varieties of canned food and, on occasion, a six-pack of beer. Mostly this was unnecessary and added greatly to the weight. But the beer was sure good for our attitude at the end of a hard, tiring day.

We didn't need the stoves and extra fuel, and we should have done without the fancy canned tidbits. It is hard to break old habits and learn new ones, especially when people think they need all the extra convenience items to survive in the woods. We should have been building fires and using them for cooking, and relying totally on the lightweight prepackaged food. For some ridiculous reason, we missed these important points, probably because we had used larger cooking stoves and real food on the Outward Bound program in North Carolina. At that time, we had more people to feed, but we also had more backs available to carry gear, a very important factor.

I can only assume we must have thought it was best to continue with this same method of cooking our meals and that we wanted to learn how to properly use our new Peak pack stoves, which could be contrary at times, depending on the weather and elevation. Eventually we would get it right and reduce the load we carried, but it would take time and lots of soreness before the realization of how we were unnecessarily torturing ourselves fully settled into our hardheaded minds.

We visited the mountains several times during the summer months and then had a quiet hiatus from the woods until late October. The leaves in Georgia begin their transition at this time of the year, and the spectacle of all the changing variations in colors creates a spectacular rainbow of sheer beauty normally occurring around the last weekend of the month. This colorful display, more prominent in the mountains, seems to reach its apex over a three-day period, and then starts an imminent decline as its vibrant color scheme fades and the leaves begin falling from the trees.

We learned the forecasted color change of the leaves would occur over a specific weekend and quickly decided we should be in the most fortuitous place possible to see this phenomenon—the North Georgia Mountains on the Appalachian Trail. Another hiking trip in the mountains was now seemingly evolving in our minds, and before it was finalized, we invited two additional friends to join us on this adventure. Mack Butler, an attorney with the Atlanta-based firm of Troutman, Sanders, Lockerman, and Ashmore, and legal counsel for our bank, who incidentally had been trying to get me to go on a hiking trip for quite some time, would join us, along with his brother Terry, who worked as a branch manger for the bank.

The date was set, agreements and plans were made, and provisions determined; we would soon be on another outdoors adventure trip, but most, I repeat, most of our plans did not work as initially perceived because, yes, you guessed it, rain and plenty of it came cascading down from the heavens above.

Mack was an excellent outdoorsman, in good physical condition; however, his brother, an avid smoker but outdoors-knowledgeable, was another issue. I think Mack was trying to whip Terry into some better level of conditioning, because he nearly killed the boy when he led the hike by walking at a much faster pace than his brother could maintain. Every time we took a break during the hike, poor Terry nearly collapsed from exhaustion. While resting, he always managed to sneak a few hidden puffs from a cigarette. I suppose he was not quite ready to be encouraged by his big brother to mend his ways and seek a healthier lifestyle. Brotherly rivalry likely prevailed, though, as is common among most siblings. The entire issue was not a pretty sight, and when the trip was finished, poor Terry looked like death warmed over. But this wasn't the worst of it, as time and the weather would later unveil.

We spent our first night in a cabin nestled in the mountains and had a steak dinner at an inexpensive, remote-country greasy spoon. This was punishment for our digestive tracks. Upon arising the next morning, we discovered that it was overcast, misting rain with a light fog permeating the area. Prior to this journey, before departing Atlanta, we had reviewed the weather forecasts, and they had indicated only a "slight" chance of rain. Our worst suspicions were now sadly being confirmed.

We had planned to hike on the southernmost part of the Appalachian Trail in Georgia and end our trip at the terminus approach trail beginning at the base of Springer Mountain, the official Georgia trailhead for the Appalachian Trail. Our starting point was about twenty-four miles north of the trailhead near Suches, south of Blairsville, Georgia. After reaching Springer we would still have eight miles to walk down the mountain to complete the hike, ending at Amicalola Falls State Park. It would be a long hike—three days and thirty-two miles of trekking. We planned to spend two nights in the woods.

Nonetheless, in good spirits and eager, even with the bad weather, we dropped off one car at the park and then drove together in a second car to our starting point. The longer we drove, the worse the weather became until we could barely follow the road because of the obscure, mucky, and rainy conditions.

Upon arriving at our trail entrance and entering the woods, we were amazed at just how bad the visibility was and how dripping wet the woods were. It was a foggy mess, and we could only see about fifty feet through the overcast wet conditions.

The entire area was fully socked in and the resulting dampness numbed our shivering bodies, but there was no turning back at this point. We were on a mission.

Finally someone in our group, obviously trying to offer some cheer and encouragement not too brightly remarked, *"This fog and rain will lift later in the day when the sun comes out."* Obviously, his statement and unqualified weather analysis was utterly ridiculous. But hope springs eternal. So, we all agreed, and in our own foolhardiness, started our trek. The more we hiked throughout the day, the worse the weather became. It was so overcast and murky that you could not see the leaves hanging from their water-laden branches. The conditions were actually so bad that we had a difficult time staying on the trail.

Mack Butler was the first leader of our inglorious group, and within one hour he had poor Terry, his brother, who brought up the rear of our not-too-tight column, huffing and puffing like an old worn-out or overloaded locomotive. Naturally, being the sagacious big brother with something to prove to his younger kin, he never slacked off his pace at any time while in the lead, regardless of what was happening to Terry or Jim, or me for that matter. On and on we sloshed throughout the day as we worked our way through the messy weather and over the undulating trail. Naturally, we were complaining constantly, which was our normal group *modus operandi* on most of our expeditions.

When strong-minded men are thrown together in most any endeavor, a clash of wills is certain to occur. Someone in the group will always have a better plan or even an agenda to express to the group in hope of having his way. This is human nature, and we had plenty of that—most of the time, and it was obvious. Arguments always surfaced about any new idea or plan presented by another member of the group, and these friendly but pointed altercations would last throughout the entire trip. Amazingly, some of them still continue today. Oh well, this was part of the fun, experience, and numerous but inflated stories that evolved from these experiences and explorations.

We hiked twelve miles in the gloom of that first day, finally agreeing on a camping spot in an open area in the woods adjacent to the trail. It was so hazy and cloudy, we did not want to wander too far off-course because we feared we might lose our sense of direction.

Pitching our tents quickly, we prepared dinner, wolfed it down, and climbed into our sleeping bags. With all the wetness around, there was nothing else we could do except mill around outside and soak up more water on our already rain-drenched bodies.

When we awoke the next morning, we found the same conditions and knew we would face another day of long, damp hiking, with little respite from the weather. Unfortunately, it would get a lot worse before we concluded that day.

From our trail map, we knew there was a shelter located on the top of Springer Mountain, and we thought we should try to get there before nightfall. It would take most of the day to hike the necessary miles to reach our objective, and we would have more difficult terrain to traverse than the previous day.

Later in the day, a heavy downpour descended on us just a few miles from the shelter. We continued to march toward our destination with the deepest hope that when we arrived at the hut, there would be room at the inn for our soaked four-man group. We suspected that other hikers along the way, who were also struggling in the rain, would have similar intentions, and the shelter might be filled to capacity. It would only accommodate ten people adequately. It was about four o'clock when we found the refuge. Luckily we found only five people huddled inside the open-sided hut. We quickly crawled in out of the downpour and established our sleeping niches in a vacant corner of the shelter for the night.

Everyone had their cooking stoves going in the hooch trying to get some food down their gullets to help them warm up from the wintry, wet conditions. This was certainly one occasion when it paid a huge dividend to carry a stove and extra fuel with us in our backpacks. Everything was so wet it would have been impossible to find any wood that was even partially dry to start a fire.

▼

On patrol during the war, we never built a fire because the light could give our position away to the enemy and possibly provoke mortar or artillery attacks. Most of the time while in the bush, we actually tried to hide when we stopped for the night.

Frequently our unit would move into a position before dark and then relocate to another spot a short distance away after the night settled. We hoped this maneuver would confuse the enemy and aid in concealing our exact location or, better yet, our hideout. This ploy must have worked, because we were never attacked at night, except when we had been in a set-piece (fixed) camp or an open area for any protracted period. This static condition gave the enemy ample opportunity to zero in on us with their weaponry.

When cooking our C rations, we used the small heat tab that came packaged in the box to heat our various cans of foodstuffs. We did this by a punching a couple of holes in the bottom of an empty can with a knife, placing the tab at the bottom of the can, lighting it, and then balancing the can of food that was to be heated on the top of our rudimentary makeshift stove. This method of cooking would only emit a small, bluish glow. To conceal this light, we placed the contraption at the bottom of our foxhole. It worked perfectly, and we could usually enjoy a hot meal for breakfast and dinner, other conditions permitting.

It was from this background of cooking in the war that I now preferred to haul the stove and fuel with me, rather than risk starting a fire, failing, and then eating uncooked, cold food.

▼

With the present situation, we were damned glad we had brought our stoves on this particular trip to the mountains.

After we had been entrenched for a couple of hours in the shelter, another two people arrived—a father and his young son. The boy was about eight years old, and both he and his father were in bad shape. They had hiked the eight miles up the mountain in the drenching rain, and their clothes and other gear were wringing wet. We made room for them, and they crawled to a corner space in the shelter; it was then that we actually noticed the sad condition they were in and their lack of equipment, food, and preparation for their outing. They were wearing tennis shoes, had little rain gear of any quality, no change of clothes, and had brought blankets that were now too wet to provide any warmth. We were appalled and pissed off at the father for his shortsightedness; nonetheless, we began immediately to share our extra provisions and clothing with them. They were in serious trouble, nearing hypothermia, needed hot food, to dry out, and to get some warm clothes on their shaking bodies. Otherwise, we would have a major medical catastrophe on our hands—the man's son for sure, and most likely, his father also.

We were able to get some hot food inside of them, some wool clothes on their shivering bodies, and among the group in the shelter, found enough bedding items for them to sleep warmly. Everyone in the hut strongly suggested that they go back down the mountain as soon as the rains abated the next morning. The father agreed. Frankly, he had no other choice, and he was given none.

We spent sixteen long, boring hours sequestered in that hut. When dawn finally arrived after a very weary and uncomfortable night, I crawled outside to check on the weather situation. It had finally quit raining, although the fog and mist were still hanging over us like a thick blanket and we still could not see the sky. Of course, we had not seen it for two days anyway, so there was no surprise with that breakthrough observation.

I thought to myself, *"It's time to get the hell out of here."* Our group rousted from our night's quarters, fixed some coffee, ate some cold protein bars, and in total agreement, packed our gear and headed down the mountain. There was no arguing and no bickering; everyone was in concurrence. Perhaps this was the first time on the trip that we had reached full agreement on any issue. In our haste to get off the devilish mountain and out of the foul weather, we probably hiked this final eight-mile leg in record time. We didn't stop for anything, except to pee a couple of times—we had to discharge the coffee—and reached our car in the parking lot by late morning.

As we drove back to our starting point to pick up the other automobile, we talked about the trip and concluded it had been a dreadful experience, almost a disaster, but we all agreed, except for Terry, that we had benefited from this experience.

Mack's brother was still with us bodily, but his mind was almost depleted from the efforts he had put forth. He received no adulations from his big brother, who was obviously disappointed with his physical status.

We had not seen any beautiful scenery, so as far as we knew, the turning of the leaves never happened or just passed us by surreptitiously. So much for our planning. We didn't return to the Georgia mountains for some time. Our backcountry interests were evolving rapidly with each new experience; we would soon begin to undertake more diverse activities in more distant locations. Actually, we began thinking and talking about heading out to the western mountains. The thought was intriguing!

FOUR

THE EVERGLADES

In early December 1983, I received an intriguing brochure from the Outward Bound School in North Carolina announcing a nine-day canoeing course that was to be conducted early the following year in the Florida Everglades. The brightly colored pamphlet had a compelling, picturesque photo on the front cover showing two people, with their shirts off and in shorts in canoes, holding their paddles exuberantly above their heads as if they were celebrating a special summer event. The sun was shining brightly with a warmish tint, outlined in the summerlike background by a beautiful blue sky.

Needless to say, I was taken by this scene and thought how wonderful and refreshing it would be to travel to a warm climate in mid-February, enjoy the sun and sand, and leave the Atlanta winter months and demanding work schedule behind for a few days.

In my mind's eye, I visualized the trip as a great getaway, with beautiful scenery, interesting flora and fauna, and a unique opportunity to learn something new about canoeing. More outdoor-water adventures, but perhaps a little more awe-inspiring in scenery and probably less physically demanding than the last Outward Bound program. At least, that's the way it was presented and the way it was perceived by me from this persuasive announcement.

I showed the brochure to my other adrenalin-seeking junkies, Jim and Mack, and we all agreed that we should immediately enroll in the course. Another adventure was now on the horizon, and by the time it was over, it would test our mettle and challenge the very core of our character and strength. Of course, we had no idea of the trials that lay in store for us. Clueless, I believe, is the most descriptive and accurate term I can conjure up from my personal vocabulary that defined our understanding and outlook at that moment.

As scheduled, we caught a plane to Miami for our new endeavor; full of excitement, we were ready and in need of a break from our daily corporate grind. We managed to charm the Delta stewardesses on our flight—at least we thought we did—with our inflated stories and, importantly, the need for foodstuffs to help us through this new challenging and demanding undertaking. They reciprocated our crude advances and ominous stories by giving us bags of candy bars, sandwiches, and other goodies for our novel adventure. We were always afraid we might run short of foodstuffs, as the result of our first experience with Outward Bound, and end up hungry, weak, and possibly disoriented—meaning, not doing what we were supposed to do according to the rules.

This point was especially important to Mack, who constantly seemed to be starving and in search of food. His concern really piqued after we told him about the meager food supplies that had been provided on the first Outward Bound program.

We essentially carried our *gratis* Delta-supplied goodie bags with us until they were accidentally discovered by our instructors. This was an absolute no-no for Outward Bound. Consequently, we had to share our rapidly declining stash with the other members in the course. We had been snacking on them for days, gaining weight in the process, while our companions were losing weight as a result of all the physical requirements of the challenging course.

We spent our first day in the course gathering supplies; being issued gear; swimming, which was a test to ensure that we could make it back to the shore if our canoe overturned; instruction on maneuvering our crafts; and finally loading our boats to haul them to the put-in point at Flamingo, the southern entry to the Everglades.

Around nine o'clock that night, we finally launched and headed up a small estuary to our first night's lodging site. Most nights we would sleep on an open-air, roof-covered, wooden raised platform supported by poles, built several feet above the water.

These camping platforms, called *chickees*, were designed and constructed to help protect campers from the water and any unwanted visitors, like alligators, crocodiles, and snakes. (*Chickee* is the Seminole Indian word for *house*.) In the Everglades there were few places to camp on *terra firma* due to the abundant water flow, thick marsh areas, and lowlands.

▼

The Glades were originally a slow-moving freshwater river fed by Lake Okeechobee. Now there are a labyrinth of mangrove waterways, marshes, and salt prairies. It is the largest remaining subtropical wilderness in this nation. The 102-mile-long Wilderness Waterway that we would canoe runs from the southernmost entry point, where we started at the National Park Flamingo Center, and flows north to where it ends at Everglades City.

The increased development in southern Florida has impacted this area in recent years, and still does today, because the canals are alternately drained and flooded to meet the water needs of the adjacent towns.

This reverses the natural wet and dry cycles. This situation, obviously, has threatened and endangered the variety of fish, birds, animals, and vegetation that depend on a more stabilized environment.

Everglades National Park is comprised of about 1.5 million acres of natural habitat. Our travels would take us through most of the major lakes, streams, rivers, and ponds that traverse the centermost part of the Glades, with a short canoeing trip in the adjoining Gulf of Mexico, where we would ultimately camp for two nights on the coast at Highland Beach, located on Key McLaughlin.

▼

Rare American crocodiles would be our constant companions throughout most of our travels on the wilderness waterways. Interestingly, they would watch our travels, leisurely lying in groups on the banks of secluded rivers as we paddled by. At night they would maintain a vigilant interest in us as we slept on our platforms out of their grasp, perhaps hopeful one of us might tumble into the water; then they could enjoy a meaty late-night snack. You may wonder how we knew they were around us at night. All you had to do was scan the water with your flashlight, and you could see their glowing red eyes penetrating the darkness. It was really kind of eerie. Some of those eyes appeared very close.

This was the adventure we had signed on for, and it would be one of the most difficult and trying experiences we would encounter during all of our many expeditions over a twenty-five-year period. It would also be the most endearing and impact us personally in ways that were hard to understand. For example, when the course was nearing conclusion, we did not want it to end. Go figure that attitude!

Our instructors cautioned us early that reentry into civilization might be difficult for some, because the hardships and challenges we successfully overcame would affect us in a unique way, making everything else seemingly inconsequential and unexciting. We did find this to be true. After returning to Atlanta, we felt like we were in some kind of magical daze, although we were definitely at complete ease with ourselves. It was like we were there, but we were not really there; all the while we really wanted to be back in the swamps undertaking more risks. These impressions went on for a couple of weeks before they finally subsided. How could this happen, and what was the root cause of these intense feelings?

It had to involve the deep commitment required to complete the course, the daily physical challenges that had to be overcome, coupled with the constant array of evolving risks, culminating in one hell of an adrenalin rush that went on for days. In effect, we had been on a constant high and had a difficult time coming down when it was over. Our systems had apparently been traumatized by the overbearing events we had encountered and ultimately conquered.

▼

Similar situations occur with soldiers returning home from a war or a combat experience after they have been exposed to great personal risks and witnessed unbelievable carnage. They may have a difficult time adjusting to their environment, friends, family members, or society in general. They also have been on a high, although theirs may have lasted for a year or more and been much more stressful and mentally disturbing.

Coming down, gaining control of their lives, and realizing they are no longer at risk on a daily basis and that the danger has passed is very difficult for their minds to grasp. The outside world may seem to be a humdrum place to them; problems that are of major concern on their jobs or to other people may appear to be trivial or minuscule after the distress they have recently experienced.

This situation is not totally uncommon for many and is the reason some soldiers will decide to return to the conflict. This course seems to be more palatable for them to adjust to, and it also appears to correlate with their altered and confused mentality. They may miss the thrill of combat, and even more importantly, the continuing adrenalin rush they have been required to live with and operate under for an extended period.

Sadly this decision to return to the war zone may seem to them the only path to follow in order to find satisfaction and happiness in their lives. They must be on a mental high constantly; otherwise, they have no positive direction or capability to live normally.

This occurred with several of my friends who were in Vietnam with me and had lived through and survived unbelievably dangerous experiences. A few of them made the decision to go back *in-country* for peace of mind shortly after they returned home.

▼

That first night we departed from Flamingo under a moonlit sky, nudging our canoes along at a slow pace because of the heavy vegetation, much of which was hanging over the water. It seemed as if we were traveling under a subdued, dimly lighted channel of tree limbs until we finally reached the remote Coot Bay, a large lake.

For me it was almost reminiscent of a scene from the 1950's movie *The African Queen,* staring Humphrey Bogart and Katharine Hepburn. If you saw the film, you might remember when Bogart was required to pull the boat by rope through the heavy underbrush in what appeared to be an overgrown, swampy-like, slow meandering stream. We were not pulling our canoes, but the thicket enclosing our crafts and the brackish stream delivered an uninviting message similar to that portrayed in the movie.

Just as we reached the opening into the bay, a loud, crashing noise jerked us to attention. It sounded like a small explosion. At first we thought it was some kind of a ploy or trick our instructors were playing on us. But no, on closer inspection what we saw were two bellowing manatees (sea cows) playing in the pond; when we surprised them with our arrival, they submerged with a thunderous splashing of water. This wilderness area is among the few remaining places where manatees and crocodiles are assured of a permanent and safe sanctuary.

We continued to paddle until about three o'clock in the morning, finally locating our campsite, a chickee platform located in the center of our waterway course. Crawling up the wooden ladder of the stand, we dumped our gear on the hard wooden floor and immediately began to unroll our sleeping bags for a much-needed few hours of respite. Our restless slumber did not last through the night.

Before dawn we were awakened by a loud, crashing sound just at the water's edge at the base of our chickee. It went on for a few minutes and then quickly subsided. It was too dark to determine the cause of the noise. Our instructors appropriately decided to wait until it was light to investigate the occurrence. At early dawn one of our instructors, Mary Day, ventured down the ladder to the small boat dock to check out the incident, and what she discovered was unsettling. As we watched from our safe haven high above the water's edge, she found one of our canoes bent and crushed in the center section, as if it had been struck by a heavily weighted object. Apparently a large crocodile caused the racket we heard during the night when it had tried to leap into the canoe and then had to disengage from the tangled wreckage after pulverizing it with its weight and struggle to get free.

Naturally we wondered, "*What was it looking for? Possibly one of us for a late-night snack,*" we considered. Or maybe the croc was only trying to obtain a tasty mouthful of nourishment, like our packed foodstuffs. We now understood the reason for sleeping above the water out of harm's way. The wooden floors no longer seemed so high or too hard. We were damned glad to have been on them and to have the height of the platform between us and whatever lurked below. After regaining our wilting composure and performing our morning rituals, we loaded our gear and happily started on the next leg of our adventure.

We canoed all day, crossing another large body of water called Whitewater Bay. After covering about twenty miles, we finally reached another platform in Oyster Bay, where we spent our second night.

The next day we paddled on a river that led us to our next destination, which interestingly enough, was in the middle of this waterway; it was not an island or a platform. We would spend that night with our canoes anchored in the center of the stream and would attempt to sleep in our crafts. Believe me, *attempt* is about all we could do. It was unbelievably uncomfortable trying to sleep confined on the top of our stored gear. All six canoes were tied together with ropes. Lines were then attached to the port and starboard sides of the lashed canoes and tied to trees located on the opposite shorelines. This anchoring system was to ensure that the canoes would remain stationary and not float helter-skelter downstream with the current. Then we rigged a large tarp over the group to protect us in the event of inclement weather. Our river campsite was properly named The Shark and would eventually connect with another waterway that would ultimately take us into the Gulf of Mexico.

We did not see any sharks, but Jim, while canoeing, had caught some fish earlier in the day, and he hung them over our gunnels (sides) of our outboard canoe that night, thinking we might cook them the next day. When we awoke the following morning and checked our lines, we found the fish had been mostly devoured by something in the water. A small shark probably enjoyed an easy catch for his dinner. It might have been a turtle, but the tearing teeth marks seemed to indicate otherwise.

We did not leave our canoes the entire night we were tied together. We prepared our evening meal on our camp stoves, and afterward we tried to sleep. As I noted earlier, sleeping conditions were pretty much intolerable; nevertheless, most members of the group did manage a few hours of sleep.

When you are tired, really tired, you can get some shut-eye almost under any conditions; we were, and we did.

"What about going to the potty?" you might ask. Well, there was only one way to do it, and it was over the side of your canoe—for both the men and the women. There was no way to be discreet in this situation. When you had to go, you went, mostly with your *fanny or pecker* dangling over the side of the craft. With thirteen people going at different times throughout the night, there was lots of shuffling about, followed by the tinkle of water or other nondescriptive things into the stream.

By the time morning arrived, we had become a very tightly-knit group with little to hide from each other. Overnight the women's language had developed more explosively and expletively. The men had already accomplished their own particular vindictive mode of expression. Now, after just a couple of days of hardship and stress, the entire group sounded like a bunch of drunken marines on the rampage in a rowdy bar.

This day, unknown to us at the time, would be a *ballbuster*. It would nearly bring every member of our team to their knees. We canoed for a few hours to a take-out spot on the river, and then for the next seven hours, we were required to portage our canoes across a wide, marshy, mudflat in a penetrating downpour. The mud was so treacherous that some of the people actually sank up to their waists in the mire as they pushed and pulled their fully loaded canoes across the mushy, porous soil. Several people actually lost their shoes when they were sucked off their feet by the gunk, as they trekked along manhandling their boats in the quicksand-like muck.

Late in the afternoon, we located the starting point for the next leg of the trip. It was nothing more than a trickle of seeping surface water that would grow in size, depth, and width in time. Eventually, it became a small tributary called the Harney River; it would ultimately dump into a larger stream called the Wild River.

We dragged our canoes into the dribble of water, pulling and pushing them along until the current and depth would fully support their weight. Then we crawled inside and, standing erect, grasping tree limbs, continued pulling our canoes over the shallow water.

In the next stage, as the water deepened, we were able to sit in our canoes and push them along with our paddles. Finally the water became deep enough to actually paddle our crafts. What a relief after two hours of pure misery and excruciating physical labor!

We finally came to the juncture of the Harney River. Our designated campsite, another chickee, was just a short distance down the river, but we were late getting there because of our seven-hour portage and the difficulty of locating the river entry. When we arrived the chickee was occupied; another group had arrived earlier and had already settled in for the night. There was no room at the inn, so to speak.

Our instructors sheepishly admitted they had miscalculated the time requirements by taking a route that had never been traveled before, causing us to be late; consequently, we lost our campsite. It was on a first-come basis if not occupied after a specified time.

On we went into what was known as *the Nightmare*. This stretch of the Harney River is an eight-mile mangrove tangle dividing the north and south halves of the wilderness waterway. Many paddlers are intimidated by this flooded jungle; it would be a miserable place to be stranded overnight. Thank God, we were able to get through it and not spend the night; things and critters were everywhere.

Soon it was dark, and we continued to work our way down this water passageway, which is impassable at low tide, floating under, around, through, and over broken trees and creeping, thick vegetation. The twisting river channel narrowed significantly, and as we struggled along, we could see many crocs huddled on the riverbanks watching our every movement. As it grew darker, their shiny red eyes seemed to glow more menacingly in the cool, black night.

At one point a low-hanging tree branch slapped me in the face, dislodging my cap, and it fell abruptly into the brackish water. I reached to retrieve it, but then quickly reasoned it would be stupid to put my meaty hand into that dark, uninviting stream. Looking at all the red eyes of the crocs around, I thought, *"I might just pull back a nub. To hell with the hat,"* I hastily decided; hats are replaceable, but not human limbs, especially mine.

During this phase of our lengthy, struggling, arduous expedition, Mack Butler, my companion explorer and staunch outdoorsman, capitulated to his breaking point. While engaged in the intense physical labor of the earlier, lengthy portage, he had shouldered a great deal of responsibility, caring for some of the less vigorous members of the group; consequently, he was nearly undone physically before the most recent nighttime challenge we had now undertaken in the Nightmare.

One of the afflicted was a retired marine corps general, who was the oldest member of our group, early sixties. He appeared to have suffered a near heart attack. Somehow, almost miraculously, he had recovered from the pain with a dose of medication and was able to continue with the portage, but in a weakened condition. Mack had helped care for him, carried most of his gear, and had also assisted some of the other poorly conditioned people during the portage. He had traversed the muck and mire of the mudflats several times to aid them by pushing their canoes across the swampy area. Finally, the exhaustion, tension, and depletion of his strength from the day caught up with him, carrying him to the edge of the envelope.

Very late that night, after a difficult, tiring maneuver to pass around an obstacle in the river, Butler, exhausted, broke down and began bellowing obscenities at the instructors. He cited their lack of planning and shortsightedness in the trip preparation by choosing a route that was almost impassable, and certainly not easily negotiable in the specified time, resulting in the loss of our campsite and prolonging the almost impossible day. Now, he said, people were tired, some disoriented, and many were unable to shoulder their responsibilities and contribute to the program because of their physical limitations and exhaustion.

His vociferous tirade went on for several minutes, and he stated that he was ready to hang it and conclude his involvement. He was beat, and the whole show had now become an atrocious play in his tired mind and body.

Finally, after his emotional release, he settled down, regained his composure, and made a mental adjustment, fully realizing that everyone was doing the best they could under the checkered conditions. He picked up his paddle and began to paddle his canoe once again, but not before he had made his point in no uncertain terms. By the way, this is what intelligent, trained lawyers do for a living: get their views across on behalf of their clients and themselves. It's what they are paid to do.

We all have a breaking point, including the so-called risk takers and adrenaline junkies, although they do seem to have a higher level of tolerance and greater acceptance than the norm.

In point of fact, many of us may break several times in any lengthy, difficult endeavor. These incidents may occur repeatedly; it just depends on the nature and mind-set of the individual and his or her ability to handle the so-called stress syndrome.

The personal characteristic most important in managing these conditions is how we intellectualize them and what we do to recover our senses and then get on with the mission. If we do not handle the situation properly, adjust our determination, and make up our mind to get over the setbacks, they can leave us immobilized, unable to reason properly, resulting in an unrecoverable mental state.

▼

This nearly happened in Vietnam to one of my young lieutenants when our rifle company was on a combat mission and our unit came under heavy frontal fire from an NVA unit dug in around a small unoccupied village. I gave him, my platoon commander, the task of sweeping the area with elements of his unit. They were caught in an unexpected crossfire by the entrenched enemy and had to be retracted from the ambush and withdrawn back to our defensive position. The lieutenant was badly shaken and emotionally distraught. I ordered him to immediately regroup his forces and to take his unit back into the same battle area and to sweep it clean of all remaining enemy opposition. He looked at me incredulously, but there was no other option. The position had to be taken, and if he had not returned to action straightaway, he might have lost all courage, his strength of character to prevail, and his ability to contain his fear. He went back into the attack with his platoon and performed as ordered. He won both the day and, most importantly, the restraint of his trepidations.

A similar situation also happened to me on my first combat operatiom when we came under heavy fire. For a few seconds, I was not certain that I could mentally handle the situation and do what was required of me. Fortunately, after a hasty and very serious conversation with myself, I was able to work though my panic-stricken condition and to act decisively. Honestly, this same sensation mounted my subconscious several times in that Vietnam War. Thank God I was somehow able to overcome my fears; otherwise, I might have ended up a mental cripple, second-guessing my own motives and courage each time I was stressed out by some seemingly unconquerable event. This mental condition could have haunted me for the rest of my days.

This is what breaking points are. They are character tests, gut checks if you will, requiring a willingness to prevail when you think you can't. This is equally applicable to the so-called brave and stouthearted as well. People never escape their personal fears totally, regardless of how courageous or brave they think they are.

▼

It was midnight when we finally exited the Nightmare into the Broad River. We still had three hours of paddling to make it to the Gulf Coast and our campsite at Highland Beach, just north of our exit from the river. Around three in the morning, we paddled our way through the difficult surf, as the tide was now going out, and landed our canoes on the shore. We had struggled with our crafts for more than twenty hours that day, and the entire group were now totally fatigued, including our well-conditioned, but somewhat misguided, instructors.

We put up our tents and crawled in quickly. Game over, at least for that day. There were still more challenges to overcome in the days ahead, and they would also be hellish.

▼

Summary of the day: A restless and mostly sleepless night sequestered in our canoes anchored in the middle of a river, followed by more paddling, and then a seven-hour rainy portage across a swampy quagmire of slush and unstable mud. This episode was followed by dragging and pulling our canoes over inches-deep water, and then several more hours of paddling to our next campsite, which was occupied because we were late arriving and another group had taken it. Then another several hours of paddling though a river clogged with the thickest vegetation that anyone could imagine, filled with crocs on the riverbank watching our every maneuver.

Finally, reaching the Gulf of Mexico, we then struggled with the outgoing tide and rough surf as we paddled our canoes with all the fading strength left in our bodies to our final resting place. We had spent in excess of twenty hours battling the terrain, rivers, swamps, and weather. Our mettle and will had been fully tested, and several members of the group had reached their personal breaking points. Some, but not all perhaps, had overcome them.

▼

The next morning Jim, Mack, and I went exploring before the rest of the group crawled weakly from their tents. We had been walking the shoreline for some time when our lead instructor, Mary Day, came running to catch up with us. It seems that no one was supposed to leave the group or wander off without an instructor. This was a safety rule that Outward Bound followed religiously.

In all probability we had been a bit of a pain in their ass because of our individuality and assertiveness. We, more or less, tried to do things our way, and perhaps we were not necessarily considered to be team players all the time. Therefore, she determined that we should be separated for a spell, and that would mitigate any future problems from developing while we were at the campsite.

She told Mack and me that we were to locate our camping areas at opposite ends of the group, about five hundred yards apart, and Jim was to be positioned in the center. She was pissed at us and concluded that this was the only way to control our excess energy, enthusiasm, and adrenline overflow.

Our group spent two days and nights on the island, primarily because we had missed one night at our other site and this extra day would put us back on schedule. We had one full day devoted to a solo experience, which was to be our private reflection time about the course, what we had learned, and how we might benefit from this swamp and water-oriented experience. The remainder of the time we spent on short canoe trips to other small islands and exploring around our own island home.

The following day we canoed through a bunch of small islands and had a difficult time determining our location, but finally found our chickee as night settled. The next day, after canoeing for several hours, we spent our final night in the waterways on a small peninsula. After this period of moderate rest and activity, we were fully recovered physically, and on this last morning of our trip, we started on the concluding run to our final destination, Everglades City, the northern terminus point of the Glades. On this particular day trip, our team set a record for the course by canoeing thirty-two miles in an eleven-hour period. It was a bitch, but we did it, arriving around dinnertime that evening.

At the completion, our instructors told us they had never canoed that many miles in a single day in any other course. They were as proud of this achievement as we were. It was a good feeling.

The following morning we would have our final challenge, when we engaged another, much younger Outward Bound class in a half-mile run followed by a five-mile canoe race and concluded with another half-mile run to the finish line. Our competitors, on average, were in their mid-twenties. Our team averaged in their mid-thirtiess, with Mack and me in our mid-forties. Jim was younger, at age thirty-five.

We planned our strategy, and Mack and I decided that we would go all out to try to win the event. We determined that if we could beat the others to the canoes and grab the first one, we could hopefully maintain the lead on the waterway and win the race. There was no way that we would allow a bunch of young *whippersnappers* to beat us in this competition. Personal pride is wonderful, but you must be able to deliver on your commitment; we were determined to give it our best.

In the half-mile run, the first two people to reach the canoes would team together and get the first canoe, which was at the front of all the parked boats. The next two people in the race would team together and get the next-best situated canoe, and so on. The race started, and as planned, we did beat everyone by a short distance; we grabbed the first canoe, jumped in, and began paddling like hell up the stream. We had the lead, and we hoped to keep it. It was nip and tuck most of the time. In every instance when the much younger team attempted to pass us, we increased our paddle momentum and managed to stay in front of them. After failing several times to overtake us, they more or less gave up and slacked off their pace.

Later, after the race was over, they confided in us that they were totally surprised and dumbfounded that two *old men* could paddle a canoe with the youthful determination that we had demonstrated.

Butler and I did have one stupid mishap in the race, and it was not pretty. The course took each canoe under several low-lying bridges. In order to pass under them, we had to bend over and lie horizontal, our bodies aligned with the gunnels of the craft as it floated under. Otherwise, we would have to do what most folks did: disembark and portage the canoe around them. We had derived a methodology that, if executed properly, would allow us to stay in the boat and drift casually under the obstacles. We would paddle up to within a few feet of the overpass, and then I was to lean forward, as I was in the front of the canoe, and position my chest on the front panel, while Mack, who was in the rear, would lean backward, placing his back on top of the rear panel of the canoe. Lying parallel with the top of the canoe, we would glide effortlessly under the bridge, losing no time or momentum. Once we cleared the bridge, we would straighten up and begin paddling hard again. This was not a difficult maneuver, but the timing was critical.

The best-laid plans many times go astray. As we approached the first bridge and paddled up to it rapidly as planned, we suddenly became confused, and each of us simultaneously shifted our weight and bodies and moved in the wrong direction, overturning the canoe.

Now we had to get out of the water, drag our canoe up on the shore, empty it, drag it to the other side of the bridge, get back in, and start paddling again. In the meantime, our young friends had significantly closed the gap between the two canoes.

I don't know what we looked like with our stupid mistake, but I do know how we felt. It was so typical and dumb; we had it made, and then screwed it up. Nevertheless, even in our confusion, we still had the lead—barely. Nonetheless, we were able to maintain it and, luckily, negotiate the other bridges successfully.

We ended the canoe part of the race, and in our wet socks and shoes, we ran or stumbled through the last half-mile, beating our competitors by several minutes. At least, the most important part of our disjointed plan had worked; we had won the event.

Afterward, huffing and puffing, Mack walked up to me while I was trying to catch my breath and composure. He said, "Jackson, we still have something left, don't we?"

"Hell, yes," I replied rather meekly, "but I wouldn't bet any of my money on us."

With the conclusion of the competition, the program was now officially over, and we would have one more night to celebrate our graduation, or survival, and then depart the next morning for home.

Interestingly, it was when we began our canoe approach into Everglades City, after canoeing the record distance, that we started to feel some remorse about the course ending. Collectively in our subliminal minds, we wanted to continue, stay in the glades if possible, even though we were approaching exhaustion.

This is the emotional reaction described earlier, and it was difficult to comprehend. It lasted for several weeks after we retuned home and took up our responsibilities. We had been told reentry into the real world would be difficult because of what we would experience during the program. Literally, it was overwhelming.

After we retuned to Atlanta, Jim Box told me that this was one of the greatest, most important things he had ever accomplished in his life. From these experiences, Mack Butler made a life-changing decision to eventually relocate to Montana. I would make a similar resolution a few years later to live part-time in Idaho. The three of us had the same reaction to this experience; perhaps it just affected us differently from the others. I don't know for certain, but Mary Day, our lead instructor, was on target when she told us about reentry and how these experiences could possibly impact our lives. In some ways this was an insight into ourselves whose time had come, and we must have been mentally ready to make some changes. Or perhaps, like the soldiers who had a difficult time readjusting after returning home from war, we needed to live a more exciting and adventuresome lifestyle to satisfy the cravings in our subconscious.

This course had been one of the most endearing and challenging episodes that some of us had ever participated in during our lives. I am confident that we would do it again if we could, but time and age have robbed us of the ability and strength for a repeat performance.

▼

Somewhat later, after recovering mentally and physically from the Everglades experience, we took some additional overnight hikes and camping trips in the summer months, but they were more for leisure and to keep us conditioned for our next adventure. None of these journeys seemed to feed our souls like the Everglades trip. However, these endeavors were necessary to keep our adrenalin pumping and to ensure that we would be ready for the next, best, and greatest adventure opportunity that we could find.

In the meantime Jim and I still had a mission to fulfill, and that was to find an outdoor wilderness program for First Georgia Bank's Executive Training Program. We put our attention to that task, and it slowly, but surely, began to materialize in our minds.

In the interim, while continuing our search for the most suitable curriculum, we scheduled several groups of our bank officers for some whitewater rafting trips on the Chattooga River. During the summer weekends, members of our management team would depart by bus to the river for a special day of team building and physical challenge. We thought these trips would be a great way to indoctrinate our folks for the forthcoming outdoors challenge they would ultimately face, that being a wilderness experience or something like it. The movie *Deliverance* was shown on the bus trip to heighten expectations and interest for the day. As expected, it always captured the participants' wide-eyed attention.

When we took to the river, the managers, grouped in teams of six-to-a-raft along with an instructor, would battle and paddle their rubber rafts across the swirling waters of the gushing wild river for five hours, often being dumped in the cold mountain water while attempting to shoot the rapids or maneuver their craft around a rocky crevice in the stream. It was exciting for them, and their confidence in their outdoor skills was definitely enhanced as they learned to paddle and plow their way through the churning river, despite a few, sometimes frequent, capsized introductions to the chilly water.

They had a great time, and their enthusiasm was obvious. They learned about working together, or to play on a pun, how to pull together, while they shared in the physical labor of rowing and maneuvering their unforgiving rubber rafts as they crashed about the river-laden rocks in the quixotic water of the Chattooga.

Afterward they were treated to a beer and steak dinner cooked outside, near the water's edge, to help them loosen up. By the time we boarded the bus to return to Atlanta, everyone was usually quite mellow and very, very tired.

This time spent together provided our staff folks with the opportunity to become better acquainted, under extreme conditions, and taught them how to function as collective team players by sharing a common bond in this physically demanding event. Not only did they learn the importance of working together, but also the necessity of mutual dependence in the achievement of a common goal. It required full and total cooperation from everyone in a raft for them to be successful with their quest. This was the exact mind-set and attitude we were trying to create in the working environment within the bank.

Yes, we were most definitely grooming them for more challenging training. This river experience would greatly help minimize the initial shock and anxiety that might occur when the next phase of outdoor training was introduced to them. The minds and bodies were ready. It was time to capture the moment, or as we used to say in the marine corps, *take the hill.*

FIVE

EXECUTIVE ADVENTURE

In our pursuit to find a wilderness-training course for our managers at First Georgia Bank, we heard about a program sponsored by Boston University's School of Management. Called the Executive Challenge program for key managers and staff members, it was publicized as a unique, award-winning outdoor training program for management and professional development, conducted primarily for corporations' senior management teams.

The program was operated and staffed locally by the Atlanta-based Executive Adventure Organization. The company is still in existence today and operating successfully, albeit without any involvement with its former partner, Boston University. Bob Carr was, and is still, the owner-manager of Executive Adventure.

From our conversation and investigation with some of his clients, we learned that he and his highly qualified staff ran a top-notch program, and everyone who had attended the course was most pleased and extremely complimentary about this unique training.

As an aside, Bob's enthusiasm for this training approach has never slackened in all these years. With this program he has continuously displayed a masterful attitude, devotion, and commitment to his client's needs for over two decades. It is pleasing for me to say that I continue to hold him in high esteem today and consider his friendship and professional ability above reproach.

The Executive Challenge course normally ran for three rigorous days in a remote location. This tactic ensured the participants would be removed from any workplace interruptions, allowing them to totally concentrate on their involvement in the program. Separation from their duties and the job environment provided an opportunity for the mangers to have more quality time together, which would enhance team building and camaraderie.

The course provided a blend of various outdoor problem-solving obstacles and activities that were mostly team-structured to ensure full participation by each member. The most significant and talked-about confidence-building venue provided in the program was the *treetop ropes course*, a medium also used by Outward Bound.

This component of the program consisted of six to eight different obstacles arrayed in the tops of several large trees about seventy-five feet above the ground. The students were required to pull, climb, and hoist themselves through, over, or under each of these rope-constructed barriers as they moved through the treetops. Each participant had safety lines attached to their waist in the event they miscued and fell. Naturally, these security devices would have precluded any serious injury from occurring upon falling, but the student would be left dangling in the air. That was just one of the scary parts out of many!

Upon completion of each initiative, Bob's team of professional instructors conducted debriefings on the solution process, reviewing the management principles or, in some cases, the lack of principles employed by each group of a dozen participants. The classes were purposely kept to this size to facilitate maximum participation by each individual member in the exercise.

In the bank's annual report, this program was noted as an accomplishment by the bank in the management-training efforts for the year. The Executive Adventure experience was described as follows: "Our managers were required to explore the elements of teamwork, trust, risk-taking, problem solving, and improvement in their ability to communicate, and confront personal challenges—qualities essential to effective leadership and management."

In 1983 when this program was initiated at First Georgia Bank in Atlanta, it was considered to be on the leading edge of management training. A few large organizations had begun using adventure or wilderness programs for their management staff, but they were considered to be unproven, highly questionable, and an unknown quantity at that time; however, as time progressed, more companies gravitated toward this training technique. This distinctive training method ultimately garnered a great deal of fame and acceptance in the corporate world.

At First Georgia, we were extremely proud to have had the foresight and *guts* to explore and subsequently implement this method of executive education. Over a three-year period, First Georgia Bank successfully enrolled over 250 key management personnel in Executive Adventure courses.

Several years later, while I was president of another financial institution in Atlanta, Georgia Federal Bank, the same training was introduced with similar enrollment numbers. Both organizations experienced significant improvement in their operations, enhanced their corporate culture, and gained noteworthy attention in the marketplace as the result of using this training technique.

Senior management was the first group to attend the initial course. Obviously, this was planned to indicate our top-down support and commitment to the course, as said earlier: Don't ask your people to do something you won't do. We made certain that our top executives participated in the course before any of the other staff members were enrolled. We reinforced our dedication by debriefing each group at the conclusion of their experience. Every participating member was asked to review with their fellow team members what they had learned and how they intended to use it in their professional careers.

One female branch manager cited a memorable learning experience that defines the essence and retention value of the syllabus; it is worthy of repeating here. She related the difficulty she had experienced dragging herself across a rope suspended between two trees high off the ground. This initiative required her to actually lie belly down on the rope, grasp it with both hands, and pull herself across the twenty-yard expanse to the opposite end of the obstacle. This particular hurdle, obviously, could be frightening for most people, and she admitted that it was terribly scary to her.

The woman in question told the group that, as she pulled her middle-aged body across the horizontally suspended rope, she didn't think she had the strength or courage to make the distance she was supposed to traverse. But she said, "I was determined," and finally completed the event while taking almost twice the time of her fellow teammates. Furthermore, she noted she would not have made it through her test if it had not been for her team members and fellow officers on the ground below enthusiastically cheering her on.

She was asked, "What did you learn from the experience?" Her reply was positive: "I learned that I need to be more of a cheerleader to my staff. With the same kind of moral support and encouragement, they should be able to accomplish any task given to them." She had expanded her managemt and leadership insights.

Another lady told the group, "I was afraid to stand on a chair and hang a picture on the wall, but I am no longer fearful to undertake that task. Matter of fact, I find myself more daring in most things that I now attempt at work and at home." I will add, these particular women showed marked improvement in their work, as did most of the people who attend this training.

The participants' responses were endearing and truthful; in almost every incident, they reflected improved self-confidence in themselves and their job responsibilities. This is exactly what we wanted to achieve with our staff.

Another interesting aspect of the debriefing process was the gaining of the group's agreement on the specific objectives that needed to be undertaken to improve the bank's working conditions, customer service, training, operations, morale, and most importantly, profitability. Team to-do lists were developed, with objectives, time charts, and assigned responsibilities for later follow-up by the group. This process helped create significant peer pressure and motivation that ensured the agreed-upon plans were completed on time and as assigned.

As most of the senior management members were present at the debriefing session, listening, learning, and responding, we were able to gain consensus on the future plan of attack. This obvious commitment on their part made the group more attentive. It also eliminated any departmental turf issues and barriers to performance that might ultimately surface during the follow-up work sessions. The new catchphrase that evolved from these sessions was, "If you're waiting on us, you're backing up."

▼

From my early years while undergoing Officer Candidate Training in the marine corps, I can still remember an important lesson taught to our class by an old, crusty drill sergeant.

Lecturing on tactics he emphasized the importance of timing and responsibility when involved with an enemy force. "As future leaders of men," he told us bluntly, expletives deleted here, how important it was to follow through with our plan and to be at our designated location when we were supposed to be there. He said, "People are counting on you, and your failure to meet your commitment may result in defeat or the loss of life." He then gave us one simple rule that should actually be applicable to everyone in everything they do regardless of their circumstances, their job, or the situation they find themselves in.

His rule: "Do what you say you're gonna do when you say you're gonna do it; no excuses will be tolerated."

This is an excellent personal characteristic to practice in all situations; unfortunately, it is a character and management principle that is not normally preached, taught, or promoted with any regularity. Think about it, and consider the ramifications of this code being applied commonly in your job, or for that matter, in all of your relationships and varied responsibilities, whether they be business or personal.

▼

A graduation ceremony was held for each group of Executive Adventure graduates. All of the participants were formally presented with a camouflage-colored certificate of completion, encased in a rustic wooden frame, encircled with a small knotted rope, more or less symbolizing their completion in the ropes course. It was a fitting and appropriate award that truly denoted their accomplishment.

They were asked to display this commemorative in their office for all of their employees and customers to view. We anticipated these executives would take great pleasure and satisfaction from this unique and rewarding achievement. Additionally, we wanted them to realize that few people, especially bankers, had ever completed or even attempted such a challenging training program.

The personal pride exhibited by each individual upon the course completion was obvious; their enthusiasm spread like wildfire throughout the bank, and the sense of achievement each one espoused about their individual accomplishment was contagious. These managers gained additional respect from their staff as a result of their participation and their heightened willingness to undertake and explore a more motivating business attitude within their own sphere of responsibility.

While this particular training became an integral part of our corporate culture, it also provided the bank with a personality and status in the community that few organizations could claim. We were truly "the bankers who swing from trees." This description about our staff was highlighted in several Atlanta publications.

It was a complimentary and fitting accolade for First Georgia in general; it defined our employees' tenacity and provided a reputation that helped us stand above the other bankers in Atlanta. This was an important facet to our business activities, and most importantly, our corporate value system.

In the late eighties, after I took the Chief Executive Officer position at Georgia Federal Bank in Atlanta, the identical program was implemented in that institution. It was conducted principally to help facilitate a rapid change in the culture and operating mentality of that company. It needed a revitalization shot in the arm, and it got it.

This was a significant step for that bank, since it was basically a savings and loan institution that focused its business primarily on home mortgages and savings deposits. At that time, 1986, these savings banks were situated in an industry mired down with a traditional slow-to-react mind-set and unconditioned to rapid change.

In order for the company, and me for that matter, to survive in a new position in the overall rapidly changing financial services world, it was critical for us to make a swift modification in the culture, attitude, and operations of the bank. The institution had to be more proactive in its business approach, not reactive, which was typical for the industry. It was clearly a case of continued existence for the business. The Executive Adventure Program would once again serve as the key catalyst for this transition. After implementation, the great results at First Georgia Bank were replicated at Georgia Federal, proving the perpetual value of this enterprising method of training.

These programs can produce positive results for an organization only if the company executive staff has the management mentality, drive, forward thinking, and initiative to promote them enthusiastically. As in any leadership enterprise in any kind of organization, the "thrust must trickle down from the top; it will not well up from the bottom." This same principle applies for motivation.

▼

In a convoluted and meandering way, the pursuit to locate and implement this method of training to meet the bank's needs was the catalyst for the discovery of a new destiny for Jim and me to pursue. This mission was the vehicle that drove us to that destination. When we arrived, we embraced it for twenty-five adventuresome years. It made all the difference in our lives.

Now, as fall approached, we sought new adventures to quell our restlessness. The adrenalin was again cascading through our systems; we wanted reliable and new highs to match this driving need for more risk-taking exploits. We would travel to South Georgia, only a few hundred miles south of Atlanta, to gain the relief and fix that our minds and bodies seemed to be craving. The next adventure would take us deep into the ominous Okefenokee Swamp.

SIX

THE OKEFENOKEE SWAMP

The Okefenokee Swamp covers 681 square miles mainly in southeastern Georgia, with a small overlap into northern Florida. It is the largest swamp in North America. The Okefenokee National Wildlife Refuge is a part of the Okefenokee, occupying 396,000 acres of the swamp. Geologically the Okefenokee was shaped over 250,000 years ago, when the ocean was some seventy-five miles inland of the present Georgia coast. It was originally formed in a shallow depression and later scooped out by the Atlantic Ocean. Development of the swamp occurred when ocean currents and wave action constructed a narrow sandbar about forty miles long on the seaward side, creating a shallow lagoon behind it. When the waters receded, the lagoon was drained, and the sand basin became the swamp's bed. There are only three ingresses leading into the swamp, which makes it rather remote and somewhat difficult to reach.

The Okefenokee, because of its peat moss, heavy vegetation, and abundant water, has been described as a peat-filled bog. The Seminole Indians, who lived in this region years ago, called it "Land of the trembling earth"—*Okefenokee.* Walking on this wobbly ground, with all the knotted and compacted vegetation underfoot, produces a sensation of trembling and feels as if you are walking on a shaking water bed.

It has been estimated, conservatively, that over ten thousand alligators make their home in this swamp. In the three days we canoed through the narrow, twisting waterways, we saw at least five hundred gators; and as revealed in the Glades, none of them appeared to be hospitable.

Approximately 120 miles of canoe trails crisscross and intersect throughout the swamp so, because of the thick vegetation, the meandering and wandering water flow, and the lack of identifiable terrain features to guide by, direction and location can become confusing. These boating waterways wind through cypress forests and across open prairies that are almost indistinguishable one from the other. This swamp is definitely a true wilderness area.

The languid, flat water and the many shallow trails ensure that paddling a canoe in these streams will be slow and tedious.

At times the canoeist may even have to disembark and push the craft along the narrow, shallow water artery until it becomes deep enough to once again support a fully loaded canoe.

One point is abundantly clear to all travelers: there are no free rides in the Okefenkoee Swamp. In order for your canoe to have momentum, you must paddle continuously. There are no flowing currents that will move your boat along leisurely.

The Okefenokee is reputed to be gloomy and forbidding, a place of *terror and mystery*, filled with creatures that can tear your body apart in moments and then eat the tattered remains.

Numerous horror stories told about the swamp include monsters roaming at night through the dense watery acreage to the landing of aliens from outer space. So, typical for our adventure travel choices, this was the "joyful" environment and bizarre challenge that we had chosen for our next adventure.

▼

My first exposure to this type of menacing and frightening wilderness setting was in the jungles of Malaysia while attending the British Army Jungle Warfare School north of Singapore. I can recall the feeling of dread and trepidation when I stepped into that green tangled mass of overwhelming, hellish vegetation for the first time. Four of us, me and three British soldiers, were dropped off the back of a military truck on a dirt road in the middle of nowhere and told to find our way, as soon as possible, by map and compass, to a designated location several miles distant. We were bluntly informed we would be picked up when we arrived the next day or the following day or whenever we eventually made it to our assigned objective. The British did not mince words with their instructions.

Never having been in this sort of surrounding, I was totally dependent on my Brit comrades, who fortunately had had some exposure to the jungle and were highly knowledgeable about operating in it and especially skilled in navigating in it. With our brusque instructions, we launched our march, and as I stepped into the thicket, I sheepishly wondered if a wild animal would have my young, tender body for dinner before we concluded our quest.

Prior to attending this school in the Johore Baru province in Malaysia, I had heard that the jungle is neutral. It is neither for you nor against you. It is what you can make of it.

We attempted to make as much of it as we could, but it was a struggle for most of the trip. This Malaysian jungle was referred to as secondary, meaning that much of it had been cut and had grown back twice as thick as it was when originally formed.

The aborigines, original inhabitants, were partially responsible. They would occupy a part of this jungle for a period and then slash and burn the original vegetation to create fields for growing food and for building their huts and general living spaces. Once the ground was no longer fertile, they would relocate and repeat the same process in another part of the tropical forest. This went on for years. In every case, over that time span, the new vegetation would grow back thicker and denser, making for arduous foot travel through the knotted mess.

Using our compass to navigate, we made our way though the snarled and entwined hell while leaches affixed themselves to our bodies, sucking the blood from our legs, our groins, and any other part that was available for their nourishment. Another scene from the movie *The African Queen* depicts what we experienced. Humphrey Bogart was in the water pulling his boat with Katherine Hepburn aboard through the thick swamp; he finally climbed inside and took off his shirt, exposing all the leaches that had affixed themselves to his body; she quickly poured salt on them, and they dropped off. Probably the best way to remove leeches is to apply a burning cigarette close to their hindside, or to pour salt, chewing tobacco juice, or any other caustic item on their sucking little bodies. It is inadvisable to pull them off the skin because they leave their biting mouths attached to the body; then swelling, redness, and infection will eventually occur at the bitten site; if this happens it can be lethal in the jungle, where treatment is difficult to administer.

If left embedded in the skin for a period of time, the leeches will ultimately fill up on your blood and then release their mouths from your body, fall to the ground, or down into your pants or shirt, and die from the richness of the food that had been so recently supplied. In essence, they literally drink themselves to death on *your blood*.

It was on this particular exercise that I actually learned to use the compass effectively, even though previously I had had numerous hours of instruction. Attempting to read the terrain was impractical because of the intertwined vegetation—nothing was discernable on the ground, and few terrain features could be matched with our map—we had to rely almost totally on the compass, as we had been assigned specific azimuths and distances to follow to our destination. Consequently, it was necessary to constantly estimate our pace to determine the distance traveled, so that we had some idea of our location on the map as we traveled from one point to another; otherwise, a person could wander for eternity or until *eaten* by a wild animal of some kind. We were fortunate. We made it though the course by the end of the second day. Thank God for my fellow British teammates and their knowledge about course plotting; they took the lead and educated me on jungle navigation. I never forgot it or them. It was an astonishing learning experience!

We did experience one fearsome event. On our bivouac the first night, we were awakened by a tiger's low, menacing growl; consequently, the four of us sat in a small circle around a large burning fire throughout the night with our rifles at the ready, prepared for an attack by the animal. We could hear the large cat stalking around our campsite most of that time, but when the first light crept through the canopy of the treetops, he disappeared. Believe me when I tell you, this kept our precious bodily fluids flowing in our overwrought bodies during that entire time. The jungle may be neutral, but it is also scary as hell.

▼

We had received an announcement from an outfitter in Savannah, Georgia, announcing a three-day canoeing trip for late October, and it piqued our interest. We immediately enrolled: Jim, Mack, and my son, Christopher, a student at the University of Georgia, who for the first time would join our adventuresome triumvirate on this "fun-filled" excursion. Chris, having developed an interest in the backcountry early on, was comfortable in this environment. He had gone out on many outdoor trips prior to this one, using some of my old and out-of-date marine corps equipment that he had found stored in my service-issued, musty footlocker in the garage.

He had also previously participated in a number of hiking and camping activities with some of his school friends while a student at Young Harris College, in the mountains of North Georgia. I was pleased to have him link up with us, and I thought the exposure would be of personal benefit to him, and also to me, for that matter.

Some modicum of father and son mutual involvement in outdoor activities is a good thing. I was hopeful this experience would help bond our relationship in a more mature way. After this initial outing, he would join with us on a number of future wilderness trips; I believe he learned a great deal from those experiences and the exposure gained from being in the company of older men who had a youthful outlook on life and a hardy zest for adventure. At least, I hope it was good for him, because we did a lot of crazy things, but that is what adrenalin junkies and risk takers do in their lives. More about this facet of our trips later on.

A few days before our departure to the swamp, Mack Butler, who was generally immune to any health issues, came down with a bad case of the flu and was unable to make the trip. He was certainly disappointed, but resigned to recover as quickly as he could. Not to be undone, the three of us packed our gear and headed to the swampy marshlands of South Georgia. The next three days and nights would be an interesting education; we would learn more about the swamps than we had anticipated, perhaps more than we needed.

After some detailed orientation, our group of ten people headed out the following morning, paddling along in the still water. Of course, our guides cautioned us to stay in our canoes unless the water was so shallow we would have to disembark and push or pull our crafts along to a deeper part of the stream. Otherwise, they told us, "Never get out of the boat." Frankly, we didn't need the advice about staying in our boats because, after learning more about the Okefenokee alligators, we agreed discretion would be our constant companion and we would observe them only from a distance—a good, healthy distance!

One of the three nights we would sleep on a *chickee* in the middle of a large pond; these were the same kind of wooden platforms that had been introduced to us in the Everglades. The next night would be spent on an island, and the third in a camping area near the water.

We canoed all day and finally arrived at our destination, where we unloaded our gear onto the chickee. After preparing dinner as darkness overtook the daylight, we spread out our sleeping bags and air mattress on the wooden floor and prepared for a peaceful, though hard and uncomfortable, night's sleep.

When it became dark, we gazed out over the large body of water surrounding our platform; the reflection from the starlit sky was dazzling. As it grew even darker, our guides told us to point our flashlights out on the pond. We did, and what we saw was alarming. The pond was filled with the sinister glowing green eyes of the many alligators lying about, partially submerged in the waterway, all staring, we thought hungrily, in our direction. What a sight! Although a bit eerie, it was something to behold. We were damned glad to be safely suspended on our platform above the water's edge—except for one curious individual.

When I woke up at some point during the night, I could not locate my son, who had been sleeping next to me. I assumed he was probably relieving himself on the lower landing of the shelter area, but the truth would surface the next morning when I learned that he had taken one of the canoes and paddled out into the middle of the pond for a closer inspection of the green-eyed phenomenon.

Yes, he had left the safety of the platform and by his lonesome had steered his canoe near a group of the gators, where he sat for a couple of hours reflecting on the sight. When I discovered what he had done, I had an old-fashioned southern hissy fit (explosion) and chewed his ass out until I was certain he could fully comprehend the message. I explained to him that, had his craft overturned, we would have never heard from him again; in other words he would have been a late-night snack for probably a hundred always-hungry, rambunctious, prehistoric beasts. He promised after my tirade that he would not attempt that exploit again, but who knows what lurks in the shadows of a young, wild, expanding, wondering mind. I sure as hell didn't at my age—at least, not any longer.

The next day Jim Box and I partnered up in a canoe and had two experiences that scared the hell out of us. We had been canoeing along a small waterway for several hours enjoying the scenery and watching the gators submerging in the water when we approached them. Then I noticed a large alligator resting peacefully in the sun on an adjacent shoreline. I was in the front of the canoe with my camera, and I motioned to Jim to guide our canoe over toward the gator so I could take a close-up picture. I had forgotten about keeping our distance—apparently! We slowly moved toward it, edging our canoe along slowly and silently as we approached what we assumed was a sleeping, probably ten-foot-long alligator. At probably no more than a few feet from his resting place, I pointed my camera at him to take what I thought would be a wonderful picture of this sleeping beast. I had just framed him in the camera sight when he erupted into the air, springing and propelling off his powerful tail, sailing over our heads, crashing down loudly into the water off to our flank, just a few "short" feet from the canoe.

Jim, although stunned as much as me, began to laugh loudly as the gator slid beneath the surface. He said he had heard the shutter click about fifty times while the gator was in motion sailing above our heads. In my fear and excitement, I had kept pressing the shutter button on the camera, but I didn't get one photo—except of the blue sky, my feet, and the bottom of the canoe. The gator scared the crap out of me. What would have happened if it had landed in our canoe? We would have been history and probably lunch for the gator. That was the last of any attempted close-up camera shots by me or Jim.

Well, that was my big scare of the day and of the whole trip, for that matter; I know now that *my cup had runneth over* with adrenalin at that moment. The next frightening moment belonged to Mr. Box, and I would enjoy it.

We had been canoeing along a narrow water passage for some time, with Jim still guiding the boat from the rear seat, when I heard and felt some screaming and loud thumping on the rear floor of our canoe, where Jim was sitting. I had no idea what was happening and was almost afraid to turn around and check on the commotion. Reluctantly, though, I did, more from fright than interest; he was kicking at some poor fish that had jumped into the canoe. It had scared him out of his wits; I think he must have thought it was a gator in the attack. Actually, it was a long-nosed jackfish that had sprung up out of the water when we surprised it as we glided by; tumbling back toward the water, it had landed directly in front of him at his feet. Apparently these fish hover near the surface of the water, and being somewhat skittish in nature, will leap up out of the water at the slightest provocation. This time our canoe was its landing site.

Poor Jim thought he was being assaulted, and it scared the living stuff out of him. Now it was my turn to laugh, and I did—loudly. I gave him the same insensitive treatment that he had bestowed on me when the gator leaped from the bank while I was trying to take its picture and scared the hell out of me.

That night we slept on a small island in the middle of the swamp, and nothing remarkable occurred except for the creepy crawlers and mosquitoes that pestered us most of the night. The next day we continued canoeing, exploring the Okefenokee spectacle and viewing numerous submerging gators as we glided across the water, ending this sojourn at a campsite close to our original starting point..

The following day we completed our water wilderness journey, and late that night arrived back in Atlanta. Our friend Mack had partially recovered from his bout with the flu and returned to the living. He was disappointed he had not been able to join us on the swamp trip, but he wanted to hear our stories. We told them all.

This particular adventure opened my mind on a personal issue that I had not previously considered at any point in my life. The catalyst for this awakening to my inner thoughts happened to be a major Atlanta social event held the very next night after we had returned from our swamp journey.

As president of one of the larger city banks, I had been invited to attend a prominent black-tie cocktail party in celebration of a movie, *Slugger's Wife*, which had been partially filmed in Atlanta. It appeared that anyone who was anybody or, perhaps, thought they were somebody, was in attendance. It was an event filled with celebrities, politicians, business leaders, the local gentry, and several movie stars who had starred in the film.

Only twenty-four hours prior to this event, I had been canoeing in the Okefenokee Swamp—dirty, tired, unshaven, smelly, and all the other things that can generally make someone persona non grata when they are around people of means. But now, here I was dressed to the nines, looking good, cavorting with all the bluebloods, cocktail in hand; pressing the flesh, participating in generally boring conversation about nothing of importance, while inwardly and surprisingly enjoying myself and the affair in general. It was an interesting turn of events.

As the evening progressed, with a few fortifying drinks under my belt, I began to focus on my personal feelings about what I had just completed, and perhaps in a smug and conceited way, began observing the crowd of people more closely. You couldn't miss the gadflies, the hoity-toity, the heavy drinkers, the fat bellies, the puffy cheeks, and the always present beautifully dressed and coiffured women; there was plenty of them in attendance to grab your attention—as you might guess.

I suddenly began to wonder, *How many of these people here tonight could have, or would have, participated in the adventure that I had just finished hours before?* This was an indiscriminate evaluation on my part, and possibly I was placing myself and my interests and capabilities above everyone else. This was neither a fair nor proper assessment on my part. Who was I to judge? Many of those businesspeople present could probably do many things that I was incapable of handling. But there was another significant part of this equation that surprised me when I realized that I was actually enjoying the cocktail function almost as much as I had enjoyed my time and experiences in the swamp.

Although, I must honestly admit, I probably did enjoy the canoe trip more, and if given the option, I would have preferred to have stayed with it for a few more days; but still, the party was highly enjoyable, and as I said previously, I was having a darned good time.

Nonetheless, it was a wonderful discovery on my part. It was all about living in the *moment*. Enjoying what is currently going on in your life. Making the best of whatever you are involved with at all times; relishing in every minute, learning to adapt to every situation, and making every opportunity worthwhile and meaningful. The proverb that comes to mind best summarizing this attitude and approach to life in general is worthy of an indelible etching in our minds: *Nothing is either good or bad, but thinking makes it so.*

Sometime later, when philosophizing with my son on some typical father-son issues, I shared this story with him, relating it in the simplest of terms: "When in Rome, be Roman." I told him to learn how to adapt, even if the situation is not the best or is not at the top of your priority list. There is always something new and different to gain knowledge from. Experience and variety in life are truly two of the best and wisest teachers if a person listens and observes all the things going on around him or her. My only wish was that he would grasp the redeeming value of my new awakening. Hopefully he did, and I can only pray that he will remember this during his life and relate it to his children when they are old enough to understand, just as I did with him.

▼

In those days it seemed that our wilderness adventures would go on forever, but eventually time takes its toll on the body. Fortunately, we still had several good years ahead of us, and we wanted to push our physical abilities to the utmost while we still had the motivation and energy level. Left to our own devices, we would make every effort to do so, regardless of the pain and discomfort that we regularly inflicted on ourselves with our strenuous programs. The next test and pain-enduring opportunity would almost undo us once again. But being hard learners, risk takers, adrenalin junkies, and most appropriately, totally incapable of declining any interesting opportunity, we decided to do another Outward Bound program in early 1984. This would be our first of many trips to the mountains or high country in the western part of the United States, and it would open a whole new realm of exciting exploits, education, wonderful stories, and intriguing journeys. This backcountry adventure would take place in the high desert of California at Joshua Tree National Monument. Later this area was renamed Joshua Tree National Park.

SEVEN

JOSHUA TREE NATIONAL PARK

Gluttons for punishment! There is just no other way to describe our adventuring mentality. In February 1984 Mack, Jim, and I enrolled in another Outward Bound program, this one to be conducted in the wilderness of Joshua Tree National Monument, near Palm Springs, California. This particular course would focus on desert hiking, navigation, and rock climbing and rappelling techniques.

We flew from Atlanta to Palm Springs and rented a hotel room for the first night. None of us had spent time in the desert, and we were not accustomed to the temperature drop in the winter months after the sun went down. We quickly learned about it, though, at the hotel swimming pool that first afternoon.

Sitting on the pool's edge around four o'clock clad in our bathing suits, suddenly we saw everyone get up from their chairs and dash from the pool, leaving us by ourselves. The sun had just dipped below the mountain range to the west of the city, and unbeknownst to us Southern guys, we were about to become educated on just how rapidly the warm temperature in the desert could suddenly become frosty. We immediately began wrapping our shivering bodies with towels, but that did not help. Then we jumped into the heated pool, which warmed us as long as we stayed in the water.

When we climbed out to dry off, it was another story. Somewhat reluctant about leaving our beautiful surroundings but with our bodies now shivering in the rapidly cooling air from the temperature decline, we decided we should seek out the comfort of our warm, inviting hotel room, and we did so with dispatch.

That night we wore our wool sweaters to dinner. Although we didn't have a clue about the desert, we would learn a great deal about it over the next nine days; unfortunately, much of it would be painful in one way or the other, but nevertheless, still enjoyable.

The next morning our course instructors picked us up and drove us to our jumping-off point for the trip. Most of that first day was spent receiving our gear and in general orientation about the program. There were twelve students from around the country, including four women.

After a quick dinner, our guides told us to gather our sleeping bags and rubber mattresses, water bottles, and safety ropes for a foot scramble to the top of a high rock formation adjacent to our camp. No questions were asked, and little direction about this venture was proffered by our instructors. We did exactly as we were told. In single file with one instructor in the lead and one in the rear of our column, our gear tied to our backs with the ropes, we began our hand-and-foot scramble up to the top of a slightly convex boulder perched, seemingly balanced, on the top of a large pile of rocks standing about three to four hundred feet above the desert floor.

We thought it was rather late to be starting with this particular activity and wondered how we would return in the dark, but when we topped out on the granite platform, our instructors said not to worry, because we would not be returning to terra firma this day. They told us we would spend the night on the precipice, the very apex of the granite formation. Our campsite for the night was a rock virtually suspended in midair by a column of supporting boulders. It was circular and no more than twelve feet wide at its broadest part. Impaled in the center of our stone bed was a metal spike, with only its closed circular neck protruding out of the rock.

We laid our sleeping bags with the mattresses inside of them out in a tight circle on the rock. Then we were instructed to tie our safety lines around our waists and affix them through the metal spike head. The group was almost head-to-head, just a few inches apart, in the circle, with the ropes extending around our faces no more than a couple of feet from the imbedded spike. This arrangement with the safety ropes would keep us from falling or sliding off the rock if anything went amiss during the night.

With the rock platform convex shape, we constantly slid down toward the edge as we tried to sleep, and when we ultimately did drift off, we would suddenly awaken by the straining rope tightening around our waists and pulling tightly across our faces. But we were still held securely with the ropes and the steadfast steel rod impaled deeply into the center of the stone. Without these safety devices in place tied to the spike, there would have been no way for us to stay on top of that rocky precipice, particularly while trying to sleep.

Needless to say, we didn't really rest much that night, but, totally free of any artificial light, we witnessed a spectacular display of shooting stars and a brilliant moon overhead.

Literally miles from civilization, we were suspended high in the air with no obstruction of any kind to hinder our sight. It seemed as if we were floating in the sky itself and could almost reach up and touch the shooting stars as they performed their magical, glittering performance in the heavens above. It was absolutely stunning.

▼

The only time I could recall a similar starlight display was in the marine corps sailing aboard a U.S. Navy troopship far out at sea. On occasion, when crossing the Atlantic Ocean or sailing in the Mediterranean Sea, while standing on the forecastle (front) of the pitching ship, I would be in complete awe of the never-ending, star-laden sky spreading all of its beauty though the black night. In this night obscurity, the cresting ocean waves would appear sinister-looking as they crashed into the side of the ship's steel hull, beating a constant reminder of our insignificance, as contrasted to the power of the mighty sea that supported and surrounded us.

It was a rare, intimidating experience for me; it could indeed make a person feel insecure and almost helpless. At the same time, one had to luxuriate in the sheer, mysterious beauty of the time and place. These were the types of experiences and feelings to be captured and held dearly throughout your life. Surely our airborne group, floating on this platform in the sky, had similar reactions.

▼

Relieving ourselves at night balanced on this granite platform offered additional challenges for our group of intrepid explorers. A rope attached to the impaled spike extended about thirty feet over to a small cluster of boulders on our flank. This somewhat intimate space was designated as our *open-air latrine*. In order to meet nature's call, it was necessary to remove our safety lines from the secured device and then, while holding tightly to the guide rope, we would make our way across the rock surface to the somewhat concealed potty location within the boulder formation. While no one came close to falling from our exposed, rocky roost during their nightly maneuvering, I am certain a few folks probably delayed nature's call until the morning and suffered rather than attempt to relieve themselves under these extreme, inhospitable conditions.

Joshua Tree National Park lies 140 miles almost due east of Los Angeles. It was established in 1936 by President Franklin Roosevelt as a national monument to preserve the spiny-leaved Joshua tree. This species of the yucca family was named in 1851 by early Mormon travelers, who apparently saw in the twisted branches the upraised arms of the biblical figure Joshua. It was legislated a park in 1994. When we visited in 1984, it was still called a monument.

The park covers more than 1,200 square miles of desert country, most of which is nothing more than a roadless wilderness. Elevations in the park range from 935 feet to over 5,800 feet; it is called a high desert. Temperatures varied from the mid-seventies to freezing during the time of our visit in February. In the summer months, temperatures can reach 110 degrees.

This park can shatter your notions of a vast wasteland, because life does flourish in this land of little rain; both the flora and fauna have adapted to the heat and drought. The park's largest animal is the desert bighorn sheep. No services or merchandise stores are available in the park, so travelers must carry their own water, food, and gas throughout their stay. With all the many astounding, colorful granite formations, the park has become a rock climber's paradise and a fascinating area for hikers to explore. Palm Springs, the nearest city, serves as home base for many park travelers. Other towns close by are Desert Hot Springs, home of a thousand natural mineral pools; Yucca Valley; Joshua Tree; and Twentynine Palms, home of the Marine Corps Air Ground Combat Center.

Much like in the jungle and swamp, becoming disoriented in the desert is easy because of the lack of critical terrain features to guide on. Knowledge of the compass and map reading are critical, and proper safety precautions should be practiced by everyone who enters this domain. As a result of the brutal desert heat and lack of rain and available water sources, it is recommended that every desert traveler have at least one gallon of water on hand per day to sustain them when hiking or camping in this arid park area.

▼

The next morning after preparing breakfast, we packed our gear, which included six large plastic containers each holding two gallons of water. (Each individual container weighed almost seventeen pounds.) The jugs were strapped to the top of our packs along with the rest of our gear. It was one helluva heavy load to carry on your back. If you sat down with your pack on your back, it was nearly impossible to get up unassisted. Mostly, you didn't take it off, because it was so difficult to hoist it back on your shoulders. Never have I carried that much weight on a hike, and I don't want ever to do it again.

Those containers, along with the two canteens we carried, would be our water supply for the next three days. Additional water and other provisions had been stashed at defined points along our hiking route by our guides. We would pick them up when we arrived at those sites and leave our certain-to-be-empty jugs in their place. There were no water holes or streams in the desert, and we were told to conserve our precious fluid supply; otherwise, we could suffer from dehydration.

▼

In the jungle we had found plenty of water in the various streams, water holes, and catch basins, but it was almost too rancid to drink. Traveling in that subtropical climate and stagnating heat, we had to drink fluids, and lots of them, all the time; otherwise, dehydration and incapacitation would eventually overtake us.

On patrol, after locating water, the procedure was to strain it through a piece of cloth to remove the debris, sanitize or boil it, and then gulp it down quickly, so we couldn't taste how bad it was. This took time, something we didn't always have. Often while we tried to recover water from a streambed, we'd find animal droppings near the edge, or even in the water. It was best to avoid these locations; otherwise, unless we boiled the hell out of the water, we could still end up with diarrhea or worse. Usually, when retrieving water, we would dip it out of the stream, pond, or basin with a canteen cup and strain it through our handkerchiefs as we filled our water containers. Because of the crap floating in and on the water, it would take some time to fill our canteens. We had to continually rotate the filtering cloth because it would clog up with the stuff in just a few seconds.

If we had the time and could boil the water, that was the best way to ensure absolute purity; however, mostly, we poured a couple of drops of iodine or water purification tablets in the canteen and let it dissolve for thirty minutes before drinking it. Even with this method of purification, the taste was not great, but it was better than going without, which would leave us debilitated and in a rapidly faltering state. A person can go without food for days, but not so with water; you must have it or become dehydrated, and subsequently death takes its toll. "Drink all you can whenever you can" is a good rule—essential when it's hot and you have to put forth a continuous strenuous effort battling the elements and terrain.

▼

On our first day in the high desert, we hiked for most of the daylight hours to a vertical rock formation, where we spent the next two days practicing the techniques of rock climbing and rappelling.

We used ropes during the climbs, and the safety harness we wore would mitigate any serious injury if anyone fell trying to scale the rocks. This assumes, of course, that the belay person at the foot of the cliff kept a firm, attentive grip on the support rope by holding it taut and releasing the tension whenever the climber moved. This was a great experience, although a few of us did smash our bodies against a sheer rock face a couple of times when we attempted some swinging, lateral moves and missed our handholds. Thank goodness, in every case, our belay partner on the ground held tightly to the support rope. A few of us ended up dangling in the air, unharmed except for a few minor scratches and personal dismay; however, this went with the territory and was expected.

Following this triumphant exercise, we spent another day hiking cross-country and then scaled a ledge about two hundred feet high off the floor of the desert, where we spent the night. The most unforgettable part of that experience as we slept on the hanging shelf, besides the beauty of the open sky, was the rats and mice. The ledge had obviously been used by other campers in the past and had scatterings of rotten food all around the area. These tidbits, along with our own food droppings, brought the hungry little critters out in force. They would actually venture up to our sleeping bags and sniff around, searching for dinner. We waged war with them for most of the night, but as daylight appeared, they crept back into their secure, little holes and left us with some peace and quiet.

▼

The bunkers we had occupied in Cuba during the missile crises of 1962 and then later in Vietnam were always infested with rats and other undesirable vermin. There was just no way to keep them out of the sandbagged, dank, dark, musty-smelling shelters built to protect us from enemy mortar and artillery fire; however, it was far better to live with them in those cloistered, rotting holes than to be out in the open and be pierced by a flying piece of shrapnel from a nearby explosion. At times, when we darted into a bunker during a bombardment in Vietnam—and we were damned glad to have them available—the rats would leave temporarily, but they would quickly return once the *shit hit the fan* and the enemy fire began to explode and tear the hell out of everything around us; we just had to learn to live with it. So, rats were not new to me, but still, they were nasty, disease-infested, worrisome little bastards.

▼

The subsequent morning our task was to rappel off the ledge to the warm desert sand below, and then to climb back to our perch and try it again until we got it right. Our instructors fitted us with ropes, carabineers, and safety harnesses while rappelling, and taught us the technique of properly braking our fall after we had leaped off the rock into space. Then, after stopping our flight with our braking hand, we would again launch into the air with our lowering rope, again stopping our fall with the rope wrapped around our waist; while we more or less lowered, leaped, and walked our way down the cliff.

After completing this endeavor, we launched on another desert hike through some interesting rock formations, climbing to a much higher elevation, almost six thousand feet; this was the high desert!

We encountered a minor dilemma soon after, when one of the women was unable to continue the hike. *The Three Amigos*—Jim, Mack, and I— had been carrying most of her gear for part of the day, because her sore feet prevented her from lugging it herself. She had blisters and was limping badly from the tennis shoes she was wearing. (Imagine—tennis shoes for nine days of hiking.) Why she had not brought good-fitting boots with her for this course was beyond comprehension. Late that day, when she could no longer tolerate the pain, she was unable to continue. The instructors had previously given us an objective to reach, and the three of us wanted to make it regardless of what we had to endure or the amount of time it took. As usual, we had a mission, and we wanted to finish it.

They called a group meeting and asked the students for their recommendation about her situation. We had two choices, we were informed. Leave her at our current location with food and water, and she would be picked up the next day and driven back to the base camp. The remainder of the group would stay the course, carry on the hike, and proceed smartly to our assigned objective. The second choice was to abort the mission altogether, keep the group intact, care for her feet throughout the night, and hope she could continue the hike the following day. Outward Bound has a philosophy of always maintaining group integrity; they try to obtain student consensus whenever unique choices or difficult decisions need to be made that could possibly affect all the course members or cause an alteration in the program content.

Naturally the three *Musketeers* voted to leave her with provisions and continue the march. As I said earlier, we had a mission, and we wanted to complete it as planned, regardless of the consequences. We were summarily voted down by the instructors and the other participants, who were obviously not as personally driven to succeed as we were. For us, this was a great challenge. For the others, well, it was probably drudgery. We thought the young woman would be better off not hiking for a few days and most likely would not recover from her plight overnight. Later, our instructors informed us that this was the first time in the history of their Outward Bound experience that a negative vote, like ours, had been proffered in one of their courses. Oh well, there is always a first in everything; we took the prize for this one.

We spent the night, and the next day she hobbled painfully to our final encampment for our last night in the desert. Of course, we again carried all of her gear so she could make it. Incidentally, we never made it to our original objective, a real disappointment for us.

▼

Upon graduating from Marshall University and entering the Officer Candidate Program at Quantico, our class of young men was quickly indoctrinated into the basic ideology of the corps in no uncertain terms. In one of the first orientation classes, our instructor told us that "the basic objective of the marine corps is to accomplish the mission, and to ensure the welfare of your men." He then emphasized, "But you must always accomplish the mission."

Right or wrong, this was our attitude about the young woman; we would take care of her and still accomplish our mission.

▼

Hiking in the desert during the heat of the day while carrying our heavy load of supplies and large water jugs was energy-consuming; it would drain all the strength in our bodies by evening. It was so hot during the day, a few of us removed our shirts as we hiked, but it was necessary to use suntan lotion to protect our skin at the high elevation. At six thousand feet, the thermals and sunrays can be devastating to the body and can easily burn the living crap out of you. Earlier, I commented on our experience at the swimming pool in Palm Springs and the radical drop in temperature once the sun descended below the mountaintops. It can get bitter cold and highly uncomfortable without those penetrating rays available to keep you warm and comfy. Generally, as soon as the sun began its descent in the dessert, around four o'clock, we would halt our march and begin putting on our heavier clothes. Most of the time, we would just keep layering our body with all the clothing items we had until we ate dinner. It was just amazing how cold it got in that desert in such a short period of time without the sun's radiant heat beating down.

Many mornings we would awaken to find a thin layer of ice on the top of our sleeping bags or tarps; we had to let them thaw out and dry before packing them, or else they would stay damp and be a mess the next time we used them. The ice had to be broken into small pieces so that it would melt faster on these chilly mornings; this was not the most auspicious way to begin the day.

Our final night found us with a limited and disparate food supply. Mack Butler and I were assigned cooking duties for our last supper in the desert; being somewhat entrepreneurial in nature, we cooked a fine *dinner*, in our opinion. A few of the people said it was not edible, but we thought it was pretty damned good and gladly ate more than our share.

Having eaten most of our supplies for the previous eight days, we were down to the bare bones on vitals. Not to be daunted by such a minor issue, we inventoried all of our available resources, finally concluding that we should mix everything we had together and make a stew (unknown name or unidentifiable); we were most definitely more into quantity than quality. If the remaining items were fit, or maybe not so fit, for human consumption, we still used them.

Our cohort, Jim Box, refused to eat our nameless delicacy. He said he had tried it and it almost made him throw up. He admitted later that he had buried his portion deep in the ground so no animal could dig it up and eat it and possibly become contaminated or poisoned. Unknown to us at the time, he still had some of the candy bars we had obtained from the Delta stewardesses concealed deep in his pack; he ate them instead of our purist concoction.

That dinner meal was our swan-song contribution to the course. The instructors were probably happy to see us go after this final inedible creation, along with the never-ceasing commotion we had caused during the course with our imaginative attitudes.

The next day the group was taken to Palm Springs to make connections for the trip home. However, the Outward Bound course was only part of our plan. We had made additional arrangements for a side excursion trip to San Francisco for a few days of R&R (rest and relaxation) before returning to Atlanta. It was as this point and time when things began to get messy and complicated.

We had several hours before we were to catch our plane, so we convinced our instructors to stop at a convenient bar for a few parting libations. This was the *first mistake* of several to come.

We had not had a bath for nine days, and our clothes were filthy, but that didn't seem to make much difference, at least to us. The entire group ventured into a local upscale bar and ordered, of all things, a host of ice-cold margaritas. *Second mistake!*

Under the circumstances and after what we had just gone thorough in the desert, this was the most potent alcoholic beverage we could have possibly put into our worn-out, depleted bodies. Regardless of our weakened condition and partially dehydrated situation, though, we still managed to quickly order two more drinks each, and to dispose of them, unfortunately, in record time. *Third mistake!*

As the day progressed, several members of our rapidly sinking team had to leave us and go to the airport to catch their flights home. During that faltering afternoon, we made a total of three airport runs in our van. On reflection, I could only recall the first one, but someone mentioned that I had enjoyed each jaunt. After every trip we returned to the bar for another killer drink of the same size and caliber. *Another mistake*, and they kept mounting. As the time approached for our departure, our triumvirate, rapidly degenerating, huddled together and decided to delay our trip to San Francisco until the next day. *Yet another mistake!*

Amorous feelings, alcohol-inspired, were developing between certain members of the group, and it appeared that discretion being the better part of valor, we should stay the course and investigate our options. Our *bad judgment* was now without bounds.

Shortly after we had made our liquor-inspired decision, we met a nice couple in the bar from Newport Beach. After some frivolous flirting with the man's girlfriend, which he thought was humorous and harmless, he invited the remaining members of the partially intoxicated group to dinner with him and his lady friend. His invitation was timely because the manager of the bar thought it would be highly prudent if we exited his establishment ASAP.

The Bob Hope Classic Golf Tournament was underway in Palm Springs then, so the town was crowded with people, all nicely attired. In our disheveled condition, we stuck out like sore thumbs. We still had our dirty clothes on, had not bathed or shaved for nine days, and we must have possessed an unforgiving odor on our persona, but our condition did not dissuade our new friend from his invitation; he took us to a very nice, upscale Italian restaurant. They let us in, primarily because he was a friend of the establishment's owner. After another drink we ordered dinner. I faintly recall ordering spaghetti and meatballs. That is about all I can recall about that part of the evening, Apparently I took an unexpected nap, not on the tabletop, but with my face buried in the plate of spaghetti.

Our new friend, who had somehow taken an amused liking to our little intoxicated group, offered to take me to the Thunderbird Motel, get me a room, and summarily dispose of my reeking body for the night. I don't remember much about that phase of the evening except the walk to the motel, and then it was *lights-out* for me.

When I awoke the next morning, I still had my boots and clothes on. The white bedsheet had an emblazoned imprint of my dirty body embossed on it. I had no idea were I was or what had happened to my good buddies, who had, without any forethought or concern, allowed me, in my stupefied condition, to be carried away in the night by a total stranger. My first thought was to see if I still had my billfold and airline ticket. I did, thank goodness. Then I went in search of Mack and Jim. Upon checking at the front desk, I found they were also registered and had also stayed there that night.

Ultimately they ventured out of their rooms in a condition that was not much better than mine. Then I learned the dastardly details of their fun and frolicking evening. They admitted that they had been unaware of my situation or that I had even been escorted from the restaurant. That was unbelievable, but that was their story. After they had finished dinner, they accompanied two ladies to the motel and tried to encourage them to climb into a hot tub with them. Their intentions—I leave that to your imagination. Whatever they were thinking about or hoping for didn't work.

Our fun trip was most assuredly over, and it was time to go back to Atlanta—that day. We were out of bullets, tired and hung over from our adventure trip, misadventures, and bad judgment. Now in sound mind, somewhat sober, and with better judgment currently prevailing, we scratched the extension of our trip to San Francisco and made new reservations for a return flight home. It had been a great exploration for the three of us, and we certainly made the most of it—more than we should have, in all probability.

After returning to Atlanta, my secretary, never outspoken—at least by anyone I knew—remarked that our deep-set, dark-circled eyes looked like *two pissholes in a snowbank*. She was probably right; however, we were unreceptive about her description of our current physical state. After all, what did she know anyway? Unfortunately, she probably could have assumed almost anything, and she would have most likely been correct.

Outward Bound was beginning to take a toll on our bodies, and we began to think in terms of conducting our own adventure program, a task that I respectfully wanted to undertake. It would be interesting planning these unique journeys, highly educational, and most importantly to me, I would have control—no small point. "Take what you can, whenever you can" is a wise mandate when one is uncertain of an outcome. Strangely, my friends referred to me as a control freak. This was totally unfair, and I did take offense to their superfluous criticism—which, incidentally, was totally accurate.

Naturally, competition and a thirst for recognition among high-testosterone males always results in conflict. Neither of my fellow explorers wanted to take the responsibility for planning the trips or for even offering suggestions. All they really wanted to do was to complain constantly about whatever decisions and plans I devised.

They still complain today when we reminisce about our journeys. That's just the way it is among good friends who have lived a fun life together. Later, we received an invitation from our new friend from Newport Beach to visit him—he probably needed some laughs—but we declined; we were thinking that a boating trip somewhere in the West should be our next adventure.

EIGHT

GLEN CANYON NATIONAL RECREATIONAL AREA

This trip would be the first major adventure we had planned totally on our own, and it was much more fun and challenging than I had originally anticipated. Besides the travel arrangements, food planning, and determination of dates and locations (there were many to choose from), we had to coalesce as a group. Some of our explorers would be new, and coalescing proved to be a challenge.

My son, Christopher, would join us once again, along with an untrained, partially unequipped, but highly excited manger from our bank who would make his entry into our new adventure program.

Terry Miller, a former athlete, would be trying his talents as an explorer for the first time, and the gear he chose to bring would clearly demonstrate that he did not have the slightest idea of what he was doing or how to prepare for an outdoor trip; he would eventually learn, though, as we all did after we had experienced enough pain and discomfort with our travels in the backcountry.

Mack Butler was unable to make this journey because he was either afraid of our new agenda, which is understandable, or had important responsibilities to fulfill at his law firm. Some of us did have to work, you know, from time to time! This left the old stalwarts, Jim Box and me, as the other two members. Four was an acceptable number for our group; we attempted to have at least that many on most of our expeditions, and more were even better. There was strength in numbers, as well as mass confusion, but size did help mitigate the arguments that occurred about everything from the selection of a campsite and gas-station stops to meal preparation and hiking routes. There was just no end to the disagreements that could arise.

▼

In the marine corps operational planning instruction, we were taught a very simple guideline that is applicable to almost any situation requiring some degree of detailed preparation. It was called the 7-Ps of planning: "Proper Prior Planning Prevents Piss Poor Performance." Almost everything the corps taught us had some quirky little saying or mnemonic attached to it to help us with recall, and after all these years, I can still remember many of them.

For example, *I AM U WE CAT,* was the cliché taught for the operation of the M-1 rifle. The actions described were: **I**gnition, **A**ction of the recoil spring, **M**ovement of the slide to the rear, **U**nlocking of the bolt, **W**ithdrawal of the firing pin, **E**xtraction of the round, **C**ocking of the weapon, **A**ction of the recoil spring, and **T**ermination of the movement.

We were also required to learn the 5-Paragraph Order, a great checkoff list for issuing instructions. The easy mnemonic was *SMEAC:* **S**ituation, **M**ission, **E**xecution, **A**dministration, and Logistics, **C**ommand, Communication, and Control. I can assure you that I did not have to research any of these keywords or phrases; they come totally from memory, learned over forty-seven years ago.

Mnemonics was and is a wonderful teaching technique, serving as a super method for memory recall. I often wondered why most schools don't use this technique! I used this stuff when I started the planning for our wilderness trips, and it got the job done. During my business career, this process was introduced in my organizations and used for thirty-five years; it also worked perfectly in that environment. Old habits die hard, especially those that can help get the job done.

▼

The one area where it did not apply was in the management of the bitching and complaining arena; however we were not in the military, so within our group of explorers, to a large degree, discipline did not exist in any material fashion, much to my chagrin.

We flew to Salt Lake City, rented a Chevrolet Suburban, and drove to Hite, Utah, to rent a speedboat. We wanted something fast so we could explore more of the canyon area within our limited time schedule and also to do some waterskiing.

Our boat lasted one day. We bent the propeller trying to navigate through some shallow, rocky water that we should not have ventured into. Naturally, we had assumed that we could get through it without any problem. It seems we were always going where no one else would go. The propeller was damaged rather badly, and we turned the boat in after paying for the accident. An unplanned expense for our travel ledger.

After this unfortunate mishap, we wisely decided that a pontoon boat with a flat bottom and a fifty-horsepower engine would do just fine for our ambitious travels. It would also be less susceptible to damage and would easily carry the four of us and all of our gear, and we could sleep on its deck if necessary. It worked great for our needs, was much easier to beach, and easy to manipulate in the smaller canyons we explored during our trip. We did return it in relatively good condition, except for a few "minor dents," which went unnoticed by the pavilion manager.

▼

The Glen Canyon National Recreational Area extends from northern Arizona in the Grand Canyon National Park, along the Colorado River, into southeastern Utah. Lake Powell is the name of the waterway that actually runs through the186-mile-long canyon, which is comprised of 1,986 miles of shoreline.

The Glen Canyon Dam, near Page, Arizona, at the southern end, provides power to cities and industries throughout the West and forms Lake Powell, whose main purpose is water storage. The canyon began filling in 1963, following the completion of the dam across the Colorado River, and was not completely filled until1980.

The huge dam is the second-largest man-made in the United States and is reputed to be the most scenic. In 1972 the lake and surrounding countryside were incorporated into what is now the Glen Canyon National Recreational Area.

The lake flows into numerous almost hidden side canyons, sandy coves, and inlets, and around beautiful, towering stark red sandstone cliffs, which makes a stunning contrast between the clear blue waters and the contiguous, rocky landscape.

The wandering explorer of the Western frontier, John Wesley Powell, was the first explorer of the Colorado River in the 1800s and named this canyon area the Colorado River Glen Canyon.

About two thousand years ago, the canyon was occupied by a group of farming nomads who were primarily engaged as Basket Makers. Their culture ultimately evolved into what we now know as that of the Anasazi Indians. It is currently believed that the Anasazi tribe was most likely the ancestors of the Hopi Indians.

Caves within the canyon are adorned by drawings, both pictographs and petroglyphs. Pottery shards and other miscellaneous items have also been found buried in the dirt and dust of these unusual cave structures.

Around 1300 AD, agricultural and climatic changes occurred, driving the natives from the area because they were unable to harvest their crops and sustain their way of life.

The topography and beauty of this canyon area was breathtaking, and the Indian history captured our attention. Vertical walls of the canyons, whose ledges contained artifacts and dwellings, coupled with the abundant colors of the rocks and azure water of the large lake made for a spectacular educational experience for us Southern boys from the flatlands of central Georgia.

We explored canyons and climbed some of the rock formations, finding Indian caves and drawings on numerous walls of these former cavern dwellers. Using our pontoon boat like a mobile base camp and supply point, we would land it on beach areas, cook our dinner on the sandy beach, and frequently sleep without a tent under the open sky adjacent to the water's edge.

The surrounding hills neighboring the lips of the canyons offered an array of scenic opportunities to view the beauty of the canyons and to explore the surrounding landscape. Several times hiking we lost our way; although we could still see the river, we couldn't get to it because of the concealed valleys that crossed our route of travel. The landforms, extremely difficult to navigate because of these depressions, caused us to spend one entire day bushwhacking though the dense foliage and rambling terrain while we attempted to get back to our campsite; even though we could see it periodically from our route, getting to it was another issue. It was utterly ridiculous.

We could see where we needed and wanted to go, but we were unable to traverse many of the step cliffs and protruding ledges that suddenly appeared on our route.

On one particular occasion, when we ran out of water, we had to locate a small trickle of water and use purification pills to ensure its potability. As the day progressed, we began to realize that we might have to spend the night in these hills without food or our gear.

We had brought no maps with us on our trek to help with the land navigation; consequently, we had no idea whatsoever about the terrain and any trails that might lead us around the barriers.

The 7-Ps of planning, mentioned earlier, often escaped us on some of the hikes and trips we undertook, and it seemed that we always paid the price in bewilderment and sweat. Once again we had made an assumption that it would be simple to hike leisurely in the area. *Assume* always seemed to bring the same result to us: confusion and embarrassment.

▼

An old marine corps story makes this point. A hard-nosed, tough "mustang" (prior enlisted) lieutenant colonel was the commander of a marine battalion during the Korean War. He had dispatched a reconnaissance patrol to obtain information about the enemy's disposition; it was led by a young, inexperienced second lieutenant. After the patrol returned, during the debriefing, the colonel asked the lieutenant about enemy strength and positions.

The lieutenant replied that he *assumed* the enemy had vacated the area and had moved to another location, because he did not see any obvious evidence of their activity; therefore, he chose to terminate the patrol and return to the headquarters to give his report.

The battalion was preparing to move out in the attack, and the commander was concerned as to how he should employ his troops in the possibility of enemy contact. It would not have been prudent for him to move his unit without adequate knowledge of the enemy's situation. Consequently, the colonel, after hearing the young lieutenant's response, very bluntly said to him, in no uncertain terms, "Never *assume* anything in combat, because it will probably make An Ass of You and Me." Then he told him to go back and find out what in the hell was really happening. The lieutenant left within minutes with his chewed-out butt hanging below his knees. Later, he did return with a more accurate report.

▼

Mother Nature is fickle and capable of doing the most unusual and dastardly things to the environment at the most inopportune time. It is also wise to never *assume* anything about the wilderness; if you do, that is when you will probably lose your ass.

Case in point. Carolyn Muggee, a real-time adventuress, the proprietor of an adventure company in Atlanta, and a good friend of mine, had done some work with our bank staff. Over a long weekend, we decided to take a mountain hiking trip to Standing Indian Mountain in South Carolina. This mountain was only about 5,500 feet in elevation, which was rather high for this part of the country. It was located just on the northwestern edge of the Georgia-Carolina state line.

Carolyn was one of the first true outdoor-sports women, well ahead of the curve, very knowledgeable, and highly capable in most outdoor-type venues. She was very good at handling various watercrafts, an excellent hiker, mountain climber, and well, you name it; she could do it all. She eventually moved to Alaska.

I have not seen her for several years, but we communicate occasionally by e-mail and I know that she has stayed very active, completing Iditarod races while she has lived there over the years.

Anyway, we made plans (hasty plans) and headed for Standing Indian Mountain on a weekend when the weather was supposed to be good. We also *assumed* a lot of things about the trip, the weather, and our needs. Everything we did not plan for happened to us.

Both of us thought that, because we were experienced, we could easily manufacture whatever we needed in the backcountry; we were certainly confident of our ability to take care of ourselves in every backcountry situation. This is when the mistakes began to occur.

Since the weather was forecast to be good, we did not take adequate rain gear, nor did we take a good map of the area or a compass. We thought we didn't need this mundane stuff; after all, we were not amateurs, and besides, we were only going for a few days. After parking the car, we experienced several false starts in locating the trailhead to the mountain and had to double back and start again. This took two hours of valuable time. If we had brought a trail map with us, this would never have occurred, and we would have forged straight to the trailhead after leaving our vehicle.

During the hike we lost our way a couple of times and had to depend on guesswork. Fortunately, after several misguided attempts, we figured it out—only because we had tried every possibility. I repeat, we would not have had this problem with a map or compass.

After climbing for several hours, as we neared the top of the mountain, a torrential downpour occurred, catching us totally off guard and soaking us and all of our equipment. We put on our meager insufficient rain gear and huddled together under a tree for quite some time. At the end of the storm, we were saturated to the bone, and all of our sleeping gear was a wet mess.

It was getting late, night was overtaking us, and we had not prepared a campsite. Concerned about hypothermia, we considered descending the mountain, even though it was getting dark, to avoid the possibility of slipping into this condition and to help us stay warm from the downhill hiking effort.

Everything around us was drenched, and we needed to build a fire to get warm, dry out our waterlogged gear, and prepare some hot food for consumption to get our internal engines regenerated.

We searched around on the mountaintop and finally located a thicket of heavy vegetation with a substantial canopy of overhead tree limbs that looked promising for a campsite. It was shielded from the wind by the large trees; and the ground, although wet, was not inhospitable for our needs. We were able to find some semidry branches to start our fire, and then we put a tent up quickly to protect us in case of another surging downpour.

Our sleeping bags were extremely wet, and it was necessary to dry them by the fire. Once we had eaten and our bags were dry, we climbed into the tent, stripped down to our undees, and arranged the back sides of our bags together to capture as much collective warmth as possible. We needed to share and distribute body heat, as appropriate under the circumstances and weather conditions.

There is a common misconception about sleeping bag warmth. Some neophytes think they should wear all their clothes when they are in their bag in order to stay warm. In fact, the best procedure is to sleep in the minimum amount of clothes. As a person's body heat becomes trapped in the bag, it will become toasty warm. Many campers advocate sleeping practically nude for the best results. Wearing clothes minimizes the amount of body heat that can be captured in the bag. Usually, underwear and a long-sleeve shirt are adequate. A wool hat is appropriate to help contain heat from the head and to protect the face.

The next morning we descended the mountain, walking the ten-mile route as fast as we could. As we worked our way down the steep, rocky slopes, we were damned happy that we did not attempt this hike at night, carrying flashlights to help find the way.

In retrospect, we knew we had failed in our preparations for this adventure. Carolyn and I were embarrassed that we had been so lackadaisical about this point, but we had learned an important lesson. The good part about the situation was that we had reacted properly, used our fieldcraft knowledge, acted with cool heads, and made the necessary adjustments to care for ourselves.

The obvious advice for your edification: always plan for any contingency, regardless of your experience level, and you will never be surprised or caught off guard when Mother Nature decides to add a little special flavoring to your trip. Remember this rule; you will probably hear it again as you read: "Have a plan and have a backup plan, because the first one probably won't work anyway."

Yes, assumptions can absolutely level your ass and make a fool of you when least expected; it is much better to gather whatever facts you can, even if they are sketchy, and base your decision on that information. The more you know, and prepare accordingly, the better chance you have of surviving, especially if things get critical.

▼

It was January 1967, and Mike Company, 3rd Battalion, 4th Marines had been in the same set-piece (fixed) defensive position for several weeks conducting vigorous patrols in their assigned tactical area of operations.

The base camp was about four miles south of the DMZ in the northern part of South Vietnam near the town of Cam Lo. Their location had been previously occupied by a much larger battalion- size unit for several weeks; it was a good defensible position from ground attack, with adequate visibility of the surrounding terrain.

The higher-ups had assumed that, because of the heavy patrol activity conducted by Mike Company and the mutually supporting fire bases that could supply artillery protection, the site was secure from attack and could be maintained indefinitely.

However, Mike Company had taken a beating from some previous battles and was near combat fatigue.

Their position was fortified with concertina wire, mines and bunkers. Consequently, it was *assumed* by the hierarchy command structure, and the overwrought company leaders, that they were in a tactically sound defensive position.

At 1700 hours (5:00 p.m.), having previously received a command briefing and status report on the company, its mission, and defensive location, I arrived by jeep to take over the leadership of the rifle company. Darkness was approaching when I entered the scene; only enough daylight remained for me to tour the perimeter outpost areas and meet the platoon commanders and noncommissioned officers of the unit. They provided another brief update on their role and general tactical situation. Everything was *shipshape*, they said.

The unit commanders also told me they had never been attacked by the enemy since they had occupied the base. The only instructions I had time to communicate were to my 60-millimeter mortar unit located on a prominent hill on the edge of the perimeter.

Fortuitously, I had told them while touring their position, if we were ever hit by mortar fire at night and they could see the muzzle flashes in the distance, to begin returning fire immediately using the free-tube method.

Mortars, when they are fired, emit a flash from the tube that is visible for some distance if the line of sight is unobstructed. The free-tube method of firing is done by holding the mortar tube in the hands, resting the bottom on a steel base plate, without using the supporting aiming tripod, which takes important minutes to orient toward the direction of the target. With this technique, the distance to the target is estimated visibly. The mortar crew can watch the impact from the bursting shell as it hits the earth and explodes. They make quick visual corrections to get on target rather than using valuable time turning dials on the aiming tripod to move the tube.

This is the fastest way to put this weapon into action, and it is very effective in returning fire in an emergency, even if the return fire is only close to the mark. I had learned this technique at the Jungle Warfare School—a very important lesson, as you will discern.

Then I hit the sack. Around two o'clock in the morning, all hell broke lose.

We were under attack by North Vietnam Army (NVA) enemy mortars. The first rounds shattered the tent I was sleeping in, and the only reason I am alive today to tell the story is because sandbags surrounded the tent up to five feet in height. The sandbags took a beating from the metal fragments of the bursting shells, but they saved the lives of me and my gunnery sergeant, who was also sleeping in the tent.

After being stung in the head with some small steel fragments, I jumped from my cot, pulled on my boots, and crawled at record speed to the underground bunker, where our radio operators were busily requesting counter-mortar artillery fire.

The mortar crew on the hilltop, having seen the muzzle flashes, had given a compass azimuth and appropriate distance from our base to the enemy position. We called in the data, and in seconds counter- defensive artillery fire was signaled on the way. Unbelievably, the first salvo of six rounds fell inside of our position.

Some asshole had made a real bad mistake. The wrong coordinates had somehow been programmed into the firing pattern, almost causing *friendly fire* to damn-near wipe us out. A frantic correction was quickly communicated to the artillery battery, and they adjusted their firing immediately. At least they were quick.

In the meantime, as soon as the first enemy rounds slammed into our position, the alert mortar crew began firing away with their mortars. Within minutes it was over. One hundred eighty rounds of enemy mortar rounds and six friendly artillery rounds had hit our position, mostly inside our lines, fortunately resulting in only minor casualties. The next day one of our combat patrols located the NVA position and found a large number of unfired mortar rounds and two mortar tubes. Interestingly, they also discovered a large number of mortar craters around the enemy location. Apparently these had been made by our own mortars when our crew returned fire at the muzzle flashes—using the free-tube method, no less. They had gotten on target quickly, and this rapid response had been our salvation; the enemy had been spooked and took off before firing all their ammo. Several of my men were awarded Bronze Star Medals for heroism. They had stayed at their position with rounds bursting around them, risking their lives to save the lives of their fellow marines.

The facts of this situation were simple. It had been *assumed,* that our position was a safe harbor and the enemy was unlikely to be so blatantly bold as to attack this supposedly impregnable position. It was not, and they were not. The enemy had been able to infiltrate the area undetected, occupy their hidden gun position, and initiate their dastardly deed. Only after they had attacked and had hit our position were they discovered and brought under fire by the marine forces.

Another important point learned in Vietnam: "If the enemy is in range, so are you."

In the future, more explicit measures would be taken and more nightly patrols and ambushes would be employed to ensure our safety. Lessons learned the hard way are never forgotten. The risk of death has a lasting impact on the retention of those lessons.

We concluded our explorations at Lake Powell. It had been a good experience for our first internally planned trip. Except for a few minor mishaps, like arguments, bent propellers, getting lost, a few bodily gashes from some dumb accidents, and having a few drinks too many around the campfire, we had survived and were still speaking to each other. More adventures were forthcoming, and the challenge was to do the proper planning and never again assume anything about our explorations and the backcountry, *assuming,* of course, that we would remember our shortcomings.

NINE

THE GREEN RIVER

Our next adventure covered multiple venues of exploration, all of them on and around the Green River in the northeastern corner of the state of Utah. It was one of our favorite states to explore.

Jim, Terry, my son, Christopher, and I flew into Salt Lake City, rented a four-wheel-drive Chevrolet Tahoe, and headed toward Vernal, Utah. While en route we camped and hiked in the Uinta Mountain National Forest. On the morning of the second day, high in the Uintas, at Brown's Park, my three companion wanderers decided to take our vehicle and do some exploring in the mountains; I chose to hike around and try my hand at setting some small animal traps. That was a mistake. Before they left camp, I asked them to be extra careful, since they did not know much about the lay of the land.

Little did I realize or consider that they did not have the faintest clue of where they were going or what they were doing. As a consequence a potential disaster was in the making. Within the hour they had driven the vehicle into a bog in a very wet bottom area and were mired down in mud up to the top of the tires. I happened upon them when I crossed a hilltop directly above them as they were attempting to push and pull the vehicle free of the quagmire.

Why they chose to drive the truck into an obviously damp and mushy spot is beyond normal comprehension, but who said they were normal anyway? Not my son, of course, but Jim and Terry.

As I hiked down from the hill to join them with my walking stick in hand, Jim remarked to his cohorts that I looked like a prophet from the Bible that had come to convey either a message or a miracle of some magnitude.

I had no message, but I had a question: "How could you guys be so stupid as to drive into such an obviously remote, wet, and swampy area?" Unfortunately, I did not have the supreme power to deliver a miracle. After a close-up view of their situation, I thought it would take a near miracle to get them out of the mess they had sunk into.

Jim and Terry, usually the instigators of most of our unsavory problems, immediately blamed my son, Chris, reasoning I would have mercy on them if they could redirect the fault and their stupidity.

In retrospect, I am confident they must have set a fine example for my young son with all their lying, conniving, and the Lord only knows what else may have gone on when he was in their company.

I never did actually discover who was driving, but, of course, it didn't really matter now since the truck was submerged up to its fenders in the muck. The question was how were we going to get it out? This was particularly relevant as the entire area around the truck was very wet, and even if we could free it from the rivulets the tires had created, there was no solid ground close by that would support its weight. All the adjacent soil had turned to mush.

We were now immobile, in the middle of nowhere, with little hope of redemption. We badly needed a tow truck or that miracle I was supposed to deliver. Nothing else would save us; however, unknown to us at the time, a miracle was in the making, and without it, we would probably still be there, stuck in oblivion!

We scouted around for a while looking for help of some kind—a telephone, another vehicle, or anything else that would assist us in the resolution of this adversity. Finally, we found it!

In a local campground not too distant, we located some friendly people who were on a picnic, and unbelievably one of the men had a pickup truck. Not only did he have a truck, but of great surprise and joy for our quandary, he just happened to have a one-hundred-foot-long chain in the back of his truck. It was truly providence, because as indicated, our vehicle was stuck some distance from any firm ground. In order to salvage our transportation, the recovery vehicle would need to be located at least fifty feet away. This situation necessitated that a very long chain or rope be attached to our undercarriage to pull it free from the surrounding mushy area and onto solid earth.

Our *angel of mercy*, as we later called him, had the vehicle, means, and know-how to set us free from our strife. After he had performed the most appreciated act of kindness, we tried to pay him for his troubles. He would not accept any gratuity for his efforts, but told us that we looked so pathetic and inexperienced that both he and his entire family felt compelled to help us out. This was not an auspicious beginning for our newly planned trip.

We departed the next day, thank goodness, with our bruised egos and our very muddy and dirty vehicle. I always wondered if the traps that I set produced any results. I was too preoccupied with the truck incident to even check on them; oh well, maybe at the next stop!

That next stop would be at Flaming Gorge, parts of which are in Wyoming and Utah; it is fifty miles north of the town of Vernal, Utah.

▼

Vernal is located at an elevation of 5,050 feet, and we were informed that its airport is at the highest elevation of any airport in the continental United States. Another interesting fact concerns the Bank of Vernal's building. In 1919 the bricks to build this structure were sent by parcel post from Salt Lake City, 170 miles distant, to save expense, because mailing charges were seventy cents per pound less than the railroad freight charges. Due to post office restrictions on mailing more than fifty pounds in one package and more than five undred pounds to a single address, the bricks were sent in packages of seven to twelve bricks to numerous Vernal addresses to circumvent the policy.

The town of Vernal is located in an area of ancient geological interest, where numerous American Indian petroglyphs (rock art) and mineral deposits flourish. We would have the opportunity to explore some of the locations where the petroglyphs were found toward the end of our trip when we visited Jones Hole, a remote historic recreational area on the Green River.

▼

The Flaming Gorge National Recreational Area is due north of Vernal and straddles the border between Wyoming and Utah. Lake Flaming Gorge, a ninety-one-mile-long reservoir, was chiseled by the Green River millions of years ago. The river flows from the north in the Bridger-Teton National Wilderness to the south by carving its way through the Uinta Mountain range.

Flaming Gorge Dam is located at the southern tip of the lake and controls the flow and impounds the waters of the Green River to form the reservoir. The large dam offers a spectacular view of the surrounding canyons from 1,400 feet above the reservoir.

During one of his many western expeditions, the explorer John Wesley Powell named Flaming Gorge in 1869 after he and his men saw the sun reflecting its bright glow off the red rocks that are so prominent in the canyon.

Major Powell was in charge of the last great exploration of the continental United States. His voyage of discovery through the uncharted canyons and raging rapids of the Green and Colorado rivers finally culminated in a deadly float trip through the Grand Canyon, where a number of his men lost their lives.

Prior to Powell's exploration of the West, the great canyons of Utah, Colorado, and Arizona were mysterious and unknown.

Petroglyphs and other artifacts abound in this region, indicating that the Fremont Indians lived and hunted game in this region for many centuries. Several other Indian tribes, such as the Comanche, Shoshoni, and Utes also spent time in the gorge area.

The peripatetic Green River continues its course from Wyoming into Utah, touching Colorado's northwestern tip as it flows through Dinosaur National Monument and then cuts westerly back into Utah. The river continues south until it passes through Stillwater Canyon, intersecting with the Colorado River in Canyonlands. Undulating hills, abrupt cliffs, and promontories are found in the northern section of Flaming Gorge, and numerous canyons abound in the southern section. Over the years, the gorge has become a popular recreational and bountiful fishing area.

After renting a speedboat at a local marina in Cedar Springs, we began exploring the vermillion-hued canyons. Fortunately, on this particular excursion, we did not attempt to take our craft into shallow water as we had at Lake Powell, where we had bent the costly propeller. Our river journey took us north upriver until we crossed into Wyoming, spending several days en route climbing canyon walls, swimming, waterskiing, and hiking on some of the rim trails.

After leaving our boat at the marina, we drove on some of the access roads to explore and experience more of the vibrant rock colors and formations of this canyon area. After those excursions we drove to Jones Hole, Utah, chapter three of our trip, for more rock climbing and hiking.

▼

Jones Hole is a two-thousand-foot-deep gorge that runs along the border between Utah and Colorado. It is about forty miles from Vernal and lies just north of Dinosaur National Monument Park in northwest Colorado. A fish hatchery is located at the entry of the canyon, where we found the trailhead that would take us along the canyon floor, adjacent to a rapidly running creek bed for four miles, until we reached the Green River in Whirlpool Canyon.

As we entered the canyon walls on our hike, we came upon two archaeological sites that had been recently excavated—further evidence that over the past seven hundred years, the Jones Hole area had been intermittently occupied by at least fifteen Indian cultures.

These primitive sites contained well-preserved examples of Indian pictographs on the vertical rock walls, in some shallow cave areas, and inside a few rock indentures. Actually, some of this Indian art seemed to portray imaginative creatures from outer space, fully adorned in space suits, helmets, and other related space-travel paraphernalia. My imagination can be, at times, overactive.

We hiked all the way through the canyon until we reached a lush grassy area adjacent to the river, where we set up our camp. The next day, though, we were informed by a park ranger that this location had been established as an experimental area where certain grasses and other vegetation had been planted for trial growth and subsequent observation. Because we had not seen any signs denoting the significance of the planting, we pleaded plausible stupidity. Except for a good ass-chewing, since the damage had been done, the ranger let us stay an extra night. If we had known, we would not have camped there. In all probability we most likely destroyed most of the grass and other foliage during our stay.

Prior to starting the hike deep into the canyon, we had purchased some beer, margarita mix, and tequila for our evening and predinner enjoyment. We had also acquired a bag of ice, wrapped it in an insulated sleeping pad to keep it cold, and carried it with us. This was Terry's idea; he liked everything cold. After a couple hours of hiking, we decided to store our gear near the streambed and take a short trek up an interesting-looking side canyon. Before starting out, someone in our group (Terry) decided we should put our beer in the frigid stream so that we could have a cold one when we returned. He also stupidly declared that we could probably preserve our bag of ice along with the beer. The beer in the stream was a great idea; the ice in the stream, even though it was cold, was a brainless idea.

We hid our packs and hiked for a couple of hours, crawling over the walls of the canyon, enjoying the rock art and fossil remains from an ancient sea. These old vestiges of the past were notably sprinkled throughout the sandstone and limestone formations. When we returned to pick up our gear by the stream, the beer was good and cold. The plastic bag was now filled with icy water, but no ice. Naturally, all the ice had melted. Duh!

At first, some were amazed that this could have happened, but with a little intelligent rationalization, we began to understand that if something is not frozen, it will not keep something else frozen; rather, it will only hasten the melting, which the stream did. You did not need to be Einstein to figure this out. Our stupidity was infinite.

Heading now for our illicit campsite, somewhat disquieted, we were nonetheless anxious to set things right. Unfortunately, we were a long way from achieving that goal, as time and our ensuing actions would soon reveal during the progression of the evening.

Upon locating the beautiful new grassy camping area, we spread our sleeping bags out in the open near the river's edge and began preparing our dinner. Naturally, we decided that we should have a libation or two before we had our meal. Regrettably, two drinks turned into four, and by the time we had prepared dinner, we were about pickled and on the road to perdition.

Our pots and pans and everything else were spread out all over the place, and the whole area was now in disarray. One of the small Peak cooking stoves actually burst into flames from the spillage of fuel. Chris picked it up and threw it in the river to extinguish the blaze, but later retrieved it from the water, and the next day after it had dried out, he made several attempts to prime it, actually coaxing it to work again. Wonders, sometimes near miracles, never ceased to occur on our trips. Believe me, we needed them to survive.

Jones Hole was apparently a favorite overnight stop for boaters of all kinds; earlier in the afternoon, a group of rafters ("river runners") had put ashore directly across the bisecting streambed from our camp, in an area reserved specifically for rafting tours. Why they happened to choose the campground next to ours, less than one hundred yards apart, particularly in our destabilized condition, which had to be obvious to them, has always been a question in my mind. However, we were drawn to introduce ourselves because the group encamped in such close proximity were mostly women—ten teenage girls, two attractive mothers who were chaperons, and two *not-that-attractive-male* river guides. The young women were members of a girls' club and had undertaken the raft trip as some kind of a special project.

A sizable, rapidly flowing creek separated our group from theirs, but as the evening progressed and we had imbibed enough liquor to fortify our courage and dull our senses, that—and our rising testosterone levels— motivated us to attempt a crossing.

Slowly and unsteadily we picked our way across some stable rocks in the swirling waters of the creek, reached their camp, established contact, and introduced our incoherent team from the South.

Upon our arrival at their camp, it was probably blatantly obvious to everyone, especially the male river guides, that we were not nearly as stable as the rocks we had just crossed, but the entire female group welcomed us, and as we had brought some booze to share with the mothers as a peace offering of a sort, we enjoyed their immediate friendship and hospitality.

Obviously, the younger women knew we were old men except for Chris, who was much younger and seemed to draw most of the girls' attention much better than the rest of us. But that didn't stop Terry, who considered himself as some kind of a unique woman's man and highly attractive to every female that he made contact with.

The mothers, on the other hand, liked our banter, and they humored us with conversation while we conveniently supplied them with several libations. We were sinking and sinking fast and deep, because I suddenly dozed off while sitting on a wooden table in midsentence—my midsentence. One of the mothers asked what was wrong with me, and Jim Box responded, "His *pilot light* just went out, but not to worry; it will come back on in a few minutes."

Now, as a result of that stunt and the progression of the evening to a point of no return, we had become more inebriated, both with the liquor and the exuberance of our own verbosity. The male river guides appropriately suggested that we should return to our side of the river. In other words, "Get the hell out—now!"

This mandate did not please Terry and in his druken state of grandeur was hopeful that one of the dear ladies would want him to stay and continue to socialize for a while. Of course, Terry always thought he was desired by most women of all ages; age discretion was never a part of his mentality. We did not tell him that he was not so desirable. The truth would have utterly and totally destroyed his vain, inglorious ego.

We gingerly started back across the creek, but it was now very dark and the water had risen; we could not find our former rock path. For some reason the stream had increased in velocity; we now had rushing water up to our knees, instead of our ankles as when we had earlier made our initial crossing.

Staggering along, we were holding onto each other, trying to maintain our balance and footing in the swift running water, struggling diligently not to be washed away into the raging Green River just a few yards away from our water trail. Had that happened to any of us, it would have been curtains, especially in our condition.

Terry, on the other hand, actually crisscrossed the creek several times without any regard of the severity of the gushing water, while the rest of us struggled with our single perilous crossing, because he foolishly believed one of the mothers' was beckoning to him.

The next day he confessed to us, "I felt a light on the back of my head, and I was certain that someone was signaling me with a flashlight to come back. Then I heard a whistle from somewhere, and I knew I had to go back and see who it was." Perhaps now, you can clearly understand what I meant about his ego and delusional thinking. Terry experienced fantasies about women and their attitude about him whenever he met a female. We ridiculed him about his overconfidence by telling him he was definitely a legend in his own mind when it came to women.

Ultimately we reached our camp and collapsed on our bedrolls for the night. The next morning the boaters departed early, waving to us from their rubber vessels as they glided by our disheveled camping area. Noticeably, the male river guides did not wave.

Our gear, along with several "dead soldiers" (empty beer bottles), were scattered all over our campsite, and we'd left our dirty cooking equipment and food containers out for the insects to enjoy. The area really looked appalling and unhealthy.

That was the day the park ranger came paddling by in a John Dory boat, stopped, got out, surveyed our mess, and asked us what we were doing camping in a restricted area. We looked so bad, hungover is a better description, and incoherent that he finally told us to sober up and to leave the area the next day. We did as he suggested, spending the remainder of that somber day hiking and exploring the adjoining canyons. That second night, exhausted from all the fun and games, we slept soundly, woke up the next morning, policed (cleaned) the area, and hiked out of our canyon of memories.

At that time I was a member of the Young President's Organization (YPO), which had started offering wilderness and Outward Bound programs, generally in the West, for father, son, and daughter members. I had enrolled Chris and myself in a four-day rafting trip on the Green River, and then scheduled the other segments of our trip with Jim and Terry in the same general locale.

After leaving Jones Hole, they dropped us off in Vernal, where we would meet our guides for the next phase of our adventure, and then they drove back to Salt Lake City to catch their plane home.

When they departed they looked a bit sheepish and extremely tired. Later they told me that they had slept for two days after they had returned to Atlanta. I was not surprised.

Chris and I would do three YPO wilderness trips over consecutive summers, and each time we would meet our buddy explorers, either before or after the YPO trip, for extra add-on adventures; often we would be gone for ten or more days. More was always better, and it was also good for our morale.

This particular YPO-sponsored rafting trip started at the Gates of Lodore Canyon, just north of Dinosaur National Monument in Colorado. The trip would take us though the center of the park, and we would travel almost forty miles during the four-day trip before returning to the take-out point south of Vernal.

▼

During his canyon exploration of 1868 when Major John Wesley Powell and his expedition reached the *Gates of Lodore,* they described the canyon, in their journals, as "dark and foreboding, it looked like a mountain drinking a river," they wrote. However, when they ultimately began their descent into the canyon, they were awed by the beauty of the vermillion-colored walls imbedded with a touch of green. One of Powell's crew members had come across the name "Lodore" in an English poem, and since the location was unnamed, they called the canyon opening the Gates of Lodore.

▼

The first night we camped at the entry of the Gates, sleeping in the open on the banks of the river, with a spectacular view of the river passing between the canyon walls. Around midnight a violent thunderstorm erupted, and lighting struck the hillside just across the river from our camp; the hillside burst into flames, and we just sat and watched. Some people, unfamiliar with the area, were screaming to call a fire department, but cooler folks remarked, "It won't do any good; there is nothing to burn except sagebrush." Finally, the fire burned itself out. However, I will admit that the lighting striking so close to our position would put the fear of God into anyone, regardless of their religious preferences and beliefs.

The exciting rapids on the Green River are appropriately named Disaster Falls, Hell's Half Mile, and Triplet Falls. The steep canyon walls are colorful and covered with lush vegetation and trees. We spent most of our time paddling; however, we were able to do some hiking and exploring when we stopped our rafts each day.

This area, along with many others that we visited over the years, is perfect for solitude and reflection; most certainly, the Lodore Canyon will start your adrenalin flowing and keep it flowing, especially when your craft enters the dramatic rapids of this historic river gorge and they toss your raft around like a rubber ball.

At the end of the trip, one of the other YPO members and his daughter offered Chris and me a lift to the Salt Lake Airport. The transportation was his two-engine four-passenger Cessna; we gratefully accepted, appreciating his friendliness and the opportunity of catching an earlier flight home after this extended backcountry adventure.

As we flew over the various mountain ranges, thermals shooting upward from the tops of the 13,000-foot peaks buffeted and bounced our little aircraft around quiet unnervingly. At that time in our flight pattern, we were probably no more than a couple of thousand feet above the peaks. I was glad that we had two engines; nonetheless, the light plane still jumped and bounced all over the sky. Chris and I were a bit white-faced when they dropped us at the airport, and quite happy to catch a larger, more stable, and much more comfortable ride on to Atlanta.

It had been a great trip for all of us, and there were still many more to come! The question was, would we live through them without destroying our bodies physically from all the trials, self-imposed difficulties, and tribulations that we unnecessarily cast in our path? But this is the nature of risk takers and adrenalin junkies, and it's probably good for all of us to remind ourselves, from time to time, that "when the going gets tough, the tough get going."

This is an old aphorism from my sports days that our prehistoric coaches would use to try to motivate us when some overpowering opponent was beating our asses into the ground. Naturally, this only applies in any given situation if you have anything left inside of yourself to get going.

Now it's time for a breather and a short segue on wilderness cooking. This facet of our journeys was also an adventure, and most definitely it was an exploration of sorts, sometimes good, sometimes bad, but it was always interesting. Regardless of the situation and menu, we always had enough to eat and it was usually tasty. When you're hungry, tired, and had a few drinks everything is yummy.

TEN

DUTCH OVEN COOKING

Never have so few done so little with so much. My apologies to Sir Winston Churchill for rephrasing one of his great quotes, but this is an appropriate reference to our utilization on our wilderness adventures of a cooking pot called the Dutch oven. This cooking container, as described in Webster's New World Dictionary, "is a heavy metal pot with a high, arched lid, used for cooking *pot roasts*." However, I would add to this definition that just about anything you can imagine can be cooked in this iron kettle. It only requires a little imagination on the part of the chef. But when used on expeditions like ours, you must bear the pain and strain of carrying it strapped to your backpack.

This seems to be an appropriate time to discuss this aspect of our journeys—cooking. Yes, I realize I have previously mentioned some of the trials and issues about food preparation on our trips; but as time progressed and we undertook less vigorous programs, we opted for less primitive and more domesticated techniques. In other words, we wanted to satisfy our growing appetites with more variety and better-prepared meals that would properly reward the laborious effort we were putting forth in our reduced, but still challenging, physical endeavors.

Jim Box, by far, had developed into the best chef among our exploring group. He was especially good with the dinner menu, and we universally agreed (agreement being something highly unusual in our always disparaging group) to abdicate most of our responsibility for this meal to him; the other meal preparations were up for grabs.

Unfortunately, everyone had their own idea as to how and what we should prepare. Putting together an appropriate food list for our trips was almost an exercise in futility, so we just took the same food on every trip. A simple solution! A Dutch oven seemed to be the best choice to solve our quandary. We decided to tote it on our trips and cook most of our meals in this almost indestructible, heavy, iron, flexible cooking vessel. Jim introduced the Dutch oven on one of our trips, and after experiencing the wonderment of this cooking instrument, we were prepared to haul it with us regardless of the inconvenience and overburdening weight. As I recall, fortunately for some of us less inclined, he opted to carry it on most of our trips.

This was perfectly acceptable to our group, and it empowered Jim to have some degree of control over the selection and preparation of our meals, and this is what he wanted, because he liked to cook; the group most definitely benefited from the variety of food and his tasty concoctions. Actually, everything tastes good in the woods, but it really is good when it is artfully cooked. And that's how the now-ubiquitous Dutch oven became our constant camping companion and new friend, even though it was a bit overweight, clumsy, and a burden to tote around on our adventures.

A really wonderful meal we learned to prepare during our numerous Outward Bound exposures was called Picole Pie; it also was baked in our Dutch oven. The ingredients consisted of fried hamburger meat, chili sauce, onions, crushed tomatoes, tomato sauce, green peppers, canned Mexicorn, grated cheese, tortillas, and a teaspoon each of oregano, ground cumin, and chili powder. Other items could be added based on individual tastes and availability of food.

The meat sauce, vegetables, and other sundry items were cooked together in a frying pan and then poured over alternating layers of tortillas in the Dutch oven, this was followed by sprinkling each layer with grated cheese. The top of the mixture was covered with Jiffy cornbread mix.

The pot and mix were then placed over simmering coals in the fire pit; hot coals would be bunched up around the sides and on the top of the oven lid, with little heat being directed from the bottom so as not to burn the delicacy. Delicious and filling, it was also a nourishing feast. The oven would hold a large quantity, and we always made a bunch and consumed every ounce. Somewhat like the old Maxwell House coffee slogan, "It was good to the last bite." And rest assured, somebody ate that bite; no crumbs were ever left on anyone's plate.

We also liked to serve our special slaw with the Picole Pie as a side salad, which made the meal even more scrumptious, delightful, and importantly, much easier to digest. The slaw was mixed with onions, pickle bits, green pepper, salt, and pepper, and then laced with a tablespoon or two of mayonnaise.

Spaghetti covered with our special field-made meat sauce was another delicacy prepared on many of our adventure programs. Of course, our field slaw always accompanied this heavy meal. You may question the integration of slaw with so many of our meals.

The fresh cabbage provided roughage and aided in the digestion of these weighty meals, which are highly recommended when people are physically active and require a large amount of fat and protein to keep their strength at its peak and to stay warm when required.

A combination of pancakes, biscuits from scratch, grits, bacon, and eggs, all cooked in the oven, were favorite selections for our morning repast, and frequently the remains of this meal would suffice for lunch, sometimes supplemented with beanie weenies, smoked sausage, cheese, candy bars, or trail mix; this was the meal when we were hiking and exploring vigorously that we needed for the sugary carbs to keep our energy levels going.

We could also bake cakes in this pot, and we used a ready-made mixture for these concoctions. You may not believe this, but many of the pastries we made in our Dutch oven were just as good as those cooked in a kitchen stove, meaning, perhaps, they were not burned and tasted great, especially in the backcountry.

A very important issue also learned the hard way, while on our explorations, was to ensure that all of the baking mixes brought to the woods contained the necessary preparation ingredients and required only *water*, not eggs or milk, to prepare for cooking.

The dinner meal, as noted earlier, was our major spread, and we always had an attitude readjustment period during the preparation to help us relax from the rigors of the day. Our cocktail hour could consist of beer, vodka tonics, or margaritas, depending on the amount of ice that we could keep frozen in our containers. Blocks of ice would stay frozen longer than chipped. Sometimes we would prefreeze water in plastic one-gallon jugs and carry these with us.

The key to using the oven was learning how to position it over an open fire pit. It was normally supported on rocks located in the pit suspended over sizzling ashes, with hot ashes spread on the top and around the sides of the pot so that the delicacy would be cooked slowly and evenly. The oven was never put directly on an open flame or hot coals, because the excessive heat generated in the oven from such high temperature would burn the food in just a few minutes. We scorched and destroyed a lot of good victuals before we perfected the proper method of Dutch-oven cooking, but once we learned how to use it and reconciled ourselves to carrying the heavy-weighted pot, the results were well worth the anxiety we had gone through in the early stages of our cooking trials. The oven was also very flexible because either part of the oven could also be used as a frying pan. Some makes of the oven had handles on both sections of the pot that could be locked together; this also aided in its utilization. Frankly, we used it for every imaginable type of cooking.

To clean it in the field, we usually scoured it with sand from a streambed, and that was effective, especially when we had burned some of our potential eating pleasures. Then it would be rinsed with water, and placed near the fire to dry; afterward it would be laced with Crisco to keep it from rusting. The Dutch oven is ideally suited for explorers, hikers, campers, and anyone else who likes to cook good stuff on an open fire. In addition, its versatility is almost unlimited, and its cleaning and maintenance are simple.

After returning from our trips, it was thoroughly cleaned of all the accumulated rust and dirt. Crisco was applied liberally to the inside and outside; it was then baked in a conventional oven for about an hour to cure it and make ready for the next trip.

From this description about meal preparation, you've figured out that our risk-taking group was beginning to gradually descend from the typical hard-core, wilderness adventure programs to more lenient and less-demanding routines on our explorations.

Yes, we were still active with our outdoor travels around the country, especially in the West, continuing to schedule at least two weeklong trips annually, but we began doing more sightseeing, car camping, and day hikes than mountain climbing and long-distance backpacking. Please don't think we had become *slackers*, though—not by a long shot. We still loved being in the backwoods, and our adventures were still much more than most people would ever attempt in their lifetime. As the years progressed, we would drive our vehicle off-road into a remote location, usually deep in the wilderness away from civilization, and establish a base camp; naturally, it was always the perfect location or campsite (this will be described later). From there we would launch our hikes, carrying only enough food and water for the day. Afterward we would return to camp, build a great fire, have a few drinks, engage in some controversial conversation, and enjoy a superb open-fire dinner; then hit the sack and do it again the next day.

During these later years, bad knees and other ailments were beginning to take their toll on our battered bodies, but we maintained the course as best we could by making a few adjustments in our previously stringent programs. Carrying heavy packs for long distances was no longer a viable option or necessary for us to enjoy the outdoors. Day packs and hiking poles, however, worked just great.

This fine-tuning on our trips, along with heavy dozes of ibuprofen and an occasional day off, prolonged our capabilities for several more interesting and exciting years. We even started bringing a couple ice coolers with us in our four-wheeler, filled with food to ensure freshness, variety, high quality, and of course, ice for our libations.

One particular item I personally enjoyed to the fullest was cinnamon. Unfortunately, my buddies held it and me in disdain after I had possibly gone to extremes with its use. I put it into the morning coffee, cakes, pies, pancakes, and anything else I could get away with without being summarily terminated by my camping buddies.

As an early riser, I would generally get the fire started and put on a pot of coffee for the group to start the day when they rolled out of their sleeping bags. Naturally, I always put cinnamon in the coffee and had the first cup or two, sitting by the fire enjoying the early light as it silently crept through the foliage and settled around our camp. In my opinion, probably in my fellow explorers' as well, this was the best part of the day: the dim light, the crackle and fragrance of the burning embers, the gentle rustle of the breeze against the leaves, and the enveloping solitude were inescapable and just so soothing to the mind and body.

These experiences, along with the other aspects of our travels, produced the relaxation response so instrumental in helping our team of compulsive executives handle the stresses of the work enviorment after returning to our jobs in Atlanta.

Unfortunately, the bitching, complaining, and moaning always started as soon as the first person up poured themselves a cup of my coffee from the pot resting by the fire on a convenient rock. "Oh my God, not cinnamon again!" seemed to be the standard morning lament, repeated verbatim by each person as they sipped away at their first cup of the day. Of course, no one ever expressed any gratitude for the ready coffee; they preferred to complain. That's just the way it was, which was to be expected. It was the gamesmanship everyone played when we were on expedition. It was just so typical. One of them could have built the fire and made the coffee, but that would require them to crawl out of their tent in the cold and do some work. It was easier and more fun to doze there, be served, and bitch.

Desserts were my thing, and I liked to experiment with a variety of recipes, and I used lots of cinnamon and brown sugar whenever I made them. The guys always nitpicked the ingredients and any burned parts, but they always ate every particle. The more they bitched, the more of my special featured items were put into the desserts. It was my way of getting even for having to listen to their ungrateful and unflattering comments. I believe this is called one-upmanship.

One evening in Montana, while camping along the Yellowstone River, Jim prepared a meal for five people that was absolutely beyond reproach. Using every pot and pan we had, including the oven, he fixed three kinds of pasta and various side dishes. At the end of dinner, we counted fifteen different pieces of cookware that he had soiled during the feast, not counting knives, forks, and drinking cups. Clearly, we could overextend with our meal preparation.

At times, accidents would occur during the cooking process, such as the time I inadvertently dumped spaghetti meat sauce on the ground; hastily scooping it up, I put it back into the skillet before anyone could see what had happened, I hoped. Unfortunately, Jim and Mack did see the mishap, and I heard about it for years afterward. After all of this time, it still comes up when we reminisce about our wilderness exploits. Luckily, the stuff fell on some pine needles, and after eating all they could hold, they told me how bad it was, but they liked the addition of the native pine nuts, they said.

One evening in Idaho, Mack cooked a beef stew with an array of fresh vegetables. It looked great and smelled wonderful; but as usual, he was unable to just let things be, which was his nature, and at the last moment, against our outcries, he decided to dump a bag of raw rice into his delicacy. The rice should have been cooked in a separate pot, with the stew served over it as the topping.

Eating his final product was like trying to swallow a gob of water-soaked paste. The taste was actually okay, but it was tacky, stuck together, and difficult to swallow without gulping down water along with every bite. We ate it anyway, though. It was all we had. Actually, Butler was a good cook; he just did dumb things, probably for spite and to piss off the rest of us, and he succeeded.

I enjoyed making cinnamon pancakes (there it is again) for breakfast. We normally used a mix that required only water to make the batter, and the resulting pancakes were truly quite good. Before one of our trips, Mack was asked to pick up the pancake mix along with a few other items for our cooking needs. The first morning of the trip, I broke out the fixings for breakfast, including the pancake mix, syrup, and a big slab of country bacon. When I checked the instructions on the box about the preparation of the pancakes, I discovered that all we needed to prepare the batter was three eggs, a quart of milk, and a blender! If I had been in a well-equipped kitchen, I could have easily followed the instructions, but in the woods, well, it was *Mission Impossible.* I hurled the box into the fire and let it burn to smithereens, much to the chagrin and surprise of my other partners. Of course, Mack pleaded innocence, a highly unlikely and unacceptable plea. In our minds we instinctively knew he did it on purpose just to alienate us, and probably to ensure that we would never again ask him to shop for groceries to take on a trip. I think he was happy with the results, and we didn't have any cinnamon pancakes on that trip. Come to think of it, that might have been his plan from the get-go. Oh well, I did manage to include extra cinnamon in our coffee every single morning; it's called tit for tat.

As I indicated, Box was our premier chef, and we always enjoyed his meals; however, some of the members of our crowd did nothing but eat. They gathered firewood and washed our eating utensils in the local creek, but mostly they just chowed down on whatever was made available. They seemed to be quite happy to be fed regularly, especially since they didn't have to cook. A few of them couldn't cook anything if they tried, and mostly they didn't make an attempt.

On every wilderness trip we undertook, one other issue always impacted our group. Amazingly, it was the selection of a campsite. Everyone had their own idea as to the perfect site, even those who didn't have any idea whatsoever of what it should really resemble. We spent way too much time trying to gain a consensus on the right location while driving from one site to another. However, if people are hiking with a heavy load on their back they are easy to satisfy and do not debate the selection that someone makes regarding a campsite. Everyone just wants to get off their feet and rest.

You might want to ask, "How could grown men act this way and be so selective for what typically would only be a 'one-night'event?" It is impossible to describe the degree of bitching that occurred during our search, and the many great sites we passed up while inexorably driving around in the woods in absolute disagreement, under a cloud of ever-darkening hostility.

You might also wonder, "What makes a perfect or ideal campsite?" Ideally it would be located next or close to a body of water–a stream, a lake, or a river–in order to facilitate general cleanup, cooking, washing of our cooking gear. Also, it was good to be near rushing water at night because it's a soothing sleep inducer, especially when you're dead tired and need Mother Nature's music.

We seldom drank the water at our camping areas because we were concerned that it might make us sick. Too much pollution of the streams, lakes, and rivers has occurred over the years, even in the most pristine and remote wilderness locations. We would boil it to kill the bacteria and use it primarily to clean our eating utensils.

For the perfect campsite, trees were a must for shade and protection, as was an abundance of deadwood to keep our perpetual fire going, and also of great importance was a panoramic view of the surrounding landscape. In essence, our camping area had to look good, have the aforementioned amenities, and be well-situated, preferably on or near high ground. This was an important criterion, even for our primitive camping. Our principle was to always leave our campsite in better condition than we found it, an imperative to our wilderness etiquette.

During one of our trips to the high backcountry in Colorado, Christopher was driving the vehicle on a remote dirt road that penetrated a lone plateau. Jim, Mack, Terry, and I were arguing, vociferously disagreeing on every potential camping site that we saw, while my son was rather stoic and exceedingly silent about the whole matter as he kept weaving in and out of prospective, but declined, sites. Nothing we saw seemed to please everyone. Finally, as the arguments increased and cacophony filled the vehicle, Chris had had all that he could stand. Suddenly, without any guidance from anyone, he veered off the road and came to a quick stop at the edge of a large open field adjacent to a wooded area. He jumped from the truck and bellowed, "This is it. No more driving; we're stopping here."

Silently, without any resistance to his declaration, the four of us climbed out of the vehicle, gathered our gear from the storage area, and began to set up camp for the night. It was humorous because no one offered any resistance. It was as if some kind of nasty spell had been broken, and common sense had finally overtaken the arguing and disgruntled group. Naturally, as Chris's father, I supported his decision, and his site selection turned out to be a good choice. It had a nice view of the surrounding terrain; it was level, dry, with trees and lots of firewood, but there was *no water*! Oh well, no one can be perfect all the time in choosing campsites, not even my son.

Dick and Chris bonding in
Arapaho National Park

"The Desert"
Arches National Park, Utah

Pictographs, prehistoric art, in cave
at Green River, Utah

**Rocky Mountain National Park
Dick, Jim, Terry, Chris & Mack**

**Where the Buffalo Roam,
Yellowstone Park**

Sun Valley, Idaho
Summer and Winter, both beautiful

All cleaned-up and going home
Mack, Jim, Chris, Terry, and Dick

"Sunday Morning Coming Down"
The Local Pub, Livingston, Montana

Rowing the rapids
on the Chatooga River

**The Gates of Ladore
Green River, Utah**

**Dick and Chris on the
Summit of Mt. Elbert**

Elk Mountain, New Mexico
Dick, Steve, Christopher & Jim

Summertime, Taylor Mountain,
New Mexico

**My dog Gypsy on the
Lewis and Clark Trail in Idaho**

**Jim and Andy Box at
Sawtooth Lake, in Idaho**

ELEVEN

ROCKY MOUNTAIN HIGH

When we initially started our backwoods exploration journeys, no one in our group had ever seen or been to Colorado. According to the best recollections of our now decrepit team of explorers, over the years we made six separate and distinctively different excursions into this beautiful, bold, and dramatic state.

According to some travel literature, the people who live in Colorado tend to breathe a little easier, focus a lot better, and take themselves a whole lot less seriously. I've also read that, "The higher you go, the higher you get"—and no wonder, because the scenery is awe-inspiring and the unadulterated air is just plain wonderful. With fifty-eight mountain peaks surpassing fourteen-thousand-foot elevations and the Continental Divide ripping a jagged line through the state as it rambles across, over, and through the heavily forested Rocky Mountains, a person visiting this state may feel both humbled and empowered at the same time.

The history of Colorado encompasses everything from originally being a part of the Louisiana Purchase in 1803 to the discovery of gold in 1850, raging gunfights between famous cowboys, and old ghost towns that were at one time thriving areas. This state glows prominently by offering the interested tourist some of the most breathtaking scenery on this continent. The musician and entertainer John Denver penned the song "Rocky Mountain High," which embraced many of the general feelings about this *vertically* oriented state. This music captured the imagination of everyone who had an appreciation for the wonders of the mountains and the beautiful forested surroundings.

▼

During these exploring years, our wilderness adventures would take us to a variety of Colorado locales, each one prolific, exciting, and educational. Because of these inspirational visits, we continued to return regularly, searching for even more thrilling experiences and spectacular vistas on every trip, and we usually found them. One of our earliest trips included a visit to Dinosaur National Monument, an exploratory excursion we added after a camping trip in Utah.

Dinosaur is located in the northwest corner of the state, partially situated in both of the states of Utah and Colorado. It contains one of the largest and best-known concentrations of fossilized dinosaur bones found anywhere in the world. A wide variety of prehistoric animal bones have been revealed in a single sandstone cliff at this park. The Dinosaur Quarry Visitor Center, where they are exposed in relief on an open rocky face, has been left in place for continued study by geologists and inspection by visiting tourists.

Since our initial visit, various members of our team of explorers have returned several times to visit this interesting park and to hike around the general area. It is a unique and fascinating place and is recommended for all ages; if you haven't been there, you have missed an exceptional display of zoological history.

▼

My son, Christopher, and I decided to attend another Outward Bound trip sponsored by the Young President's Organization. This time we chose a Colorado mountaineering course under the aegis of the Pacific Northwest Outward Bound School.

It was a fine program, with ten people enrolled; however, after the class had concluded, we decided that we never again wanted to experience that kind of adventurous challenge. Chris and I came to this conclusion after we had climbed Mt. Elbert, nine miles from Leadville, the highest incorporated city in this country. At 14,433 feet in elevation, Elbert is the highest, little-known peak in the state of Colorado. Although my son and I were both in excellent physical condition at the time, we were unaccustomed to the elevation change we encountered climbing up this craggy mountain. Atlanta, Georgia, where we lived, has an elevation of about one thousand feet, and the highest point in the state is Brasstown Bald in north Georgia; it is only 4,784 feet in elevation and was the limit to what our systems could handle.

We started the climb at 10,500 feet, which was above the tree line, and hiked up for four hours to reach the peak's plateau. As we started our climb, we immediately began to experience some breathing difficulty; we did not have altitude sickness, but because of breathing the thin air as we climbed, we were unable to sustain a normal hiking pace without feeling an abnormal and deleterious impact on our bodies—meaning we could not catch our breath.

Once our instructors saw our difficulty, they advised us to take only a few steps at a time, and then to vigorously expel the dead air trapped in our lungs. After trying that little maneuver, they told us to breathe in more air and continue for a few more paces, and then to stop and repeat the process. That is the way we went up that mountain: one step at a time, huffing and puffing all the way.

Chris handled the altitude much better than his fifty-year-old father, and on several occasions when he saw how much trouble I was having, he suggested that we discontinue the climb. But that was not to be. I told him, under a personal shroud of hidden anxiety, that I had started the hike and would finish it, even if I had to crawl to the top of that damned mountain. And I almost did.

When we finally reached the summit of Mt. Elbert, we were in wonder at the spectacular view; it seemed as if we could see to the ends of the earth! We rested for a period, regained normalcy of our breathing, and then explored around the elongated flat pinnacle of the mountaintop for about an hour before preparing for our descent.

Interestingly, prior to our departure, we found buried in a cairn (a vertical pile of rocks denoting direction of a trail), a small metal container. Opening the cylinder we discovered a pad of paper containing the names of people who had successfully negotiated Mt. Elbert and the dates of their climb. Chris and I added our names to the document and reburied it in the pile of rocks for future climbers to record their accomplishment. Then slowly and cautiously we began picking our way back down the rocky mountain trail. The trip downhill turned out to be a breeze, and we finally had the opportunity and strength to observe the unspoiled beauty of the surrounding mountains. The return hike took our group only about two hours to reach the original trailhead, after having spent well over four hours on the ascent.

As my son and I ambled along, we talked about the hike; I told him I would not make a hike like this again. It had been much too difficult for me. Been there, done that, so to speak. He responded, "Dad, I don't ever want to take a hike like this again." The mountain had won; the climb beat the hell out of both of us.

▼

Usually mountain hikers are advised to acclimatize their bodies to the elevation by hiking only about one thousand feet of elevation gain each day above that which they are accustomed. Using that scenario, since we had come from one-thousand-feet elevation and were increasing by more than 13,500 feet in that climb, we should have had about fourteen days to prepare for the hike; we only had three. During that time we had taken a couple of short hikes to become acclimated, but these were not high enough or long enough to condition our breathing or legs to any great extent. It was just too little too late!

Some people can adjust much more quickly to altitude than others; it depends more on an individual's body and lung capacity than their level of physical conditioning. A few of the much younger folks didn't seem to have much problem, or if they did, it was not at all obvious to me. But then, personally, I was hurting so much from the lack of oxygen, I probably couldn't even have noticed what was happening to the other hikers.

▼

Our group undertook another event before Mt. Elbert that had a harsh effect on me. It was the Pacific Northwest School's rendition of the treetop *ropes* venue. I had participated in a similar event in the North Carolina program and again when we hosted our own in-house course for the managers at the bank. These classes had been conducted by Executive Adventure, but their ropes setting was not situated at an elevation of ten thousand feet; it was more like one thousand to four thousand feet—a huge and crippling difference, to say the least.

This Outward Bound class undertook this tough course in the mountains of Colorado on the second day of the program. These obstacles were similar to those of the other programs; however, they did offer a few variations that made them more difficult to negotiate. For example, one of the obstacles required the participants to grab a type of swing in the treetops and glide across to a platform nestled between two large tree limbs. When I attempted this arduous move, I missed grabbing the cable three times before finally connecting, and found myself totally exhausted and out of breath when I finally did reach the wooden perch in the trees.

The elevation had obviously taken its toll on my body, and I had to rest for thirty minutes before continuing with the remaining obstacles. At that moment I began to realize that the elevation-gain factor would never become my ally while in the high country.

Rock climbing was another event that challenged us, and to some extent held us spellbound as we scrambled around on the vertical, granite rock faces. This activity was conducted on a steep cliff, about two hundred feet high, adjacent to an old, now-vacant, military training camp from the Second World War that had housed the U.S. Army's Tenth Mountain Division. This unit had conducted their winter and mountain training here before their deployment to Italy.

We spent most of the day scaling the cliff with ropes until we had, more or less, gained our confidence and could negotiate the obstacle with some degree of success. Finally, as the day neared its end, our instructors asked us to climb the cliff *blindfolded*. Yes, blindfolded. Only a few people volunteered to try this abnormal method of climbing. Of course, Chris and I had to make an attempt, even though we were frightened and dubious of our success. The guides tied a bandana over our eyes, affixed a climbing harness to our body, and assigned a belay person to handle our safety rope at the base of the cliff. We began climbing the sheer rock face.

It was amazing just using our finger and toe tips to find tiny slots in the rocks' outcroppings on which to grasp and pull ourselves upward. We were astounded by the sensitivity of our touch, and surprised that we could locate hand- and toeholds much easier by feeling our way with our probing fingers than by trying to make an eyeball determination of possible support points. We made it to the top—not once, but twice. It was so exhilarating after we had achieved that initial success, we just had to do it one more time!

This is the kind of stuff and risks that adrenalin junkies and risk takers do. Although in this case, the risk alternative would have only been a banged-up body, not serious injury or even death, still it was enough to get the precious bodily fluids flowing. This was one of the two highlights of the course; the other being the Mt. Elbert climb, although our success on that event was questionable.

After the program concluded, Chris and I departed with the rest of the group on a bus and headed to Denver; however, we had another adventure ahead of us, so we asked to be dropped on the roadside near Empire, Colorado, a town of about a hundred people located west of Denver in the mountains on interstate I-70. We had made plans to join up with some of the other regular explorers from our group—Jim, Mack, and Terry—and spend a few days hiking and camping in Arapaho National Forest and Rocky Mountain National Park. These beautiful areas were within easy driving distance.

After we were deposited near a convenience store, we waited several hours for our buddies, but they did not arrive as we had planned. As daylight turned to dusk, we began to think we would have to spend the night in a nearby wooded draw. Fortunately, there was a small country store situated at this wide spot in the road, so we were able to buy some cold beer and snack food during our wait.

I am certain we did not look particularly respectable as we slumbered on our camping gear by the side of the road consuming a six-pack of beer.

Things must have been tough and males must have been in short supply in Empire because, twice, women stopped their cars and asked us if they could be of assistance or give us a lift to our destination. Maybe we were the only males around the town. Frankly, I must admit they did not look any better than we did in our disheveled condition, so we very politely declined in each instance, and they drove away in utter surprise, much to our relief.

As it was getting dark, the near-improbable happened. Our mates drove up in a small rental van with a big, toothy smile on their faces. They had located the van in Denver after finding that their scheduled four-wheel-drive jeep had been inadvertently given to another group by the car rental company, not totally surprising since it was the Fourth of July weekend. It didn't look like an exploring vehicle and it had minimum power for the trip ahead of us; but, oh hell, it was a vehicle, and Chris and I were glad to get in the car and escape from the group of drive-by onlookers in the tiny town of Empire.

We headed north and finally reached Granby after dark, locating a campground for RVs on Grand Lake. After searching through the park, we found a small remote spot in the trees next to the lake and decided it would have to do, even though tent camping was not allowed. We did not always follow all the regulations when we were in the backcountry areas, especially if we thought they were without merit or superfluous. The next morning, early, we got the hell out of there before we were either severely chastised by a ranger or required to pay a user's fee for using the campground.

We didn't like to pay fees for using any of the wilderness areas, because we believed that they were to be enjoyed by all people without any additional costs to anyone. Our taxes, we reasoned, were supposed to take care of these backcountry places. But politics and bureaucracy being what they are, some things are simply beyond control unless you can find ways around the overbearing prohibitive rules. We seemed to be very good at that tactic. We simply called it *circumventing the crap.* Our next stop would be the Arapaho National Forest. Adjacent to the Rocky Mountain National Park, it was comprised of over 36,000 acres of unspoiled wilderness.

Upon arriving at Arapaho, we checked in with the park ranger, who advised us that the weather in this high country could be erratic and that it could easily snow at the higher elevations in the summer months. As it was early July at that time and we were inexperienced with this part of the country, we naturally questioned his warning.

Hiking up a valley trail for about three miles, we came to a juncture of two gushing mountain streams, both of which culminated in powerful waterfalls prior to joining together, forming a fabulous, thunderous, rapidly flowing creek filled with luscious brown trout.

Next to this creek, adjacent to the trail junction and within sight and sound of the falling water, we found the *perfect campsite,* with all the attributes we believed were important in establishing a good nest in the woods. It was also situated at the juncture of several mountain trails that offered convenience for further exploration into the high country. There was no disagreement, perhaps for the first and only time among our normally disagreeable group, about occupying this campsite for our stay in the Arapaho wilderness.

That afternoon we put our gear in order, built a suitable fire pit, gathered wood, situated our tents, and generally made our bivouac site the perfect of all places to be. Then we tried a bit of fishing in the local creek, and Mack, the best angler in the group, caught a few young, tender trout for our dinner.

▼

Many times when we camped, memories of Vietnam would find their path into my mind. Lingering comparisons seemed to continually evolve from our present-day adventures, coinciding with many of the things we did in that Asian war. For example, when on patrol, finding the best places to locate and establish secure base camps so that we could defend ourselves in the event of an attack was a critical necessity. Poor site judgment could be fatal. Mostly we had tried for high ground, which always gave us, the defenders, the advantage over the enemy, both for visibility and defensibility. If no high ground was available, we tried to hide our position, as was done frequently in the jungle because the terrain was flat and the vegetation was thick; we always tried to inhibit the enemy's knowledge of our location so that we could preclude an unexpected attack, whether by ground forces, mortars, or artillery.

On one notable occasion, my rifle company was required to protect a helicopter, shot down near the DMZ, until it could be retrieved the next morning. It was necessary to establish our position near the chopper in a small circular valley surrounded by towering hills containing several interlocking trails that led north to the DMZ; it was the worst of all places to be. In point of fact, it was an accident looking for a place to happen, and it did. Around midnight several NVA soldiers, traveling on trails that ran through this position, penetrated our perimeter and engaged our forces, resulting in a continuous exchange of gunfire throughout the night.

The situation now almost out of control, we radioed for assistance from a marine artillery battery. We needed flares dropped over our location to ensure we had sufficient light to restrain additional attacks and to help ferret the enemy soldiers inside our lines out of their hiding places. We turned night into light with eight hours of continuous artillery-supplied illumination, and it saved our ass. The next morning I was told by our command headquarters that over six hundred rounds had been used by the battery throughout the night to protect the integrity of our position. The artillery unit had used every round in their arsenal to ensure our safety—a lot of taxpayer money.

On another occasion, we had been in pursuit of an NVA unit that had decimated a marine infantry battalion, having chased them for over twelve hours as they were attempting to withdraw across the DMZ and return to North Vietnam. Finally, near midnight, we reached the highest point in the area, a small mountain with good visibility and excellent defensible high ground. *It was the perfect campsite!* As we were arranging our perimeter defense, I received a radio message from the rear regimental headquarters ordering me to move my company to another position for the night. The senior officer ordered me to relocate immediately under the cover of darkness. Why they wanted us to move remains a mystery to me even to this day.

The suggested location was an open swamp area at the foot of the mountain we currently occupied. I refused, tactfully explaining to my superior that it would be disastrous for us to move onto lower ground at that late hour and we could easily be ambushed. I reiterated to him that we held the high ground; it was the best defensive position in the battle zone. We could see everything for miles. Finally, after a few expletive-deleted words, he rescinded his order and told me to make my own decision; I was the person with the most knowledge of the surrounding terrain and situation. It was easy for me to make the decision. We stayed there–safe!

Obviously, the perfect campsite in combat did not fit the same criteria that we used on our expeditions into the backcountry, but there were enough similarities between the two situations to reignite the lasting memories of some of those old wartime experiences.

▼

That first night in Arapaho National Forest we slept peacefully, listening to the rushing water and roaring percussion of the two waterfalls. Then the next morning after a hearty breakfast of pancakes, with cinnamon of course, bacon, and hot coffee, the four of us—Jim, Terry, Chris, and me—decided to hike five miles up the mountain to Crater Lake, an elevation of 11,500 feet. Mack, after his success from the previous day's fishing, decided to cast his lot and luck in the bubbling, teeming trout-infested creek. We left early in the morning and hiked for several hours, exploring the backcountry as we steadily climbed.

The hike up to the lake was steep; the surrounding terrain and numerous alpine meadows, breathtaking. Crater Lake itself was unbelievably fascinating; glacier-carved, it nestled at the base of a large mountain, where we rested on the shore, ate lunch, and then explored around the edges of the cold, blue-green water. Suddenly, the sun vanished, and we watched some ominously, foreboding dark clouds creep across the mountaintop. The sky darkened as if night, or worse; it was obvious a storm of some enormity was approaching.

Witnessing this climatic change, the warning by the park ranger the day before about the fickle weather and how it could suddenly turn, causing a rapid drop in temperature resulting in a drenching downpour or an accumulation of that frozen white stuff, suddenly took on greater significance in our minds.

We had left camp that morning wearing short-sleeved shirts and shorts, delighting in the warm weather and cloudless sky; none of us had thought to bring rain gear. Not a smart decision, but early in the morning, it had been beautiful, especially at the lower elevations. But now we were at a high elevation, and as they say, *crap happens*. We decided to hastily depart the lake and took off running down the mountain trail as the weather conditions continued to worsen. Within minutes a torrent of rain fell from the sky, catching us about a quarter of a mile from the lake. Yes, the weather could certainly change quickly, we sadly discovered, just as the ranger had predicted and we had pooh-poohed. We tried to protect ourselves from the heavy downpour by huddling under some large cedar trees; the water cascaded through their branches and soaked us thoroughly, and then we began to chill. At that point, we decided to make another run for it, hoping the effort would stir up the circulation, warming us a bit; otherwise, we knew, we would be susceptible to hypothermia. After about an hour, we had either outrun the rain or it was contained at the higher elevation, so we continued our march at a rapid pace, finally reaching our campsite, where the sun was shining brightly. I guess we looked like old horses that had been "rode hard and put up wet."

When Mack saw us, he was surprised and thought we had accidentally fallen into the lake. We explained what had happened with the weather. Naturally, for him, it had been beautiful the entire time he was fishing! The good news, he proudly related, was that he had caught over three dozen brown trout while we'd been gone. He was elated with his catch and spewed forth a bit of braggadocio about his fishing talents. We had to agree with him. He was good!

Naturally, being a very bright attorney (a legend in his mind, just like Terry), he chastised us for our stupidity for taking the hike without the proper gear. Of course, he reminded us that he had made a better decision by staying at the camp and fishing. No matter, though, we gladly ate some of his trout for dinner, and they were delicious. The next day he cooked the remainder and seasoned it so we could enjoy it as hors d'oeuvres with our evening cocktails. As I recall, we ate on his catch for three days, carrying the tasty fish with us everywhere we went. We had hauled some beer in our packs to our perfect campsite; however, it didn't take us long to dispose of it, what with all the fish Mack had caught and our continuing physical activity. On our last night in camp, we decided we needed more liquid refreshment to help us celebrate the wonderful trip and the fantastic experiences in the Arapaho Forest. (Actually, we just wanted a drink, and that was the sum of it.) We had left a case of beer in the van at the parking lot, and someone needed to retrieve it; otherwise, we would go without. That was not a satisfactory solution. This group of hard-core risk takers and adrenalin junkies voted unanimously for my young baby boy, Christopher, who was a student at the University of Georgia and in better condition than the rest of us, to carry out this mission of mercy.

The hike to the trailhead was six miles round-trip; he was encouraged to leave early to ensure that he would be back before dinner so that our frantic, thirsty group could enjoy our cocktail hour. He probably ran most of the way, even with a case of beer on his shoulders on the return trip; he seemed to make the trip in record time, but most importantly, he made it in time for drinks.

The next day we spent the early morning policing up our camp, to leave it in spotless condition; it had truly been the perfect campsite, and we wanted future campers to enjoy it and to give it the same kind of loving care we had during our stay. Unfortunately, there is a sad ending to this particular aspect of our trip.

▼

A couple of years later, while on another trip to Colorado, we passed by the Arapaho Forest with some other fellow explorers and decided to take a small detour to visit our old, but perfect, campsite. We wanted to show our new companions where we had camped and to spend one night there for old-time's sake. Also, we wanted to reminisce a bit and tell a few likely inflated stories to the new guys.

Naturally, we had bragged about the great campsite and the special efforts we had put into improving the grounds and camping conditions. We were proud of our environmental instincts and took great satisfaction in our fieldcraft capabilities.

Hiking up the valley trail, we crossed the wooden bridge at the juncture of the two streams and began searching for the camp; finally we found it, or what was left of it. It was now littered with bottles and cans; the fire pit was in shambles, filled with broken glass and other trash, and many of the trees had been cut down, probably for firewood. The site harbored no resemblance whatsoever to what we remembered about it. We stared around the ground in disbelief.

Why do people do this? They treat the wilderness like some slum area or a public dump, offering no consideration for other campers or for people who want only to enjoy the beauty and serenity of this ever-shrinking outdoor world. If you should ever witness campers mistreating the backcountry, try to guide them in another direction if you are so inclined, or at least remember to do your part in keeping your camping areas beautiful. Make it a point to honor and respect what Mother Nature has given to us to enjoy whenever you spend time in her wonderful playground.

We have never returned to the Arapaho because we wanted to remember it as we first found it, and we still do. Even now after all these years, we still talk about it whenever we are together. This is the stuff that makes lasting memories, and we plan to keep ours alive as long as we possibly can.

The next day we drove across scenic Trail Ridge Road, which traverses Rocky Mountain National Park. This section of the park, one of the highest regions in North America, is truly representative of the grandest in American mountain scenery. More than sixty named peaks of twelve-thousand-feet elevation or higher are situated in this area, with Longs Peak the highest at 14,259 feet. This mountain county is truly *vertical* Colorado at its best. Over the years we made several recreational trips to enjoy the beauty of the area.

Reaching the east entrance of Estes Park, a beautiful mountain city of about ten thousand people, we did more sightseeing, and then headed south toward Boulder, a full-blown sports town and home of the University of Colorado. After a short visit to the downtown section, lunch, and a libation, we headed south on I-25 toward Denver. We had to catch a plane to Atlanta the next day, but before that we wanted to enjoy one more night under the open sky rather than be cooped up in a motel room.

A few miles from mile-high Denver, we found a great spot off the highway in an open sagebrush area located in a remote box canyon. It was called Rabbit Canyon, and there we savored our last night of the expedition with a great dinner; yes, it was cooked in our ubiquitous Dutch oven.

Reaching the Denver airport the next morning, we checked in our loving van with Hertz; it looked as if it had been through a war zone. Actually, all our vehicles did when we finally relinquished them to the car rental agency at the end of each trip. Many times they were so filthy we had to scrub them down before returning them. I suppose we were afraid they wouldn't take them back or we would have to pay an extra cleaning fee. Soon afterward we were Delta-airborne back to civilization. Civilization was home, and civilized were we—until the next trip.

Some months later we came back to Colorado, but this trip was more like a motor tour, because we drove through much of the southern part of the state, taking the better part of a week's time. One of the newer members joined our group for this trip; Steve Georgeson, another Atlanta attorney, accompanied Jim, Mack, and me on this particular expedition. Steve liked our adventures and the stories with which we had often regaled him with on numerous occasions. Arriving in Denver we rented our standard four-wheel-drive vehicle and immediately headed west on I-70 to Georgetown, then south into the mountains toward Guanella Pass, stopping at the base of Mt. Evans, a 14,264-foot mountain, and spent the night under the stars. We took a short hike that afternoon to help with the elevation conditioning, but frankly, it probably served no useful purpose; we just didn't have enough time to acclimate to the conditions. Our climb up Evans the next morning would start at about nine thousand feet, at our campsite. We would meander upland five thousand feet to the crest over several hours of hiking

En route, heavily loaded with water because we knew it was highly unlikely we would find any flowing streams at the high elevation, we found an old rusty iron cooking grate lying on the side of the trail. Stupidly, we picked it up and carried it with us to our campsite, reasoning it would be useful for our cooking needs. Initially, we didn't think it was that heavy to carry—about twenty pounds, we calculated. After toting it up the mountain for some time, we knew it was much heavier than we had guessed; we began to question our judgment about carrying it with us. After struggling along with all the extra weight—the grate, Dutch oven, and extra water—for much of the day, we finally reached an open green meadow just below the top of the mountain. That is where and when we concluded that we had experienced enough pain; we would stop here and make camp. Although it was only about another one-thousand-foot climb to the top of the mountain, we just couldn't continue to haul all our heavy gear and cooking equipment that day. We had had it!

We decided to continue the hike to the crest the next morning with just water and day packs; this was the first sensible decision we had made all day. That night we fixed a great dinner in our Dutch oven with it perched on the infamous iron grill. These two items alone were more than enough weight for any one man to carry on a mountain hike without adding any other gear to his burden.

The next morning we began the second part of the climb without all the heavy stuff, reaching the summit within about two hours. In a small valley crevice, we made a grisly discovery; we found the wing and some scattered parts of a fuselage from an airplane that had apparently crashed some time back. The scene was holding secret its story; we tried to conjecture what had occurred, but unfortunately we were left wondering. Scouting around for quite some time, we took in the scenery, with its variety of rock formations and wonderful distant views. Later in the day, after crawling around on all the rock formations until we were too tired to play anymore, we began our descent, picked up our gear from the previous night's camp, and hiked back down to our first night's campsite, arriving around dinnertime.

Not surprisingly, we left the cooking grill on the mountain. From now on we would cook all of our meals in the ashes of a primitive fire pit constructed from rocks found wherever we camped. Who needs a grill anyway? Certainly not seasoned explorers like us. Fortunately, thank God, we got more seasoned, or maybe I should say smarter with each trip we took; however, it did take some time.

From Mt. Evans we headed south, driving to a small agricultural town called Westcliffe. As we neared the town outskirts, we drove over a small rise in the highway and unexpectedly found ourselves looking at the *Sangre de Cristo* mountain range. These mountains seemed suddenly to have risen up out of the ground, popped up, and come into our view. The mountain range, running for miles, was stunning; there were fourteen 14,000-foot-plus mountains within view of this small community of only 750 people.

We spent one night there in a driving rain, but fortunately secured a small garage apartment from a local real estate agent who had shown us some land during the afternoon and obliged us with a dry place to stay. That night, our juices flowing, we invited ourselves to a local party, and did some western dancing and drinking with the local cowgirls. Early the next morning, before anyone could catch up with us, we left town. Not that we had misbehaved, mind you, but there was more we wanted to see and do rather than just play around. It was just our nature, if you please.

Next, we headed toward Silverton, a restored old cowboy town, where the first silver strike occurred in America, in 1871. Somehow, during our wandering around trying to find the best route to the town, we drove into a small town called Lake City, located on the eastern side of a mountain that we needed to cross to get to our destination. When we stopped for gas in the town and asked for directions, we were informed by some of the local residents that there was a shortcut on an improved dirt road that went on a direct route through and over the mountain, and it would save us several hours of driving time. We were also told that there was a lot of snow in that area, but the snow plows most likely had that road cleared by now, as they had been working on it for some time.

Finding the road out of town was no problem; we drove through the snow-crusted countryside for about an hour. Yes, the local gentry were correct about the snow plows; the road had been cleared and was definitely passable—that is, up to a point. Snow was piled up along the roadside the entire route, but when we came to the highest point of the trip, Engineer Pass, at an elevation of 12,800 feet, we encountered a snowbank in the middle of the road that was at least twelve feet high.

Although the snow plows were hard at work, they had not cleared the final two hundred yards of the road. We were informed from this location it was only three miles to Silverton. The town was in a valley on the other side of the pass, but there was no way to get through the mound of snow. Disgruntled, we turned around and headed back to our original starting point at Lake City. Yes, we had been warned about the snow and had relied on the assumptions of the locals. Being the risk takers we were, we *assumed* we could overcome the possibility—perhaps I should say probability—of any obstacle that we encountered along the way. We thought this way most of the time.

▼

Remember the story about the marine colonel in the Korean War and what he said to a young officer about his recon report on the enemy? After a faulty effort on trying to gain information on the enemy he gave his incomplete report with a number of assumptions. The colonel sent him back and told him, "Never assume anything because it can make an ass of you and me."

▼

This mistake cost us a couple of extra hours' drive time. Taking the circuitous route through Pagosa Springs and then Durango, the home of the great Western fiction writer, Louis L'Amour, we saw that all of the mountainous terrain we passed through was covered with snow. However on this route, we came to a snow-covered mountain that looked interesting, and we decided to hike to the top. We had run into some backcountry skiers who had been hiking up the mountain and skiing down, and they told us it was safe and an easy climb to the crest. Of course, we believed these young people.

Personally, I wanted to climb this mountain because it was called by the same name as my only grandchild, Chris's son, *Richard Taylor*. Also, it just happened to be his fourth birthday on that particular day, and that made it kind of special for me, like I was celebrating or sharing it with him it in some unique way even though we were separated by two thousand miles. It took us over two hours to make the climb, and we ended up walking through some devilish snowbanks, but we finally made it. It had been an exhausting hike, but the views at the top were unforgettable.

It would have been easy for us to have been trapped in some dangerous snow bowls, which our friends, the young skiers, neglected to tell us about (I don't know where they got the idea that it was safe and easy), but somehow luck was with us and we avoided any disaster, other than leaving my glasses on the peak, which we didn't discover until we had tediously worked our way back down the mountain. Jim Box offered to go back with me to retrieve them, but I graciously declined, and told him, "You must be out of your frigging mind to think I would go through that pain again for a pair of damned glasses." We certainly didn't go back for my new $300 spectacles; they were replaceable, but my lungs and knees weren't.

When we finally arrived at Silverton, we just had to drive up the mountain to check out the pass from the town's side to know exactly how close we had come to our destination before running into that snow obstacle in the road. Yes, the people clearing the road were correct; another couple of hundred yards, and we would have been over the top of the mountain free and clear to descend into the town.

It seems that most of our lessons in the wilderness, and perhaps in life also, have been learned the hard way. If we could have only remembered them; however, one point is clear: pain does reinforce memory eventually, particularly after enough pain is experienced.

After leaving Silverton, we drove toward Telluride, located in a bowl with towering mountains around it, and spent the night on a mountain overlooking the town, took another hike the next morning, and then proceeded on through the towns of Ouray and Montrose.

Our final night was spent camping in the Black Canyon of the Gunnison National Park. It had rained most of the day, and when we entered the narrow canyon, we drove along the Gunnison River gorge on a very unstable gravel road, about one hundred feet above the riverbed.

The rain had somehow loosened the soil, and the mushy road seemed to quiver as if it might just slide off into the abyss of the canyon at the slightest provocation. It was a weird sensation, and we were somewhat unnerved by these unusual road conditions; the continuing heavy downpour of unrelenting rain seemed to be slowly sweeping it into the gorge below us. Would we be washed into the canyon also? This question seemed worthy of consideration.

Finally, after several miles of perilous driving, we elected not to continue any farther into the dark canyon; when we came to a wide spot off the road in a clump of trees, we stopped and set up, erecting large tarps to protect us from the rain, and cooked our dinner under this shelter. The four of us then slept under the tarps that night. Staying warm and dry in the rain proved difficult, but we finally arranged our tarps to angle the water away from our sleeping area. After some experimentation and about ten adjustments to place them at the correct pitch, we finally got it right. We did stay dry.

Next morning, we left the area as soon as it was light enough to see. The rain continued to pound down on us, and the road had become treacherous, so we drove slowly and cautiously out of the canyon, overjoyed when the wheels of our vehicle finally touched the concrete highway. We had had our fill of the Black Canyon, and even though we were told it was beautiful, we have never returned.

Despite the setbacks, our weeklong tour of Colorado came to a fruitful conclusion. Yes, we had traveled and toured through a large area of the mountains by vehicle, but we had also taken some interesting and challenging backcountry hikes and gained more of an in-depth knowledge about the countryside.

Over the next few years, we wanted to visit as much of this Western backcountry as we could. We wanted to know what was out there, to experience the grandeur it held for those who were willing to spend the time and make the effort to *just do it.* We would keep on until we couldn't go any longer. Is there any other way? If there was, we were not interested in pursuing it at this stage of our lives.

▼

Our wanderlust drove us in ways that are difficult to describe to the less enthusiastic. Each adventure added to our knowledge base and enticed our passion for even more exposure to this wild and wonderful hinterland of America. These expeditions enabled us to express ourselves openly, to loosen the chains of convention, to make us mentally and physically stronger, and in our work situation, more productive and stress-free. A byproduct of our trips was the cultivation of a youthful mental approach to life. Maintaining this young-at-heart mind-set is important, particularly as we grow older and are required to make lifestyle changes and acquire new friends.

A good friend and fellow workout nut, Doc Ben Garner, who exercised religiously at the downtown Atlanta YMCA until his death in his mid-eighties, put some of these things in the proper perspective when he told me, "Dick, hold what you got; you can never replace it." He was right! So my advice is the same as we tried to follow in our lifestyle and as Doc Garner emphasized in his: never grow old mentally; hold tightly to all of those things that you have worked so hard during your life to build. Most assuredly, your body will age, but keep your attitude youthful; you'll have more fun, and your life will be richer and ever so much more enjoyable. Doc Garner, wherever you are in heaven, I know you agree.

Many of our friends and business acquaintances thought we were crazy to put our bodies through these trials; they couldn't understand our mentality about living a hardy life, particularly later in our lives. Their attitude was of no concern to us, because we were seeking something better and more fulfilling in life. We found it, cherished it, and I believe some people were sorry they didn't possess the vision, energy, and courage to join us in these explorations.

Certainly, we did weird and crazy things. We took risks, went outside the box, we *lived* outside the box—but it was a good run, and we enjoyed every minute, regardless of the difficulties we created or encountered. We were not the kind of people to sit around and do nothing but talk and eat or drink; we tried to fill every moment with some interesting activity. Naturally, being men of great energy, we enjoyed having fun, of all kinds, but there was a deeper feeling within us to pursue something beyond our normal reach, perhaps even our grasp.

A kind of internal restlessness drove us in multiple directions, almost simultaneously. Chasing some poetic dream, expelling the physical energy that constantly erupted from our bodies, wanting to know what was over the rainbow, and trying to fulfill that pulsing need for knowledge that coursed so vigorously through our inquiring minds. We were virile, driven, hardy men, and that is the way we wanted to endure life.

TWELVE

BIG SKY COUNTRY

Did you see the movies *The River Runs Through It* or *The Horse Whisperer*? If you did, then you had to notice the colorful, giant Montana sky varying among shades of azure, turquoise, and peacock blue. Even though the sky is overwhelming, and it is, it was the expansive prairie grasslands of the state that were instrumental in the adoption of the state's nickname, "Big Sky Country." Actually, the name Montana actually is derived from the Spanish word *montana* ("mountain"), referring to the craggy peaks in the western part of the state. Granite Peak, with an elevation of 12,800 feet, is the highest mountain in Montana.

Montana occupies a huge landmass of almost 150,000 square miles and is the fourth-largest state in physical size in the nation, but it has a population of less than one million inhabitants. This part of the country offers stunning views and a wide assortment of interesting locales to visit. A trip to the various mountain ranges and Glacier National Park is certainly an adventure that should be on everyone's agenda. Modern-day nomads should also visit Yellowstone National Park, with its pristine setting and roaming herds of buffalo. Yellowstone touches the southern edge of Montana, although the majority of the park area is found in the adjoining state of Wyoming.

Also, the Little Bighorn Battlefield National Monument is a must-see for everyone, especially history buffs who are interested in the American Indian wars, specifically Custer's Last Stand. A canoe trip though what is now called the Upper Missouri National Wild and Scenic River will provide not only an exciting outing, but also exposure to a large number of historic sites from the Corps of Discovery expedition.

The Lewis and Clark Discovery Expedition of the early 1800s passed though this unknown area on their way to the West Coast by way of the Missouri River. After an unbelievable portage of crafts, supplies, and men around Great Falls, Montana, they crossed into Idaho for their final and perhaps the most difficult leg of their two-and-a-half-year, 2,700-mile round-trip journey. After experiencing the beauty of this state, the great writer John Steinbeck wrote, "I am in love with Montana. For the other states I have admiration, respect, and even affection, but with Montana, it's love." The residents of Montana are making every effort possible with the passage of stringent environmental laws to protect what are some of the last vestiges of the wild American West and what was once called the last frontier of this continent.

▼

Along with personal issues and the desire for a change of lifestyle, these magnificent attributes seduced one of the explorers of our group away from us—temporarily at least, until we also found Montana and tracked him down. After retiring from his legal practice, Troutman, Sanders, Lockerman & Ashmore, Mack Butler left Atlanta on New Year's Day in 1989 on a jeep trip across the country to start a new life. He was not only in search of a new beginning in a new setting; he wanted to return to a lifestyle similar to what he had experienced as a young boy growing up in Camilla, Georgia.

In my mind, and I think in his, he was looking for something that would allow him to express himself in a more rudimentary and practical way of life. He was looking for a simpler way of living, away from all the confusion and annoyances of a large city with multiple and never-ending distractions. In simple terms he believed it was time to do something different with his life rather than face the daily routine of business in which he had performed so well for so many years. Ultimately he chose to acquire land in Bozeman and become a kind of gentleman farmer. He decided to remodel an old farmhouse, just as he had gone about remodeling his own life.

Starting out, he lived in a tiny, old rustic cabin on the outskirts of town, and then later bought a house within the city of Bozeman, before finally locating to his personal "perfect" base camp, his farm and a couple hundred acres of land with unbelievable views of the surrounding mountains. Please note—it also had water. That's important and a major requirement for the perfect campsite, as noted earlier in the last chapter.

It was while he lived in his cabin that our peripatetic group decided we needed to see and experience his new digs and learn more about this part of the country. In late May of that year, Jim, Terry, Chris, and I flew to Bozeman for a weeklong camping and investigative sightseeing trip to visit our old fellow explorer, whom we had not seen for several months. This was the first of at least eight visits we would make to Montana over the next few years. During these journeys one or more of us would visit all of the places I described in the introductory part of this chapter, including canoe trips down the Upper Missouri River.

Years later, whenever Jim and I went west for any reason, we stopped by Bozeman to visit Mack, reminisce about our past lives, and vicariously relive our exploring adventures. After a couple of days of fun, camaraderie, and our inflated stories (they did get better with time and repetition), Jim and I would head out just like we did on our explorations, driving to the next destination.

Perhaps as I previously indicated during these narratives, this is one of the principal reasons our stories get better and bolder with time. I cannot even venture a guess as to the number of times they have been retold under the influence of a slight libation during the hours we have subsequently spent together. Without question this must be the reason we have also now become "mountain men—and legends in our own minds," much like Terry in his mind believed that every female he met was romantically attracted to him.

Although comfortably ensconced in Montana, Mack still participated for a number of years in all of our travels and expeditions. Although two thousand miles distant, he was not to be left out, besides it was easier for him to travel to our western haunts.

Several years ago when Jim, Mack, and I were on one of our less strenuous trips, meaning on a true R&R sojourn, we saw a quote by Robert Louis Stevenson on a sign in the front of a travel/sporting goods store in Sausalito, across the Golden Gate Bridge from San Francisco. It struck me as being the perfect description of our group's mind-set. It read: "I travel not to go anywhere, but to go. I travel for travel's sake. The great affair is to move."

I have always thought this was grand advice for compulsive wanderlust types; my associates and I considered ourselves prime examples of people with *itchy* feet, who had the inherent need to keep moving, exploring, and seeking new challenges.

Mack showed us around Bozeman the day after we arrived. That first night, though, we set up camp in his backyard and cooked our spaghetti dinner over an open fire. Naturally, it had to be spaghetti—what else is there for hungry explorers? Nothing, it seems to me.

His log cabin was quaint and small, with only one bedroom, but it was perfect for his needs. We were happy to be under the stars in the cool Montana weather. When we had left Atlanta, the temperatures had consistently been in the sweltering midnineties, with identical readings in humidity. The nickname *"Hotlanta"* is a truism in many ways; the summers in this southland are always blazing hot.

▼

Interestingly to us, Bozeman was named for a Georgia native, John Bozeman, who brought the first wagon train of pioneers to Gallatin Valley in 1864. His trail became a major byway for future settlers. Previously, the valley had been inhabited by Native Americans, who called it the "Valley of the Flowers." The area is ripe with history, of course, and as you will recall from the fishing scenes in the movie *The River Runs Through It*, the local streams help make it one of the best, if not the best, trout-fishing area in this country.

The next day we rode horses into the mountains behind Mack's cabin and were introduced to a fantastic view of Bozeman and the encompassing Gallatin Valley. That evening we packed up and left for our new Montana adventure. We spent that night in Highlight Canyon, a beautiful setting not far from the city limits of Bozeman.

Intuition is a great attribute to possess if you will only listen to it; at times it can be the best advice you will ever hear, as you'll soon read. We camped along a creek that night, parking our vehicle on a sloped hillside just below a dirt road near our campsite. Later that evening we decided that, in case of inclement weather, it might be wise to move it to higher and more stable ground. We did, and it rained and then snowed as the temperature plummeted to near zero. Welcome to Montana! We had no idea how frequently that could happen in the summer months, but we would soon learn.

Initially it started to rain heavily; then a few hours later, after pelting and beating the rain flys over our tents, no sound was detected on our tents so, obviously, we thought the rain had ceased. You know, it's just no fun to be in the mountains when it is raining like hell. Anyway, the temperature had dropped, and the white stuff quickly replaced the wet stuff. When we climbed out of our tents the next morning, the ground was covered with several inches of snow. It was beautiful! I don't think any of us had ever seen snow in May; certainly not in the South, anyway.

We were sure happy we had moved our vehicle from its original parking spot the night before; otherwise, we would have probably been marooned there for several days. After a hot food/cold weather breakfast, we hiked several miles around the Highlight Reservoir and then drove to the Gallatin River, near Yellowstone Park, which was to be our next area of exploration. Our camp was set up on the banks of the river. After these preliminary arrangements were settled, we hiked up into a broad plateau that led to the top of a mountain overlooking the river valley.

Often on these wanderings, our little group would splinter off in various directions because of diverse interests or individuals' desire for personal space, or for peace and quiet. On this particular hike, three of us chose to push on up the mountain toward the top, while Chris decided to hike off in another direction, who knows where, and Terry was seriously lagging behind for reasons unknown to us at the time. After about an hour of climbing, Jim, Mack, and I heard a scream or loud distress cry somewhere in the distance behind us. Our only response was, "Who and what was that?" and we continued on our trek. Obviously, we must have believed that our seasoned group was much too experienced to have had a problem hiking up a simple incline that was basically open ground, except for a few inconsequential, but very deep, hidden ravines.

Sometime later, after we had returned to our base camp, we discovered that we had miscalculated and made an incorrect assumption about one of our fellow explorers. The distant cry we had heard earlier was actually our dear friend and fellow explorer Terry. During an early part of the hike, we climbed up a steep rise to the ascending trailhead. Terry had made it satisfactorily, and then gradually began to fall behind until he finally made a decision to return to camp. As he tried to find his way back, he stumbled and fell off a small cliff into a bushy, hidden gully. His distress cry occurred during the fall. We could only imagine what sound he emitted when his body crashed into the thick, tangled, bristly bushes below. However, they must have helped to cushion his fall and mask his ultimate scream to some small degree!

When we arrived back at the campsite, Terry was asleep. When he finally woke and stood up, somewhat awkwardly, his body was all bent, scratched, and crooked. He looked like he had been beaten-up by a group of wild-ass hoodlums. Notwithstanding his pain and general condition, he was still in good sprits, as was his normal temperament, but as always, he still had that dumb, effusive smile.

After he told us what had happened to him, he finally admitted to the real problem. It seems the night before we departed Atlanta for Bozeman, he had gotten into an altercation of some kind with his wife, and she had hit him in the chest with a broom handle. I think he told us that she had broken the handle when she smacked him. That had to be quite a whack! It hurt us just hearing about it, but not like it hurt Terry. She must have been really pissed; about what, we did not inquire. The blow had apparently cracked one of his ribs, and he was in pain when he moved about, exerting himself physically. As he was climbing down from the hillock, the pain overtook him and he eased up, losing his grip, and fell into the thicket below. He did tell us that he bounced off of a couple of small trees and bushes while falling, which probably saved him from any serious injury.

Incidentally, after he returned home from the trip, the two lovebirds resolved their differences—to some very slight extent.

Several years ago in Idaho, while hiking with a geology study group, we had traversed some mountainous terrain and were high above a lake when my footing gave way during a rockslide. Before I could regain my balance, I found myself tumbling down a cliff with a steep drop-off about a thousand feet above an alpine lake. I had been carrying a walking stick, but had tucked it in my belt behind my back while we were crossing an exposed area that required the use of both hands for passage. As I tumbled downward toward disaster, the stick stopped my fall when it became trapped between two stationary rocks when I rolled between them. After recovering my senses to some small extent and taking an inventory of my situation, I discovered everything I had worn on the hike was ripped and torn, including my body. At that moment, I probably looked as ragged and disoriented as poor Terry after his plunge off the cliff.

▼

Back in Vietnam I was blown off of a dike in a rice paddy, and I've remembered that incident vividly over the years. As with the aforementioned tumble in Idaho, it also could have been the end of me, and possibly several other marines.

We were on a search-and-destroy mission south of the DMZ, passing through a series of rice paddies and small villages searching for the Viet Cong, who often hid in small tunnels to conceal themselves from detection by US combat units. Several of us were standing on the top of a sizable rice dike about ten feet high, which separated two large paddies, discussing our next troop movement. Suddenly, one of my officers thought he heard a sound of some kind immediately below us.

He began to investigate and found a small obscure opening on the top of the dike. When he began to open it, an explosion occurred just to our immediate flank. The VC hiding inside the mound had thrown a concussion grenade through an air vent on the side of the dike to disrupt the search and to create confusion so he could escape. Fortunately, concussion grenades do not disperse a large amount of shrapnel, but they do create a loud noise and a violent shock wave when they explode.

This shock wave blew me off the dike, and I landed smack on my back in a puddle of water, which did help cushion my fall of about ten feet from the top of the dike. A small piece of the steel shrapnel wounded the officer slightly in his foot. If the grenade had been any other kind of explosive device other than a concussion grenade, several marines, including me, would have ceased to exist at that precise moment. At that close proximity, a fragmentation grenade would have riddled our bodies with tiny bits of steel pellets.

Lying in the puddle, struggling to regain my sensibilities, I looked up and saw this small, lithe brown body in bare feet and short pants hurdle over me and take off running with his rifle and bandoleer of ammo. He was sprinting as fast as he could across the paddy for salvation, water splashing from his feet with every step he took. The small rice field, no more than forty yards wide, was encircled by fifty marines who were all trying to figure out what had happened. They did, very quickly, and all fifty of them began leveling their rifle sights at that moving target. If anyone had fired erratically, someone in the rifle company could have certainly been hit in the cross-fire shooting.

Scrambling to my feet, I screamed, "Don't shoot," and luckily no one did. The VC finally cleared our perimeter, and as he did, I bellowed "shoot him" and a marine on the flank fired one round, hitting him below the knee. We took him prisoner, administered first aid, and sent him to the rear in a Medevac chopper for further treatment and interrogation. Then we continued on our mission. It was all in a day's work over there. I was hopeful we wouldn't have that frightening experience again, and we didn't; they got progressively worse.

▼

Our team liked to be on the move in one form or another, so the next day we drove into Yellowstone National Park and toured the entire park area in both Montana and Wyoming. When we saw a herd of buffalo grazing in a low meadow near the road, we parked the car and walked out into the pasture about twenty-five yards off the road, near the herd, but not too near, to have a group picture taken with the animals for the background. Mack had the camera and offered to take a snapshot. About fifty yards from the nonchalant pack of buffaloes, we assumed our group position, and Mack positioned himself ten yards from us for this photo opportunity.

Suddenly, he looked up, frightened, and began to sprint back toward the road as fast as he could. Upon seeing him execute his maneuver, we broke like wild horses and began stampeding toward the road as fast as we could run. A rather large group of tourists were watching this drama unfold, and when we reached the road, we noticed that the entire group of onlookers was laughing hysterically. Then we glanced out into the pasture and saw that the herd had not moved. They were still peacefully filling themselves on the green grass, just as they'd been doing when we had approached them to have our picture taken.

Butler had duped us, and the tourists saw it all; this was so typical of the ruse that someone in the group always tried to inflict on the others when we were in the wilderness. Incidentally, they always worked. As I have frequently said, "We were hard learners."

A couple of days later, we woke up to a driving downpour and decided to seek refuge until the rains ceased. As previously mentioned, it is no fun to be in the mountains when it is pouring rain. Don't do it unless you have no other option. It is hell to just lie around in your tent all day when the weather is so bad that it prohibits any activity.

It was a wet Sunday morning when we drove into Livingston, near Bozeman, and found a tavern open. We thought this would about do it for us, so we hauled our damp bodies up to the bar and ordered some drinks to improve our sprits and attitudes. A few locals, having drinks when we arrived, immediately befriended us when we sat down, and we began to engage in some affable repartee.

We shot pool most of the day and with our jovial demeanor entertained some of the "buffalo" girls, as some of these very stout woman are frequently called out in the West. Later in the afternoon, when the rain finally stopped, we headed into the Spanish Peaks, which actually overlooked Livingston. We were determined to spend our last night of this adventure in the wilderness. On a slick, wet, almost washed-out dirt road, we drove up the mountain for about an hour. Near the summit we were besieged with another rainstorm and speculated on the possibility of the rain turning into snow. If it did, we knew, we would not be able to get out the next day, or possibly ever.

At this point we decided to give up the ghost and head for lower ground to search for a dry place to spend the night. We decided that a vacant barn would be appropriate for this cold, wet night if we could find one and haul our butts in undetected. Driving for a bit, we searched diligently, but could find no shelter of any kind along the road. Finally, Mack suggested that we nestle down in a barn adjacent to his cabin. So, when we finally arrived, it was getting dark, and we carried our gear up a ladder to the second-floor hayloft and started dinner. The barn was dry and the loft filled with hay; this would provide us with a warm, comfy bed for that night. When we sacked out, the driving rain was playing a musical tune on the tin roof, and it lulled us into a peaceful slumber. Sometime during the night, the rain stopped, and silence prevailed throughout the barn. Up at daylight, we opened the barn's loft doors to check on the weather, and what to our wondering eyes should appear but a foot of thick fluffy snow covering the vast Gallatin Valley! It was a beautiful sight.

During the night the temperature had plummeted, and the rain turned into our seemingly always-present nemesis, the white stuff. The thought struck all of us: *What would have happened if we had stayed in the mountains that night?* At that elevation of around ten thousand feet, snow and freezing temperatures would have rendered our only egress, the muddy road, impassable; we would have been there for days, perhaps forever, or at least, our bones would still be there, probably to this day.

That afternoon our company jet arrived to take us back to Atlanta; we had been recalled because of a pending acquisition of the bank. It was necessary to return early to handle some regulatory issues. The fun and games were over. So, we cleaned up as best we could and left Mack and the Big Sky Country with a foot of snow and temperatures in the mid-twenties.

When we arrived in Atlanta five hours later, it was ninety-five degrees under a bright sunny sky. It was May 31; summer was in full bloom. Had we been dreaming?

Butler never left Montana; he is still there today, but part of his heart may still reside in South Georgia. On a later camping trip, Jim, Mack, and I were sitting around our campfire, a bit overwhelmed with firewater, and he asked us if we would carry him back to his hometown of Camilla to be buried when he expired. We thought that was reasonable and agreed. We told him the trip back would be much the same as what the Captain did with Gus's body in the western TV movie *Lonesome Dove*. We'd drag his carcass across country on horseback in a wooden coffin just like in the movie when Gus's remains were taken from Montana to Texas. Our response to his dumbass request seemed to mollify him, at least for that moment in his inebriated condition.

Future trips to Montana would take some of us into a number of diverse areas of the Big Sky Country, including a couple of canoe trips down the Upper Missouri River in northern Montana. This, of course, is the river Lewis and Clark navigated with their Corps of Discovery expedition across this unexplored land in the 1800s as they searched for a waterway passage from the East to the West Coast. One of the most scenic parts of this section of the river is the White Cliffs between Fort Benton and Judith's Landing, where a river that intersects the Missouri was named by William Clark for his cousin Julia Hancock. These cliffs are still today like they were when the men on the expedition first laid eyes on them.

Lewis's partial description of these cliffs, as expressed in the book *Undaunted Courage* by Stephen Ambrose, is classic. "The hills and river cliffs we passed today exhibit a most romantic appearance; they are two to three hundred feet high, nearly perpendicular, shinning pure white in the sun. The water in the course of time in descending from those hills has trickled down the soft sand cliffs and 'woarn' it into a thousand grotesque figures—as we passed on it seemed as if those scenes of visionary 'inchantment' would never had 'and' end—vast ranges of walls of tolerable workmanship, so perfect indeed that I should have thought that nature had attempted 'herre' to rival the human art of masonry had I not recollected that she had first began her work."

In his book Stephen Ambrose said, "Of all the historic and/or scenic sights we have visited in the world, this is number one. We have made the trip ten times."

Other trips would take us from Bozeman north on scenic Highway 89 to Glacier National Park and on to historic Virginia City, an early gold-mining town where over 190 people were murdered in a six-month period of rampant lawlessness. History has noted that the local miners formed a secret group called the *Vigilantes* to stop the carnage. This peace-seeking group captured or hung over twenty-one criminals, including the outlaws' leader, the sheriff.

Our continuing travels to Montana took us into the Lolo National Forest and into the Big Hole National Battlefield. Several times we followed Lewis and Clark's passage across the Bitterroot Mountains from Montana into Idaho by way of the famous Lemhi Pass, where Lewis became the first American to cross the Continental Divide.

On another occasion Butler and I took two journeymen, wannabe explorers on what was to be a ten-day trip starting in Bozeman, with the termination point to be at my house in Sun Valley, Idaho.

The first day was cold and clear, but as usual, on the second day, it started to rain. We worked our way through Montana, staying the night in Beaverhead National Forest, and then moved on to Idaho, where the rain continued. The third day, we lost one of our explorers when he received a call from his wife telling him that she had been admitted to the hospital for some exploratory analysis. Obviously, he was shaken and decided to leave the trip. Fortunately, she was not deemed to be in a serious condition. We took him to Missoula, Montana, about a two-hour drive, to catch a plane back to Atlanta.

After that emergency side excursion, we drove south back to the trailhead at Lolo Pass to spend the night before exploring Lolo Trail the next day.

This trail was the route the Corps of Discovery traveld across Idaho on their trip and is as pristine today as it was in 1805 when they cossed it on the way to the Pacfic Ocean.

It was still raining, and was now dark when we arrived. We put up our tents and a small tarp on the side of the road for protection from the rain while we fixed dinner in a downpour. Our meal was peanut butter and jelly sandwiches and cans of tuna fish. Not great, but filling and fitting under the current conditions.

While we were dining, our other first-time explorer huddled under the tarp shivering, eating his cold meal, and he asked Mack and me how many times we had camped in bad weather like this. Without much thought I looked at Mack and said, "Wouldn't you think about three hundred times over the years?" He said, "That's probably pretty close." Our response was maybe a bit too thoughtless at the time, considering this was his first trip and it had not been an easy one so far. In retrospect, I think we should have been a wee bit more subtle and not so cavalier with our reply, but we were honest.

Soon afterward we crawled into our tents and got some shut-eye. The next morning it was still raining. Our buddy crawled out of his tent into the continuing downpour and informed us that his ears were hurting from the high elevation. He did have tinnitus, and I am certain he was experiencing some amount of discomfort. He asked us to take him to Missoula so that he could fly back to Atlanta for treatment and to escape the elevation and rainy weather. For the second consecutive day, we made a trip to the airport and then returned to the Lolo trailhead. Yes, it was still raining as we arrived.

We had now lost 50 percent of our group, and since it was still raining, we decided to visit the Lolo Hot Springs, which incidentally was also a stop Lewis and Clark had made for a few days on their expedition. They called it Travelers Rest. We spent most of that afternoon comfortably submerged in the hot springs, discussing our next course of action. I asked Mack if he wanted to continue with our exploration. He asked me pointedly, "How much food do we have?" I responded, "Enough for four people for six days." Without any hesitation he responded, "Let's go." Food, for him, was a critical necessity, and he could eat whatever was put on his plate! We scurried out of the pool, climbed into the jeep, and headed west on a road adjacent to the Lolo Trail, going much deeper into the Idaho wilderness. Luckily, when we left the hot springs it had finally stopped raining, and what followed were six of the most beautiful days in the backcountry that anyone could ever hope to experience. As an old saying runs, I would rather be lucky than good.

Truly we had gone through some difficult weather experiences during our times in the wilderness, but we had always survived and it made the experiences interesting and memorable.

In the woods it is essential to learn how to adapt to unforeseen circumstances and to have several contingency plans. It is important to be creative, imperturbable, and flexible and to maintain a positive attitude and adjust your plans whenever the situation dictates. If you don't you'll be SOL (shit outta luck). As I said earlier, "Have a plan and have a backup plan, because the first one probably won't work anyway."

THIRTEEN

THE NORTH COUNTRY

Most of our explorations took place in the Western states, but we did mange to take two trips to the North Country. The first was into northern Michigan, and the other was a combination trip to Maine and New Hampshire. It seems that whenever we had the opportunity to visit a new region of the country for whatever reason, we always managed to work an outdoor adventure into our travel plans. This was the case when we were in the process of purchasing some new office furniture for First Georgia Bank's operations center.

Jim Box and I had been in conversation with the local Atlanta office of the Steelcase Company, which was based in Grand Rapids, Michigan, and the local manager invited us to the home office to view their product line. Upon accepting their offer, we decided to work in a four-day expedition through the northwestern part of the state, so we selected a couple of locations that seemed interesting to us, that offered a variety of outdoor experiences, and that were close to the Steelcase headquarters. Jim, Mack, and I would make this trip along with my son, Chris, and Jim's twelve-year-old son, Andy.

After visiting the Steelcase operations, viewing their product line, and being treated as royalty, we placed an order and headed out on our excursion. We had scheduled this trip to include a weekend in conjunction with our business activities. We were pretty good at planning trips and could be creative and enterprising under most any circumstances, especially if they involved a wilderness adventure.

On the second day of the journey, we were taken fishing by our Steelcase host on an inlet near Lake Michigan, where we fished for flounder most of the day. It was a great experience for the boys, and they were excited by this particular opportunity. (Frankly, these young men were excited about most anything they did with us on our rambling expeditions.)

Actually, I think their experiences on these varied trips with us helped them to mature. They certainly had plenty of opportunity to observe the good, the bad, and the ugly when they were in our company. Seriously, though, I think most of what they saw and experienced was pretty damned good, and it was also real-life stuff. I'm confident the other people who joined our group felt the same; I was very pleased and proud, as were they, that the boys went with us on our trips, were treated as equals, and obviously enjoyed themselves.

These journeys were excellent learning opportunities for them because the challenges they faced in a variety of situations under the guidance of knowledgeable, passionate professionals gave them some background experience upon which to base decisions about their future lives later on. Naturally, they were encouraged to select from those experiences the facets that agreed with their own views of the world and of themselves.

The following day, we headed north toward Traverse City. Our ultimate destination was Sleeping Bear National Lakeshore on Lake Michigan. While en route, we came across a small, remote historic park that had an old, rustic log cabin, probably 150 years old, situated in the center of the park. We decided to spend the night in the park, and while we were putting up our tents, it started to rain; we quickly determined that we needed a better place to cook dinner and to sleep. Eyeing the cabin, as it was now dusk and no one was around, we thought the porch looked inviting, but the cabin was off-limits except for day-tourist visits according to the posted rules.

We ignored the rules, and the five of us, after dark, relocated from our established soggy campsite no more than two hundred yards away to the porch. We spread out our sleeping bags, cooked dinner, and prepared for an uneventful and well-deserved dry night of peaceful slumber under the tin roof of the large porch. We got it. We guessed correctly that the local park ranger would not be out in the heavy downpour. However, we did leave our original campsite in place, with our tents up housing most of our gear, in the event we were summarily evicted from the cabin porch during that rainy night.

Driving along the next day, we found an interesting canoeing opportunity in a recreational area and decided to rent canoes to navigate a fast-moving stream called the Wild River. It was wild, overgrown, and very, very fast. The current of this narrow, shallow stream, only about three feet deep with a rocky bottom, was flowing between five and six miles per hour. In case you are wondering, typical flat rivers and streams flow from one to two miles an hour, unless they're filled with rapids or cascading down from a mountain range. We would soon discover just how difficult it was to maneuver our crafts in this very fast water immediately upon launching them in this rapidly flowing stream.

Jim, Mack, and Andy set out first, and as soon as they pushed away from the shore, the swift current grabbed their boat and crashed it into some sunken tree limbs before they could even pick up their paddles and master any control whatsoever of their surging canoe. The super-fast water actually penned them against the exposed branches, and they had to struggle to unwind from the tangled mess, gain control, and start up again downstream.

Chris and I followed their folly and fared no better than they had. The high-speed current spun us around a couple of times and then dumped us into the water before we knew what was even happening. By this time in our travels, we were experienced and capable in handling canoes; however, this was a totally new water experience for us. Frankly, we had never seen anything like the velocity of this stream, except in the rapids of the Chattooga River.

Finally, we were able to adequately manage our boats and proceed downstream toward the take-out point. A trip that we thought might take four hours to complete only took about two hours. (Normal canoe speed on flat, slow water will usually produce a distance of two to three miles per hour, unless the canoeists are really pushing.) After our violent boat ride, we decided to go on to Sleeping Bear Dunes, a national lakeshore area approximately thirty-five miles off the northwestern shore of Lake Michigan's Lower Peninsula. This recreational area also includes two offshore islands, called North and South Manitou.

▼

The name Sleeping Bear Dunes is derived from a legend originating from the Ojibway Indian tribe. The myth tells the story of a bear and her two cubs who were forced to swim across Lake Michigan to escape a forest fire. The mother bear reached the shoreline first and awaited the arrival of her two cubs while resting on a large sand dune. The cubs never arrived. According to the legend, the mother bear still maintains her vigil in the form of a dark hill of sand on a plateau overlooking the lake. The two cubs are now known as the North and South Manitou islands.

Dunes on the lakeshore are the product of glacial attacks, over eleven thousand years ago, when rocks, sand, and silt were deposited on the shore. Some of these hills rise almost five hundred feet above the lake. We learned that the largest sand dune in North America was located here at Sleeping Bear.

▼

For two nights we camped on the lake in a slightly defilade area among some bleached and windblown trees that provided protection from the blustery weather. We had planned to take a small boat to one of the islands for a day of exploration, but the winds became so erratic (a normal occurrence) and the water so choppy that small-craft warnings were issued, preempting our boat trip.

Another surprising experience was the water temperature of Lake Michigan and the height of the waves on what is basically a lake surrounded totally by land, although the lake does have one egress at Mackinaw City, its northern tip, where it flows into Lake Huron. We tried to bathe in the water one morning, and except for Mack, who apparently has no nerve endings in his skin like most dogs who are impervious to cold water, we could not even stand barefoot in the water up to our ankles for more than a few seconds at a time. The water temperature had to be in the low forties, at best.

▼

Our other exploration to the north was to the states of New Hampshire and Maine, and it almost undid our team of explorers in a couple of ways. Matter of fact, two of our party behaved so badly we put them in the penalty box and kept them from going on the next trip. At least, that was our story, and they believed it.

The guilty were no other than Jim and Terry. From the time I had started planning the trips, these two paid little or no attention to the destination nor involved themselves in any of the details. They only wanted to go and have a good time doing whatever it was that we were going to do, but Mack and I took things a little more seriously. What would you expect from a lawyer and a banker?

Soon after arriving at the airport, we learned that the weather in Boston was terrible. It was raining, of course—nothing new for us—so our flight was delayed for several hours. This interruption meant that we would now arrive sometime after midnight. Although it was not an auspicious beginning, it was perfectly typical for our travels.

Over the years I have often thought that the most complex part of our journeys was twofold: first, the logistics of just getting to our destination, and secondly, disentangling ourselves from whatever happened to capture our attention so that we could get back home on schedule. This would be the case for this particular journey.

During the extended delay, Mack and I spread out our maps on the floor in the waiting area and began to develop a contingency plan based on our projected late arrival. We did not think we could get to our first night's planned campsite; as a result, we might have to alter all of our plans on the trip. Jim and Terry, on the other hand, were oblivious to the entire situation; they had become busily engaged in some friendly repartee with two young ladies who were on their way to Florida. When our flight was finally announced for Boston, they suggested that we should go to Florida and enjoy the warm weather for the week. When they were reminded we were going to Boston, and then on to New Hampshire and Maine, they acted surprised; they really were! (You can probably now understand how our trips could sometimes become confusing and a real test of mental fortitude for some of the more serious explorers.)

We caught the plane north, not south as they had recommended; they obviously wanted to explore something else besides the wilderness. I will say they would have most likely been in a different kind of wilderness, a kind that they would not have been able to handle, if they had accompanied these two young, energetic women who, incidentally, looked as if they could handle almost anything very adroitly, including two funky wilderness explorers. Arriving in Boston after midnight, we decided to rent a vehicle and drive through the night to our original destination, a campground in New Hampshire. Some four hours later, after driving through the rainy night, we arrived at our location in the White Mountains, Franconia Notch State Park; it was still raining, so we quickly put up one tent for the four of us to share for some much-needed sleep.

Franconia Notch is considered to be the most celebrated mountain gap in the northeast. It is heavily visited by tourists because of its popular recreational activities and scenic viewing. The noted poet Robert Frost purchased a home here in 1915 after returning to the United States from England.

After a couple hours of sleep, the rainwater penetrated our tent. In a rush to get some sack time after our exhausting trip, we had neglected to put the rain fly over our shelter, so after a couple of hours, we awoke nearly submerged in a pool of water that had flowed in from the leaking tent top and accumulated around our sleeping bags. We had no recourse but to get up, gather our gear, and locate a self-service laundry to dry our clothes and bags, after which we drove across the scenic Kancamagus Highway to Conway. This was to be a touring and recovery day for us; our only mission for the day was to rent canoes and to spend the next two days canoeing the Saco River. We located the outfitter in Conway, and the next morning, after a needed restful night, headed east on the river toward Maine. The beautiful and winding Saco originates from and flows out of Ossipee Lake in New Hampshire and into Maine, and continues east across the state of Maine until it dumps into the Atlantic Ocean.

The one problem with the trip that we were warned about prior to departing in our canoes was the black flies and mosquitoes we would encounter swarming on the riverbanks. *Encounter* was not the correct word; *kamikaze* attacks would have been much more accurate. In all of our backcountry trips, we had never experienced such aggressive insects in our lives; bug repellent was like dessert to those critters, with our flesh the main course. We would stand in the middle of our fire pit with the black smoke curling around and over our bodies to escape their attack, but they would actually dive-bomb into the smoke and bite us. It was unbelievable! We used every drop of three bottles of bug repellent during that two-day trip. When we were in our canoes on the river, the bugs did not come after us, but as soon as we stopped and climbed up on the riverbank, they hungrily attacked us.

The Saco is a beautiful, slow-moving, pristine river with a large number of small tributaries and lakes that connect with the main channel. We explored most of these during our travels, passing several old, rotting, unoccupied dwellings nestled along the bank. It was difficult to understand how anybody could have lived in what had to be an unpleasant, remote, almost junglelike, bug-infested environment. Ultimately, we reached the take-out point of our trip, Hiram, Maine, where our outfitter picked us up and took us back to Conway for our next adventure, which was to be a two-day hike into the Presidential Range of the White Mountains. Mack had some friends from Boston who joined us in Conway. They were familiar with the mountain range and were going to accompany us on the hike and guide our group to the best locations.

It was at this point, as we were packing our gear for the hike, that a mutiny occurred within our team of hardy explorers. Frankly, the mutineers were no longer interested in hiking. Their petite minds had been diverted by a conversation occurring earlier that day when some locals told them that they should visit Tuckerman's Ravine. Apparently on some weekends, a large group of athletic women often visited this remote area in the mountains and frequently hiked or skied for most of the two days. That was it. Jim's and Terry's minds had been captured and were now held hostage by some unexplainable fantasy.

As we were completing our preparations for the mountain climb, they informed us they were tired and needed a few days to recover from the canoe expedition. We had two cars—Mack's friends had brought theirs—and so we began to divvy up the food so our buddies wouldn't starve after they left us. (Not that we really gave a damn)

Personally, I didn't like the idea of splitting up the team, but they were determined to exploit whatever new opportunity they might find at the ravine. Actually, we were pissed at them, and in my anger, as I was backing up our vehicle to unload the food, I backed into the front end of Mack's friend's parked car.

Terry, always quick with a spurious comment, especially if it helped his cause, said to Jim, "Look sad, look sad." This was supposed to placate my anger. Terry could be a real wimp and kiss-ass at times, but he was always funny. Shortly afterward they were underway, with three cases of beer they had purchased to sustain them through their imaginative ordeal. We four remaining members left in the other car for the trailhead to start our climb up to the 5,715-foot Mt. Jefferson. The starting elevation was one thousand feet.

▼

The White Mountains of New Hampshire are the highest in the Northeast. Within these mountains, the Presidential Range contains the highest peaks. Mt. Washington, the loftiest peak, rises to 6,288 feet, while Mounts Adams, Jefferson, Monroe, and Madison each exceed five thousand feet in elevation.

Mount Washington offers unusual weather conditions year- round. The average annual temperature is below freezing, and the highest wind velocity ever recorded on the summit occurred in 1934 and was noted at 231 mph; conditions there can change in minutes from balmy to subfreezing weather. Ominous weather-warning signs are posted for hikers along the trails leading to all the mountains within the Presidential Range. This signage received our undivided attention, but the weather, for a change, served our needs perfectly.

This hike up to Mount Jefferson was the most difficult that I had ever undertaken because of a physical problem. By the time we reached the summit, my right leg had become so painful and stiff that I had a difficult time walking. It had actually tightened up to a point that I could no longer bend it, and I was almost dragging it when we finally stopped at the end of the day. Mack said my pack load was too heavy, but actually the fascia enclosing the tendons and muscles had tightened so much that I no longer had any flexibility around the joint. The cause was more from overuse than anything else. My knee was somewhat tender when we left home; this condition was caused by the extensive jogging that I had been doing for quite some time.

That hike was the *coup de grâce* for my injury, and as a result, many of my physical activities, such as long-distance walking and running, were curtailed for nearly two years. I had to undergo extensive physical therapy, which included weekly sessions of painful, deep massage, which left me totally exhausted after each session; this therapy included extensive stretching and was continued until my muscles and tendons became pliable once again, allowing me to return to my normal physical lifestyle. I experienced the same condition with my other leg a few years later (for the same reason).

There is a message here for every active person. If you want to stay active, don't be compulsive and obsessive with your exercise program; overuse will eventually lead to a physical disability of some kind. I learned this the hard way. I hope you don't.

After hiking up to Mt. Jefferson, we came upon a small vacant hiker's cabin perched on a high ridge with a fabulous view and decided to spend our two-night stay at this inviting spot. My three friends hiked up to the summit of Mount Madison the next day, but I was unable to accompany them due to my aching, stiff leg. I spent most of that time massaging my knee, but to no avail. The following morning we hiked down and returned to Conway to meet our errant friends. The trek down was almost more than I could take, but perseverance, aspirins, and frequent rest periods enabled me to complete the descent. Jim and Terry met us looking like death warmed over. It was from the booze, not from any mischievousness. They admitted they had struck out and had no stories to report. We were not surprised; if you knew them, neither would you be. They were officially declared traitors. With all my leg pain, I was sorry I didn't go with them; the next two years would have been more enjoyable.

FOURTEEN

THE GRAND CANYON STATE

Because of their treacherous, traitorous, women chasing ways, the turncoats, Jim and Terry, did not make the next trip, but Mack Butler, Chris, and I did. It was a short expedition over a long weekend, planned around a corporate business meeting that I attended in Phoenix, Arizona. As I have said previously, we would grasp every opportunity to engage in some kind of exploration whenever possible.

Christopher and Mack flew in to join up with me after the meeting concluded, and we immediately set out for the Grand Canyon via a number of planned explorations along the way.

Our circuitous route would take us through the lush gorges of Oak Creek Canyon to Sedona and then to the breathtaking Grand Canyon. On our return trip, we would include the Kaibab, Coconino, and Prescott National Forests, where we would encounter some interesting camping experiences, before returning to Phoenix. We undertook this particular trip during January, when the weather can be a bit dicey, and of course, we would learn this the hard way, as usual. We had not visited Arizona on any of our previous journeys to the West and were stunned at the amazing red rock conformations that we saw around the Sedona countryside.

Sedona's colorful rock landscape offers a multitude of colors, landforms, shapes, and configurations. The various monoliths' shifting hues and colors range from bright red to pale sand, and these colors change continuously as the sky casts its rays and clouds across the vast landscape. The sandstone buttes, rock caps, and other significant formations have been appropriately named to match their distinctive profiles; some of the better known are Cathedral Rock, Coffeepot Rock, Snoopy Rock, and Courthouse Butte. These wonderful rock formations in Sedona and nearby Oak Creek Canyon have been the site of a number of Western movies, including several of John Wayne's classic films such as *She Wore a Yellow Ribbon* and *The Searchers*.

When we first visited the area, we'd found it somewhat sparsely developed, but when I returned twenty years later, I could not believe how much urban sprawl had changed it—except for the prominent landforms on the outskirts of Sedona, I would not have thought it was the same place that we had visited many years ago on our expedition. Although it is sad to see natural beauty like this blemished with stores, signs, and highways, this seems to be the norm for many areas of our burgeoning country.

For the locals, however, much of this scenery must still be wonderful to view on a regular basis. Let us hope they appreciate what they have and understand what this king of progress has cost others, who still seek the solitude and wonderment provided by Mother Nature.

For the Spiritualists, Sedona is also thought to provide a home for several energy fields that emanate from this natural splendor. These fields, referred to as a vortex, are thought to emit energy upward from the earth's surface. Supposedly, there are three energy types found in a vortex: magnetic (feminine), electrical (masculine), and electromagnetic, which is considered neutral. These natural power fields, reputedly found at several locations around Sedona, are thought to provide inspiration and energy to help promote life-changing experiences for persons who believe in these phenomena.

Interestingly, a few years ago, I was hiking on a ridge that looked directly across a small depression at Cathedral Rock, where a vortex is supposedly located, and on the ground found a symbol made of small stones arranged in a three-foot circle. At first it startled me—I thought it was a sign of devil worship—but later, after learning about the vortex phenomenon and symbols, I determined that a group of practitioners had apparently marked and used this location as a place to encounter the spiritual and mental effects of these energy sources.

▼

After traveling and touring most of that first day, we found a superb, remote campsite in a thicket of woods several miles off the main highway. Because it was fenced in, we knew it was private property, but that has never stopped us in the past, so we pulled our vehicle into the wooded area and hid it from the road. Our concern was minimal because we always left our camping areas in better condition than we found them, and we hoped the owner would not be aggravated by our good intentions—and the use of his land. We made one of our favorite meals, Picole Pie, and then sacked out in our tents with the cold evening breeze dancing on our tent flaps.

The next morning after breakfast, we cleaned the campsite, leaving it in spotless condition, and then finished our drive through picturesque Oak Creek Canyon, where numerous Western flicks have also been filmed in the past; then we drove on toward Flagstaff, and from there we drove northwest to the Grand Canyon. The drive to the canyon was about 150 miles. Entering the national park in the vicinity of Grand Canyon Village, we immediately drove to the South Rim's edge and peered into the vast abyss of the gorge. The view was absolutely overwhelming.

▼

The Grand Canyon is considered to be one of the world's outstanding spectacles. Almost 280 miles long, it averages ten miles in width across the chasm from the South Rim to the North Rim. The canyon bottom, almost six thousand feet below the North Rim, is, on average, about five thousand feet below the South Rim. The various strata of rock formations indicate geological periods of the earth's history from 2 billion to 250 million years ago. The first sight of the canyon was recorded in 1540 by a member of Coronado's expedition, guided there by Native Americans. In 1868 John Wesley Powell led the first expedition to fully explore the length of the canyon in what was to be his final western discovery journey.

Although there are a number of hiking trails that lead into the canyon, we did not have the time, unfortunately, to undertake a lengthy and physically challenging round-trip jaunt to the Colorado River at the bottom of the gorge and retrace our steps the same day.

▼

We spent most of that day touring along the thirty-five-mile road paralleling the South Rim, which afforded us with incomparable views of the entire canyon area. Us Southern boys had never seen anything like this! We could have spent days exploring every aspect of the canyon area; it is so devastatingly colorful and dramatic, it will almost take your breath away. It did ours.

We finally forced ourselves to leave and head to the next destination. We were on a mission, as usual, and we had miles to go before we slept. Driving due south from the canyon, we crossed Highway I-40 and found a scrubby dirt road leading into the backcountry outside the town of Williams.

It was getting dark when we decided on the *not*-so-perfect campsite in the middle of a field, with no water, though it did have one large oak tree with spreading, dangling limbs conveniently located for our cover and an open view looking out across a flat plain of cornstalks. Settling in we pitched our tents, had a relaxing beverage, cooked dinner, talked about our visit to the canyon, and shortly afterward crawled into our tents under a cloud-laden sky, with the moon shining brightly in the background where it pierced the mottled clouds. Peaceful tranquility was ours for the taking, and we soon drifted off to sleep.

About midnight the circumstances changed dramatically when we were awakened by the most *bloodcurdling* noise imaginable; it reverberated through our campsite and across the surrounding open fields. It sounded like some kind of animals howling; they seemed to be no more than two hundred yards from our camp. The racket continued for some time, and then, after we had flashed the headlights of our vehicle in the direction of the screaming, it stopped almost as abruptly as it had started. Although the three of us had spent a lot of time in the backwoods over the years, we still could not positively identify what we heard on that particular night. Coyotes typically howl just before daylight, and dogs, well, I suppose howl whenever they want, but we never heard anything like that before or since.

When the commotion stopped, we were uncertain if the animals had smelled our food, or us for that matter, and were silently stalking our camp with the intent of snatching a midnight snack. Concerned, we considered climbing up into the large, sprawling oak tree for a spell or into our vehicle until we could figure out the situation. Finally, cooler heads prevailed; we built a fire that would last through the night, and after conquering our apprehension, we retired once again to our tents. Although the rest of the night was quiet, we dozed fitfully. This may have been a prelude of things to come, because the following day we had another unusual experience in a town that had a strange reputation for unusual activities.

The next morning we searched the area from which we thought the howling had originated, but could find no evidence of any animals, tracks, or anything else for that matter. Whatever it was that made those terrifying sounds the previous night was long gone. Or as Edgar Poe almost wrote in his poem, The Raven, "Twas the wind and nothing more."

We left the area then and drove for a couple of hours until we found another dirt road that would take us on a long shortcut across a mountain to our next destination, the town of Jerome.

We had read about this small settlement in some travel literature we had procured prior to starting the trip, and this place had captured our fancy. The document included a small mention about witchcraft being practiced in this isolated town of about four thousand people in the mountains of the Prescott National Forest; it was not far from the town of Prescott. It sounded interesting, so we decided to visit Jerome and make our own evaluation.

The one-lane, dirt, mountain road was barely wide enough for a single vehicle, so that when we met another truck on the road, we had to pull off onto a steep hillside in order for both vehicles to barely scrape by each other. The trip took nearly three hours, driving very slowly and cautiously. The road itself was not in horrible condition, though there were numerous bumps and rivulets to negotiate. When we finally dropped down off the mountain, drove into town, and parked our SUV, we noticed that one of the back tires had suddenly gone flat. It was an inauspicious arrival for us that immediately raised questions in our minds about the town. If we were going to have a flat, why didn't it occur on the mountain? Why here? We fixed the tire in our parking space in the middle of the town and then visited a western jewelry store adjacent to our parking spot.

The whole stopover was fascinating. People seemed to watch us wherever we went; although we thought it might be our imagination, we were nonetheless uneasy about their continuous staring as we patrolled through the town. Chris made an interesting observation about their facial features; he said they had an unusual look or uncharacteristic eyes, and he didn't think they appeared normal-looking. Maybe he had read too much about the town and its reputation, or perhaps he had read too much into the article. He was young and impressionable, but extremely observant.

Most probably our heads were playing mind games with us because of what we had read about Jerome. I make no assertions as to the validity of that information; however, we did feel uneasy and decided to leave after having lunch. Maybe those people had never seen anyone enter their town from the horrible mountainous dirt road. They may have thought it was peculiar or perhaps crazy for anyone to travel into town on that narrow, treacherous road when other risk-free thoroughfares were available. Our route probably was atypical. Maybe *we* were the ones who seemed unusual. We will never know the truth about the town, but it was an interesting visit.

With one more night to spend in the wilderness, we had planned to hike an eight-mile canyon trail near the town of Prescott, the first seat of government in Arizona. Abraham Lincoln established the town in 1864 during the Civil War, because goldfields were near and the Union was cash poor at this time. Obviously, he had hoped the North would reap the financial benefits from this political move.

But the day passed us by, and it grew late; we had to find a campsite for the night, so we decided to bypass the hike. Another dirt road took us into Castle Creek Wilderness, about seventy-five miles north of Phoenix, where we four-wheeled deep into the woods and found a small depression nestled along a thundering creek. We established a campsite there, put up tents, and cooked dinner while thick, dark clouds shifted across the sky toward us and the temperature began to drop. As we crawled into our tents, it began to snow. This was not good because we were camping in a low area with a steep incline leading up the hill to our only egress (escape route).

We had driven cross-country to get to our site. Now, with snow beginning to cover our tracks, we knew that if we stayed there and snow continued to fall, we probably could not gain sufficient tire traction to make it back to the dirt road. It was dark and late, but it was also time to go. We convened, discussed the situation, and made a decision to get the hell out of there as quickly as we could. We decided to drive toward Phoenix and find another campsite in a more propitious location. Although this was a good plan, it was just not workable; locating and establishing a proper camping area in the darkness with no knowledge of the terrain is virtually impossible.

Hastily gathering our gear, we threw it in a big bundle in the back of our jeep and slowly crawled up the hill, our wheels spinning most of the way. The snow kept peppering us until we had driven south for several miles, and then it stopped. It was so cloudy and dark, we could not see the area around us even though we left the main road on several occasions, disembarked from the vehicle, and walked around in the darkness. We found nothing but holes, rocks, and thick bushes, so we finally gave up and decided to drive the seventy-five miles to Phoenix and get a motel room near the airport. Our scheduled flight to Atlanta was at noon that morning.

In many ways our trip had been less than perfect, but as usual, we made the most of it under challenging and even strange circumstances. We had visited some new and interesting places in the backcountry of Arizona; our four-day trip had also included an unannounced visit by some wild animals near our camp one night, followed by a peculiar pause in Jerome, and finally concluded with our laborious getaway in the snow and late-night three-hour drive to Phoenix while looking for a midnight campsite. Oh yes, let's not forget, we had also visited the breathtaking Grand Canyon for a day.

Perhaps fate had precipitated all of these odd events because we had stayed on private property that first night; maybe fate was also telling us not to do that again. Or maybe the people of Jerome had cast a spell on us; perhaps it was the influence of the vortex (energy fields in Sedona) that brought on our bizarre experiences. Who knows? For certain, though, it was a highly unusual trip, and we would most definitely remember every part of it. Interestingly, we never went exploring in Arizona again after that trip. Perhaps we thought we might become *bewitched.* You never know!

▼

Over our twenty-five years of exploration, we had made a large number of short trips, like this one to Arizona, by taking advantage of various business obligations or lengthy holidays. In every case we always enjoyed the experience and made the most of it regardless of its difficultly, strenuous conditions, or unexpected nasty weather. Some of those trips were too numerous and too short to include here, but most were highly adventuresome and always genuinely unique.

For example, one summer Chris and I enrolled in a four-day YPO-sponsored father and son horseback and backpacking trip in the Canyonlands of Southern Utah. Conducted by Outward Bound, this was my sixth and final OB experience and my son's third. We were picked up at Green River, Utah, and taken to a ranch near the town of Hanksville, located smack-dab in the middle of the desert.

The principal instructor, whose name I can no longer recall, had been an All-American rodeo rider at the University of Utah. His photo and accompanying comments about his accomplishments had appeared on the cover of numerous magazines. At the time of the course, he was now principally a rancher, who periodically handled these outdoor riding programs for Outward Bound. After giving us some detailed instruction on horsemanship, he assigned us our mounts, and our group of ten headed south from his ranch, just outside of Hanksville, to connect with the famous (or infamous) Outlaw Trail. You may remember that Butch Cassidy, the Sundance Kid, and the rest of the Wild Bunch used this trail to escape from the law after they had perpetrated train or bank robberies in this part of the western frontier. The trail runs close to the town of Hanksville and then southeast to Robbers' Roost, one of the outlaws' hideouts, and then on into northwestern Colorado. Their main hideout, and the one best-known in history, was the famous Hole-in-the-Wall.

This is a hard, desolate country; the landscape is barren and unforgiving, with little or no available water sources. A maze of canyons stretches for miles; the entire area is peppered with caves. The outlaws could easily disappear in the vast array of canyons and avoid their pursuers, which they did on numerous occasions.

We rode our horses into these canyons and located several known places where Butch and his gang hid out during their heyday. At night we placed our bedrolls on the open canyon edges, which offered an unbelievable view of the surrounding canyons, as well as the dancing, shooting stars streaking across the expansive sky.

Perhaps the most frightening part of our trip, at least for me, was riding the horses down into the bottom of the canyons. How those animals could maintain their footing on the rocky, narrow trail was amazing, but they were as sure-footed as mountain goats and easily able to negotiate the slip-rock paths without much problem. The entire time in the saddle descending into those canyons, I would only put the toe of my boot in the stirrup; I wanted to be ready to disengage from the saddle and the horse if his footing gave way and he lost it and fell. I don't know where I would have gone had I leaped off—probably over the side and rolled over the rocks until I hit bottom—but at least I would not have had a 1,200-pound horse tumbling on or over me. The horsemanship training by our instructor had been all-encompassing; after we had completed this program, I felt quite comfortable and knowledgeable where horses were concerned.

The canyon and desert terrain was awesome. Outward Bound had again provided an experience and memories that would remain with both Chris and me forever.

The Southwest and the desert provided interesting and educational experiences; the history of the country was intriguing. Consequently, we decided that we should next explore New Mexico, Arizona's eastern neighbor state, visiting both the desert areas and the mountains. It would be another whirlwind trip, but they all were.

Actually, the more things change the more they remain the same. What else could explorers expect to happen when they did their thing in the wilderness.

FIFTEEN

NATIVE AMERICA

Native Americans have been living in New Mexico for some twenty thousand years. They were originally immigrants who probably came from Siberia to Alaska by walking on a land bridge that crossed over the Bering Strait. During the Ice Age, the waters had receded, permitting foot travel over this temporary crossing. They came in pursuit of food—deer, elephant, and any other beasts that could provide sustenance for their survival.

After crossing into the North American continent, they migrated southward, passing through the melting ice toward the warmth of the Southwest. Ultimately the ice sheets covering much of this land melted, and the sea rose back to its original level, covering the land bridge with water and cutting off these migrants from the rest of humanity.

The culture of Native Americans is rich with stories and legends dating back from their misty origins. These tales and their way of life in ancient history are supported by numerous artifacts, petroglyphs (rock or cave art), and ancient dwellings throughout the Southwest. During our travels in the northern part of New Mexico, we would be able to explore some of this Indian culture as well as to observe their lifestyle.

We visited a few pueblos (a group of people, a community, a town, or an architectural style) during this journey. On our wilderness hikes in the remote canyon areas, we also passed through several isolated villages, where we observed some of the ancient rock art. In New Mexico today, the Navajo nation, this country's largest Native American group, administers a reservation that covers more than 14 million acres.

Although New Mexico, with a landmass of 122,000 miles, ranks sixth in size in the United States, its population is only 1,800,000 people. Interestingly, New Mexico has more sheep than people! There are only twelve people per square mile, and more than 25 percent of the state is forested. The 3.3-million-acre Gila National Forest in the southwestern part of the state is the largest forest in the United States. The tallest mountain in the state, located in the Taos ski area, is Wheeler Peak, with an elevation of 13,161 feet. Much of the northwestern part of New Mexico is low, flat, scrub-like, arid land. Except for information on the region and the Indian reservations we saw, the area offered little to us as far as camping and hiking were concerned. We were definitely more interested in the backcountry mountain terrain. I guess we were just not good flatlanders.

▼

After leaving Albuquerque, where we had arrived from Atlanta, we headed into this barren, arid section of the state, spending almost the entire day touring the countryside. Then we drove northwest into Bloomfield, which was settled in 1876 and quickly became a classic Wild West town, complete with a gang of rustlers headed by the ex-sheriff. The town was about seventy miles from the Four Corners, where the state boundaries of Arizona, Colorado, New Mexico, and Utah join together. This is the only location in the United States where four states meet at a single place. Theoretically, a person visiting this location, can put their two arms and two feet in four different states at the same time, more or less.

About eight miles north of Bloomfield is the Aztec Ruins National Monument, built around 1100 AD. They are the largest and best-preserved ancestral Pueblo ruins found in the Southwest; the largest building in these historical remains contains over four hundred rooms.

Unable to find an appropriate campsite in this hot, harsh country, we continued touring and drove into Carson National Forest and on across the Rio Grande River in search of cooler temperatures and, ultimately, the mountains. The Rio Grande, the longest river in New Mexico, actually flows across the entire state. The bridge across the river offers spectacular views of the surrounding area and of the deep, colorful river canyon. On a later trip, I rafted in this river.

This first day was tiring and disappointing in some ways. We had driven for almost nine hours touring the various towns and countryside and were a bit disheartened that we could not find a good location to call home for the night. I had planned this trip several weeks in advance; remember, I had taken over this responsibility for our group some time back so that it would give me some amount of control, which I believed was necessary, but I failed miserably on mapping this first day's route, and it didn't go unnoticed by my fellow explorers.

After that first long day in the vehicle, and had finally found a satisfactory campsite, Jim Box told me that if he had been given permission to look at the map before departing on our marathon ride, he could have determined by the blanched shading and elevation contours that our intended route would not take us through scenic country. Naturally, I acted as if I was offended; after all, it was my plan. So, what was the big deal about my miscalculation? We had seen a lot of New Mexico in a single day, and that had to offer some merit to our exploration. Surely, it wasn't all that bad; yes, it really was, because we were all totally exhausted from the driving, but I would never admit it—that was not part of my character makeup.

Of course, I told him that his comment sounded like sour grapes and second-guessing; nonetheless, I kept the map under wraps and my control. "Let him bitch"—after all, no one is perfect, especially him, of which I continually reminded him on numerous occasions when he attempted to offer inane suggestions about our travels.

▼

As mentioned earlier we always wanted the perfect campsite. Perhaps we were spoiled, but each and every trip we took was special to us; we wanted to maximize every day and night, and every hour if at all possible. We wanted instant gratification in everything we did and every place we visited in the backcountry. We didn't think that was too much to ask, considering the time constraints and circumstances surrounding our expeditions. Each journey we took seemed to end too soon; perhaps that is the reason we took so many over the years. We fervently believed and wanted to make the most of our limited time on these expeditions.

Sir Winston Churchill, the prime minister of Great Britain, while making a speech at one point in his fabulous career was asked by a lady in the audience about his frequent drinking habits, adding that she thought he had consumed enough alcohol to fill the room they were in halfway to the ceiling. Noticing the distance existing between the ceiling and wall, sadly shaking his head, Sir Winston responded, "So much to do, and so little time in which to do it." This is exactly how we felt about our trips.

Concerning these adventures our group was definitely compulsive and obsessive; maybe you could call us *monomaniacs with a mission*. These explorations provided nourishment to our souls and added balance to our lives. We needed to experience them regularly, in order to survive the stresses that were cast upon us and to help force out any of the haunting ghosts of our past. The wilderness experience was the salve for our souls. Simply stated, most of us craved being in the wilderness, taking the hikes, the camping, enjoying the morning coffee, and the sheer beauty that engulfed us; all of it nourished us mentally, spiritually, and physically. Every night was special, almost like one of splendor and contentment. Our explorer team wanted to experience the best that nature had to offer. Yes, we were spoiled, but we would go the extra mile, if necessary, and we often did—just like we did on this particular journey—to satisfy our unrelenting hunger for perfection in those backcountry things that were so important and necessary to us.

▼

Late in the day, we located a campsite near the small mountain community of Valdez. Factually, there are five wilderness areas in this region, all of which are surrounded by the remarkable Sangre de Cristo and San Juan mountains.

The next morning we climbed Wheeler Peak, the tallest mountain in the state, at 13,161 feet. After this strenuous hike, we drove on SR 38, the scenic byway loop, which encircled the entire mountain area north of Taos, offering panoramic views of the southern Rocky Mountains, including Wheeler Peak.

Our first stop was the small, remote sports and recreational town of Red River, with a full-time population of only four hundred people. This former frontier town, originally settled by gold seekers, is located on the edge of the Red River. At an elevation of almost nine thousand feet, it is one of the most pristine, beautifully situated, youth and athletically oriented places I have ever visited. This would be a great place to have a second home for those inclined to these kinds of physical diverse activities; however, it would not be the easiest place to travel to and from, because of its remote mountain location. When we arrived the town was filled with young hikers, campers, and bikers. In the winter months, it is a haven for people who like to ski and snowmobile.

We spent the second night ensconced in a mountain hideaway camp near the town; this location met all of our requirements for the perfect campsite. To celebrate our success of the day and the great site, I baked an upside-down pineapple cake in the Dutch oven. However, there was one small problem in my efforts to create this gastronomical delight. We were camping at an elevation of about ten thousand feet, and I neglected to take this into consideration after mixing the cake batter. I let it set up for about forty-five minutes during our cocktails before I began to bake it in the oven; consequently, the cake mix did not rise properly. Later, while reviewing the cooking instructions on the box, I discovered that it was suggested that at high elevations the mix should stand no longer than fifteen minutes prior to baking; otherwise, it might not rise and cook properly. They were correct; this was a major oversight on my part. However, we hardly ever read the instructions on most of the things we cooked anyway. We preferred to just wing it, except when making pancakes for breakfast. As I said earlier, I always read those instructions in fear that someone, like Butler, would introduce a confusing new recipe.

When the batter was put in the oven to be baked, it was supposed to rise about six inches, but it rose only about two inches, and rather than becoming solid like a normal cake, it remained somewhat soft and mushy. Have you ever eaten a cake with a spoon? We did. Actually, it was delectable, but it was more like eating pie. Rather than pour it out into our metal eating plates, the four of us just lay on the ground on our bellies and spooned it out of the oven pot like four old dogs sharing and licking on a common bone.

My three fellow explorers bitched the whole time they were eating, but they ate every morsel. Finally, after realizing nothing was left of the cake, not even any mushy crumbs, they gave in and admitted it was delicious. It seems that even in our own stupidity, we were lucky enough to come out okay most of the time. As I often say when things are questionable but work, my standard comment is, "I would rather be lucky than good." That should have been one of our slogans, because it was a recurring theme in many of the things we attempted while in the wilderness.

The next morning the four of us—Jim Box, my son, Christopher, a relative newcomer to our trusty group Steve Georgeson, an attorney from Atlanta, and I left on the next leg of our marathon driving escapade.

This was one of Steve's earliest trips. Although he had been on a couple other trips, he was somewhat inexperienced with the outdoors, but he always gave it his best and tried to learn how to survive in the backcountry, and probably most importantly, in our company. He was also a bit nervous about certain kinds of activities, like driving on narrow mountain roads; hiking, standing, or crossing ground near the edge of cliffs; and a few other things, like camping in grizzly-bear country.

Of course, these were only accidental occurrences on our part; we reiterated this point to him each time they happened—after we had once again failed to follow our own spotty counsel. We did know better, but we always had to push toward the edge of everything we did or tried just to see what would develop.

Steve's outdoor skills were not refined because he had not had the same level of opportunity or experience that we had in the backcountry; however, he made every effort to involve himself and contribute when he was with us on our adventures. He was great fun, and we had a lot of laughs together when we were on our adventures. He grew into and out of our exploration program over time, but that was the nature of it. As people came and people went, Jim, Mack, and I remained constant.

My son, Chris, on the other hand, had become quite comfortable both in the wilderness and in our company. He enjoyed the outdoors, having attended Young Harris College in the mountains of North Georgia during his freshman year. He and his school friends had spent much of their free time exploring in these mountains, so he had learned through his varied experiences to adapt and function efficiently in the backcountry, with all its unexpected challenges.

The trips that he took with us broadened his perspective on life, enhanced his maturity, provided insight into different areas of the country, and introduced him to new and diverse outdoor experiences. I believe his adventures with us served as a rite of passage toward his manhood. The same could be said for Jim Box's two boys. At various stages each of them has accompanied us on journeys. They had also gone on independent trips in various parts of the country with their dad. After all these years since the passing of those adventures, these young men will tell anyone who asks that these outdoor experiences were some of the best, most interesting, and fun things they did in their younger lives, and they still like to tell stories from the trips. They have become chips off the block.

The next morning we decided to complete the scenic byway loop road back to Taos and spend the night on the town, not that we needed any additional inspiration or fun and frolic.

As we were driving thorough the Moreno Valley of the Sangre de Cristo Mountains, we passed through the remote year-round resort of Angel Fire, a small community of a thousand people, and were surprised when we came upon a curvilinear Vietnam veterans' memorial structure located on a hilltop adjacent to the byway. Initially upon seeing it from our jeep in this remote setting, we thought it was situated in the wrong place; we thought it should be in a more heavily traveled area. But after reflecting on what it represented, we agreed that this commemorative honoring men who were killed in the Vietnam War was truly located in the best of all places—in this isolated, peaceful, and unspoiled mountain village.

We stopped the jeep, got out, and began to read the epitaph noted on the monument. It was built as one family's memorial to their son who was killed in that war. In 1987 President Ronald Reagan acknowledged the monument as a national memorial; the chapel was dedicated in recognition of all the casualties of that god-awful war. I doubt this memorial has been seen by many, as compared to the Vietnam Memorial in Washington, but it is certainly meaningful; beautifully sequestered as it is in a serene location, it is a fitting tribute to those soldiers who lost their lives in that conflict.

▼

Years after leaving the marines, I attended several reunions hosted by the battalion that I served with in Vietnam. Close to two hundred veterans who had been members of the Third Battalion, Fourth Marines, attended many of these meetings to renew acquaintances and to honor our fellow marines who had lost their lives in the war.

When the meetings were held in our nation's capital, a troop formation of about two hundred former marines, was usually assembled at the Washington Vietnam Memorial, a marine corps band contingent played taps, and flowers were placed at the center of the wall to acknowledge the fallen heroes of our battalion. It was an impressive ceremony of honor and respect. Afterward, we strolled along the black-marbled, name-laden wall and commiserated with one another.

Several of the men who had served in my rifle company in Vietnam were in attendance at many of these reunions. At the time of the war, they were probably in their late teens or early twenties, while at the ripe old age of thirty, I was considered ancient, I am confident. Throughout the reunion meetings, they still referred to me as Captain Jack; this is what I was called by most of my troops, and I loved it. Old habits and traditions die hard, especially in the marine corps.

During one of these reunions, one of my men asked me to join him so that he could show me where the names of several of his friends and men, who had been in our company, were inscribed on the wall. As I stood beside him at the black-marble wall, he told me how they had died; suddenly he broke into tears and began shaking violently. The next minute we were in a tight embrace, with his arms draped around me as I tried to console him. It was too much for me, and within minutes tears were also flowing down my cheeks. Standing there holding onto him sharing in his emotion, my own passion and feelings began to surge forth, suddenly bursting inside of me in an unexplainable emotional release; I had never felt anything like it before. Somehow, deep within my subconscious, the realization struck me that I could finally let go of that damned war and live my life without any more regret or remorse. The war and my role in it had been a job handed to me, and I had done my duty. It was as simple as that; now it was finally over.

I suppose my friend's grief somehow implanted strength within me as we shared the bond of comrades-in-arms. I have not seen nor heard from him since, but I sincerely hope he has also come to terms with himself, his own personal demons, and the deep sorrow and regret for his fellow marines. Unfortunately, there are probably many stories very much like this, and there always will be as long as conflict exists on this war-torn planet.

▼

The city of Taos, with its population of nearly five thousand people at an elevation of 6,950 feet, has a prominent ski area. In many ways it is a quaint and artistic community located somewhat off the beaten track. After searching for a camping site, we finally settled in a campground on the outskirts of town. This was fine for the night, since we had decided to have a Mexican meal at one of the local restaurants and enjoy some downtime, do some people watching on the front porch of the restaurant, and have a few margaritas to improve our attitude. Perhaps the highlight of our visit to Taos was a side trip to the Kit Carson Park, with the cemetery where Carson and some other historic western figures were buried. It also housed some interesting artifacts from the western heydays of the 1800s.

Ultimately, after we had achieved a somewhat liquor-induced sleepy mentality, we decided to return to the campground and catch some shut-eye amid the other drinking, fun-loving inhabitants.

Early the next morning, we left for our next destination. We were on our way to Santa Fe by way of another scenic road—SR 76, known as the High Road to Taos, which took us through several small, intriguing villages. Chimayo, the oldest, settled in 1598, was also the largest, with a population of three thousand people. Upon arriving in Santa Fe, we decided to spend some time shopping and playing tourist. Initially we visited the famous Town Square in the center of town, a lovely spot to rest and reflect, and then we toured a few art galleries for cultural enlightenment; afterward we purchased some trinkets and other paraphernalia to take home to friends and family.

One of our stops there was to visit the oldest Catholic church in America, the chapel of San Miguel, located at the edge of town on the Old Santa Fe Trail. It was built by Tlaxcala Indians under the direction of the Franciscan padres circa 1610. Jim Box, who consistently complained that I would not share our trip maps with him or anyone else in our group, said that this particular stop must have been a watershed event for me; I must have experienced a sudden awakening or an epiphany of sorts because I tossed the keys of the jeep and map to him when I came out of the church and said, "Go wherever you guys want, but do it before I change my mind."

They did just that. He and the other two explorers looked at the map and decided to drive up to Elk Mountain, with a peak of 11,661 feet, outside of Santa Fe in the Sangre de Cristo Mountain Range. It was a good decision, but the narrow, twisting, rutted, one-lane dirt road that took us to the top of the mountain was extremely difficult and dangerous. This was one of those tricky mountain drives that frightened Steve. Actually, it scared the hell out of all of us, but we did it anyway. Each time we stopped the vehicle, Steve exited the jeep and tried to guide us around obstacles or ensure that we didn't roll over the steep edge of the cliff when we had to back up to navigate the twists and turns in the road. Some of the time we didn't know if he was in the truck or not; we would look in the backseat, the door would be ajar, and he would be gone. The next thing we knew, he'd be standing on the road behind the vehicle attempting to give directions. I think he was a bit nervous about the trip; he had not yet adapted to living on the edge. Or perhaps I should say to driving on the edge.

When we finally reached the top of the mountain after a couple of hours of hair-raising corkscrew driving, we located a campsite in a wooded area just below the mountain crest. Well-situated, it would protect us from the elements, primarily the fifty-mile-per-hour wind. On the peak it was so gusty we could not stand or walk erect without leaning into the wind; the views were breathtaking, as you can see from Jim Box's photograph on the cover of this book. Snowdrifts had accumulated on the mountain edge, and we walked through them to peer down into the wide valleys below. This was too much for Steve, and he excitedly expressed his concern about the dangers and possibility of us falling into the deep crevices below. Although we tried convincing him that we knew what we were doing and were confident we could maintain our footing and protect ourselves, he didn't buy into our explanation and refused to get within shouting distance of the edge. *Oh well*, we thought, *maybe the next time.*

Actually, Steve was a good soul, who added greatly to our group; he was extremely intelligent, humorous, in good physical condition, and an excellent conversationalist. Most of the time he was game for almost anything that our team wanted to do, but he was not mentally prepared to be a risk taker as we were (but how many people are?); this is not a criticism about him, just a fact. He had other strong personal characteristics, though, and we appreciated his interest and commitment to these journeys, particularly in light of his lack of experience in the backcountry and more conservative mind-set about some of the things we attempted. Nonetheless, we enjoyed kidding him, and he always took it with a grain of salt; it was all in good honest fun, and he was a great sport about it. We missed him when opted out of our program!

We spent the next day exploring around the mountain, the top of which was covered with slate and shale rock outcroppings. Discovering several pieces of rock with imbedded impressions of very small animal fossils, the type found in water, we could only guess that this eleven-thousand-foot mountain had at one time been covered by the sea. Apparently either an uplift of the earth's surface or faulting or thrusting of the earth's surface forward had shoved it up from its sea-bottom bed. While hiking around Chris, who has the best eye I have ever seen for finding stuff anywhere, picked up three very nicely sculptured arrowheads made of obsidian (volcanic glass), a magma that has hardened into solid rock. Later he took them to a local jewelry store to determine their value and was told they were not that valuable because they were only about five hundred years old. He was told they might be worth $300. He kept them for his collection.

After our foray up to Elk Mountain, we drove very slowly and cautiously down the mountain and on to Albuquerque to catch our plane home. Steve did not jump out of the vehicle on this part of the trip. He was either asleep or had adjusted to our travels. Actually, I think he may have been sleeping, because it was very quiet in the back of the vehicle and he was probably mentally and physically exhausted from looking after the rest of us for the past week.

SIXTEEN

YELLOWSTONE COUNTRY

Plate tectonics! If you know what this term means, you've probably taken some geology courses in school. For the uninformed, though, this is a geological theory about what happens to the earth's outer crust and has been happening for billions of years. This scientific hypothesis suggests that the earth's outer exterior, part of which we inhabit, is essentially supported by a dozen or so large pieces of matter or plates well below the earth's surface, which move independently and ride on slippery molten rocks.

This highly regarded speculation implies that these plates are in constant motion and can pull away from each other or collide with each other as they randomly move about. This plate movement may create or destroy ocean floors, sink or raise new mountains, and even dismember or assemble new continents.

Somewhat like large pieces of ice floating on a slow current of water, the plates, like ice floes, can meet in many different ways; they may grind against each other, pull away, or slam violently into one another. The heavier of the plates generally forces the lighter of the two downward, causing the heavier to be thrust upward, thereby forcing the landmass above to respond in varied and unusual ways. This conjecture about plate movement has supposedly played an important role in creating Wyoming as we see it today and as I will discuss in the next chapter, "Lewis and Clark Country."

About 100 million years ago, give or take a few thousand, the North American plate, where we live, broke away from the growing Atlantic Ocean and jammed the western edge of this continent squarely against the floor of the Pacific Ocean plate. The heavier western-moving North American plate rode up over the Pacific plate, forcing it downward into the mantle of the earth. When this occurred, molten matter rose from the sinking plate and flowed upward into the North American plate above it and melted large amounts of granite. Ultimately the thick, molten slabs collapsed and slid eastward, bulldozing up mountains in their path, finally coming to rest on each other, like shingles on a roof, creating the Northern Rocky Mountains we know today.

The Teton Mountains in Wyoming and many of the other mountain ranges in North America were formed from this bulldozer action, subsequent faulting in the earth's surface, and rock slippage.

Now, for the Yellowstone Park development. Some 17 million years ago, a migrating hot spot, created when a large meteorite slammed into what is now southern Oregon, began burning a swath across southern Idaho in the Snake River Plain. This collision from the meteorite blasted a mass of rock loose from the earth's surface and allowed much hotter rock to rise up from below. As the North American plate moving westward slid over this stationary hot spot, old volcanoes died out and new volcanoes were formed above the hot spot; these new volcanoes eventually migrated into more eastern locations as the plate continued its movement westerly. The remnants or chain of these inert volcanoes, caused by the moving plates, can now be seen spread across the Snake River Plain in southern Idaho. Ultimately, as the plate movement continued westward, altering the earth's surface, the hot spot moving eastward finally established the Yellowstone caldera in Wyoming.

As a matter of supposition, if the western plate movement continues, the Yellowstone hot spot will continue its volcanic track until the fires below eventually burn out. Of course, this will not occur in our lifetime, but it will most likely occur over millions of years. Perhaps someday this hot spot may even be situated on the northeastern seaboard if the plate continues its movement.

In 1807 John Colter, a member of the Lewis and Clark Discovery Expedition, was the first white man in Jackson Hole. Originally called Colter's Hell because of its geysers, in 1829 the entire area was named after David E. Jackson (Jackson Hole), a fur trapper who had spent several years working in this general locality before he sold out after making a sizable profit. His partner, William Ashley, named the valley in his honor. Mountain men called a low-lying valley that was surrounded by mountains a "hole."

In 1872 Colter's Hell became Yellowstone, the world's first national park. The Grand Teton National Park was established by Congress in 1929. The town of Jackson was named after David Jackson, the fur trapper.

This is the country we came to visit on one of our Western exploring expeditions. As time progressed and we learned more about the fascinating history, beauty, and geologic development of the area, we made many additional trips to hike, camp, and explore the surrounding terrain that makes up *Yellowstone Country*.

Our initial excursion team included Jim Box, Steve Georgeson, and me. We flew into the city of Jackson, in Jackson Hole, which is about seventy miles south of Yellowstone Park. The first night we camped in the National Elk Refuge Wilderness Area, a plateau just outside of the city limits. The 24,000-acre refuge is the winter home of 7,500 elk. As we drove up the mountain, we did see a large number of elk grazing along the dirt road. We also saw a few moose that had taken advantage of the safety of this locale and were ambling about enjoying a meal on the thick vegetation. It seems that these animals are more commonly seen in the backcountry, but viewing a moose up close was a rarity for us, so we were intrigued. Of course, we knew it would be unwise to encroach on their privacy as they have been known to attack or charge intruders if they get too close to their space. We stayed in the vehicle, took pictures, and continued on our peaceful, protected way.

We spent the night on the expansive plateau, enjoying the city lights dancing below and a display of stars overhead that seemed almost within our reach. These lights, both above and below us, provided an unusual spectacle; seeing them arrayed like this in the wilderness was an amazing and unusual occurrence.

We hiked around the next morning and found some bear scat on the edge of the woods not far from our campsite. This was an interesting state of affairs; we had not realized we were in bear country, particularly since we were so close to civilization.

Later that day we visited a ranger office in Jackson to obtain trip information and additional maps for our planned travel route. The ranger was helpful, but alerted us that our intended travels would take us into grizzly bear territory and we should be watchful, avoid contact if at all possible, and keep our campsites clean and free of any food particles. We were also told to hang our food by rope in trees above the ground at night, so it would be out of reach of the animals, and not to sleep in the clothes we had worn when we prepared our meals. Otherwise, we might have an unannounced visitor crawl in our tent looking for a midnight snack; sleeping in our clothes and smelling like food, we could be it.

Additionally, we were advised that if we encountered a bear in the backcountry, especially if it was a female who had her cubs with her, to back away slowly—no running—and to maintain eye contact with the animal, if possible. If the bear advanced toward us, he suggested that we climb a tree if one was available and try to get at least fifteen feet off the ground. Bears cannot climb very well, but they can run like hell, almost forty miles an hour for a short distance. Obviously, trying to run away from a bear in hot pursuit would be foolhardy. Before we came to Jackson Hole, Jim, who had recently read a book titled *Bear Attacks*, had already developed a keen appreciation from the book about what these huge animals could do to a human being when provoked or surprised.

After our indoctrination about bears by our Smokey Bear ranger, Jim, a bit spooked, suggested we purchase a rifle to take with us on our trip. He may have been a bit overcautious, if that is possible, when going into the wilderness where these fearsome creatures dwell. After some discussion and venting of emotions, we decided to stay on the edge, not buy a gun, and hope for the best. As I recall, Steve was ready to purchase several guns. Luckily everything worked out just fine. We avoided most of the areas that seemed even remotely attuned to the propagation of bears. We also followed the ranger's advice almost to the letter. We often did wild and crazy things, but certainly not stupid things.

We found the eastern side of the Tetons around Jackson to be crowded with people, automobiles, and recreational vehicles; the traffic flow was terrible. Many of the tourists visiting Yellowstone must drive through Jackson, both going and coming to and from the park, because it offers the only egress from the south. Consequently, during daylight hours, the main street of Jackson seemed to house a steady stream of tourist vehicles.

This is by no means meant to degrade this wonderfully situated multipurpose town. Jackson has culture, great night life, art galleries, fine restaurants, and easy access to a variety of recreational summer and winter sports throughout this mountain-rimmed valley. I have numerous friends who have second homes here, and they believe it is one of the finest of all places to spend their free time. We did enjoy many of these activities during our many visits.

For our wilderness experiences, we much preferred to separate ourselves from the crowd and to venture into more secluded and less populated areas, so we chose to take most of our hikes into the Teton Mountains from the Idaho-state side, only a few miles from Jackson, usually entering this section of the backcountry from the town of Driggs, Idaho.

▼

After visiting with our new friend, the ranger, we drove north on Highway 89 toward Yellowstone. Just before West Thumb, we headed west on a dirt logging road toward Idaho, unbelievably into one of the places where the ranger said we might encounter bears. Undaunted we camped in this area for the night, and no bears were seen, thank goodness. The next day we proceeded on into Idaho and then south on Highway 20, paralleling the Teton Mountains.

We had planned to do a loop of the Jackson Hole area by starting at Jackson, proceeding north to the edge of Yellowstone, then west into Idaho, hike on the back side of the Tetons, and return to Jackson. This road journey was to be followed by another loop from Jackson, south to Pinedale, and then across the Wind River Range in the Bridger Wilderness. From here we would head west once again toward Jenny Lake for a hike, and then south back to Jackson.

We believed it was necessary to reconnoiter an area thoroughly, both for education and future exploration. This broad excursion, along with our hikes and overnight stays, would provide us with a good overview of the Jackson Hole area and the knowledge of places to visit or possibly revisit on future trips. We accomplished our mission, and we did in fact locate several areas that various members of our team revisited on later journeys.

These explorations were important because we did not want to waste our time visiting wilderness areas that were not acceptable to our standards and piqued our interest. However, every trip we made did offer something of value about the backcountry, and this certainly made our recons (inspections) worthwhile.

▼

Detailed reconnaissance either by map or helicopter, if time and conditions permitted, was a way of life before going into battle. It was important to know exactly where you were going, how far, the critical terrain features, barriers, routes, or trails, and most importantly, your *exact* location on the map at all times. It was too damned easy to walk into an ambush if you had no conception of the terrain. If artillery was needed in an attack or to get you out of a difficult situation, it was critical to know your specific location on the ground and on the map, because a fire mission was called in by radio based on the coordinates of your location or that of the enemies, as identified from your map. If you miscalculated or used the wrong coordinates, your unit, and not the enemy's, could be potentially blown away by your own *friendly fire*. This did happen a few times to uniformed unit commanders. Similar errors could also occur with the firing battery, just as they did when we called in counter mortar artillery fire and the artillery unit mistakenly put their first six rounds on our position. *Murphy's Law* exists, especially in war—"If anything can go wrong, it will, and at the most inopportune time."

When Mike Company was on search-and-destroy missions in dense terrain, my artillery forward observer was required to carry his map in his hands and to note every few minutes our exact location on his map. His job was to get the heavy stuff delivered when we needed it and where we needed it. When the crap hit the fan, there was no time for guessing; you had to be right, or you would be history. I also had my map readily available, constantly checking on our position and route of march. It was the smart thing to do.

It was from these past military habits and experiences that I had a difficult time giving up the map on our trips, and so this practice was carried over into our excursions. My fellow explorers complained constantly, saying it was a type of control. It really was not, but it did save us time and confusion about our travels and helped with insight into our areas of exploration. What's more, no one else had any interest in studying maps. It was kind of kooky on my part, but I found reading maps interesting, and besides, I really didn't care what they thought—too much.

▼

We drove south on Highway 20 in Idaho until we reached SR 32. This was a small road that took us to SR 33 and south on to Driggs. At Driggs we drove east into Teton Valley, where we would spend a couple of days camping and hiking on the back side (western slopes) of the Tetons; this was to become our preferred entry for future trips into these mountains. A wonderful, thunderous creek runs down from the mountains and surges through Teton Valley, which is enclosed by a large stand of lodgepole and sycamore trees. We set up our campsite on this watercourse, laid out our sleeping bags on the banks of the stream, ate dinner, and were lulled to sleep listening to the lullaby of the rippling water. Next morning we hiked several miles up the valley to a trailhead junction and began to climb the Devil's Staircase. This was a steep 1,500-feet vertical mile-long climb up a dirt trail that had steps dug into the side of the mountain. It was appropriately named and was a bitch of a climb. The *Backpacker's Guidebook for this area* provides this description on the "stairs" as follows: "It doesn't take much imagination to see how the trail got its name. It is so steep horses cannot navigate it and backpackers may wish they hadn't tried."

Captivated or stupid, we went back and climbed this trail on several later visits to the Yellowstone area. I guess we must have liked the challenge; that, or we just enjoyed the strain and pain. Nonetheless, it was beautiful country, and the panoramic view of the valley going up the stairs was stunning. Perhaps that, plus the privacy of the valley, brought us back to this location multiple times; the beauty and seclusion of the area were a strong draw for us.

After making it up the staircase, we hiked though a high glacier-formed valley (shelf) in the direction of the Grand Teton peak. After about two miles, we reached a saddle at Mount Meek that opened into the eastern side of the Tetons. It was at this time we decided that we had experienced all the pleasure we could stand for that day.

Several hours later, after descending from the mountain via the staircase and hiking back though the valley, we arrived in camp for a much-needed restful night. We had hiked fourteen miles that day, half of which was uphill, and that was more than enough for our group.

The next day we hiked up the valley to another trail that took us up toward Table Mountain, elevation 11,106 feet. This mountain peak also provided unbelievable views into the Grand Tetons.

The following day our travels took us back through Jackson, thereby completing our first loop, and then forty-eight miles southeast to Pinedale for our second planned travel tour. From Pinedale we drove into the Bridger Wilderness and camped on the Continental Divide near Downs Mountain at an elevation of over eleven thousand feet. This was the Wind River Range. Next morning the three of us hiked out into this wilderness to explore. Bears were still on our mind, although we had not yet encountered any. Perhaps they were mostly on Jim's mind because, as we were hiking though a thickly wooded area adjacent to a fenced field, he bellowed out in a frightened tone, "Bear!" We didn't look back, and all three of us took off in a dead run across the open field, naturally having completely forgotten the ranger's advice. Finally, after running about four hundred yards, we paused to survey the situation and to see if the beast was chasing us.

Have you heard the story, surely it is not factual, about the two young men who were hiking in the mountains and a large bear began chasing them, and one stopped and pulled a pair of tennis shoes out of his pack. The other boy halted momentarily and asked him what he was doing; the first boy responded, "I'm putting on a pair of tennis shoes so I can run faster." The second boy said, "Don't you know you can't outrun a bear?" And the first boy, hastily tying his shoelaces, responded, "I know; all I have to do is outrun you."

This story likely corresponds with the mind-set that we harbored at that scary moment: "It is every man for himself." This probably should have been our explorer-team refrain for most of the things that we did in the wilderness.

▼

As we visually scanned the area from where we had started our mad dash, we saw a slow-moving old cow slowly emerge from the woods! Apparently Jim had seen the hindside of the animal in some nearby thick brush, and his deep-rooted concern and overactive imagination gave him the impression that it was a bear tracking us. Now, winded from our quarter-mile sprint but greatly relieved, we had a big laugh over it.

Think about it; it's much better to overreact than to *assume*, especially when you have doubts about something in the wilderness that can possibly inflict bodily harm on you. We walked slowly back to the camp, mentally and physically exhausted after that experience.

The next day we completed our exploratory travel loop by driving through the *Gros Ventre Wilderness* and on to Jenny Lake, a few miles north of Jackson. We had decided to experience one hike from the eastern slope of the Tetons, but after about two hours of walking, we became overwhelmed with the crowds in this popular area and called it quits. It was just not our thing. As I reiterated early, we preferred a more tranquil backcountry area, and after bumping into so many people on the trail, we decided that entering from the Idaho side and hiking the western slope would be more to our liking. We never came back to hike from this side of the Tetons. But we did return to Wyoming several times to hike, camp, and visit Yellowstone Park. Later on, several of us took family members to Jackson for recreation. On each of our hiking expeditions, many of which included various team members, we always went back through Driggs and into Teton Canyon for part of our backcountry entertainment in the Yellowstone area. You can tell that we really liked this location because of the beauty and privacy it offered. It was a great place to get lost, stay lost, and avoid the crowds.

Sometime later, Jim Box, his son, Andy, and I made an unusual trip over a long weekend. I met them at the Jackson airport, and we immediately returned to our old familiar surroundings in Teton Canyon; Jim wanted Andy to see this great area. Our first night out, we decided to camp in a somewhat remote campground; it was empty, which surprised us because it was extremely clean and nice.

It was Jim's birthday, and he asked me to bake a pineapple upside-down cake to celebrate. I did, and this time when it came out of the Dutch oven, it looked like a cake and not like a smashed-down, soft, mushy pie, like the last one I had baked. Our campsite established, we fixed dinner, our traditional very meaty spaghetti, primarily for Andy, along with our sweet-smelling cake, and were preparing to settle in for the night when a park ranger visited us.

We shared stories for a time, then he casually mentioned that we should be watchful, because the previous night some grizzly bears had come into the campground while a group of Boy Scouts were camping and rummaged through their trash. He did say that no one was attacked. Jim then remarked, "It's no wonder the grounds are vacant tonight." Apparently we were the only *feast* in the campground at the time. Supposedly he was trying to be funny when he asked the ranger if bears could smell freshly baked pineapple, cinnamon cake. The ranger replied, "Oh hell, yeah. They can smell it for miles." That did it. Our motivation and plan for sleeping under the stars that night was immediately squashed, and the three of us slept in the truck. It was a miserable night, but it seemed like the right thing to do under the circumstances. We had no hirsute visitors, at least we didn't hear any growling or odd noises, and if we did have visitors, we didn't want to know about it.

The next day we undertook the Devil's Staircase and again hiked up the open plateau to catch a scenic look into the Tetons. Later we located another campsite, not the one the bears liked, and the following morning, after a big breakfast of cinnamon (again) pancakes, we drove to the Darby Canyon Wind and Ice Caves, located North towards Yellowstone. The caves were a steep four-mile hike from the trailhead.

▼

The Wind Cave snakes through a layer of 350-million-year-old dolomite rock formation by way of a two-mile-long underground subalpine stream. It connects with an adjoining ice cave, an underground cavern tunneling though forty feet of ice—remnants of the last glaciation period, ten thousand years ago.

The front entrance of Wind Cave has a waterfall that flows over the entrance, exposing this forty-foot cavern, where wind often whistles through the large front opening and rock tunnel, giving the cave its name. The stream and cave system, starting at the ice cave, contains seven drop-offs, thirty-three-degree air temperature, and waist-deep wading through Crotch Lake inside of the mountain as it flows from the ice cave to Wind Cave. This multifaceted cavern was a wonderful spelunking (cave exploration) opportunity for those persons with the equipment, fortitude, and knowledge to explore the entire cave complex and the wandering underground stream. It was also emphazied that the connecting passage between the two caves should not be attempted by the inexperienced or the ill-equipped.

▼

We did not possess the expertise or interest to be spelunkers. Matter of fact, none of us liked to be in enclosed areas under the ground that offered little light, or the possibility of losing our way and never returning to humanity. We went into Wind Cave and looked around, but stayed close to the front entrance. Afterward we tramped up a steep incline for about three miles toward the entrance of the ice cave, but stayed on the fringes of the entryway.

Afterward I left Jim and Andy in Jackson, where they met with two of Jim's relatives for another few days of camping. Unfortunately, they had come totally unprepared, although they were supposedly accomplished in the backcountry. Matter of fact, they lived in the mountains of North Carolina; go figure! Jim had to take care of them and feed them during the entire trip. *Better him than me,* I thought after hearing the sad story after they returned from their trip. This is how people get into serious trouble in the backcountry—going unprepared and hoping for the best. They went back to the Alaskan Basin, the same area we had just left, and spent the next several days hiking and camping with the bare essentials. They were damned lucky to get through this trip without some serious problem. I don't think Jim and his son went on another trip with them after that experience, and they probably should not have.

Jim also took his second oldest son, Alex, into Teton Canyon for an outdoor experience. Alex was starting his last year of high school, and Jim wanted him to have the opportunity to experience the western mountains. They left on their adventure the first week in July, starting their hike in Teton Canyon, and then climbed the Devil's Staircase and trekked through Hurricane Pass at an elevation of 10,372 feet. The pass traverses close to the largest, most spectacular, and probably the most photographed mountain in the West, the Grand Teton, with an elevation of 13,770 feet. After crossing the pass, they descended into the Jenny Lake area in Jackson

Hole. The hike was twenty-four miles long, and they had intended to spend one night in preparation and three days and two nights on the trail.

Later, as Jim related his experiences and their trials on this venture, I recalled a lecture from Officer Candidate School. A crusty, battle- tested sergeant was giving a talk on tactics. He was explaining the necessity of good planning and proper follow-through when in a combat situation. The sergeant went on to tell our class of wannabe lieutenants, with numerous expletives used to reinforce his points, that it was critical we learned early in our careers the marine corps did not operate on good intentions, but on getting the job done. His final comment summed up his lecture perfectly when he said, "The road to hell is paved with the bones of dead lieutenants who had good *intentions,* but failed to follow through."

▼

Prior to departing on their journey, Jim had called a ranger station to inquire about the weather conditions in the mountains. He was told there was lots of snow at the higher elevations, but the trails were passable. However, the ranger recommended that, if they were going to cross though the pass, they should carry ice axes to help with their footing and traction, so Jim planned to purchase two of them for this outing before they departed. When they arrived in Driggs, they stopped at a local outfitter's store and were again told they needed axes for their hike, and it would cost $300 for two. This is when his good *intentions* went to hell, and Jim and his son almost followed. He later told me that he had intended to purchase the axes, but he was too cheap, and he decided to cut two wooden poles and use those in lieu of spending money for something they would probably never use again. Frankly, he admitted this was a bad decision.

The next day they had a strenuous eight-mile hike up the basin to the top of a shelf on the mountain. The trail was void of people that day, which was somewhat unusual. Now, this is a good point to cogitate when you're in the wilderness and you don't find anyone else around, just like we did at our campground and Jim and Alex did on their hike; there is probably a *reason* no one else is around, and it's probably not a *good reason.*

In our western travels over the years, we have discovered a number of lakes, mountain peaks, roads, and trails named "Fourth of July," and this is probably because it is almost impossible to reach them until *after* the Fourth of July. Keep this in mind if you plan to hike the backcountry in the West and you come across the name "Fourth of July." As a case in point, Jim and Alex started their hike on the eighth of July, and snow was everywhere they hiked.

Jim will freely admit that he made several mistakes with this particular adventure. First, he did not take an ice ax, and this could have resulted in a disaster. Second, he had been in the West several days before his son arrived, so he was acclimatized to the elevation, while Alex, on the other hand, had only two days to acclimatize before they started their trip. He had gone from an 800 feet elevation level basically to ten thousand feet in twenty-four hours. Sometime after they started hiking, Jim noticed Alex was struggling and having a difficult time keeping up. Afterward Jim said he never considered the altitude equation before or during the hike. "It wasn't bothering me; I just neglected to consider it as a possible problem. I guess I was just a dumbass at the time."

The first day they headed up the mountain to the pass and ran into sleet and snow near the top. Jim said that his son was looking kind of bad at that point. He was also throwing up, but Jim said he didn't learn about that issue until after they had completed the hike. Alex did not complain or tell him he was ill. They finally stopped for a break; Jim said he offered to turn back because of the weather conditions, but Alex said he wanted to finish what they had started, so they continued to hike through the bad weather and the snow.

One of the most frightening parts of the hike occurred on this day, when they had to cross 150 yards of ice and snow on a steep slope. This is when they badly needed ice axes to help them maintain and stabilize their footing to keep them from going over the edge of the cliff if they slipped on the icy terrain. Using their poles and moving cautiously, with Alex following in Jim's footprints, they finally made it across safely.

As they began their descent on the east side of the mountain, snow covered the trail, making it difficult for them to find their way. They had planned to camp one more night, but Jim, concerned for Alex's health and worried about the deteriorating weather conditions, decided that they should continue the march and get off the mountain as soon as they could. They hiked sixteen miles that day in all the muck and crap that Mother Nature could toss at them.

After this quest Jim confided in me and his son just how proud he was of Alex and how much he admired his courage and perseverance. He also told me he was disappointed in himself for not considering the treacherous situation before they started, and later for not recognizing the nature of the mountain sickness that Alex experienced when they reached the higher elevations.

Much later, after some reflection on the trip, he said, "This was the most worthwhile thing I had every done with my son. He would not give up or tell me about his problem, because Alex said we had not accomplished our mission." On hearing that comment, I told Jim that Alex would certainly make a mighty-fine marine.

Jim believes that the personal challenge and adversity that Alex overcame on that trip went a long way in forming his character and building confidence in his abilities to succeed.

Folks, this is a wonderful father-and-son story, indicative of the learning and growing that can occur in the wilderness, even under the most trying and physically testing conditions. Yes, assuredly, mistakes were made along the way, but importantly, life-molding lessons were learned by both of them—the hard way. This shared experience helped create a bond between a father and his son that cannot, and will probaly not, ever be severed in their lifetimes.

Alex's problem, acute mountain sickness, typically strikes unconditioned, high-elevation hikers at about eight thousand feet. This malady is the body's way of coping with reduced oxygen and humidity at high elevations. The symptoms include headaches, shortness of breath, loss of appetite, insomnia, vomiting, rapid heartbeats, and lethargy. Once this condition becomes evident, the affected should stop their climb and begin to descend immediately. Actually, a quick descent will end the problem very quickly and is probably the wisest course of action. Proper physical conditioning provides the best preparation, and it should always be accompanied by several days of acclimatization prior to the climb. The rule of thumb advocated by most experienced hikers is one day of acclimatization per thousand feet of elevation gain if sufficient time is available. Alcohol and certain kinds of drugs will definitely intensify the symptoms once they occur and should be avoided.

In all my trips to the West, the only time I experienced acute mountain sickness was *not* when I was on an expedition in the wilderness. Before starting our expeditions, I attended a three-day business meeting at the

Keystone Ski Resort in Colorado at an elevation of 9,300 feet. I had never been above six thousand feet elevation at that time and was not knowledgeable about the effects of acute mountain sickness (AMS), nor was my body conditioned for this elevation change.

Upon arrival at the lodge, I went to dinner with friends and had three glasses of wine with my meal. When dinner was over, I left for my room. Walking up a few stairsteps, I found myself totally winded. This concerned me, and I thought I should walk around so that hopefully the sensation would pass. It didn't. My pulse began to speed up, and my heart pounded inside my chest cavity. I thought I might be having a heart attack. With growing concern I went to my room to call a doctor.

While searching in the resort telephone directory for a name, I noticed a caution printed on the back cover about altitude sickness. The article listed all the conditions that were affecting me at the time. Furthermore, the piece advised people new to high elevations or prone to altitude sickness to avoid alcohol for several days until they became acclimatized. It stated that one drink at a high elevation was like three at sea level. In other words, at a high elevation you could easily get on a cheap drunk. The three glasses of wine I had consumed at dinner had my body feeling and behaving like I had consumed nine. In my ignorance I had undone myself, so I immediately went to bed, relieved it wasn't a heart attack. I will never forget this scary experience; once was enough. I had learned my lesson and would make certain that I didn't repeat it.

SEVENTEEN

LEWIS AND CLARK COUNTRY

Idaho remains one of this country's most isolated and rugged regions. To the earliest explorers, both before and after Lewis and Clark, the territory was practically impenetrable. Meriwether Lewis and William Clark headed the Corps of Discovery's trek across this land in 1805, exposing this vast unknown and unexplored territory. This expedition took twenty-seven months, and their discoveries subsequently provided the impetus for trappers, traders, and prospectors to travel to this region in the pursuit of wealth and personal riches.

My first visit to Idaho was in the summer of 1986 to attend a bankers' conference hosted by Merrill Lynch Investments of New York at the famous Sun Valley Resort. I must admit that, at that time, knowing nothing about this part of the country, I was surprised upon seeing how beautiful it was and how rugged the mountainous terrain was that surrounded this fabulous resort area. Sun Valley Resort was founded in 1935 by Averell Harriman, Union Pacific Railroad Chairman, who had hired an Austrian to find a scenic spot somewhere in the country for a ski resort. He found Sun Valley, and of course, the Union Pacific Railroad carried the tourists to the newly developed resort.

I liked the area so much that I eventually purchased a second home here and lived part-time in Sun Valley five months a year for the better part of eight years. I eventually sold my house, but I still visit the valley every summer and spend two enjoyable months hiking in the five different mountain ranges that are part of this general area of Idaho.

Unfortunately, many people, especially in the South, do not have a good perspective of some of the Western states; probably people in the West suffer the same dilemma about the Southern states. For example, upon mentioning Idaho, some eastern folks have asked where it is, or they think it is in Iowa. I would venture to tell you that many of the folks I have met in my travels have demonstrated limited knowledge about the lay of the land or even the location of the states on our North American continent.

An example will help illustrate my point. My home state is West Virginia. Whenever people ask where I am from originally, I tell them; almost invariably, most of the people, both on the East and West Coasts, will ask me if it is in Virginia. Humorously I will then go into a long dissertation about the Civil War, the secession of the states from the Union, and how the western part of Virginia and its population seceded from

Virginia in 1863, because of the slavery issue and ultimately became the state of West Virginia. I will not continue my normal, lengthy, rambling explanation for you here, because it would probably bore you to death. But you get my point.

▼

In some ways Idaho, the Gem State, is a *mess* geologically speaking. Few states have had such a variety of land-shaping events occur in the historical formation of their topography. For example, about 800 million years ago when the tectonic plates shifted apart, Idaho was on the West Coast, separated by a wide ocean from any other landmass on its western border. When the North American continental plate shifted west 100 million years ago and collided with the Pacific plate, as I discussed in the previous chapter, new landmasses were created when huge chunks of vagrant scraps of crustal rock came ashore and extended the continent westward as it is predisposed today.

The Seven Devils complex on the western edge is an old chain of squashed volcanic islands that formed somewhere out in the Pacific Ocean and then crashed into North America during all the tectonic plate activity, joining what is now part of western Idaho after separating from the newly created land that formed Oregon. Hell's Canyon on the west side of the Seven Devils is composed of many of these old rocks and runs between Idaho and Oregon. It is the deepest canyon in this country, considerably deeper than the Grand Canyon of the Colorado River, which may be surprising to some.

The Snake River, originating in Yellowstone Park, runs across the southern plain of Idaho, then north through Hell's Canyon. The Salmon River, the River of No Return, originating in south-central Idaho, runs north and then west across the state and converges with the Snake. Ultimately the Snake, the Columbia River's largest tributary, connects with the Columbia in Washington State and flows to the Pacific Ocean.

When the tectonic plates collided, the Pacific plate was driven down into the earth by the heavier western-moving North American plate. A tremendous amount of heat was generated by the sinking Pacific plate, causing it to melt, forming basalt magma.

Eventually this magma intruded through the earth's crust to the surface and crystallized into an enormous mass of granite, forming a huge batholith, the rock now found in most all of central Idaho. It is estimated that 17 million years ago, a meteorite struck southern Oregon, creating a hot spot deep in the earth's mantle that traveled across the Snake River plain in southern Idaho as the North American plate continued its western shift. Leaving traces of visible volcanoes, now called buttes, it finally came to rest in Yellowstone.

Subsequently two different ice ages, going back some 130,000 years, etched the land, gorged the valleys, eroded the mountains, and dumped sediment into the valleys. Finally about fifteen thousand years ago, a lava field was started in the Snake River Plain when volcanic eruptions began. These flows ultimately covered an area of 640 square miles; the sinuous lava oozing from twenty-five vents produced some forty lava flows during that volcanic activity, whose most recent eruptions occurred only about two thousand years ago. The flows and lava creations from these volcanic eruptions can be seen in the Snake River Plain along Highway 75 between Twin Falls and Carey and along Highway 20 between Carey and Idaho Falls; they are especially prominent in the Craters of the Moon National Monument and Preserve, situated between Carey and Arco.

Geologists tell us that Idaho has some of the best rocks they have ever seen, comprising beautiful mountains and some of the most interesting and lovely landscapes in this country. Is it any wonder Idaho, so fascinating and beautiful, can still be depicted even today as a geological *mess*, all resulting from its history of cataclysmic molding disturbances?

In 1987 I returned to Idaho to attend another bankers' meeting and spent the better part of my free time hiking and biking in the mountains around Sun Valley. This part of the country had captured my imagination by the end of the trip, and I had, more or less, decided I wanted to find a way to spend much more of my time in this locale involved in the outdoor activities that were so meaningful to me. It took seven years, but it finally happened in 1995, and I was able to afford to purchase a second home in this beautiful valley.

In September 1989, we launched our first exploration into Idaho. Jim, Mack, and I made an initial seven-day trip in conjunction with a corporate business meeting conducted at the Sun Valley Resort.

It was an interesting backcountry trip, my first outside of the immediate Sun Valley and Ketchum area. We arrived around midnight on a Friday in the town of Ketchum, adjacent to Sun Valley (one mile separates the two towns, but for all practical purposes, it is one community), and visited a popular local watering hole, Whisky Jacques, that we had heard was usually wild and crazy on Friday nights. Arrangements had been made to take advantage of this partying opportunity. It is probably obvious to you by now that we enjoyed exploring *everything* in the area when we went on our expeditions.

The first night, after we finally retired rather late in the night or early in the morning, whichever, was spent at a local motel. The next day we were a little under the weather; the lengthy travel had most likely done us in! We rented bikes and toured for most of the day, trying to recover from the trip and the previous night. We did finally manage to purchase provisions for our wilderness trip that was to begin the following day. We also retired early; it was necessary.

▼

Ketchum, a small resort town with a population of about four thousand people, is actually part of the Sun Valley resort complex, although the two communities are considered to be separate towns. The year-round population of Sun Valley is about a thousand people. Ketchum was founded in the late nineteenth century, and it was formerly a shipping and smelting center for the ore mines located in the surrounding mountains. It is the gateway to the Sawtooth National Recreational Area, located only seven miles north of this community.

Bald Mountain, adjacent to Ketchum, with an elevation of 9,100 feet, was and is the cornerstone venue for downhill skiing in this part of the country. The immediately adjacent valley floor, at an elevation of 5,700 feet, offers a unique contrast with the mountain topography. The original ski lift, the first built in America, is still visible on one of the smaller hills in Sun Valley.

The Sawtooth Scenic Byway, SR 75, runs from Ketchum north for about sixty miles to Stanley, Idaho, a town with a population today of about a hundred people. The road through the valley and mountainous terrain offers spectacular views of the countryside and is possibly one of the most unspoiled and stunning drives that I have ever taken in all my years of explorations in the backcountry.

Ernest Hemingway at one time lived in the adjacent community of Warm Springs, another ski complex and part of the Sun Valley/Ketchum resort area. He died here in 1961 of a self-inflicted gunshot wound and is buried in the Ketchum Cemetery.

▼

Anyway, back to our trip. When we departed the next morning, it was raining heavily. Bad weather conditions never seem to change much, at least for us, but we headed out nonetheless. Our plan was to drive, explore, camp, and hike on a circular route for six days as far north as we could travel within this time constraint. We intended to see as much of this particular region as we could, and then to return to Sun Valley in time for my business meeting.

The route from the valley, Trail Creek Road, took us to Copper Basin at its 9,000-foot elevation, located east of the two towns. This was a high plateau surrounded by the extremely rugged mountains of the Pioneer Range. We had hoped to do some hiking in these mountains, but the pelting rain dictated that we should keep moving.

At Borah Peak, the tallest mountain in Idaho at 12,662 feet, we stopped to investigate remnants of an earlier earthquake. The quake occurred in October 1983, when the Big Lost River Range abruptly rose a foot or more while the adjacent valley dropped four feet. The earthquake, with a Richter magnitude-reading of 7.3, had occurred, forming a scarp (steep cliff) about six feet high running for several miles along the base of the mountain range. This happened when the continuity of the rocks on opposing sides of the resultant fault line were displaced. One side fell and the other side surged upward, creating the ditch-like scarp. As previously noted, Idaho is still *messing* around, ingeniously rearranging its landforms.

Everyone throughout the Northern Rockies felt the quake, which destroyed some buildings in the town of Challis fifty miles distant. It snapped chimneys in western Montana and even affected the eruption of Old Faithful, the geyser in Yellowstone Park. As far as Mt. Borah itself is concerned, only about 250 people hike up to this peak annually, because it has some difficult sections to negotiate and experts recommend that only experienced, well-conditioned climbers attempt the trail ascent. There have been several fatalities noted because of hiker inexperience and bad weather.

What with the rain and the mountain's reputation, our decision was easy to make: no climbing that day; instead, we drove north toward Salmon, finally leaving the rainy weather, and camped along a small creek in a tree-enclosed pasture. After a dry and peaceful night's rest beside the gurgling stream and a breakfast of hot pancakes and thick, juicy bacon, we drove a few miles farther north to where the road ended, about eight miles off the main highway, at the remote and tiny community of Shoup, whose country store was its lone building. The main fork of the Salmon

River turns west in this vicinity and eventually connects with the Snake River, which ultimately joins the Columbia River on the western edge of Idaho near the recreational town of Riggins. Historically the Salmon River has produced about 40 percent of the steelhead and Chinook salmon of the Columbia River Basin.

Upon seeing this section of the Salmon River for the first time, with the many rock obstacles in its heavily forested canyon channel and the fast-moving water, we could understand why it is called The River of No Return. Lewis and Clark started their trip down this river but turned back because it was impossible to navigate safely. They opted to go overland on heavily forested mountain ridges, which should demonstrate further evidence of the river's severity.

Mack and Jim, their sweet tooths aching from the lack of dessert, decided to purchase large ice cream cones at the North Fork country store and indulge their ravaging appetite for sugary sustenance. Frankly, I was amazed that this little, remote store would have homemade ice cream for sale. Finally sated after consuming their treat in record time, we left and headed south toward Stanley through Yankee fork by way of Challis on a cross-country dirt road. This scenic drive took us off the beaten path through the remote ghost towns of Custer Centennial Park and Bonanza, homes of a mining museum and gold dredge.

After exploring these locations, we drove south to the Salmon River, about eight miles from Stanley, and located an open campsite by the edge of the river, where we would stay the night. The next day we drove through Stanley and into Iron Creek Canyon to hike up to Sawtooth Lake, in the Sawtooth Mountains; this is one of the most scenic lakes in this part of the country. As we started the hike, we met some cowboys on horseback carrying rifles and pistols. They were not on a hunting trip, they informed us, but were doing some recreational horseback trailblazing. We asked about their weapons, and they told us cougars were roaming the area and had recently attacked some local domestic animals. They were not hunting the cougars, they said, but were carrying the weapons for self-defense. They also said the cougars had recently been so bold as to track several hikers in the area, too. *Here we go again, into the valley of death,* we thought. The cowboys told us to be watchful and we should be safe; however, *they* had guns and we didn't.

With that warning we started our five-mile climb up the nine-thousand-foot mountain to the lake. We had hiked some two hours when we came to a stream that we were unable to cross because of the heavy water runoff from the melting snow accumulation. After several unsuccessful attempts to ford the torrent of water, we gave up and hiked back to the trailhead at the Iron Creek campground. We did not normally give in that easily and we were determined to reach the lake, so studying our maps, we discovered another trailhead about fifty miles away in the recreational community of Grandjean. This little sporting area is considered to be the back door into the Sawtooth Mountains.

After driving to the trailhead and starting up the mountain, once again, after two hours of climbing, we ran into another stream on that side of the mountain that was even more treacherous than the previous one. We were unable to cross and finally retreated back to Granjean to lick our wounds and put salve on our pride. It was bad! Here we were, three seasoned outdoor aficionados, and we couldn't get across a couple of small streams, albeit, fed by piles of snow that that had accumulated through the winter.

We had hiked for more than four hours and driven fifty miles without coming close to our ultimate destination. There had been a record snowfall that year, now it was in the middle of June, and it was still melting. Most all of the mountain waterways were overflowing. This small fact was discovered later, after we had returned to Sun Valley. The only positive of the day was that we had seen no cougars. Of course, they probably heard us beating around.

We drove back toward Stanley, as it was getting late, and decided to camp on a barren hill overlooking the town. We had a great view of the Sawtooth Valley, the surrounding mountains, and even the flickering lights from Stanley, about three miles east of our site.

Jim and Mack positioned their tent on the highest point of the hill, to command the wonderful view of the surrounding terrain. I found a small depression on the edge of some trees, on the hillside, and set up under a large pine tree. Then we put up a tarp to shelter or cook in the "remote" possibility of rain. Entertainingly, those other two experienced explorers had insisted on placing their tent on the hilltop, even as extremely dark clouds were rolling up the valley directly toward us. Casually I remarked that I didn't think they were in the choicest of locations if that storm was to continue on its present course. Being smart-asses, they ignored this wise sage and persisted with their efforts in creating a disaster looking for a place to happen, and it would. The disaster, in the guise of the ever-darkening sky, moved inexorably toward our campsite. Then suddenly, it slammed us with all of its wild, frenzied fury, a violent wind smashing arsenals of rain and hail into our camp.

It was so brutal and overwhelming that we jumped into our jeep for protection. The wind rocked the vehicle back and forth as if it might be blown over on its side. We sat and watched as it ripped my buddies' tent with all their gear—sleeping bags and packs—from its moorings, catapulting it past the front of the car into the trees, whose branches held it tight, but the rest of their stuff was flying in every direction. As their things flew by the front of the car, I was reminded of a scene from the 1939 movie *The Wizard of Oz*, when Dorothy was looking out the window of her house, which had been snatched up by a tornado, and saw all sorts of things—chickens, animals, buildings, and farm equipment—being carried away by the blistering wind. Our scene from the car was much like that, although the vehicle, thankfully, stayed on the ground. It was really a very funny sight, at least to me.

After all these years, I can't remember exactly what I said, but it was probably something like, "I told you what would happen, but no, you guys wouldn't listen to me." If those weren't my exact words, they had to be pretty similar. By the way, my little one-man tent remained secure on the opposite hillside under the tree, where I had "naturally" so perfectly placed it. After the rains had passed, they gathered the tent and their gear off the tree limbs and ground and set up again in a more appropriate location, probably under my tutelage; at least that's my story, and I'll never let them forget it.

We fixed a beef stew and cabbage slaw for dinner under our tarp, which fortunately had also been erected on the opposite side of the hill also, away from the oncoming storm. It had also stayed erect. We ate every morsel of food and then crashed in our sleeping bags. It had been one of those days to remember, and we had done about everything we could, both good and bad (mostly bad), to make it so. The next morning we headed back through Stanley and then south toward Ketchum and Sun Valley on the scenic byway.

▼

Stanley is a tiny settlement sequestered between the Sawtooth Mountains and the Salmon River. When I first visited, the population was only eighty-three people, according to the welcome sign on the side of the highway, and that was probably an overstatement of the facts. It has dirt streets, rustic log buildings, a few convenience stores, a couple of eateries, some outfitters, and an old hotel with hitching posts at the entrance. The town is located about 120 miles from Boise and sixty miles from Ketchum on Scenic Byway 75.

Upon entering Stanley from the south, the road forks; Highway 21 goes west toward Boise, and Highway 75 travels north along the Salmon River toward Challis and on to Salmon. It is situated in a wide river valley, carved by the Salmon River, surrounded by the Sawtooth Mountains. The views are unrivaled. This small outpost hums all summer with hikers, campers, river runners, and tourists. In the winter months, it is frequently contained within its own borders and closed off from any traffic, going or coming, because of the heavy snowfall. Although beautiful, it must be lonely there during those months. One of the major activities in the winter, coordinated by the local female population, is quilt-making.

▼

Driving south toward Ketchum through Sawtooth Valley, we reveled in the magnificent views of the Sawtooth Mountain Range. These mountains are part of the Idaho Batholith; the extruded granite was formed millions of years ago from the hot magnum released from below the earth's surface during the tectonic-plate movement. This entire region is part of the Sawtooth Wilderness. Glacial ice sculptured these mountains, whose sharp peaks resemble the cutting edge of a serrated saw. The mountains are best viewed from Galena Summit, from its elevation of 8,771 feet, located on Highway 75 halfway between Ketchum and Stanley. The Sawtooths, eighteen miles wide and thirty-two miles long, contain over two hundred lakes and literally hundreds of hiking trails crisscrossing this rugged topography. We hiked into several of the larger lakes—Redfish, Alturas, Petit—as well as Hell Roaring Lake, which was enclosed by mountains and a unique rock formation called the Fickle Finger of Fate.

The trailhead to this lake is reached by traveling on the worst dirt road that I have ever experienced in all my years in the backcountry. It was so rutted from snow and water drainage, we could only creep along at about ten miles an hour, and still we thought our jeep was going to come apart from all those bumps and deep holes in the road; a passenger car could not negotiate this road under any circumstances.

Arriving at the trailhead, we hiked up to the lake, surrounded by gorgeous mountains; the view of the Fickle Finger of Fate rock formation was awesome. We spent considerable time exploring around the water's edge and then returned to our vehicle for another bone-shattering drive back to the highway. Unfortunately, this access dirt road has never been repaired even after all these years, so I have never returned to the lake; it was just too much trouble and too uncomfortable to undertake again; however, it is a beautiful area and a must-see if you can endure the terrible drive.

We then drove farther south to the base of Galena Summit and established a campsite in a valley just below the summit, where the headwaters of the Salmon River originate, flowing down from the mountains to the south; and it follows the descending terrain and flows north.

The river forms here from the water runoff of the Smoky Mountain Range, immediately south of our location, and is fed by several larger rivers as it flows north. At 425 miles long, the river flows through north-central Idaho and drops more than seven thousand feet in elevation from its headwaters at Galena before it collides with the Snake River in Hells Canyon on the Oregon border.

The Sawtooth Fish Hatchery was located just a few miles north of our campsite on the Salmon River. The hatchery traps and holds Chinook salmon and steelhead trout, which produce eggs for transmission to other hatcheries. Each year the hatchery releases millions of small fish and eggs into the Salmon River, and they migrate from Idaho through the river system of the Columbia Basin and on to the Pacific Ocean, where the fish sexually mature. Afterward they return to their original habitat in Idaho, traveling almost nine hundred miles upstream, gaining seven thousand feet in elevation, where they spawn.

That night I fixed spaghetti for the troops, inadvertently spilling the meat sauce on the ground in a pine tree grove of trees. (I had hoped my buddies wouldn't see my mishap, but they did, damn it.) We ate it anyway, of course, after a bit of hazing and slander was tossed my way. It was still tasty, and Jim Box said that he liked the natural pine nuts mixed in with the pine straw off the ground. I told him it was natural fiber and was good for his health. He didn't buy my story. The next morning we drove south across Galena Summit, enjoying the final views of the Sawtooths. One more hike was planned in the Boulder Mountains, just a few miles north of Ketchum. This seven-mile round-trip hike started at around 7300 feet and had an elevation gain of 2,200 feet and would take us into Boulder Basin to an eventual elevation of 9,500 feet.

In the basin, which was enclosed by steep mountainious terrain, we found remnants of Idaho's mining history in an old historic mining town, Boulder City, built in the 1890s, which had remained active until 1950. Several dilapidated buildings still stand, along with a large, primitive wooden trough used to move the mined ore down the side of the mountain to mule-driven wagons for transportation. There was also some old rusty mining equipment found lying among these remains. A few cabins used by the miners were still standing, and some were in fair condition. It is a great hike for the curious explorer! We searched around the old city in hope of finding some interesting artifacts, took pictures of the old structures, and climbed up on a few surrounding ridges to get a better view of the entire basin area. Afterward we hiked back down the mountain on a gravel road to our vehicle and then drove on to Ketchum.

I was desirous of making another hike that day and suggested to my companions that we take a short trek along the Big Wood River, which runs directly through Ketchum. The headwaters of this river begin on the southwest side of Galena Summit, flows South, and ultimately empty into the Snake River near Twin Falls, some seventy-five miles distant.

It is a great fly-fishing river and is known for its abundant population of rainbow trout. We chose the Fox Creek Loop Trail, only four miles from town. I must admit that I tricked them, because after walking on a flat trail along the river, the trail meandered into the Smoky Mountain Range, requiring a few steep climbs on several switchbacks as we gained almost a thousand feet of elevation.

We finished the six-mile hike a bit hot and sweaty. (I had told them it was only three miles.) The boys were somewhat disturbed with me, but I suppose I wanted to get even with them for the slanderous comments they had made about my cooking abilities after the accident with the spaghetti sauce the previous night. Be that as it may, this is one of the most scenic and popular hikes in the area. Besides its route along the river, it also passes through high-altitude aspen groves, fields of sage, and wildflowers. I took them to a shower to clean up, then to a restaurant for lunch, and after all that attention, I'm pretty certain, but not totally, that all was soon forgotten. The entire trip had been a big success. We had seen some interesting terrain, learned a great deal about the area, taken scenic hikes, and camped and visited some great locations. Jim and Mack flew out later in the day, and I went to my business meeting.

We would not return to the Sun Valley area for a couple of years, but as I have indicated, I had pretty much decided this was the place for me to spend more of my leisure time. However, to be on the safe side, I also thought it would be a good idea to keep exploring other possibilities; after all, something better might just be out there someplace; however, if it was, I couldn't find it.

We continued with our explorations, though, and I kept searching. Finally, in 1995, after visiting many other parts of the West, I bought a townhome in Sun Valley. It was to be the start of a beautiful friendship that still exists today, although I no longer own the house. I still visit the Sun Valley area every summer for several weeks and hike as much as my aging and creaking knees will now allow. Various members of our explorer group probably made more than a dozen trips to different sections of Idaho over the years of our peripatetic journeys, and while I owned my home, it served as a kind of base camp for us to operate from in Idaho, as did Mack's home in Bozeman, Montana.

▼

The terrain around the Sun Valley area offers an unusual blend of features. Five mountain ranges lie within the region, which is located on the northern edge of the Great Basin Desert. Because we hiked and camped in all these ranges, it may be helpful for me to describe their location, proximity to each other, some idea of their sizes and elevations, and the general climate.

The Pioneer Mountains are located east of Sun Valley and are only twelve by twenty miles in total size. These rugged mountains range in elevation from nine thousand feet to eleven thousand feet, offering wonderful hiking trails with fantastic views.

The Smoky Mountains got their name as a result of a fire in the 1800s that left a constant cloudy-like haze over them. Located west and northwest of Ketchum, they have several peaks over ten thousand feet elevation. Bald Mountain, at 9,100-feet elevation, is part of this range, and along with the Sun Valley Resort is possibly one of the most popular skiing locations in the West.

The Boulder Mountains, where Boulder City is located, are situated north of Sun Valley and south of Galena Summit. They are prominently viewed along Scenic Route 75 heading toward Stanley. Ryan Peak is the highest in this range, at an elevation of 11,714 feet.

The White Cloud Mountains are north of the Boulder Mountains on the northeastern side of Galena Summit in the Sawtooth Valley. Many of the mountains in this range are over eleven thousand feet high, with Castle Peak rising majestically to 11,815 feet. They lie opposite the Sawtooth Range, immediately to their west.

The Sawtooth Mountains, first seen when crossing Galena Summit traveling north, run for thirty-two miles to Stanley. Their serrated peaks, carved from glacial ice, provide a fitting name for this range because the peaks resemble the cutting edge of a saw. Thompson Peak is the tallest mountain in the range at 10,751 feet.

The area's semiarid climate results from several factors: the moderate snowfall, spring water runoff, minimal rain, and the high altitude, ranging from 5,700 feet in the valley to almost twelve thousand feet in the surrounding mountains. This high elevation can create serious skin problems for unwary outdoor enthusiasts during the summer months, because of the sun's thermals; using sunblock is a must.

Lodgepole pine covers many of the slopes, while cottonwood trees grow along the valley streams; abundant groves of golden aspen are found snuggled in the valleys and on the mountain slopes. The numerous alpine lakes and mountain meadows flourish with wildflowers in the summer. Many of these features offer marvelous views of the surrounding landscape, as well as the perfect location for a peaceful respite for the wandering explorer. Snowfall can easily exceed two hundred inches, and the heavy snowmelt runoff is the reason why many of the trails are closed until midsummer.

▼

On one of our later trips, we opted to drive from Sun Valley and again attempt to climb up to Sawtooth Lake. It was in July, the snow and runoff were no longer a problem, and we finally made it on what was then our third attempt. It is one of the most beautiful hikes in the area, and the five-mile ascent offers superb views of Stanley and parts of the Sawtooth Valley. Several members of our group have made this hike more than six times. It is strenuous and the downhill takes its toll on the knees, but the scenic reward makes it all worthwhile. After spending the night, we drove to the westernmost part of Idaho, to Hell's Canyon and the Seven Devils Mountains.

These mountains extend along the Oregon and Idaho borders for approximately forty miles. They are bounded by the Snake River on the west and the Salmon River on the east, and they rank high among Idaho's mountain ranges for their ruggedness and beauty; they are the state's most precipitous mountain range. Named after a Nez Perce Indian legend about a young brave who supposedly encountered seven devils, one after another, while hunting in these mountains many years ago, the mountains are appropriately named Devils Tooth, Tower of Babel, She Devil, He Devil, The Goblin, Mount Ogre, and Devils Throne.

The dirt road leading to the mountains was a near-repeat of the one we took to the Fickle Finger of Fate, very rutted and nearly washed out. It took an inordinate amount of driving time to make the trip up to a camping area. There was a better route, but of course, we took the worst one in the entire area. We must have had either a high tolerance for pain or a terrible propensity to find the most horrid roads available to take us into the wilderness.

We saw no devils during our stay, but we heard noises and thought we had seen an apparition prowling in the night. These unusual events occurred after several cocktails. The sprits were definitely there, but they were probably all in our tin drinking cups.

We stayed two days, camped in a small saddle to protect us from the wind, and hiked around the ledges and across several interesting high-elevation plateaus. General mountain hiking and climbing in this region is a combination of sloshing through talus (rock rubble), boulder hopping, and climbing up short, broken ledges.

After all the hiking and climbing, we headed toward Sun Valley across a maze of dirt roads that took us through the small community of Atlanta, Idaho (not Georgia), in the middle of nowhere, spent one more night camping, and finally emerged in our filthy, dust-covered vehicle in Warm Springs, the ski area next door to Ketchum.

On one of these overnight stay-overs while reconnoitering the area, I was walking along a trail on the low side of a ridge when an unusual sensation struck me. A sudden urge compelled me to crawl under the drooping, limbs of a large fir tree. For some reason, still unknown to me, I felt that something was concealed beneath those sprawling branches. It just didn't look natural, if that is possible. So, I crawled under the limbs to look around; inside it had the makings of a shelter, born of Mother Nature, and was about the same shape and size of a small two-man tent; this arrangement would have provided excellent protection from the elements. It appeared as if someone had used the space for that purpose—how long ago, it was impossible to tell. But true to my earlier feelings, I found a small rolled-up bundle, almost like a pillow, lying next to the trunk of the tree. Curious I unrolled it and discovered a North Face weatherproof jacket that was like new and in excellent condition.

Had someone forgotten it when they packed their gear, possibly in the dark, after having spent the night under the limbs of the tree for protection from the elements, and would they return looking for it at some later date? It was impossible to make a judgment. We were far into the wilderness, and after considering the choices and the amount of gear that I had lost on my many backcountry trips, I considered it to be a fair trade-off and decided to keep it as a memento. The jacket is in my closet today, is still in great condition, and is worn frequently. Just the other day, Jim Box asked me about it, and we replayed the story about how and when it was discovered. Frankly, I believe he was trying to talk me into giving it to him.

▼

Intuition is an unusual feature of the mind. It can be very helpful if one listens and responds properly. It can also lead a person into harm's way if they are not careful. One example was when I stepped on the trip wire of a booby trap in Vietnam as we approached a village on a small trail during a search and destroy mission. Immediately my intuition told me to get the hell out of there when I saw the wire under the toe of my boot leading over to a suspicious- looking bush on the trail where the device was concealed. I did quickly and that saved my life.

On another search-and-destroy mission, I was searching though some woods when I noticed an odd-looking spot on the ground; what was odd about it is impossible for me to say. It just did not resemble the other ground around it. I probed it with my knife, thinking it might be a hidden explosive ready to kill or harm the first person to step on it. As I sank my bayonet-type knife into the ground looking for a wire or some other distinguishing feature, it struck something solid that sounded and felt like wood. I carefully and slowly cleared the debris away, naturally, not wanting to set it off if it was an explosive of some kind. Beneath the cleared area, I found a small square, wooden door no more than two feet wide. Using the edge of my bladed knife, I checked for wires; finding none, I slowly lifted the door. A brown face with a small, partially clad, lean body popped up out of the hole, almost scaring the crap out of me. It was a North Vietnamese soldier in hiding.

To this day I don't know why I didn't immediately, mostly out of my own fear, plunge my knife into him. Perhaps he scared me so badly that I was unable to do anything but grab him. Probably as frightened as I was, he did not resist. He had a rifle and ammo with him, so he could have easily shot me without any premeditation whatsoever. I kept his rifle, just as I kept the jacket found in Idaho some years later, and sent it home as a war trophy—a reminder that it could have ended my young life at that very moment. Incidentally, it was an American weapon, a 30-caliber carbine rifle.

After I took him prisoner, he was sent to the rear area for interrogation. But before we released him, he did tell us where a cache of arms, supplies, and munitions was buried. We dug them up and promptly disposed of them with some explosives before they could be used against any other American troops.

Was this stupidity on my part? Or was I just doing my job, considering that we took a prisoner and gained vital information about locating hidden arms, maybe even saving some lives in the process? I don't know the answer, but I would like to think my actions were proper. I do know that I followed my intuition, and it worked that time. Thankfully, it worked for me and not my enemy.

On another combat mission in Vietnam, we were pursuing the NVA when we came to a fork in the trail. One section of the trail went north toward the DMZ, only a few miles away; the other went off in a westerly direction. My lead platoon commander asked which way to go. I looked at the ground, the trails, and for no reason that I could specify at the moment other than the northern trail looked somehow unusual to me, I told him to proceed north.

We had gone no farther than five hundred yards when we took rifle fire on our rear security unit from a sniper who was hidden in a concealed spider hole. He jumped from the hole and ran as soon as we determined his position. Several of us nearby gave chase across a wide, open plain, but we could not catch him or bring him down with our firepower. He was in short pants and running like a sprinter.

Returning to our original position with the rest of my command, we resumed our march, and within one hundred yards, my company ran into a unit of NVA soldiers heavily concealed in fortified positions. A firefight ensued, and we permanently eliminated seven of the entrenched enemy. Several of the NVA soldiers jumped out of their bunkers and ran. We could not determine the exact number or bring them down as they scattered and ran like zigzagging rabbits through the dense foliage. The first enemy contact had obviously been their listening or security outpost, tactically situated to alert the others of our approach. We did not realize that at the time. Fortunately, we did not take any casualties during these hostilities.

However, a few hours later on the return trip to our base camp, several miles distant from the first enemy contact, we ran into another bunker. Three more enemy soldiers were eliminated during a heavy firefight and grenade-tossing exercise by both parties. My unit, Mike Company, took two casualties during the attack, but thankfully, their wounds were minor and they were fit for full duty within two days.

Please keep in mind that our job was to search for and destroy the enemy. We had done just that and accomplished our mission on that particular day primarily because of a hunch, an instinct, or more appropriately, from a deep-seated intuitive consciousness. I have always believed that a person's feelings or intuition are probably the best advice that one can ever hope to receive. They should listen to the message very carefully and cautiously when they hear it. But it must be evaluated and acted on maturely and intellectually. I have been fortunate, as my internal messages have served me well in some highly unusual situations and importantly to me, saved my life.

One summer when I was living in Sun Valley, Jim, his oldest son, Andy, and my son, Chris, flew out for some exploration in the mountains of Idaho. It would be a trip to remember, because over a five-day period, we would hike over sixty miles in some of the most rugged mountainous terrain in the entire area.

My scheduled program, which could be questionable at times (meaning pushing everyone to their limit, including me), incorporated a hike within two hours after they had arrived from Atlanta following their six-hour early-morning flight. Upon arriving around noon, they purchased food stuffs, packed their gear, and filled water cans; and at about three o'clock that afternoon, we hit the trail for a nine-mile hike in the Pioneer Mountains. Afterward the guys referred to this trek as the Idaho *death* march. Actually, they were beat when we started the hike.

The first leg of this loop hike went up to an old skier's cabin (pioneer cabin) built in 1937 to house people who liked to trek up the snow-covered trail to ski the powder bowls of the various mountain ranges. It was a challenging and difficult climb because of the steep five mile trail starting at about 6,000 feet to the summit at 9,500 feet. Once the ascent to the peak was completed, the trail traversed around a mountainside and then steeply descended into a deep ravine. It was necessary to make the descent by mostly scooting down to the bottom on our fannies. At the bottom the trail went up one side of an abrupt incline to a saddle, and then followed a very long downhill path for two miles that pounded and stressed the knee joint into near submission. This part of the trail was called the Long Gulch Pioneer Cabin Loop.

We completed the hike as dusk was settling, around eight o'clock, and then drove for forty-five minutes up a steep, scenic, car-battering road to a rustic campground at Summit Creek in Copper Basin. Tired and dirty after the strenuous hike, with darkness rapidly descending on us, we wanted and needed to find a quick and easy campsite to pack in for the night.

After that exhausting day, my ill-conceived plan backfired on me when I was awakened by the worst leg cramps that I had ever experienced. I was screaming with pain so loudly that Jim thought a bear had gotten to me. In fact, it hurt so terribly and my hamstring had tightened up so much that I was incapable of pulling myself out of the tent. Jim and his son had to drag me out so that my leg could be straightened and then massaged to alleviate the constricting pain. It took almost thirty minutes' massage before the cramps released and I could walk around. I deserved what I got, though, because I was not conditioned for that much climbing and stress on my old beaten-down legs and should have planned an easier first day—for all of us.

Of course, the problem may have been easily caused as well by a slight case of dehydration. The day had been very hot, and we had been on the go for the entire time; we did not even take a break after we reached Pioneer Cabin. Also, I had not been in the area myself for more than a week and was not acclimatized to the elevation, and neither were my fellow explorers for that matter. Nor did any of us drink much water during the hike, perhaps no more than a quart or one canteen. In the future I would keep my body hydrated—a good lesson learned the hard way.

The following morning, a bit refreshed after the ghastly nocturnal experience, the four of us hiked into Kane Lake, at an elevation of 9,260 feet. This hike was located only a few miles distant from our previous night's campsite. The drive into the trailhead was extremely rough, and we were forced to ford a stream in our vehicle on three separate occasions. The road is so bad that it is impassable until midsummer.

This hike was eight miles round-trip and was rated as difficult. After the first two miles, the trail, more or less, just goes up, up, and still more up, never stopping its ascent until topping out at the lake. There were three talus-slope crossings to navigate, which added some interesting flavor to our struggles as we clambered over the fields of boulders. Numerous cairns were located among the rocky features for direction (bless the souls who construct these stone markers); otherwise, it would have been very difficult to find our way. Later, we learned Kane Lake had an unusual nickname. Because of all the boulder crossings, steepness, and the terrible road into the trailhead, it is often referred to as Pain Lake.

We returned to the same campsite for a second night and slept peacefully, although our group was somewhat exhausted from the two days of challenging hikes and breath-sucking elevation.

The next morning would be somewhat easier when we undertook our third hike in the Pioneer Mountains; however, on this hike we would see a large brown bear eating his breakfast (brown bears are frequently found throughout Idaho). We hiked into Summit Creek, with its elevation of 9,400 feet, and this trek was not as difficult as the previous hikes. We were rewarded with a comfortable walk through a high-altitude meadow before reaching our destination, a spectacular alpine lake nestled in a valley at the base of a mountain.

It was on the way in when we saw the bear, fortunately at some distance away, foraging along a small creek. Watching closely we waited until the animal moved away into a thicket before working our way around the area by climbing into an open space on the side of a steep mountain slope. This high ground provided a good view into his domain, and we felt a little safer as we quickly and wisely put as much distance as we could between us and him. On the return we stayed in the open as much as possible and ended the hike by climbing high into a saddle and crossing over another mountain to ensure that we did not have another friendly encounter with the bear. It worked. We did not see him again.

That night we repositioned our campsite closer to our fourth and final hike in the Pioneers. After driving twenty miles up a deserted canyon to the end of the North Fork of the Big Lost River, we established a campsite on the banks of the stream in a group of trees. This site was convenient to the trailhead of our next hike; it had water, cover, and a view, so it was just fine.

The Big Lost River has rightfully earned its name, because it does get lost flowing out of the Pioneer and Boulder Mountains. It flows south onto the Snake River Plain and then submerges into the porous basalt flows. Once underground the water continues through the rubbery zones in the basalt before finally emerging to join the Snake River near Twin Falls, Idaho some ninety miles distant.

▼

We had planned to hike up to Herd Peak, elevation 9,860 feet, and return on the same trail for a total of ten miles. The elevation gain was almost 2,700 feet. Because of the almost vertical climb of the last two miles of the hike, it took us several hours to negotiate the trek to the barren mountaintop. Frequent rest and drinking stops were the order of the day; after my experience with the cramps, everyone in the group made certain they consumed plenty of water during the entire climb.

Once on the treeless plateau-like summit, the vastness of the land below and the scenic views of the surrounding Pioneer and Boulder Mountains held us in awe. Walking around looking for whatever we could find, I came across a discarded geological marker lying on a pile of loose rocks. It no longer served any purpose, as far as I could determine, and it, like the jacket I had found under the tree on that earlier trip, quickly became a coveted memento of this trip. Now we had to decide on the route we wanted to take back to the trailhead, for we found no joy in our hearts for backtracking on the laborious trail we had just walked.

Studying our map we decided to bushwhack across several ridges, saddles, and finally down some switchbacks that would take us into Tool Box Canyon, where we would exit a half mile from our original starting point; all of this was easier said than done, we would soon discover. What we could not or did not discern from the map was the number of hidden, steep drop-offs, unassailable rock walls, and dense thickets that we would encounter and have to negotiate around after we started our trek down the mountain. We were required to backtrack on several occasions, sometimes totally retracing our steps back to our last departure point and starting over again in a different direction.

Finally, reaching the canyon bottom, we had a two-mile relatively benign hike down a dry streambed to the trailhead. The first three miles, as previously described, were a ballbuster. Lesson learned: If you don't know how to read and interpret a map or a compass, learn or suffer! We did, and we still suffered. It was a bitch of a hike, but fun nevertheless.

In four days we had now hiked over thirty-five miles at high elevations. Needless to say, the group was doing very well with the challenging wilderness program that had been forced on them. The car-battering treacherous road we traveled from Sun Valley to Copper Basin, where we initially started our hikes, is very rough and full of sharp, pointed rocks. It is also dangerous because it is a narrow, slippery gravel road with a step drop-off on one side that falls three thousand feet. The trip up to the summit from the valley floor below is fourteen long miles. This road is a disaster looking for a place to happen, and it usually does in the form of a rock-punctured flat tire. It did for us; we ended up with two flats, one a result of the trip into Kane Lake the other fom the mountain road.

After our hike to Herd Peak, we returned to our campsite by the Big Lost River and spent the night. The next morning we found the first flat tire and, on inspection, saw that another one seemed to be headed in the same direction. Our only spare tire, now in use, we knew we needed to get to a gas station ASAP; otherwise, we would be doing a lot of unnecessary walking. Immediately we drove out of the basin, about forty miles to the town of Mackay, hoping to find a service station. It was Saturday morning and we did find one, but we had to wait almost five hours to get the two tires patched.

Our travels then took us toward Stanley, a one-hundred-mile drive through some beautiful backcountry. Nearing the town we stopped at a pool of hot springs bubbling in the Salmon River on the Scenic Byway SR 75. Heaving our tired, worn bodies into the hot river water of about 110 degrees, we enjoyed a most relaxing and revitalizing soak until we were soothed and mellow. It was pretty much standard fare for our group to both bathe and soak in any hot springs whenever we came upon them. Sometimes that would be the only bath we would have for several days, unless we had encountered other streams along our travels. This soaking helped restore our tired muscles for the continued arduous activity ahead.

▼

On another trip, Jim, Terry, Steve, and I were on an excursion in northern Idaho when we stopped for provisions and learned that some hot springs were near our ultimate destination. Within record time we had found the trailhead, grabbed our bathing suits and towels, and hiked back into the woods toward the springs. About a mile down the trail, we suddenly emerged from the woods into a broad opening with a stream flowing though the center with pools of steaming, hot water scattered throughout the streambed. Much to our surprise, most of the pools were occupied by people—all in the *nude*! Apparently these people either belonged to a nudist colony or practiced nudity as a wilderness lifestyle.

Shocked and amazed, we four stood there letting it sink in. Finally, regaining our composure, we looked at each other. "Oh hell, when in Rome, be Roman," we said. Dropping our suits, towels, and clothes on the ground, we walked nonchalantly toward the pools, each of us selecting a different one, and climbed in with the rest of the people and enjoyed the day. Actually, we *really* enjoyed it. No more details are needed about this experience, except to report that everyone was friendly and comfortable with themselves and us, the wayward intruders. After about an hour, our eyeballs, had absorbed all the pleasure they could stand. We packed up and hiked out.

This was the only time during all of our wilderness adventures that we had this kind of experience, although there was one similar episode that occurred on a trip with Mack, Steve, Jim, and me on one of our many trips to Colorado.

Somehow we ended up in Steamboat Springs and decided to visit Strawberry Park, seven miles from the town, with its fabulous hot springs pool. It was snowing at the time and quite cold as we drove up the mountain toward the park. When we arrived, the attendant directed us into a large Indian teepee; this was the dressing area!

Hitting the hot pool of water, we enjoyed ourselves for a while, although the other people's behavior did seem a bit unusual. It was hard to describe, but somehow they were different. Or maybe we were different. Anyway, when I went back to the tent to change clothes and was sitting on a bench fully exposed, a woman walked in, surprising the hell out of me. She sat down immediately across from me and began to change her clothes, seemingly oblivious of my presence. Frankly, I didn't know how to handle the situation, so I covered my privates with a towel while she dressed calmly and casually, apparently not realizing that she was simultaneously both entertaining and embarrassing me. The only communication that passed between us was "hello." Were other options available? Who knows, and I didn't care to ask. When she finished she left me sitting there with my towel still on my lap, wondering what that was all about. Apparently this was one of those places that were also liberal about nudity, although everyone in the pool was clothed, but still suspicious-looking. Oh well, it takes all kinds to make a world.

▼

After our relaxation in the steaming hot water of the Salmon River, we drove to Iron Creek, a few miles west of Stanley, to select a campsite close to the trailhead of our backcountry trek. We found a great site in a wooded area near a small stream, far from the crowds.

The next morning Jim and I planned to take our boys on a climb up to Sawtooth Lake, their first visit, our fifth. It would turn out to be the longest hike of the trip, over eighteen miles. Usually this hike is ten miles round-trip; the elevation gain is 1,720 feet, and the high point is 8,430 feet. The lake is located in the Sawtooth National Forest, and as indicated earlier, is the most scenic and photogenic of all the lakes in this distinctive mountain range. It is also one of the most remote lakes in these mountains. It is a steady uphill climb to the top, but the scenery along the way, the views of the Sawtooths and the deep valleys below, occupy a lot of space and time in your mind as you hike along this steep, winding trail.

Once we reached the lake after about a three-hour scramble up the mountain, still feeling refreshed from the previous day's soak in the hot springs, we elected to continue the hike through a pass at the far end of this large body of water toward Mount Regan, which has an elevation of 10,190 feet. This trail, climbing high above the southern bank of the lake, provided a wide-angle panoramic view of the entire basin as we walked along. As we neared the far edge of the lake after walking the entire length of Sawtooth, the trail descended sharply, taking us closer to the sparkling-clean, azure water.

I believe this lake, with its clear, sky-blue color, surrounded by mountains, with an open-ended scenic pass at the far edge of the lake, is without question one of the most picturesque spots in the Western mountains. I have made this hike at least a dozen times over the years and will continue to visit this lake yearly as long as my badly worn knees will allow me to make the climb. It is just too beautiful to pass up; every trip is an adventure within itself.

We hiked through the pass and emerged into a barren, desertlike landscape that represented some distant planet; it seemed as if we had momentarily departed the earth. After some exploratory hiking, we retraced our steps along the edge of the lake and returned to our original staring point. Continuing on, we decided to hike on toward McGowan Lakes; this trail took us up a steep hill crisscrossed with sharp switchbacks. Upon reaching the crest, after about two miles of the strenuous climb, we stopped and were pleasantly surprised by the far-reaching views of the town of Stanley and on into the Sawtooth Valley.

Concluding this was a good turnaround point in our trek, we rested briefly and then started downhill, departing Sawtooth, and headed to Alpine Lake, which was somewhat off the main trail, hidden on the side of a deep ridge. It is also a lovely lake to visit, sequestered at the end of a heavily forested ravine. After a short rest and some trail mix, our only meal of the day, we hiked back to the main trail and continued our walk back to Iron Creek where we had camped. As we approached the trailhead, our final destination, the four of us were limping badly—from both the long hike and the downhill knee-crunching trail which does contain switchbacks.

During the hike I had promised Jim, Andy, and Chris that if they completed this *killer* day, I would take them to Stanley for a night on the town. Motivated by the opportunity to relax a bit and have a juicy steak dinner, they were lured into the challenge and gave their best during the entire day. There was no bitching or complaining by anyone. After returning to our camp, we washed off our sweaty bodies, doctored our sore feet, and went to town in our cleanest, dirty clothes; it was not a long drawn-out evening, we had dinner and that was it. We were far too worn out to engage in much merriment of any nature.

The next day we were still tired and sore, so we spent most of the afternoon swimming and napping at Alturas Lake sequestered between two mountains about half-way back to Sun Valley. It was about all we could do with our tired, sore, beaten-up bodies. Recovering somewhat we drove farther south toward Galena Summit and established a campsite with a great view of the Sawtooth Mountains. One more hike was left on our schedule, and if we were physically able, we would tackle it the next day.

When the morning rolled around, we pulled our still-tired bodies out of our tents. (It was not a pretty sight; we were all creaking a bit when we stood up and walked around.) Fixing coffee and breakfast while procrastinating heavily, we finally decided to just go do it. Breaking camp we drove ten miles up a dusty dirt road called Fourth of July to the trailhead. (This was one of those places in the West that no one could get to until about mid-July, because of its elevation and snowmelt.)

Our hike was an eight-miler round-trip trek that would take us to the Fourth of July Lake and then cut sharply uphill to a long flat ridge at 9,800 feet. From there the trail descended precipitously down a twisting series of extremely steep switchbacks into Ants Basin. After reaching the basin floor and hiking across this drainage, we stopped for a prolonged lunch of beanie weenies (beans and franks) and candy bars; we needed protein and lots of carbohydrates to keep us going and to get us back to the trailhead.

This is a very nice hike in the White Cloud Mountains (one of the five mountain ranges I described earlier in this commentary), but we were just too damned tired from the efforts put forth over the past several days to fully enjoy this particular quest. Our steps were slow and deliberate trudging back across the basin floor, traversing up the steep mountainside, reaching the top, and working our way back down to the canyon and then on to the jeep. The trip was now officially concluded; we headed back to Sun Valley.

Our explorer group had hiked in excess of *sixty* miles during the week and camped out six nights; except for the few hours of much-needed rest by the lake on the penultimate day of our expedition, we had been on the go the entire time.

Jim and I were extremely proud of our sons, Andy and Chris. They had done a grand job, probably better than the two of us, in handling the demanding program that had been delegated to them. Actually, they were still enthusiastic and full of sprit, and would have continued if time had permitted. Both of the boys were excellent in the backcountry and in good shape, and they knew how to take care of themselves under the most trying conditions. Sure, it had been fun and exhausting, but it had also been oh, so worthwhile! I like to think this was, and is, the type of legacy that a father should share with his son. It is also the kind of learning experience they can later pass on to their own children. Chris has already started to do this with his two boys, and Andy will probably do the same in due course. Sadly, this was the last time the four of us took a wilderness trip together; however, it was one of the most challenging we had ever done, and these experiences would leave each of us with memorable and compelling memories for the rest of our lives.

There was one other adventure trip in Idaho that also had a major impact on several of the explorers; as a matter of fact, it may have been a "Life Changing" point in our lives. Jim, Mack, and I were the "usual suspects" for this particular journey. While I was doing my part-time thing in Idaho, we met in Sun Valley to start our journey. Mack was now living full-time in Bozeman and had driven over to meet Jim, who had flown in from Atlanta, and me for the journey.

For this summertime trip, we had planned to explore northern Idaho more deeply; this was an area we had partially visited on our first jaunt to Idaho. Initially we drove to the Idaho-Montana state line at Chief Joseph Pass and spent that first night on the road camping in the Challis National Forest. Unfortunately a large number of forest fires were burning in the various mountain ranges in this area; consequently, the sky was filled with black smoke, and even the fresh, clean air was inundated with the smell of smoke where no fires burned; the wind could carry the smoke for hundreds of miles. It had been a bad season for fires that summer, and the firefighters were out in force trying to contain them. For some unknown reason, upon arriving at Chief Joseph Pass, we decided to alter our northern advance and proceed though the pass about thirty miles to the Big Hole National Battlefield in Montana.

▼

This site commemorates the battle fought in the summer of 1877, when US calvary troops staged a surprise attack against several bands of Nez Perce Indians, who were led by Chief Joseph. By way of this remote, hidden pass on the Nez Perce trail from Idaho to Montana, the Indians were trying to escape the United States' planned relocation to a reduced-size reservation in Idaho. They had lived for thousands of years in the valleys of the Clearwater and Snake River and their tributaries, and along the Lolo Trail. The Indians had refused to sign a treaty that, because gold had been discovered on the land it was being appropriated by the US government, and would sifnificantly reduce their reservation boundaries to one-tenth of its original size.

The Nez Perce were trying to reach Canada, where they thought they could live peacefully and without any constraint to their way of life. Army troops had pursued them across Idaho for several months until finally engaging them at the Big Hole. Although the native tribes won this bloody battle, they sustained large losses, including the deaths of numerous women and children. After the Big Hole battle, they were finally trapped forty miles from the border of Canada and surrendered. Chief Joseph, after losing so many of his people during the bitter fighting, reportedly said after their capture, "I will fight no more forever."

We viewed the battlefield area, a large open field that contained a number of uncovered teepees (only the tent poles used for supporting the fabric were tied together and standing) erected to memorialize the Nez Perce Indian's trial by fire in Big Hole and ultimate forced dispossession. The entire scene was was very moving and so very sad, because it depicted the unfair practices of our early government in their treatment of the Native Americans of this country over many trying years.

We drove on to the small community of Wisdom, with a population of one hundred people, only a few miles from the battlefield, and found a suitable campsite for the night. The Big Hole River actually flows through this town. Several outfitters located here provided float trips on this popular valley river, along with hiking and camping equipment for the adventure-minded. A small dirt road on the outskirts of Wisdom took us up on a high plateau, which provided an expansive view of the entire Big Hole region. Actually, the Big Hole is often referred to the Valley of Ten Thousand Haystacks, because when the local farmers harvest their enormous crop of hay in July and August, they fill the entire valley with the hay that has been harvested.

We hiked around our mountain base camp that evening and found an outcropping of boulders, and these rocks became our front-row seats for the panoramic view of the valley and the massive sky with its nocturnal dazzling starlight show. The next morning, after a breakfast of cinnamon pancakes and bacon cooked by yours truly, much to the continuing complaint of my associates who ate voraciously, we packed and drove south along the Big Hole River to Jackson, Montana.

It seemed our wandering intuition was now taking us toward a destination that was not yet discernible in our minds. We were apparently on a mission, but to what end? We would find our answer sooner than later. Stopping in Jackson, a small, quaint cow town, what to our wandering eyes should appear but a log lodge building with a large pool fed by some local hot springs. This location and springs were noted in the Lewis and Clark Journals on July 7, 1805: "[A]t the distance of 16 miles we arrived at a Boiling Spring. Situated about 100 paces from a large easterly fork of a small river in a level open plane which heads in the Snowy Mountains to the SE & SW of the springs." Lewis added, "too hot for a man to endure his hand in it for more than 3 seconds." During their stay here, some of his men even cooked meat in the hot, sulfur-tinged waters.

Were we now tracking on the course of Lewis and Clark? It was not apparent to us at that moment, but perhaps subconsciously we had chosen previous explorations that had touched on their trails, but we had not really focused on the depth of their travels or the Corps of Discovery and their contribution to our nation, but soon we would. But now, a dip and a soak in the hot springs seemed like the right thing to do. This was followed by a hot shower with some locally made sweet-smelling soap. It all felt good to our tired, bodies. Then it was time to continue on our undefined quest toward the historic gold and ghost town of Bannack, Montana.

▼

This town was established in 1862, when gold was discovered in the creek where Bannack stands today. This discovery was not only the beginning of the town, but also the state of Montana, which is considered to be one of the last frontiers. Over the years this mining town became a home to ten thousand miners and a haven for outlaws, with the local sheriff leading the gangs. In 1940 it was abandoned and became a ghost town.

Interestingly the ghost-town description may be more appropriate for Bannack because of the cold spots or ghostly images that have reportedly been sighted over the years. An apparition of a teenage girl, killed in a dredge beside a pond, and crying children have been reported a number of times in the old Hotel Meade, built in 1875. The sightings and contacts date back over a hundred years. Numerous other sightings of this young girl have been reported over the intervening periods, along with sightings of ghostly women dressed in their finery of those times. Sixty old structures still stand in Bannack; The state of Montana made it a state park in 1954.

▼

We visited this interesting old town located in a remote, desertlike area along Grasshopper Creek, where gold was initially discovered, and walked around for some time looking at all the old structures. Considering its age and high tourist traffic, the town was in good condition. Obviously a great deal of maintenance had been performed on many of the old buildings; however, it was certainly the real thing, reflecting the *cowboy west* as many of us might recall from our history books and the old western movies we used to watch at our local hometown theaters in years past. Concluding our visit we headed south toward Clark Canyon Reservoir, located on Interstate 15, twenty miles south of Dillon, Montana.

The Reservoir area was where the Lewis and Clark Discovery expedition established a camp in 1805, after proceeding down the Jefferson River, now called the Beaverhead River on most maps, and headed overland by foot. They called it Camp Fortunate, but it wasn't so fortunate after all, because the original campsite is now under the waters of the reservoir. The Discovery expedition spent six days at this location reconnoitering for a path over the Beaverhead Range of the Bitterroot Mountains and what was to eventually become a demarcation point of the Continental Divide. They found an old Indian trail that led them to an opening, now called Lemhi Pass, which took them through the mountains. The passage, at an elevation of 7,371 feet, still looks the same today as it did in 1805 when the Discovery Corps crossed over it on their trek westward. This site is now the boundary line between Montana and Idaho.

▼

After leaving the Reservoir, we drove on a steep winding dirt road, part of the same general route that Lewis and Clark took from Camp Fortunate up to this now national historical landmark. At the top of Lemhi Pass, we saw the same view that the captains of the Discovery Corps observed when they reached this spot over two hundred years ago! Lewis's description of the terrain as he looked across this vast landscape of what was to become the state of Idaho is recorded for posterity in his trip journal: "We proceeded on to the top of the dividing range from which we discovered immense ranges of high mountains still to the west of us with their tops partially covered with snow."

What he had expected to see was either an open plain extending to the Pacific Ocean or a large river that would carry them to the ocean. Factually, the most difficult part of the twenty-seven-month round-trip still lay before them in the form of the Lolo Trail, located several miles north of their crossing of the pass. This trail extended some three hundred miles across mountainous land in Idaho that is so rugged that no road bisected this terrain until 1961. At the pass there is a historical marker with another remark that Lewis recorded in his journals. He wrote that he descended the mountain for a short distance on the western side "to a handsome bold running creek of Cold and Clear water." The sign contains the remaining part of his entry: "here I first tasted the water of the great Columbia River."

After crossing the pass, we proceeded on down the same route as the Corps, now a winding, twisting, steep gravel road to a campsite on a creek with the characteristics Lewis had described in his journal. We located another marker at this location designating their travel route north and assumed this was same site where they had spent their first night in this newly discovered land. The next morning we hiked up a steep mountain, also indicated by a sign as part of their trail, to a ridgeline overlooking a broad valley to the west, thinking we were following in their two-hundred-year-old footsteps. If we weren't, we were damned close.

On our descent from the mountain that previous day, as we drove down the dirt road from Lemhi Pass, we saw another sign on the edge of the road indicating the location where the Red Rock stagecoach had been robbed several times in the late 1800s after it had crossed Lemhi Pass; its route was from Bannack, Montana, to Salmon Idaho, covering roughly sixty miles. Sitting around our campfire that night, we discussed all the history we had encountered during the day. As the fire burned with a bright glow in our secluded camp under the darkened sky, we begin to think that we had somehow become witness to a part of that history. It was almost as if we were now living in those days, and our imaginations began to play fanciful tricks with our minds.

Since we had located our camp in the approximate location where they had also spent the night, we thought we could faintly hear the men of the Discovery Corps rummaging around through their gear, eating, talking, and walking in the thick brush around the camp. Voices seemed to resonate though the chilly night air from the road above us, where the Red Rock stagecoach had been frequently accosted by outlaws one hundred years ago. Of course, no one was within miles of our location— or were they? It had now become ink-black dark, the clouds blotting out the stars and moon; an ominous feeling pervaded us as we walked around the area and then made our way about a mile up the steep trail road in a daze to the sign where the Red Rock stage had been repeatedly stopped by bandits. We were now searching for some semblance of balance in our minds, trying to prove to ourselves that we had actually somehow been propelled back into the past and that everything we felt and heard was real. Ultimately all of these feelings passed as the night wore on after we had returned to our camp. Sometime later during that *ghostly* night, our minds returned to the reality of the present day. I don't recall if we were happy or disappointed, but we had definitely been under a spell, and yet there was still more to come. The blanks in our minds would be filled in the next day by an unlikely encounter in a remote country store and local post office.

The following morning, after our hike up the Lewis and Clark trail, we drove to Tendoy, Idaho, no more than ten miles from our campsite, where we stopped at a roadside country store to replenish our food supplies. Here our mysterious quest would end; the blanks would crystallize in our minds, and a new destiny began to evolve in our lives. An elderly woman was tending the store, and as we poked around looking at the merchandise, we came upon a display of books, many about Lewis and Clark's adventures. While we inquisitively explored their contents, an older woman who was running the store and post office, asked us where we had been. Why she had asked at that precise moment since she had other customers in the store is question without an answer. Nonetheless, we told her of our recent travels and experiences from the previous night, and how we had seen and learned so much about the travels of the Discovery Corps over the past few days. Suddenly she stopped with her chores, looked at us in earnest, and said, "You know, of course, if it had not been for Lewis and Clark, there would be no Idaho." Then she began to tell us more about their adventures, facts that we had no knowledge of whatsoever. We were like little kids in a candy store absorbing every sweet morsel of information that she presented.

Her discourse lasted for at least thirty minutes as we stood there fully engrossed with her improvised lecture; practically astonished, we asked how she could know so much detail about their journeys. She said she was over seventy years old, and she had taught American history for many years around Salmon, Idaho. Naturally she had devoted much of her instruction to Lewis and Clark's wilderness adventures.

After listening to her weave her insightful story, combined with our previous experiences, especially those from the previous night, we were overcome with the need to know more. Yes, we had studied about Lewis and Clark in school, but the information had come from a book—not providing any real insight as to the importance of their travels and the impact they had had on the future development and growth of America. An intriguing urge to know more enveloped our minds, so we purchased several versions of their story from the elderly history-teller, all of which were ultimately read in detail after returning home from this recent, mind-expanding journey.

What we had been unknowingly searching for during our travels had now become a reality in our lives. We had to grasp it and use it to foster more knowledge about our great country. Combining this mentality and thirst for information about this land, its history, and its evolution would sustain our level of enthusiasm for the continuation of our wilderness explorations for years to come.

Just as Outward Bound launched us on a life of adventure travels and Executive Adventure provided the momentum to promote a vibrant new culture for our employees at the bank, the adventures of Lewis and Clark provided a similar impetus for us to increase our efforts with our exploring mentality and not to slacken the pace in any fashion, which at that time was being considered. We never stopped, even with our advancing years and sporadic infirmities; although it is fair to say that as our activities may have slowed considerably, our passion has continued to burn inexorably.

This particular adventure truly became a "Life Changing" event for the three of us and would never have happened without our consuming explorer interest over the years.

Sometime later, after Stephen E. Ambrose had completed his book *Undaunted Courage, the Story about Lewis and Clark's Discovery Corps Journey,* and it had become a best seller, I had the opportunity to meet him in Atlanta. When I asked him why his book had become so successful in such a short period of time, he said, "Americans were in need of, and looking for, heroes. The story about Lewis and Clark filled that need. If the book had been published 15 years ago it would not have received the attention, nor would it have been as successful." His timing, although accidental, he admits, had been perfect, and the book had captured the imagination of the American people.

Later, when Ambrose gave a speech at the Atlanta History Center, he told the audience that he had met and read about a lot of great leaders in his life. He said that each one of them had different physical characteristics and dissimilar value systems, but the one constant attribute of all of them was *attention to planning.* He then told his audience that Meriwether Lewis, with all of his personal limitations and character faults, also practiced this same undeniable trait. Without it, he said, the Discovery Corps would have never completed the difficult mission assigned to them by Thomas Jefferson, President of the United States.

This trip to Lemhi Pass and to other parts of Lewis and Clark's trail across Montana and Idaho was only the tip of the iceberg. During our personal years of discovery, several members of our expedition group made a number of deeper forays into this wilderness. We visited Lemhi Pass and the adjoining valley at least five more times. During one summer interlude, Jim Box celebrated his fiftieth birthday on the pass with his family and my wife and me. We revisited our old campsite on the western slope two more times, and my wife and I were members on an interpretive tour visiting some of the locations Lewis and Clark passed through. We also camped overnight on Lemhi Pass. This was the only time any of us chose to actually camp on top of the mountain near to the pass.

Mack and Steve Georgeson, along with several others, took a canoe trip down the upper Missouri for several days, as did my wife and I with another couple. This river is quite challenging, and we were canoeing downstream; how the Discovery Corps were able to navigate it upstream was beyond our wildest imagination. Mack and I also visited the Lolo Trail and traveled across the Scenic Lewis and Clark Highway, US12, which runs a few miles south, but roughly parallels the Lolo Trail and the Nez Perce route across the Bitterroots; this is the same trail the Indians took when they were attempting to escape from the army on their way to Canada.

We hiked, camped, and explored in this area and also in the Selway-Bitterroot Wilderness, a part of the Clearwater National Forest, the second largest wilderness area in the continental United States. This terrain is rough, steep, and damned-near impassable, and is where the expedition was threatened with extinction and almost derailed from their mission when they tried to cross through this wilderness in the winter of 1805 after the Lemhi Pass crossing.

▼

The steep mountains sent horses and equipment tumbling down the numerous gullies, and then a snowstorm hit, halting the march for several weeks. They survived during this period by eating candles, bear fat, and a few of their horses, until they finally stumbled into a Nez Perce village suffering from starvation and dehydration. The village was located in the Weippe Prairie on the western edge of the Bitterroot Mountains.

The Indians saved their lives and helped them to recover and to continue up the Columbia River to the Pacific Ocean. In his journals Lewis wrote the following description about this segment of the trip: "we suffered everything cold, hunger, and fatigue could impart."

▼

After Mack moved to Bozeman to live and I purchased a second home in Sun Valley, we began to spend more of our time in these locations rather than traveling around the country to more distant spots. The education we received from the schoolteacher in Tendoy incited our interest and provided a reference point for these travels. It was, without doubt, an idea whose time had come, and it had come to us at the precise moment that we needed motivation to continue our travels. The timing of that particular trip was perfect, because at that point in our lives, we were starting to lose interest in our backcountry wilderness adventures; instead of winding down, we now began to speed up. It absolutely changed the direction of our lives.

Looking back at that specific period, it is obvious to me that we were searching for new, different, and unique adventures to undertake. Thank God the lady store keeper was there in Tendoy to help us through our maze of restlessness and confusion. In that remote backwoods country store, her discourses on the Discovery Corps and Lewis and Clark caught our attention, ultimately opening up an entirely new spectrum of possibilities for our journeys. We will always be grateful to her for what she did for us. Unfortunately, she will never know how much she helped these three wayfarers who unwittingly entered her establishment many years ago in search of something they could not define. That elderly lady was most definitely our own personal Ms. Destiny, a clerk in a country store located on the side of a dirt road. Thank you, ma'am, for helping us find our way, and for the wonderful education you provided to us about the building of America, you helped make us who we are today.

EIGHTEEN

LE CINQUE TERRE

By this time we had finally begun to slow down somewhat with our wilderness adventures. Some members of our explorer group had moved away or just lost interest, and this was not unexpected, especially considering the vast number of trips we had taken over the years. Mack and I, after years of sports, hiking, jogging, and graceful aging (there is no other way I want to describe it), began to lose a step or two from the beating we had imparted on our knees. By the time 2000 rolled around, we were finished hitting the pavement altogether; actually, we had been through for a few years. Jim, on the other hand, had not been a jogger or an athlete in school; consequently his legs were sound and are still in pretty good working order today. As we were going through certain physical and mental changes, several of us experienced matrimonial alterations in our lives; at this time I will only mention mine, when it occurred and how I attempted to handle the pain and frustration.

Every individual trying to live a fulfilling and productive life must find within themselves their own personal methods to deal with the misgivings and disappointments that befall them along the way. My approach was to go into the backcountry and to use it as a source of strength and redemption, particularly after experiencing my surprising divorce that I did not expect or want to happen. It was a second marriage for both of us; consequently, there were no children from that marriage. The anxiety and pain only affected the two people who were personally involved in the separation. There are no recriminations to account here; however, each of us had to make our own way through the morass of readjustment, and I believe that, over time, this was suitably accomplished. My approach was to get away and to try to put the divorce behind me as quickly as possible. I planned a monthlong trip to France and Italy in conjunction with a corporate board meeting. My plans included a week in Florence, followed by a week's stay in a wonderful house in Tuscany with my immediate family, including my children and two grandchildren, who would share the first two weeks of this trip. After their departure and return to Atlanta, I would go on an eight-day hiking trip along the coast of Italy with a touring group, and then to my board of directors' meeting in France. Altogether I would be gone for thirty days, enough time for me to begin to get my head screwed on straight.

The hiking trip was principally oriented to *the Cinque Terre* ("Five Grounds") region on the Italian Coast of the Ligurian Sea, and it was superb; it provided a full medicinal dose for the healing process to begin.

▼

The Cinque Terre is a stretch of rocky coastline on the Italian Riviera. The name refers to five self-contained villages, which seem to dramatically cling to the very edges of the steep, vertiginous cliffs ranging along the shoreline. The villages—Monterosso, Vernazza, Corniglia, Manarola, and Riomaggiore—are not connected by any road, although a train does pass through each community. Also, an ancient footpath, known as the Sentiero Azzurro (Blue Trail), follows the coastline and traverses through all five villages. The trail, high on the ridges, offers fabulous views of the sea and countryside. This was one of the key trails our group undertook during our visit.

That summer Europe was experiencing a tremendous heat wave, and if my memory serves me correctly, over three hundred people died of heat strokes during that time. The smothering heat in the Cinque Terre was so horrific that our tourist group opted to hike only two sections of the trail on two different days. Most of them spent the remainder of their time touring the small villages by train, but I decided to challenge myself by hiking the entire trail in a single day, heat notwithstanding. The entire undulating, hilly trail running between the small villages requires about five to six hours to complete one way. This decision was almost a mistake.

▼

Early one morning the others went on their tour of the little towns starting with Riomaggiore, the southernmost village, while I splintered off by my lonesome and began hiking north up the coast toward Monterosso al Mare (Monterosso by the Sea), the end point and the town where our small hotel was located.

After only a short time walking, I was uncertain if I could complete my goal because the heat was nearly overwhelming. There were no friendly encounters of other hikers on the trail that day, nor were there any trees or large bushes to crawl under for a brief respite from the blazing sun. Hiking in short pants and a T-shirt, I carried two liter bottles filled with cold water. One bottle was for drinking, and the other was to pour over my head and down my back to help mitigate the withering heat and to cool my heavily perspiring body. As I came to each village on the route, I left the trail and went downhill into the community to purchase fresh bottles of cold water, to rest in the shade, and to soak my entire body in the cool Ligurian Sea. Stripping to the waist, I sat on the shoreline and splashed water over my myself, soaked my shirt until it was filled with the chilled water, and then wrapped it around my head to lower my body temperature in preparation for the next leg of the hike.

The locals probably thought I was nuts to be hiking in that weather; my shenanigans on the water's edge, which was always at the villages' harbor in town center, probably raised some eyebrows. For certain my waterside activities probably fit their portrayal of one of those *wild* and *crazy Americans*.

After completing the route, my body was whipped and partially dehydrated, even though I had consumed seven liters of water during the trek. That night at our Italian dinner with the other members of the group, I drank a bottle of white wine by myself without any deleterious effect; I guess it was my personal reward for the day's challenging effort, and obviously, my system must have needed it. At least, *that's my story and I'm sticking to it.* (The trail was about five hundred feet above sea level, so I did not have to contend with issues of acute mountain sickness.) The next morning our tour director took us to Santa Margherita Ligure, a popular touristy town three hours up the coast from the Cinque Terre.

Santa Margherita Ligure is a seventeenth-century village, whose aristocratic architecture hints of *old* money. It is a lovely and personable small town with a fun resort character. Another highly enjoyable hike on the Italian Riviera was a ten-miler from Santa Margherita (Saint Margaret) Ligure though a mountain range high above the coast that terminated at the most exclusive harbor and resort town in all of Italy—Portofino. Hikers call this one of the best and most scenic hikes on the Riviera. Portofino, with sleek shops along the waterfront in its cove-like piccolo harbor is crammed with yachts of the rich and famous, and its classic Italian architecture reeks of *new* money. Both of these small unique towns, cuddled along the coast, are appealing and enjoyable to visit for some serious people watching.

▼

Once again, not all the members of the touring group decided to make this lengthy trek. I went along with a family from Ohio with two teenage children and had an enjoyable, but fast, stroll through the lush forest area that opened up with views of the sea and the coastal towns. Many of the hiking trails in Italy have stone steps at the trailheads for both the ascent and decent to and from the tops of the mountains. It is a costly addition for most trails, but certainly a pleasure to walk on. I can only assume the Italians didn't believe in switchbacks, which are so common to the mountain trails in the United States. The kids were a joy for me; they were full of youthful zest and enthusiasm and were also great hikers. The three of us decided to hike off from their parents, who did not seem to mind, and do the course our way. It was a fun day and interesting walking down the staircase mountain trail, and then suddenly emerging in the main part of the exclusive little village of Portofino.

After this trip we drove back to Florence for a few days. I took a group biking trip in the hills surrounding the city for one day, and then it was on to more mundane stuff—my board meeting in France.

Upon returning to Atlanta after the trip, I left immediately and flew to Sun Valley. Since selling mine, I also rented a house during my normal two month visit. Much of that time was spent hiking in the various mountain ranges and visiting with my friends, most of whom lived there on a permanent basis. Thank goodness I had these physically challenging outlets and supportive friends to call upon; without them, I am not certain what my mental outcome from the divorce might have been. The trips cleared my head, provided a new perspective, and enabled me to move forward with my new and dramatically changed life.

As I had been taught by my former athletic coaches, "No pain, no gain." I had now learned firsthand that this bit of wisdom applies to emotions, as well as physical exercise. I had experienced plenty of physical pain from my hardy activities, and I discovered that the same kind of activity did help eradicate the mental anxiety and uncertainty of the domestic problems plaguing my mind.

My inner ghosts were finally beginning to dissipate. Time and activity are great curatives for many personal problems; at least they were for me at that particularly difficult time in my life.

EPILOGUE

TRAIL'S END

As we were sadly winding down one of our lengthy exploratory adventures, Mack Butler, my old friend and companion explorer, said, "All things finally do come to a natural end." I have thought about that statement over the years and have concluded that he was only partially correct. I would counter and say things end only if you encourage or let them. As long as we remain vertical and have our senses, we should have some level of control over the termination of our activities and any changes that may affect our participation.

Of course, everybody knows that change is a way of life, and we must all learn to live with it—or else! Changes occur as we mature and age; consequently, we attempt to follow divergent paths in our pursuit of new goals and opportunities. In most cases we choose these paths, but sometimes uncontrollable obstacles impede our way, just as trails in the wilderness sometimes become impassable because of surging streams, excessive snow melt, and fallen trees. When this occurs we must then alter our direction and seek out other traversable routes to take us to our destination. This is life and the way it works, and we should travel it as we think best. Just as a hiker must sometimes climb a tree or move to higher ground for better visibility so they can determine the proper direction, we must also periodically move to a higher plateau in life to gain an enhanced perspective on any changes we need to make to continue with our advance.

The game of football has often been described as a metaphor for life; its thrills, chills, pain, sacrifice, hard knocks, teamwork, and complete personal dedication are the same issues that routinely beguile humanity. The game serves as a symphony of life, with much to be learned from the way it is orchestrated.

Life changing adventures in the Wild may also be a proper metaphor for life and a way to reinvent yourself to meet the challenges in our lives. Learning how to function in the backwoods serves as an example for living, coping, tolerating hardships, and surviving under extreme conditions. Need I remind you that these are the identical issues we face today, living in our changing, perplexing, and demanding world? The enlightening experiences gained from the outdoors can be applied to the requirements of work, friends, family, or any other worthwhile endeavor. I have always considered my efforts in the backcountry as something special, somehow giving me the edge in every difficult endeavor I encountered in my life.

My friends would likely offer the same response about their outdoor experiences. Perhaps it was nothing more than added confidence, but I suspect there was more to it than that!

Revisiting Mack's comment, allow me to posture it another way: death is the only true natural end, and it concludes everything, right? Or does it? What about those significant pieces of our personal life—our accomplishments and lives that we helped bring into this world, and importantly, that will survive and be perpetuated after we have passed through our mortal coil? Have we not left something of importance for posterity? I think we have. All of the substantive things that make up our morality and character are worth something to someone at some point; they just have to find their place when they are needed the most. We leave these aspects of our life, along with all the good things that have been accomplished, for others to have, to use, and to hold dear in their lives. I am happy with this thought, and it makes me feel better now that I have expressed myself by putting it in writing for others to read, and perhaps even to ruminate on at some point in time—when that time is right.

Poets have inspired or confused our thinking with questions like: "Is it the end of the beginning or the beginning of the end?" and "Is the glass half full, or is it half empty?" Upon examination of questions like these in the recesses of your mind, you might wonder what is real. For certain, your perception is real; it is what you see through your personal prism, your own rose-colored glasses. It is the way you see the world, right or wrong. No one can take that away from you, although external events can certainly influence it.

Speaking metaphorically, is the end of the trail really the end, or does it just close out one phase of an experience and open the door for a new undertaking in another direction?

Trail's end, as applied here, is nothing more than the end of these particular adventure stories; however, it does *not* necessarily denote the end of an adventuresome life, or as Yogi Berra, the great baseball player, said when he was asked about their chances of winning a game they were losing, responded with one of his most famous Yogiisms, saying, "It ain't over till it's over." I think my fellow explorers, to a man, would agree with Yogi's sentiment. Within our particular attitude about living an exciting life, as it should be with everyone, there was no end to any of the trails we trekked, only the challenge to locate new trails whenever the old became impassable, useless, or took us completely off course.

Living *on the edge* as we did for twenty-five years was truly an idea whose time had come for us. It started with Outward Bound and then took on a life of its own. In addition to all the benefits we received, our experiences were also a legacy to leave to our children. In making this decision to live as explorers, we made the sacrifice, endured the pain, and relished in the joy and satisfaction of these efforts. Most importantly, we chose a strenuous life as the way to express ourselves, and it was agreeable to our needs, regardless of what others considered appropriate or within civilized conventions. Frankly, more people could increase the joy in their lives through similar experiences if they would only open their minds to adventuresome activities and the possible long-lasting benefits.

Yes, perhaps for some of us, our pilot lights have dimmed a bit with time. Unquestionably, we no longer possess the physical characteristics that once were so easily exploited or brought to bear under the harshest of circumstances, but that is unimportant. These human elements are expected to decline over time, and wise people accept that; but some hardy-minded folks fight on, suppressing this unwelcome visitor with all the power remaining in their minds and bodies. This is as it should be and can be if a person has the moral fiber, energy, and personal drive to undertake the task. That is what we explorers did. We needed to get away from stress and to breathe the fresh air, sleep in the open spaces under the sky, climb mountains, and bring our bodies into submission in order to release the internal demons that resided in us, as they do in most people.

This is how we coped with the confining aspects of life and work. You might ask, "If this approach is so wonderful, why don't more people do it?" Some do, but many don't. That is just the way it is, always has been, and will probably always be; it is human nature. Many people do not understand or comprehend the importance of living their lives under some degree of self-imposed duress; they don't realize that meeting challenges builds confidence. Also, there are some folks who don't consider this kind of life normal, particularly those who have lived a sedentary lifestyle most of their lives. However, we did. Were we normal people? Probably not, but we were fun-loving creatures, respected for our individuality, creativity, and business acumen. Notably, there are folks out there today just like we were, doing just what we did; our approach to living a vigorous life is not new and different, but it was unusual for the time, especially for a group of business professionals.

Jim Box, my other old friend and fellow explorer, has told me on numerous occasions that he has always wanted to create a graphic representation of our travel routes on a map of the United States; that is, to compile a linear travelogue that would *clearly* illustrate our explorations over the past twenty-five years. He has tried, he says, but each time he attempted to sketch out the numerous journeys and destinations, his depiction resembled an unintelligible, intertwined, jumble—something like the circles and symbols we drew in our early Palmer writing classes in grade school. The reason for his indecipherable diagram was because of the meandering, wandering, overlapping, and zigzagging nature of our travels. He is correct. His images might even resemble the maniacal actions of the frenetic Keystone Cops of the old silent-movie days; whenever they left their police headquarters on a mission, they always seemed to be out of control, confused, disoriented, and traveling in disjointed and bewildering circles. But, they finally got to their objective.

▼

There should not be a *trail's end* for hardy souls; all of us need to learn to attack in another direction. The words *retreating* and *quitting* should be cast to the winds, eliminated totally from our vocabulary. Understand that locating the proper trail to take you to your destination does require commitment, dedication, and effort. However, it's the person who loses interest, their sense of urgency, energy, and personal motivation, who can't find the trail; then they get lost, stay lost, give up, and finally become one of life's casualties. Please, don't let this happen to you.

Your trail will never end as long as you are prepared to continue to search and do all that you're capable of doing. You will just do it differently as time and your age progress. This should not be a limitation to you unless, of course, you allow it to happen. It is up to each of us to make certain that we don't allow ourselves to age out or give up, especially mentally. Our strength, endurance, and mental faculties may falter; our knees may become unsteady, and our breathing more laborious; but we can still advance on a different trail, although it may be in a new direction with different objectives.

At times we may find ourselves like the hero in battle, who charges an enemy position with no regard for his life; his only thought, many times his last, is simply to respond to the crisis. He does not know how he did what he did; many times he can't explain it. He will tell you only that it seemed like the *right* thing to do, or I had to take care of my people. This is what a hero or a great leader would do normally.

I would encourage you to be unafraid to venture into unknown territory, to be an energetic, enthusiastic explorer of life. This is how the unknown becomes known. It is also how we discover new elements about the world and ourselves, and how to live in more fulfilling ways. Wherever your explorations may take you matters not; what does matter is that you keep moving—searching, exploring, and questioning. This may be the only truly real *fountain of youth*; it is readily available for us to drink from whenever we choose, and the amount we drink and the frequency with which we drink is entirely our own decision.

Find the trails, explore vigorously, and leave obvious trail markers (your footprints or fingperprints) on the path for the next person to follow. This is our legacy for future generations.

Now, to conclude, I will return once again to Lewis Carroll and his story about *Alice's Adventures in Wonderland*. When Alice was trying to find her way, she asked the king for directions. He said, "Begin at the beginning and go on until you come to the end: then stop." Sounds like good directions to me, and I shall follow them.

Happy trails!

CPSIA information can be obtained at www.ICGtesting.com
Printed in the USA
LVOW11s0304180915

454655LV00001B/40/P